A SIMPLE STORY

broadview editions
series editor: L.W. Conolly

Elizabeth Inchbald, by T.S. Seed after an unknown artist. Reprinted by permission of the National Portrait Gallery, London.

A SIMPLE STORY

Elizabeth Inchbald

edited by Anna Lott

broadview editions

Library and Archives Canada Cataloguing in Publication

Inchbald, Mrs., 1753-1821.
  A simple story / Elizabeth Inchbald ; edited by Anna Lott.

(Broadview editions)
Includes bibliographical references.
ISBN-13: 978-1-55111-615-0
ISBN-10: 1-55111-615-4

  I. Lott, Anna, 1963-   II. Title.   III. Series.
PR3518.A73 2006   823'.6   C2006-905174-7

Broadview Editions

The Broadview Editions series represents the ever-changing canon of literature by bringing together texts long regarded as classics with valuable lesser-known works.

Advisory editor for this volume: Morgan Rooney

Broadview Press is an independent, international publishing house, incorporated in 1985. Broadview believes in shared ownership, both with its employees and with the general public; since the year 2000 Broadview shares have traded publicly on the Toronto Venture Exchange under the symbol BDP.

We welcome comments and suggestions regarding any aspect of our publications—please feel free to contact us at the addresses below or at broadview@broadviewpress.com.

North America:	**UK, Ireland, and continental Europe:**	**Australia and New Zealand:**
PO Box 1243, Peterborough, Ontario, Canada K9J 7H5	NBN Plymbridge Estover Road Plymouth PL6 7PY UK	UNIREPS, University of New South Wales Sydney, NSW, 2052 Australia
PO Box 1015, 3576 California Road, Orchard Park, NY, USA 14127	Tel: 44 (0) 1752 202300 Fax: 44 (0) 1752 202330	
Tel: (705) 743-8990 Fax: (705) 743-8353 E-mail: customerservice@broadviewpress.com	E-mail: enquiries@nbninternational.com	Tel: 61 2 9664 0999 Fax: 61 2 9664 5420 E-mail: info.press@unsw.edu.au

www.broadviewpress.com

Book design and composition by George Kirkpatrick
PRINTED IN CHINA

This book is for
John David, who inspires me,
and is dedicated to the memory of
John N. Whitaker, M.D.

Contents

Acknowledgements

I cannot possibly acknowledge all the friends and colleagues who have helped me work on this edition. I am grateful for and humbled by their generosity and encouragement. I am especially indebted to Aileen Douglas, who first introduced me to the work of Elizabeth Inchbald when I was a graduate student at Washington University in St. Louis. Since then, she has been a source of friendship and support. I am also greatly indebted to the participants of an NEH summer seminar at Cornell University directed by Mary Jacobus. The fruits of that seminar continue to influence my thinking and research. I appreciate especially the support of Bonnie Nelson, who remains a close friend and advisor. Betsy Bolton and Catherine Burroughs read early versions of some of the material that made its way into this edition. Comments made by Broadview's anonymous reviewers greatly influenced the shape this edition finally took.

I am grateful as well to my students and colleagues at the University of North Alabama (UNA) who have helped in surprising and often delightful ways while discussing Inchbald with me inside and outside the classroom. I have benefited from the generosity of Laura Harrison, whose endowed professorship allowed me a much-appreciated reduction in my teaching duties for a year while I worked on this project. My colleagues at UNA continue to encourage me with their support of this project and others, and I am especially grateful to John Roth and Larry Adams, both of whom read *A Simple Story* and discussed it with me shortly after I came to UNA. John's questions about Catholicism in the novel inspired me to learn more than I knew when he first asked; Larry's interest in the mirror in literature and art has influenced my work on this edition. My department Chair, Ron Smith, loaned me a departmental laptop and arranged my schedule so that I could find pockets of time to write. Eleanor Gaunder, dear friend and colleague, has been a constant source of enthusiasm and support throughout the project. Terri Craft, editorial assistant *par excellence*, typed the entire text of the novel, and helped, throughout the project, with proofreading and editing. Research grants from

UNA helped with copying expenses and allowed me to travel to various libraries.

Annibel Jenkins has been generous with her time and conversation, and her recent biography of Inchbald has been an invaluable resource. I am grateful to the editors of previous editions of *A Simple Story*. I have benefited especially from the Oxford edition (edited by J.M.S. Tompkins and introduced by Jane Spencer) and the Penguin edition (edited and introduced by Pamela Clemit). Thanks to the librarians at the Bodleian Library, the British Library, the National Portrait Gallery, London, the Folger Library, the Library of Congress, Emory University, Washington University in St. Louis, Cornell University, the University of North Alabama, and the University of Alabama at Birmingham. I am thankful for your expertise and for your patience.

Numerous friends and family put me up while I was doing research. I am especially grateful to Norman Prentiss, Jim Gernert (who sacrificed a very nice jacket to the cause—sorry), Phil and Shin Liang, and Frances Sowers. I know there have been others, and I appreciate their amazing hospitality. Carolyn Smith has been a trusted friend and supporter, even before this particular project took its current form. Most recently, she faxed on short notice some material I desperately needed from Washington University in St. Louis. Polly Price and Kara Bryant graciously postponed a long-scheduled party when I was overwhelmed with deadlines. Thanks to you all.

Above all, I am grateful to my immediate family, especially my parents, John and Sandra Lott, who have been role models, friends, and unfailing supporters. They give more than they know. My husband, David Haws, grudgingly helped with this project but came through magnificently in the end. He never wants to see this manuscript again. John David has been as brave as any three-year-old can be whose mother keeps disappearing to work on "the book."

Introduction

Inchbald Biography

When Elizabeth Simpson Inchbald was thirteen, she announced that she "would rather die than live any longer without seeing the world."[1] Five years later, she left a rather cryptic note for her mother—"should I ever think you wish to hear from me, I will write,"[2]—and took the forty mile stagecoach ride from Suffolk to London. There she began her long career, first acting on the stage and then later writing plays, novels, and critical essays. When she went to London in 1772, she found it difficult to convince managers to speak to her seriously, much less to offer her a position. Her determination to succeed, however, is demonstrated by an instance in which she threw a basin of hot water in the face of a manager whose offer of employment turned out to be a subterfuge for his sexual advances. Inchbald's perseverance, in this instance and in others like it, allowed her to have a versatile and lengthy career. She achieved and maintained a prominent position in the theatrical and literary world despite a wide range of obstacles, including hostile managers and her own speech impediment.

Inchbald was born 15 October 1753, the seventh of eight children. Her parents, John and Mary Rushbrook Simpson, were farmers in Standingfield, a small community in Suffolk, near Bury St. Edmunds. The family was Roman Catholic. John Simpson died in 1761, leaving Mary Simpson in charge of maintaining the family and the farm. When Inchbald decided to pursue a career on the stage, she followed the example of her younger brother, George, who had already left his family to become a strolling player. George's letters to his family solidified Elizabeth's resolve to succeed on the stage, and on several occasions she visited him and two of their married sisters who were already living in London. During one such visit, she met her future husband, the actor and

---

1 Quoted in James Boaden, *Memoirs of Mrs. Inchbald; Including her Familiar Correspondence with the Most Distinguished Persons of her Time* (London, 1833) I, 7. All references to Boaden will be to this text.
2 Quoted in Boaden, I, 18.

painter, Joseph Inchbald, nineteen years older than she and also a practising Roman Catholic. He was immediately smitten with her, but her decision to marry him came only after she had tried for several months to succeed on the stage as a single woman. The marriage secured Elizabeth's entrance into the theatrical world and provided her with protection from the jeers and innuendoes that she had experienced as an unmarried woman within that world. After a few engagements in Bristol, the couple acted with several companies—first with West Digges in Scotland, and, after a trip to France, with Tate Wilkinson in Leeds and York. During these years, Elizabeth developed life-long friendships with prominent actors and stage personalities such as Sarah Siddons and John Philip Kemble. Although the Inchbalds' marriage was turbulent, with frequent arguments and public disagreements, Elizabeth was apparently fond of her husband and was genuinely distressed when he died suddenly in 1779. She records his death with the following notation in her pocket diary: "Began this year a happy wife—finished it a wretched widow."[1]

Some of Inchbald's disagreements with her husband stemmed from her desire to help her family financially, a need that continued throughout her life and contributed to the financial necessity that she invokes as a muse in the Preface to *A Simple Story*. In the Preface (which was removed in 1793 after the novel's first two editions), she comments on the particular details of her life and work, including her early education and, at least indirectly, her financial disputes with her husband. When she welcomes necessity as "the instigator of many bad authors and actors," she refers to her own financial need, evidenced by the careful accounts that she kept in her pocket diaries and elsewhere. John Taylor, a long-time friend, journalist, and editor, gives an illustration of the effects of Inchbald's life-long financial need. He describes the frugal lodgings she took in The Strand at age fifty-two and explains that he warned her that her parsimonious lifestyle was causing others to suppose her miserly and even insane. Inchbald's response was angry:

---

1   Folger Library, M.A. 149.

Because I choose that retirement suitable to my years, and think it my duty to support my two sisters, instead of one servant, I am accused of madness. I might plunge in debt, be confined in prison, a pensioner on "The Literary Fund," or be gay as a girl of eighteen, and yet be considered as perfectly in my senses; but because I choose to live in independence, affluence to me, with a mind serene and prospects unclouded, I am supposed to be mad.... Retirement in the country would, perhaps, have been more advisable than in London, but my sisters did not like to accompany me, and I did not like to leave them behind.[1]

Her strong reaction illustrates the unusual closeness felt by the entire family, a bond that led her to support her sister Debby, who had turned to prostitution, and her brother George, whose gambling debts ultimately caused him to lose the family farm. Inchbald's fierce refusal to leave her sisters behind was probably inspired by her mother's own dedication to her children, particularly her six daughters, whom she actively encouraged to read and to learn. Her mother read aloud to her daughters and wanted them to act in informal productions of plays.

Although she seems in the Preface to *A Simple Story* to disparage her early education as "confined to the narrow boundaries prescribed to her sex," she claims in another context that she and her sisters were able to transcend these limitations: "it is astonishing how much all girls are inclined to literature, to what boys are. My brother went to school seven years, and never could spell. I and two of my sisters, though we never were taught, could spell from infancy."[2] In her Preface, however, she suggests that her inadequate education is quite debilitating and is one of several factors (including her speech impediment and her dislike of the hard work necessary for writing) that inhibit her novel's chance for success. She argues that her plays have been popular because she has been lucky—"good fortune" has been "substituted in the place of genius"—and that the only chance

---

1 Quoted in John Taylor, *Records of My Life* (London: Edward Bull, 1832), II, 404-05.
2 Quoted in Boaden, I, 209.

for *A Simple Story*'s success is a continuation of that same "good fortune." Despite these protestations, Inchbald was, as Annibel Jenkins has argued, "exceedingly well read—perhaps more so, or indeed more so, than anyone in her circle" (299), and Inchbald's informal statement that girls are actually "inclined to literature" was probably more sincere than the apology she makes in her Preface. Her deferential stance places her in line with women writers such as Frances Burney, who offered a similar prefatory apology for her first novel, *Evelina* (1778). Burney claimed to present her writings to the public "with a very singular mixture of timidity and confidence ... trembling for their success from a consciousness of their imperfections," and yet "happily wrapped up in a mantle of impenetrable obscurity," because the novel was published anonymously.[1] Burney's and Inchbald's positions are both devious: Burney, by announcing her novel's imperfections in advance, deflects her critics' power to ridicule it; Inchbald, by listing her own personal limitations as explanations for her novel's flaws, attempts to diminish any criticism of her novel before it can occur.

Perhaps facilitated by Inchbald's self-protective stance, *A Simple Story* was extremely popular, going into a second edition in March 1791, one month after the publication of the first edition. Critical response to *A Simple Story* was likewise overwhelmingly positive: *The Critical Review* proclaimed enthusiastically that "Mrs. Inchbald has discovered the true path which she ought to pursue" (See Appendix B1). Despite these enthusiastic affirmations of the novel's merit, she substantially revised each subsequent edition. Many of the changes were probably reactions to the published reviews and to informal responses she received from friends, but her revisions also reflect the cultural changes occurring during the thirty years between *A Simple Story*'s original publication and the final 1810 edition. The changes also seem influenced by Inchbald's own changing political and religious views—she had essentially abandoned the Catholic Church during the years she was composing early editions of the novel, but she became more

---

1   See Frances Burney, *Evelina, or, a Young Lady's Entrance into the World*. Ed. Susan Kubica Howard.

devout during the later years of her life. Her continuing revisions allowed *A Simple Story* to remain popular in the midst of disputes about the moral value of fiction, and her novel has remained in print almost continuously until the present day.

During the month following the first edition of *A Simple Story*, Inchbald edited her novel to correct grammatical errors and to remove colloquial phrases. These early revisions were probably influenced by more than one reader, including, as Jenkins has suggested, her long-time friend Francis Twiss, a circuit judge who was a friend of the entire Simpson family. We know from Inchbald's pocket diaries that Twiss was reading and commenting on her work as early as 11 December 1780, when she reports that she "received a note from Mr. Twiss, with my novel."[1] Later, in a series of letters about Inchbald's comedy, *I'll Tell You What* (1785), Twiss made suggestions about the content and style of her play that seem consistent with the kinds of changes she later made for the second edition of *A Simple Story*. Before Twiss had even seen a staged performance of *I'll Tell You What*, he complained that her language in "the serious part" was "low and groveling; and that the pathos of the scene (at least my feeling spoke so) is not a little impaired by the humility of the style."[2] Although she did revise *I'll Tell You What* according to Twiss's suggestions, her near-contemporary biographer James Boaden was later to disagree with Twiss's assessment of her prose. Exclaiming that "intense anguish is never verbose," Boaden noted with relief that "Mrs. Inchbald happily persevered in her easy natural expression, and we have the *Simple Story*." But Twiss's (and other public figures') influence over her work may have been greater than Boaden acknowledges; when Inchbald formalized the diction of *A Simple Story* in later editions, she may have been doing so in response to Twiss and to suggestions in published reviews (see Appendix B1 for selected reviews). Inchbald was a successful writer (that is, she made money) largely because she did not hesitate to alter her products to suit

---

1   Folger M.A. 150. Whether or not this 1780 novel was an early version of *A Simple Story*, the notation indicates that Twiss was reading Inchbald's work early in her career and is likely to have continued doing so when she revised *A Simple Story* after its initial publication. On this point, see Patricia Sigl, 1-2.

2   Quoted in Boaden, I, 210.

the responses she received from her audience. Because Twiss was neither a manager nor a publisher, he had no professional authority over Inchbald, and thus, as Ellen Donkin has noticed (210), she was able to take his advice freely without compromising her position in the theatre.

Twiss and a few other close friends represented a microcosm of the larger audience that Inchbald needed to please in order to succeed as a writer. Twiss, in another letter written to Inchbald after he had seen a performance of *I'll Tell You What*, articulated a widespread dispute about the theatre's didactic purpose: Twiss complained that she was not distinguishing clearly between moral and immoral characters and was thus creating a "poison which is imperceptibly, indeed, taken in, but which never fails to work its passage till it undermines the very vitals of morality."[1] Although the performances on the stage were considered especially pernicious because of their physical enactment of immorality, the novel—because of its verisimilitude—was likewise dangerous, as Samuel Johnson argued in issue number 4 of the *Rambler*: "when the adventurer [in a fictional work] is leveled with the world, and acts in such scenes of the universal drama, as may be the lot of any other man; young spectators fix their eyes upon him with closer attention, and hope, by observing his behaviour and success, to regulate their own practices, when they shall be engaged in the like part (69).

Some of Inchbald's later revisions indicate that she felt pressure to clarify *A Simple Story*'s moral lesson. Several revised descriptions of Miss Milner seem designed to lessen some of the ambiguity that is central to her nature from the beginning of the novel—her character is ambiguous enough that Dorriforth must struggle "inquisitively ... to gain intelligence of his ward's disposition before he saw her." Although in the revised editions Dorriforth remains confused about his ward's essential nature, Inchbald adds the words "dissipated" (in the second and third editions) and "vain" (in the fourth and fifth editions) to an early

---

1   Quoted in Boaden, I, 221. Twiss's statements are relevant to eighteenth-century discussions about the morality of the stage, a point Inchbald addressed in her 1809 letter to Prince Hoare's *The Artist*, in which she defended the stage against charges that it promoted immorality.

description of Miss Milner. These changes seem designed to prepare readers for Miss Milner's later adultery and perhaps to keep readers from sympathizing too much with (or, perhaps, from imitating) her behavior.

As a novelist, Inchbald was following the legacies of Samuel Richardson and Henry Fielding, who defined their own work in opposition to earlier works of fiction that were considered not only formulaic but also immoral and dangerous to young readers. Richardson claimed to have created a "new species of writing" that was didactic rather than corrupting,[1] and Fielding responded to Richardson's *Pamela* with his own "new province of writing" a province grounded in a tradition of classical rather than popular literature. By the latter part of the eighteenth century, when Inchbald was composing and revising *A Simple Story*, an audience would have expected a novel to be at once scholarly and didactic, and Inchbald's revisions reflect this general expectation.[2]

Politics

Inchbald's pragmatic efforts to please her audience were occasionally at odds with her own sometimes radical political views, including her support of the French Revolution and the rights of women. During the years immediately following the publication of *A Simple Story*, her close friends included such liberal thinkers as philosopher and novelist William Godwin and playwright and actor Thomas Holcroft, the latter of whom was Inchbald's close friend from when the two acted together in Canterbury in 1777. In the early 1790s, after the first edition of *A Simple Story* was published, Inchbald, Holcroft, Godwin, and the publisher J.G. Robinson met frequently for tea and conversation. These meetings probably stimulated ideas for her novel, *Nature and Art* (1796),

---

1   For considerations of didacticism in Richardson's novels, see J. Paul Hunter, 225-302 and Mary Patricia Martin.

2   As a woman, Inchbald was under particular pressure to instill her writing with a didactic message. As Janet Todd explains, "Female novelists united in their effort to use fiction for interventionist purposes, to comment on life as it was lived at the particular historical moment and to provide a moral or political critique that would help the reader to bear or change her conditions" (*Sign of Angellica*, 229).

and for her essays and plays. During these years, Inchbald also read early versions of Godwin's *Enquiry Concerning Political Justice* (1793) and his novel, *Caleb Williams* (1794). Godwin's ideas may have significantly influenced her revisions to *A Simple Story*, but it is now generally acknowledged that her influence on him was also profound.[1]

Inchbald broke off her friendship with Godwin in 1797 when he married Mary Wollstonecraft. Wollstonecraft, a public supporter of women's rights, had developed a reputation for promiscuity, partly because she gave birth to a child, Fanny, out of wedlock. After the marriage to Godwin, Inchbald and others such as Sarah Siddons avoided contact with both Godwin and Wollstonecraft because of Wollstonecraft's scandalous reputation.[2] Her public avoidance of the couple demonstrates the precarious nature of her own reputation as a public, professional woman. Inchbald could not risk being seen publicly with Wollstonecraft or Godwin, but her private feelings about them must have been more complicated than her public avoidance might indicate. Her private and public writings demonstrate her support for both Wollstonecraft's and Godwin's ideals.

In March, 1791, Wollstonecraft reviewed *A Simple Story* (see Appendix B1), and the review was one of several factors that contributed to Inchbald's dislike for her. Wollstonecraft complained that Inchbald's novel was not explicitly didactic, particularly concerning women's education: "Mrs. I. had evidently a very useful moral in view, namely to show the advantage of a good education; but it is to be lamented that she did not, for the benefit of

---

1   As Patricia Sigl notes (228), Godwin's diary entries (Bodleian Library, Lord Abinger Manuscripts, Reels 72-73) indicate his admiration for *A Simple Story* in particular, which he read and re-read in September 1793, June 1798, September 1799, November 1804, December 1818, and August, 1831. Inchbald read and commented on Godwin's *Caleb Williams*, explaining in a letter that "Your first volume is far inferior to the two last. Your second is sublimely horrible—captivatingly frightful" (quoted in Charles Kegan Paul, *William Godwin: His Friends and Contemporaries*. 2 vols. Boston: Roberts Brothers, 1876, 1:136).

2   When Wollstonecraft's lover, Gilbert Imlay, refused to marry her, Wollstonecraft simply introduced herself in English society as "Mrs. Imlay," in order to give her daughter a name. When Wollstonecraft, pregnant again, married Godwin, it became clear that she had never married Imlay.

her young readers, enforce it by contrasting the characters of the mother and daughter, whose history must warmly interest them." Inchbald was deeply offended by Wollstonecraft's review, and she made the following complaint to Godwin in 1797 after learning of Wollstonecraft's death: "I did not know her. I never wished to know her; as I avoid every female acquaintance, who has no husband, I avoided her. Against my desire you made us acquainted. With what justice I shunned her, your present note evinces, for she judged me harshly." Inchbald never reconciled with Godwin, although he continued to correspond with her throughout her life.

Religion

Between 1770 and 1810, the years of *A Simple Story*'s composition and most of the revisions, Inchbald had essentially left the Catholic Church, explaining, in a 1777 letter to her friend, Friar Jernigan, that her own religious doubts prevented her from taking the sacrament:

> In the outset it appears nearly impossible to admit to the sacrament of the Eucharist one who professes to have doubts, and even strong doubts, not only as to that sacrament, but even as to revealed religion itself, and the truth of the Scriptures. It should seem that such doubts can but little accord with those profound sentiments of adoration, of love, and gratitude which the *real presence* both inspires and exacts.[1]

Inchbald's struggle, apparent in this 1777 letter, seems to have been resolved during the last decade of her life. She returned to the church, reporting in her final diaries that she attended mass regularly and followed certain dietary restrictions. Her final revisions to *A Simple Story* and her revisions for the third edition of her later novel, *Nature and Art*, reflect her newly energized religious faith. For the final edition of *A Simple Story* (1810), for example,

---

1   Quoted in Boaden, I, 80.

she added a quotation from Burke's *Reflections on the Revolution in France* (1790) that directs readers to view the novel from a more unambiguously conservative position than they might have been inclined to do when the novel was originally published. Burke's description of a clergy who seemed "beyond the clerical character, liberal and open" commemorates a benevolent, paternal, Catholic authority—the very authority that Miss Milner challenges throughout the first half of *A Simple Story*. Inchbald's changes for the 1810 edition of *Nature and Art* may also reflect her increasing religious faith. When she changed the heroine's name from Hannah to Agnes, she may have been attempting to impose an explicitly moral message on her narrative by invoking the Christian heroine Agnes of God.[1] Inchbald spent the last years of her life in relative seclusion, and we have no explicit discussions of these fairly significant changes to her novels, but the emendations may have been attempts to remove some of the ambiguities of her complex narratives.

Inchbald was fairly isolated in her last years, losing contact with her theatrical and literary friends. Her writings, however, had gained a prominence that led others to seek her company, sending her letters and visiting her privately. Despite her self-imposed seclusion, she developed stimulating relationships with a few prominent people, including novelists Maria Edgeworth (see Appendix B3) and Madame de Stael. Inchbald recorded these and other visits and activities in her letters and pocket diaries, which she kept until her death on 1 August 1821.[2] Her compositions, from the pocket diaries to *A Simple Story*, present a multifaceted portrait of an author who, in the words of James Boaden, "became an object of anxious request among all who could admire powerful talent, graceful manners, and the urbanity of native wit" (2:290-91).

---

1   See Patricia M. Taylor.
2   See Annibel Jenkins, 496-97. Jenkins notes that "In the end [Inchbald] had two ceremonies [Catholic and Church of England]. When she was buried, the rites of the Catholic Church were administered, although she was given a Church of England funeral service, just as she had had two ceremonies when she and Joseph Inchbald were married."

Composition of the Novel

Because information is limited about Inchbald's early, unpublished work, critics are divided about exactly when *A Simple Story* was first composed. We know that Inchbald corresponded with Kemble in 1777 about a novel she was writing, and we know that in 1779 she tried unsuccessfully to publish it. Inchbald mentions this early novel in her pocket diary entry for 5 December 1780, but she offers no details concerning its substance, remarking simply that she had been paid a visit by Dr. Brodie, a physician friend who read and commented on many of her plays: "Dr. Brodie called and came after to tea—brought my novel and went through all my Farce." In her diary entry for the next day, she writes that she sat before a warm fire in her dining room and "Looked over my novel c & c."[1]

Boaden, Inchbald's near-contemporary critic and her earliest biographer, assumes in his 1833 biography that the novel Inchbald mentions was an early version of *A Simple Story* ("the Miss Milner/Dorriforth story"),[2] but recent critics have questioned this supposition. Bonnie Nelson suggests that the novel Inchbald composed in the 1770s and tried to publish in 1779 may actually have been *Emily Herbert*, an epistolary novel published anonymously in 1786.[3] Nelson's argument implicitly lends support to critics such as Patricia Sigl and Gary Kelly who situate the concerns of *A Simple Story* later in the century, arguing that the novel is derived from the specific social and political milieu of the 1790s. Sigl also argues that because the characters of Miss Milner and Sandford are more fully developed than similar characters in the plays Inchbald was composing in the 1770s, even the first half of *A Simple Story* must have been completed long after those early plays. Influenced by Sigl's argument, Jane Spencer, in her introduction to *A Simple Story*, suggests that it is "most probable"

---

1 Folger Library M.A. 150. After Dr. Brodie returned Inchbald's novel, she gave it to Francis Twiss to read. Inchbald notes in her diary that on 11 December 1780, that Twiss returned the novel to her with his comments.
2 See Boaden, I, 75, 92-93.
3 See Bonnie Nelson.

that "if the novel was an early version of *A Simple Story*, the work was given an extensive revision, if not recasting, in 1789-90" (xi). William Godwin's[1] journal entries for the end of 1790 and the beginning of 1791 seem to support Spencer's argument. Godwin indicates that the early version of *A Simple Story* he read in 1790 was a "series of letters."

A change in the novel's format from epistolary to narrative is, of course, significant, even if the plot and characters of the novel were left exactly as they were when Godwin first read it, but Godwin's entry leaves unresolved the question of whether the novel that Inchbald was composing in 1777 was the same novel (or even a drastically different version of the same novel) that he read in 1790. There are some convincing arguments that *A Simple Story* was not composed in a short time. Jenkins[2] points to Inchbald's method of composition as a strong indication that she worked on *A Simple Story* gradually for at least ten years. Since Inchbald typically put aside plays that she was writing and returned to them months or even years later, Jenkins argues that Inchbald is not likely to have written *A Simple Story* quickly "in the last months of 1789 and the early months of 1790" (273). But perhaps the best evidence that *A Simple Story* was written over a period of many years is found in the evolving literary form of the novel itself. The two very different halves of *A Simple Story* illustrate how quickly novelistic conventions were changing even as Inchbald was completing her manuscript. *A Simple Story* is characterized not only by sympathetic emotion typical of the eighteenth-century sentimental novel but also by more disturbing elements of the emerging Gothic novel, particularly the inclusion of a female victim who was oppressed and often imprisoned by a despotic man.

The Gothic novel became trendy in the 1780s and 1790s,[3] and the timing of this surge in popularity offers a clue about when the second half of *A Simple Story*, clearly influenced by Gothic

---

1   William Godwin (1756-1836) was a "radical" social philosopher, journalist, and novelist who associated closely with Inchbald during the early 1790s.
2   See Jenkins, 273-74.
3   See, especially, E.J. Clery.

conventions, was composed.[1] Matilda's obsession with her despotic father Elmwood is typical of late eighteenth-century Gothic literature: Elmwood's cruel demand that Matilda live in his house without ever seeing him creates an air of longing combined with mystery and danger; the danger becomes overtly sexualized when Matilda gazes obsessively at her father's hat and at his portrait, and later when she faints in his arms. Elmwood's absurdly literal taboos, his attempts to govern Matilda's movements, seem almost inevitably to create an incestuous energy between him and his daughter, an eroticism that a number of critics have identified as central to Gothic literature: as Ruth Perry has recently argued, "incest implies the violation of genealogical principles and hence the attempt to short-circuit true succession and disrupt history" (193). Elmwood's unreasonable prohibitions, which are designed to erase all memory of Matilda's mother and to displace Matilda from her rightful place in his family, ultimately fail. Elmwood's "history," his marriage to Matilda's mother, is made only more obvious by his futile attempts to remove all traces of that history.

The Gothic characteristics of the novel's second half seem even more striking when we consider that they are so entirely absent from the novel's first half, which relies heavily on the satiric conventions and exaggerated gestures and emotions that characterized the sentimental novel, popular from the middle of the century. The first half of *A Simple Story*, with its exploration of the power inherent in female sensibility, is reminiscent of the novels of Samuel Richardson.[2] Miss Milner quite successfully

---

1   Eleanor Ty points to the Gothic overtones of the novel's second half to emphasize Matilda's passivity: "If anything, compared to her energetic mother, Matilda is a figure of compromise and resignation. She is a descendant of Horace Walpole's Lady Matilda of *The Castle of Otranto*, who is erroneously murdered by her own tyrannical father Manfred, and prefigures Mary Shelley's heroine in *Mathilda*, which depicts the pseudo-incestuous love and reunion of a sheltered adolescent girl and her cold, distant father" (87-88).

2   See Michael Boardman, 207-22, who offers an analysis of *A Simple Story* "as a particular kind of innovative plot that develops a number of previously untried possibilities available to novelists since Richardson pioneered the form in 1740" (209). *A Simple Story*, Boardman claims, "shows clearly in what it essays and what it avoids the influence of other attempts, all the way back to Richardson, to construct serious plots out of romantic materials" (211).

gives Dorriforth, as Terry Castle observes, "a sentimental education" (205). Just as Pamela teaches Mr. B., so too does Miss Milner teach Elmwood to acknowledge his own feelings, even when such an acknowledgement means the disavowal of already established codes of conduct.[1] And like Pamela, who teaches Mr. B. to "speak from the heart," Miss Milner "stimulate[s] passion in place of propriety" in her guardian/lover Lord Elmwood. Both women are rewarded with marriage to their pupils: Pamela submits her will to Mr. B. only after she is convinced that he has learned from her how to be an authority she can trust, and Miss Milner marries Lord Elmwood (submitting herself to an authority which Sandford hopes she will not "dare to violate") only after she is convinced that he has learned to value and even to imitate her own unruly patterns of behavior.

The often satirical tone of the novel's first half could well have been influenced by earlier writers such as Frances Burney or Henry Fielding.[2] Janet Todd, among others, has noted Inchbald's use of satire in *A Simple Story*'s first half and he has suggested that Inchbald "followed a seemingly satirical first section of *A Simple Story* ... with a sentimentalized version [in the second section] in which the actors are father and daughter" (228). The objects of Inchbald's satire are multifaceted and include female coquetry, social constraints against eighteenth-century women, constrictions implicit in the Catholic Church, and the binary world view held by Dorriforth and his mentor, Sandford. Miss Milner, placed under the dominance of Dorriforth, a person she has met only recently, is forced to rely on satiric laughter to gain a measure of control.[3] When, to cite

---

1   Several critics have considered Dorriforth's sensibility in the context of late eighteenth-century debates about masculinity. Candace Ward argues that Dorriforth's submission to his ward "dramatizes the late-century concern that sensibility undermined masculine authority" (2). Against this view, Caroline Breashears argues that Dorriforth's authority is actually enhanced instead of lessened by his sensibility: "Dorriforth is ennobled, but not enervated, by the civilizing process" (457).

2   Of course, the satiric impulse was clearly evident in works (including Inchbald's plays) throughout the eighteenth and nineteenth centuries, so the tone of the first half does not prove definitively when the novel might have been first composed.

3   On Miss Milner's laughter, see Catherine Craft-Fairchild who argues, "Any form of masculine constraint or animosity is subject to Miss Milner's mirth, as laughter becomes her woman's weapon against oppression" (82).

just one of many examples from the novel, Dorriforth mentions the rather ordinary Frederick Ashton as a possible suitor for Miss Milner, Inchbald's narrator comments that "a laugh of ridicule was the only answer." As Catherine Craft-Fairchild has noticed, Miss Milner's laughter unsettles Dorriforth's system of binary oppositions, which does not admit uncertainty or ambiguity, especially in his perception of Miss Milner. In the darker, more somber atmosphere of the novel's second half, however, there is none of Miss Milner's laughter; instead, Inchbald relies on more sinister Gothic conventions to convey the bleak situation of Miss Milner's daughter Matilda. The strikingly different tones of the novel's two halves indicate that they were probably composed separately, possibly over an extended period of time. However, the exact dates of composition remain uncertain.

Catholicism

Inchbald noted in her pocket book entry for 6 June 1780, that the day was cold and that she "drank tea with Mrs. Cummings." She then added matter-of-factly that she "read the account of the riot in London." What Inchbald called simply "the riot" was a particularly violent response to the 1778 Catholic Relief Act, a legislation that had relaxed some of the legal restrictions against English Catholics. The Act had immediately practical benefits when it was passed, because England was in the midst of the American Revolutionary War, and the Act allowed English Catholics to join the army without taking a religious oath. However, despite the obvious need to strengthen the military, public response to the Act was hostile. On 2 June 1780, Lord George Gordon, a retired navy lieutenant, led approximately 60,000 people to the House of Commons to present a petition in protest. The ensuing week of violent riots caused widespread destruction of property (including private homes and public chapels) and over 200 deaths in London and the surrounding area. Victims of the Gordon Rioters included practicing Roman Catholics and certain people and institutions (the Bank of England, for example) thought to be sympathetic to the Catholic plight.

Inchbald's casual mingling of details in her private pocket diaries, the familial and private (drinking tea with a friend) with the public and political (the Gordon Riots) is typical of the daily accounts she kept throughout her life. It was not unusual for Inchbald to record in a single entry news about a family member and news about a public figure or event. Jenkins has suggested (59-60) that Inchbald's casual mention of the "the riot" in her journal indicates that she probably did not understand the extensive devastation the riots were causing. (Inchbald was in York at the time, acting in Tate Wilkinson's company, four days away from London.) Even before the Gordon Riots, however, Inchbald, as a Roman Catholic, considered herself part of a group that was socially and legally marginalized throughout eighteenth-century England. The marginalization of Catholics dated as far back as the Reformation of the sixteenth century, when Henry VIII broke with the Catholic Church over the issue of divorce. Henry's Supremacy Act declared the Church of England the official national religion—with the King, not the Pope, as its head. Subsequent attempts to restore the Catholic monarchy to power were disastrous. The reign of Mary Tudor (Henry's daughter, a devout Roman Catholic who succeeded her brother Edward VI to the throne in 1553) serves as perhaps the most notable example. During Mary's three-year reign, 280 heretics were burned at the stake in an attempt to reestablish the supremacy of Catholicism. More than a century later, in 1685, James II (a convert to Catholicism) attempted again to reintegrate Catholicism into mainstream English society, but the public ignored his calls for toleration—James was deposed from the throne by the Glorious Revolution of 1688, after which Catholics were barred from succession to the British monarchy.

During the first half of the eighteenth century, however, newly energized movements to restore the Catholic Stuarts to the throne caused widespread anxiety about the return of a Catholic monarchy that many assumed would be despotic. The growing unease about the possibility of another Catholic ruler led to the stricter enforcement of old laws (enacted during the Reformation of the sixteenth century) meant to prohibit Catholics from owning property and voting. The long-standing Toleration Act (passed in 1689) had given certain rights to most dissenters from the Church of England, but the act specifically excluded Unitarians and Roman Catholics. Catholic priests (represented by Sandford and Dorriforth in *A Simple Story*) were not allowed to be educated in England and were barred from holding public services in established places of worship even if they had been trained elsewhere (usually in France). By the end of the eighteenth century, some laws (including the 1778 Catholic Relief Act) had relaxed penalties against Roman Catholics, but the more relaxed laws often led to resentment and had occasionally severe repercussions, as was the case in the violent 1780 Gordon Riots.[1]

Given that Inchbald was living in such an unsettled political context, her fictionalizing of Catholicism in England was a double-edged sword. Certainly, *A Simple Story* demonstrates Inchbald's personal discomfort with intolerance towards Catholicism: Dorriforth and his tutor Sandford are essentially placeless, apparently conducting marriage and funeral services in private homes. Miss Milner's marriage to her guardian, which Castle describes as an "ecstatic, extra-logical union,"[2] is facilitated by a scarcity of English Catholics and a perceived need to protect the religion (the circumstances of the marriage would have reminded readers of the marginal status of contemporary English Catholics). When Dorriforth is released from his vows and given the title Lord Elmwood, it is with the intent that he marry and have sons, thus continuing the Catholic lineage.

Despite Inchbald's personal interest in the treatment of the Catholic minority, however, the novel also demonstrates her uneasiness with the constrictions inherent in the religion itself: she suggests that the Catholic Church sanctioned the repression of individuals, especially women. In Dorriforth's household, Catholicism is the dominant religion, and Miss Milner, as a protestant, is clearly in the minority. If, as George E. Haggerty has

---

1   For considerations of Catholicism in eighteenth-century England and, particularly, of the Gordon Riots, see Colin Haydon and David Mathew.

2   Castle, 295. Castle's study explores Miss Milner's (and her daughter's) authority. For Castle, *A Simple Story* is "a rhapsody of transgression, in which masculine authority is insistently demystified, female aspiration rewarded, and the conventional world of eighteenth-century representation transformed in consequence" (293).

argued, "Miss Milner's situation becomes abject as a result of Lord Elmwood's arbitrary tyranny" (660), then her misery is also authorized and enforced by the Catholic Church that Dorriforth represents. Dorriforth's mentor Sandford, another representative of the Catholic Church's authority, has an unwavering ambition to control the conduct of others and to define their identity; he is "possessed of steadiness to accomplish the end of any design once meditated, and of wisdom to direct the conduct of men more powerful, but less ingenious than him."[1] His despotic rule over his male pupils results in a loyal, homosocial relationship that is antipathetic to a strong female presence such as Miss Milner's. Sandford, as the former tutor of Dorriforth and of his cousin, the first Lord Elmwood, is by "this double tie," now "entailed upon the family."

Sandford perceives Miss Milner as a threat to his male enclave, and he works diligently to neutralize her challenge to his authority. Imagining himself sanctioned by his religion, he insults Miss Milner until she feels "an inward nothingness she never knew before."[2] On several occasions, Sandford attempts to define (and thereby control) Miss Milner by classifying her as deceptively evil; at one point, he even compares her to Lucifer, "the most beautiful angel in paradise." Near the end of Volume II, when Sandford advises Dorriforth (who, after the death of his cousin, has now been given the title of Lord Elmwood) to marry Miss Milner, he thinks, again, that the marriage will help to control her: "such ties from offending you, she shall not *dare* to violate." Sandford's advice is entirely predictable and is anticipated in Volume I when he warns Dorriforth that "a proper match should be immediately sought out for [Miss Milner], and the care of so dangerous a person given into other hands." Although Sandford might have preferred that Miss Milner's anarchic tendencies be

---

1 On this point, see Jenkins, 283-84, where she argues, "The whole subtext of the conflict between Miss Milner and Sandford allows Inchbald to develop Miss Milner's character and to show Sandford as the most extreme example of the Catholic Church in his belief that he had absolute authority to regulate her conduct and to impose his views on her every move" (283).

2 Craft-Fairchild reads the power struggle here as manipulated by Dorriforth, "the hidden controlling patriarchal force between all of Sandford's and Miss Milner's skirmishes" (93).

controlled by someone less closely connected to him than Lord Elmwood, Sandford chooses her marriage to Elmwood as an acceptable compromise to the more disruptive alternative of her remaining anarchically single.[1]

Theatricality, Performance and Gender

Influence of the Theatre

The eighteenth-century novel, still a developing form in 1791, self-consciously defined itself in opposition to other genres, even while it borrowed from or reinterpreted them. Ann Radcliffe,[2] for example, heightened the suspense in her Gothic fiction by interspersing her narrative with poetry, and Laurence Sterne[3] and other writers of sentimental novels in the eighteenth century relied heavily on dramatic conventions such as gesture, emotion, and *tableaux*.[4] Inchbald's *A Simple Story*, extremely popular throughout Europe and the United States, also borrowed from other genres, including drama. While Inchbald was composing *A Simple Story*, she was discovering that the form of the novel allowed her to explore the intricacies of her characters' emotions, motives, and even physical appearances in much more detail than she had been able to do as a playwright. As Diane Osland has argued, the "intelligible but simple signs" that Edgeworth admired in a talented actor's performance, or that she herself would have used onstage, "may convey the *force* of those feelings, [but] they cannot convey the exact nature of those feelings—or at least not as Inchbald conceives of them" (83). Osland notices that Inchbald effectively conveyed ambiguous feelings and motives by listing alternative, equally plausible explanations for her characters' actions. When Sir Edward Ashton visits Miss Milner early in the

---

1 On this point, see Castle, 298.

2 Ann Radcliffe (1764-1823), a writer of Gothic novels best known for her mastery of the terror and suspense that typify the Gothic genre.

3 Laurence Sterne (1713-68), a popular novelist who pushed the limits of conventional narration, interspersing his narrative with reflective pauses forced by images—a marbled page, a blank page, or a black page.

4 I.e., theatrical conventions where actors presented silent, unmoving scenes on the stage.

novel, for example, Inchbald's narrator simply offers two separate explanations for his reluctance to speak: he is "either so unwilling to give pain to the object of his love, or so much intimidated by her frowns, that he seldom addressed a single word to her." In the theatre, conveying the exact motivation for uncertain or ambiguous gestures, such as Ashton's unwillingness to speak, would have been difficult, if not impossible.

Inchbald was keenly aware of the forms in which she was writing, and she discussed the freedoms and limitations for both the novelist and the playwright in her 1807 letter *To The Artist* (see Appendix A1). In the letter, Inchbald argues that a novel's details can convey "unwelcome news" such as the reader's fading beauty, her malice, or her greed, without risking offense. The playwright, conversely, is subject to uncertainties such as official censorship or actors' unpredictable performances, either of which can significantly alter the perception of a play for a particular audience. Inchbald writes in the letter that "whilst the poor dramatist is ... confined to a few particular provinces ... the novel-writer has the whole world to range."

As several critics have noted, Inchbald used her experience in the theatre to create what Edgeworth described as "a belief in the real existence of the characters."[1] In *A Simple Story*, Inchbald detailed theatrical movements and gestures, demonstrating, as Nora Nachumi explains (332), "that bodies express emotions more authentically and more persuasively than words alone." However, though writing novels allowed Inchbald to describe indefinite and sometimes inconsistent motives, she also recognized the unique power of physical representation on the stage. In a frequently cited essay on Shakespeare's *Macbeth* in *The British Theatre* (1808), Inchbald writes enthusiastically about John Philip Kemble and Sarah Siddons (her friends) in a particularly memorable performance of the play. The long list of specific details in Inchbald's description indicates how personal and immediate the stage was for her:

> But to those who are unacquainted with the effect wrought
> by theatrical action and decoration, it may not be superfluous

---

1   See Edgeworth's letter to Inchbald in Appendix B3.

to say—the huge rocks, the enormous caverns, and blasted heaths of Scotland, in the scenery;—the highland warrior's dress, of centuries past, worn by soldiers and their generals;—the splendid robes and banquet at the royal court held at Fores;—the awful, yet inspiring music, which accompanies words assimilated to each sound;—and, above all,—the fear, the terror, the remorse;—the agonizing throbs and throes, which speak in looks, whispers, sudden starts, and writhings, by Kemble and Mrs. Siddons, all tending to one great precept—*Thou shalt not murder*,—render this play one of the most impressive moral lessons which the stage exhibits.

Inchbald tried in her novels to recreate the spectacle that she admired in popular plays. In *A Simple Story*, she included, as much as she could in the form of the novel, elements of theatrical action. Inchbald allowed her narrator to detail the looks and whispers that she appreciated on the stage, but she remained aware, as Nachumi points out, that a performance "was designed to provoke an immediate emotional reaction while reading encouraged reflection" (330). In many ways, *A Simple Story* is Inchbald's attempt to merge two forms, the novel and the play. She seems, in effect, to be creating a permanent stage performance. That early reviewers of *A Simple Story* often commented on the theatrical qualities of the novels is not at all surprising. (See Appendix B1 for sample reviews.)

One of the earliest critics to make an explicit connection between *A Simple Story* and the theatre was Boaden, who compared the seventeen-year hiatus between Volume II and Volume III to the sixteen-year interruption in the narrative of Shakespeare's *The Winter's Tale*. Perhaps Boaden's comment was motivated by Inchbald's own argument in *The British Theatre* (see Appendix A4) that the complex plot of *The Winter's Tale* (spanning two generations and containing several subplots) is best experienced through reading. When the play is performed, Inchbald argues, the audience does not "so feelingly unite all they see and all they hear into a single story, as he who, with the book in his hand, and neither his eye nor ear distracted, combines, and enjoys the whole grand variety." Of the many explanations that have been

offered for Inchbald's choice to combine the two strikingly different halves of *A Simple Story*, Boaden's leads us to one of the most
obvious starting places. If a writer wants to consider the disastrous
and long-lasting effects of separation and betrayal (or *apparent* betrayal, in the case of *The Winter's Tale*), then that writer needs an
audience who will read and consider, not just passively view, the
narrative. When Inchbald states that the novelist has "the whole
world to range," then, she may be referring (at least in part) to the
attention she could expect from a reading audience.

Tableau

In Inchbald's own plays, she often avoided the confusion inherent
in *The Winter's Tale*'s complex plot by avoiding lengthy portrayals
of courtship and marriage, focusing instead on more concentrated
moments when changes occur in the later stages in life—betrayal, divorce, aging, and death. In doing so, she asks what Misty
Anderson considers a "fundamental generic question.... What did
it mean to write in the seemingly romantic, Greek new-comedy
style and *begin* a play with a divorce?" (275). Inchbald's play, *I'll
Tell You What*, is illustrative. In the play, Inchbald isolates and explores startling moments when the family is revealed to have been
disintegrated by a divorce and subsequent remarriage. George's
uncle is at first simply stunned at his nephew George's uncanny
change of circumstance. "Did not I leave you one of the happiest
of men?—married to one of the most beautiful women in the
world?—Did not I give you my blessing and a large fortune, and
did I not stay and see you father of a fine boy?—Then only just
stept over to visit my estate in St. Kitts, and, now I'm come back,
here I find you married to another woman—and your first wife
still *living*—and, egad, she is married to another man." Certainly
the literal disappearance of an entire family leaves dizzying questions for George's Uncle Euston and later for his Uncle Anthony.
Both of these men intend to leave large inheritances to George,
and for practical purposes the recipient of such an inheritance
must be legitimately settled and must produce heirs who can
themselves receive the inheritance when the time comes.
    For Inchbald, the abrupt disturbance of the marital structure

also raises fundamental questions about gender roles. Inchbald's audiences, familiar with the social conventions of the time, would have understood that any man who had simply "stept over" to an estate in St. Kitts, could legitimately have expected everything to remain in its proper place until he returned. As Inchbald's play opens, George has clearly failed in his duty as a man: he has protected neither his own personal circumstance nor the circumstances of future generations in his uncles' absence. The uncomfortable position of George's two uncles in the play parallels that of Lord Elmwood in *A Simple Story*. After Elmwood has "stept over" to the West Indies for three years, he, like George's uncles, discovers upon his return that things have changed. In *A Simple Story*, the moment of return and discovery is presented as a tableau, similar to the beginning of *I'll Tell you What*. Volume III of *A Simple Story* begins with the following statement:

> Throughout life, there cannot happen an event to arrest the reflection of a thoughtful mind more powerfully, or to leave so lasting an impression, as that of returning to a place after a few years absence, and observing an entire alteration in respect to all the persons who once formed the neighborhood—to find some, who but a few years before were left in the bloom of youth and health, dead—to find children left at school, married, with children of their own—some persons who were in riches, reduced to poverty—others who were in poverty, become rich—those, once renowned for virtue, now detested for their vice—roving husbands, grown constant—constant ones, become rovers—the firmest friends, changed to the most implacable enemies—beauty faded.—
> In a word, every change to demonstrate 'All is transitory on this side of the grave.'

Of course, in *A Simple Story*, it is the narrator who has left the neighborhood, but the statement must also refer to Elmwood who also returns after a few years absence to discover the many changes that are revealed at the beginning of Volume III. The scenes of discovery in both the play and the novel are suggestive, as Alison Conway has noticed, of the "tableau vivant," a popular form of entertainment in the eighteenth and nineteenth centuries (195-209). In the tableau, a scene was presented on the stage by actors who posed, unmoving, as if in a painting; in fact, the tableaux often were intended to signify or evoke *actual* paintings.[1] Tableaux had been traditionally presented in private homes, but by the nineteenth century the presentations had developed into public, theatrical performances, performed either at the beginning or the end of a play.[2]

Gender in the Novel

In the tableau that marks the beginning of Volume III, Inchbald seems to suggest that Miss Milner's transgression (her adultery) is simply another inevitable life change, along with children growing up and beauty fading: Miss Milner is "no longer beautiful, no longer beloved, no longer, tremble when you read this, virtuous." But only one of the changes is inevitable—Miss Milner will lose her youthful beauty. In *A Simple Story*, however, the loss of virtue is also inevitable, given the system of governance that Dorriforth (who becomes Lord Elmwood) creates and maintains; Miss Milner's femininity (and by extension her beauty) is a scripted, well-controlled performance, constrained by those in authority, Dorriforth and Sandford.

Similarly, because Dorriforth's masculinity is dependent on his ability to act, to hide his feelings from members of his household who constitute an "audience," it also is performative. The two halves of *A Simple Story* are strikingly different, but the despotism of Dorriforth (continued after he becomes Lord Elmwood) progresses inexorably throughout the novel. Despite the narrator's description of Dorriforth as having "an inexhaustible fund of good nature," his actions seem to indicate that he either does not have

---

1   Richard Schoch notes that a "tableau, whether presented as a discovery at the opening of a scene or as a concluding image of arrested motion, was a frozen stage image recreating or suggesting a recognizable painting through the composition, relation, and gesture of its figures" (37).

2   A related theatrical convention was the pantomime, a silent, moving presentation containing elaborate costumes and scenery. Inchbald often performed in the trendy pre-show pantomimes, although her diary entries suggest that she did not enjoy participating in them (see Jenkins, 117-18).

or is concealing the "*genuine* passion" (Inchbald's emphasis) that Inchbald praised in an 1805 letter to Godwin.[1] The hegemonic masculinity that Dorriforth creates and maintains prevents him from revealing, or even recognizing, any sort of "refined sensibility" or "genuine passion." In one startling example, Dorriforth holds his nephew Rushbrook fondly in his lap until he realizes his relationship with the child:

> Just, however, as the coach stopt, [Miss Milner] had the forecast and the humility to say, "we will not tell Mr. Dorriforth the child is his nephew, Miss Woodley, unless he should appear fond, and pleased with him, and then we may venture without any danger."
>
> This was agreed, and when Dorriforth entered the room just before dinner, poor Harry Rushbrook was introduced to him as the son of a lady who frequently visited there. The deception passed—Dorriforth shook hands with him, and at length highly pleased with his engaging wiles, and applicable replies, took him on his knee, and kissed him with affection. Miss Milner could scarcely restrain the joy this gave her; but unluckily, Dorriforth said soon after the child, "and now tell me your name."
>
> "Harry Rushbrook." Replied he with great force and clearness in his voice.
>
> Dorriforth was holding him fondly round the waist as he stood with his feet upon his knees; and at this reply he did not throw him from him—but he removed his hands, which supported him, so suddenly, that the child to prevent falling to the floor, threw himself about his uncle's neck.—Miss Milner and Miss Woodley turned aside to conceal their tears. "I had liked to have been down." Cried Harry, fearing no other danger.—But his uncle took hold of each hand that had twined around him, and placed him immediately on the ground; and dinner being that instant served, he gave

---

1   Elizabeth Inchbald, letter to William Godwin, 1805, Oxford, Bodleian Library, [Abinger Deposit] Dep. c. 509. Barker-Benfield posits that "Dorriforth's exquisite sensibility makes him deeply susceptible to 'love'—in effect, susceptible to women and to sexuality. Nonetheless, he exercises self-control for several chapters…" (256).

no greater marks of his resentment than calling for his hat, and walking instantly out of the house.

In the novel's second half, Dorriforth (now Lord Elmwood) protects himself from any similar paternal moments by allowing his daughter Matilda to stay in his house only on the condition that he never see her or even hear her name—he threatens to banish her from the house if she disobeys. Within such constraints, Sandford, Miss Woodley, and Rushbrook can only surmise that Elmwood's cruel system is not, in fact, "genuine" but is instead a kind of performance that helps him to hide his love for his daughter and, by extension, for his now-dead wife. When, for example, Matilda first arrives at Elmwood house, Sandford imagines that Elmwood shakes his hand with more warmth than he ever has before, and Sandford assumes (correctly, the narrator implies) that Elmwood is thinking of his daughter Matilda. When Elmwood carefully chooses books from his library for Miss Woodley, the narrator tells us that Miss Woodley "reasonably supposed Matilda's reading, and not hers, was the object of his solicitude."

Later, a well-known scene (in which Matilda faints in Elmwood's arms and his "long-restrained tears" finally burst forth) removes any doubt that Elmwood possesses the "genuine feeling" that Inchbald claimed to admire in Godwin. In the scene, Matilda hears footsteps as she is descending a stairway and is not sure if she should turn back or continue going forward:

—She hesitated a single instant which to do—then went a few steps farther till she came to the second landing place; when, by the sudden winding of the staircase,—Lord Elmwood was immediately before her!

She had felt something like affright before she saw him—but her reason told her she had nothing to fear, as he was far away.—But now the appearance of a stranger whom she had never before seen; an air of authority in his looks as well as in the sound of his steps; a resemblance to the portrait she had seen of him; a start of astonishment which he gave on beholding her; but above all—her *fears* confirmed her it was him.—She gave a scream of terror—put out her trembling hands to catch the balustrades on the stairs for support—missed them—and fell motionless into her father's arms.

He caught her, as by that impulse he would have caught any other person falling for want of aid.—Yet when he found her in his arms, he still held her there—gazed on her attentively—and once pressed her to his bosom.

At length, trying to escape the snare into which he had been led, he was going to leave her on the spot where she fell, when her eyes opened and she uttered, "Save me."—Her voice unmanned him.—His long-restrained tears now burst forth—and seeing her relapsing into the swoon again, he cried out eagerly to recall her.—Her name did not however come to his recollection—nor any name but this—"Miss Milner—Dear Miss Milner."

That sound did not awake her; and now again he wished to leave her in this senseless state, that not remembering what had passed, she might escape the punishment.

Elmwood has indeed been "unmanned" by this sudden contact with his daughter, but the "unmanning" is significant only, the scene makes clear, if Elmwood's behavior has been witnessed by someone other than himself. For an instant, before Elmwood realizes that his moment of weakness has been seen (Giffard, his servant, appears immediately at the bottom of the stairs), he thinks that his daughter "might escape the punishment" that he himself has decreed, of banishment from the house. His hope that his daughter "escape the punishment" must also be seen as a hope that he has not revealed his own powerful sentiments, kept hidden for most of the novel.[1]

Inchbald's interest in the despotic father figure is evident in several of her plays, the form of which allows her to represent her characters' emotional struggles without narrative interruption. In one such play, *Every One Has His Fault*, the father, Lord Norland, is confronted with his penitent daughter kneeling before him in a scene that is reminiscent of the meeting between Matilda and

---

1 Nachumi discusses Elmwood's attempts to conceal his own emotions, attempts that are thwarted because "the heroines' intrusive bodies constantly undermine his emotional reserve" (334).

Elmwood in *A Simple Story*. In the play, we are given no signal that Norland is moved by his daughter's plea. He simply tells her that "your prayers are vain." The audience is given no hint from the text that he will eventually reconcile with his daughter.

Inchbald's *Wives as They Were and Maids as They Are* (a play that Inchbald herself compared to *A Simple Story*)[1] offers a more nuanced portrayal of a conflicted despotic father figure. In the play, the father, Sir William, reveals his paternal love in an aside where he muses that "perhaps I could forgive you. But I must not." As Osland notes, in this scene, "Inchbald is reduced to some fairly cumbersome theatrical effects to convey Sir William's emotional turmoil." In each play, the form of the drama allows Inchbald to emphasize (with the immediacy that a staged performance allows) the frightening power of the despot; however, because the fathers in both plays ultimately reconcile with their daughters, the form of the drama also enables Inchbald to suggest that the despot's masculinity is simply an affectation, a kind of performance that disguises the actual paternal feelings that in the end drive his choices.

In addition to the obvious similarities between *A Simple Story* and Inchbald's earlier plays, the last two volumes of *A Simple Story* were, as already noted, almost certainly influenced by the emerging popularity of the Gothic novel. Lord Elmwood is, in many ways, a typical Gothic villain—Lady Elmwood's ultimate destitution derives directly from Elmwood's almost complete power—but his position as villain is less than comfortable or happy. It seems obvious from early in the novel that Dorriforth/Elmwood genuinely loves Miss Milner, though his behavior in the last couple of volumes of the novel would suggest otherwise, and he is obviously deeply hurt by his wife's betrayal. We know from William Godwin's 1791 journal entry that he read an early version of the novel, which he described as a story about Dorriforth and his nephew: "It was in this year that I read and criticized this Simple Story in ms." A notation on the same page, written sideways on the other side of the page, says: "The story/whole in alternate letters between two confidantes./Miss Woodley relating the story

---

1   See Appendix A for Inchbald's review of the play.

of Dorriforth & the other the story of Rushbrook."[1] Godwin's entry might, as Annibel Jenkins has suggested (310), simply reveal Godwin's own interests in the male characters, but it also might suggest that the novel's earlier version was focused more on the male characters than on the female ones, or that we might want to consider more fully Inchbald's own interest in constructions of masculinity.[2]

Characters in *A Simple Story* often seem to be struggling with conventional notions of masculinity and femininity, acting in ways that disguise their true feelings. This notion of gender as a performance is probably most evident in the novel when members of the second generation try to step outside of existing behavioral paradigms. Matilda may well possess the "manly resentment" of her father (in fact, she tells Rushbrook that if he enters her thoughts at all, it will be as an object of envy), but as a woman she cannot compete with the more forceful presence of physically powerful men such as Margrave, who abducts her, or even with the less-threatening Rushbrook, who forces himself "into her presence and shocks" her with "offers of services which she scorns." Rushbrook's behavior is in many ways imitative of his uncle's, and it is not surprising that Matilda, Sandford, and even Miss Woodley resent him and his position in Elmwood's house.

Inchbald, however, made Rushbrook a more complicated and sympathetic figure by allowing him to tell Miss Woodley that "if you knew the sensations of my heart, you would not treat me with this disdain." Inchbald also gave Rushbrook her mother's maiden name, suggesting, at least, a strong connection with a female lineage. Caroline Breashears has argued that *A Simple Story* "explores the consequences of competing masculine ideals" (453), and these consequences seem particularly evident in Rushbrook's struggle to break out of his uncle Elmwood's powerful familial system. Rushbrook discovers that his existence as a man, and certainly as Elmwood's nephew, amounts to complicity in a hegemonic masculinity no matter what he does or tries to do: in a moment of

---

1 Oxford. Bodleian Library, [Abinger Deposit], Dep. e. 197-99.
2 Critics who have begun to consider masculinity in *A Simple Story* include Caroline Breashears and G.J. Barker-Benfield.

desperation, he cries to Matilda, "What can I do?—What am I to say, to make you change your opinion of me?" Inchbald explores a similar theme of competing masculine ideals in her play *Every One Has His Fault*. When Lord Norland's grandson is forced to make an immediate and unexpected choice between loyalty to his grandfather and love for his mother, he "stands between them in doubt for some little time: looks alternately at each with emotions of affection" before choosing to go away with his mother.[1]

Elmwood, with partial seriousness, offers a solution to Rushbrook's frustration by remarking to Sandford that Rushbrook and Matilda could exist happily on love without Elmwood's approval, consent, power, or money, "for genuine love will make him happy in banishment, in poverty, or in sickness; it makes the poor man happy as the rich, the fool blest as the wise." Of course, happiness based on "genuine love" is the model for *The Winter's Tale*, in which Florizel defies his father's wishes because he loves Perdita. Yet Rushbrook's inability to leave what is essentially a masculine regime emphasizes the impossibility of him achieving any sort of healthy masculinity. The ending to *A Simple Story* is ambiguous about how happy Matilda and Rushbrook will be, staying as they apparently will within the confines of Elmwood Castle. Inchbald's narrator asks the reader to surmise "whether the heart of Matilda, such as it has been described, *could* sentence [Rushbrook] to misery." The statement leaves ambiguous not only whether Matilda had it in her power to actually sentence Rushbrook to misery, but also whether any misery Matilda might inflict on Rushbrook would come from her refusal or from her consent to marry him. The novel's final sentence only increases the ambiguity. If the reader is inclined to assume that Matilda's heart did not sentence Rushbrook to misery, then she "has every reason to suppose" that Matilda and Rushbrook marry and are happy. But the novel itself does not answer the question.

---

1 Norland's grandson assumes the decision will be permanent, but Norland reconciles with his family by the end of the play.

In *A Simple Story*, the ambiguity of Elmwood's self-protective system, and his incongruous paternal or even conjugal love, is most evident in the portrait that hangs in Elmwood Castle. The portrait is displayed publicly, as if in a museum, ostentatiously displaying Elmwood's status as owner of the painting and of everything around it. Elmwood probably would have worn a wig for the portrait,[1] and the formal pose is intended to maintain a distance between the subject (Elmwood) and the viewer (in this case Matilda). We are not told when the portrait was painted—before or after Lady Elmwood's death—so we can only guess at his intended audience. But since Elmwood had originally been released from his vows of celibacy in order to preserve a Catholic lineage, and since he has stated that after his wife's adultery and subsequent death he will not remarry, the portrait can be seen to function as a kind of substitute for a direct male descendent. As John Berger has argued, "The oil painting was thought of as a permanent record. One of the pleasures the painting gave to its owner was the thought it would convey the image of his present to the future of his descendents" (144).

Of course, Elmwood does have a direct descendent in his daughter Matilda, and, ironically, the oil painting is exactly what allows her to achieve a kind of intimacy with her father. The formal pose would have been meant to impose a distance between subject and viewer, but the painting's verisimilitude would have also provided a kind of intimacy—even complete strangers could study the minute features of the subject's face. Whatever Elmwood might have intended with the portrait, it allows his daughter Matilda to "discern the exact moulds in which her own appeared to have been modeled."

Matilda's unauthorized, intimate, gaze at her father gains her a veiled authority, but earlier her mother claims a more immediate and direct power by positioning herself as subject of the male gaze. As Conway argues, "Miss Milner enjoys her power as a

---

1   See Marcia R. Pointon, *Hanging the Head: Portraiture and Social Formation in Eighteenth-Century England*, New Haven, CT: Yale UP, 1993.

spectacle and the freedom to which she is entitled as an unmarried woman" (197). This power and freedom are particularly evident when she attends a masquerade ball, and the masquerade has been the subject of much of the critical attention *A Simple Story* has received.[1] The masquerade was considered dangerous because of its tendency to camouflage or remove barriers caused by social class, physical appearance, age, or even gender. (See Appendix C for sample responses to the masquerade.) Miss Milner's attendance at Mrs. G.'s masked ball unsettles Elmwood not only because her attendance defies his explicit command, but also because it places her in an uncertain situation where her beauty will be displayed to an indeterminate, possibly large audience. As Elmwood states, "she does not know, herself, what company she is in." Miss Milner's costume exemplifies the ambiguity inherent in the masquerade. She is dressed as the goddess of chastity, but the narrator explains that "from the buskins, and the petticoat made to festoon far above the ankle, [the costume] had, on the first glance, the appearance of a female much less virtuous." Miss Milner's boots render her costume sexually ambiguous, so that when she returns from the masquerade, the servants cannot determine whether she left the house dressed as a man or as a woman. This confusion is reminiscent of Dorriforth's own uncertainty about Miss Milner's moral character when, at the beginning of the novel, he questions people she has known in an attempt to "gain intelligence of his ward's disposition." The answers he receives to these early questions are as contradictory as the answers he receives later to his questions about Miss Milner's masquerade costume.

Miss Milner's beauty (and its inherent power) becomes evident almost simultaneously with her realization of its limitations. When, shortly after Dorriforth and Miss Milner first meet, Dorriforth asks Miss Milner incredulously if she really believes she is not handsome, she responds by saying, "I should from my own opinion believe so, but in some respects I am like you Roman Catholics; I don't believe from my own understanding, but from what other

---

1 For extensive discussions of the masquerade in *A Simple Story* see Castle, Conway, Craft-Fairchild, and Schofield.

people tell me." Miss Milner's sarcastic response is, of course, a direct challenge to the authority of the Catholic Church, and by extension, Dorriforth's personal authority, but it also emphasizes the limits of her own power. When others admire her beauty, she gains a kind of authority over them, but her control over people's perception of her as subject is limited at best. If people who gaze at Miss Milner do not recognize her beauty—either because she has married, grown older, transgressed, etc.—then her beauty affords her no power. Dorriforth affirms these limitations when he warns her to "let this be your criterion.... that what we teach is truth; for you find you would be deceived did you not trust to persons who know better than yourself." Later, when after complicated preparations Miss Milner finally arrives at the masquerade, her entrance seems almost passive. Her impression of her own appearance is based on others' reactions: "she *perceived* she was the first object of admiration in the place" (my emphasis).

The few times that Miss Milner actually does look at her appearance in a glass might bring to mind the many portrayals in literature and art of frivolous, vain women admiring their own reflections.[1] Miss Milner, however, seems inevitably disappointed either because what she sees in the mirror does not correspond to the façade she wishes to present or because her intended audience simply does not appear—such as when Elmwood dismisses her would-be lover lord Frederick before he is able to see her, or, later, when Elmwood almost leaves the country after breaking off their engagement. At this point, she says, "after all ... I dare not see him again." Later, when Elmwood has broken off their engagement, Miss Milner, trying to feign indifference, "Scarce able to crawl,... rose, and looked in the glass, as if to arrange her features, so as to impose upon him."

Miss Milner's daughter Matilda never consults a mirror at all[2]—evidence perhaps that she accepts her own abjection in a

---

1 See, for example, in Burney's *Evelina*, Evelina's cousins, the Braughtons, interrupt her and her companion Miss Mirvan dressing before a mirror. The cousins are delighted to have caught Evelina "at the glass" (185).

2 The mirror itself was an expensive commodity and would probably be an unavailable luxury for Matilda.

way that her mother never does.[1] Miss Milner's attempts to "arrange her features" in the mirror are echoed when Matilda stares obsessively at her father's portrait, imagining that she sees a version of her own features. The inadequacy of her fantasy, however, is evident when Elmwood accepts his nephew as a surrogate offspring, even "heir apparent," regardless of his daughter's physical resemblance to him. Like Miss Milner, Matilda gains Elmwood's love only when she positions herself (or is positioned) as subject, not as viewer: when she faints in her father's arms and later when she is rescued after her abduction by Lord Margrave. In both cases, Elmwood's acceptance of his daughter is initiated by her vulnerability (which neutralizes her threat to his self-protective system of governance), but, more importantly, by her physical resemblance to her mother, not to him. When Elmwood catches Matilda in his arms, he invokes his dead wife's name, calling, "Miss Milner, my dear Miss Milner." At this moment, his daughter has been rendered unconscious by the sight of his face, an image that she has studied repeatedly. *A Simple Story*'s concern with these images—real and imagined, male and female—is made explicit by Inchbald's descriptions of the mirror, the masquerade, and the portrait, each of which illustrates the power afforded by appearance and disguise.

---

1 See Haggerty's discussion of abjection in *A Simple Story*, (655-71). In *Nature and Art*, Inchbald addresses directly the limitations of female beauty. At the end of the novel, the fallen Hannah, drastically altered by poverty and aging, has changed so much so as to become unrecognizable to others and even to herself. When she accidentally sees her own reflection, she "start[s] back as if it [is] some other face she s[ees] instead of her own." [*Nature and Art* (London: G.G. and J. Robinson, 1796), 90]. Her former lover William, now a judge, sentences her to death without ever realizing who she is.

Elizabeth Inchbald: A Brief Chronology

[Unless otherwise noted, dates given for Inchbald's plays are dates of first performance.]

1753   Born on 15 October in Standingfield, Suffolk, England, seventh of eight children born to John and Mary Simpson.

1760   George II dies. His son becomes George III.

1761   John Simpson (Inchbald's father) dies.

1770   George Simpson joins Norwich players. Elizabeth applies unsuccessfully to Richard Griffith's company in Norwich.

1771   First visit to London. Meets Joseph Inchbald, actor and painter.

1772   Leaves for London on 11 April.
Marries Joseph Inchbald on 9 June. Catholic wedding ceremony followed by an official Anglican ceremony.
Inchbalds go to Bristol on 4 September, where Elizabeth plays Cordelia to Joseph's Lear.
Inchbalds join West Digges's company in Scotland in October.

1773   Parliament appoints Warren Hastings governor general of the East India Company's possessions in India.

1776   Inchbalds leave Scotland to search for new work on 12 June.
Inchbalds go to Paris on 23 July. He paints; she studies French.
Inchbalds return to London in August.
Meets John Philip Kemble, actor, former priest, and perhaps the model for Dorriforth in *A Simple Story*. Begins work on novel that some have argued was an early version of *A Simple Story*. The Inchbalds go to Canterbury, where they meet Thomas Holcroft.

1777   Inchbalds join Joseph Younger's company at Liverpool in October. Begins lifelong friendship with Sarah Siddons.

1778　First Catholic Relief Act.

1779　Finishes novel that is turned down by Stockdale. Joseph Inchbald dies suddenly at age 44 on 6 June.

1780　2–8 June, the Gordon Riots. Joins Thomas Harris's company at Covent Garden in September.

1780–81　Writes *Antient Law* (never performed or published).

1782　Treaty of Paris ends American Revolutionary War.

1783　Mary Simpson (Inchbald's mother) dies.

1784　Performs in her own play, *A Mogul Tale; or, The Descent of the Balloon* (published 1786). East India Company placed under England's jurisdiction.

1785　*I'll Tell You What* (published 1786). *Appearance is Against Them* (published 1785).

1786　*Emily Herbert* (epistolary novel that has been attributed to Inchbald). *The Widow's Vow* (adapted from Joseph Patrat's *L'heureuse Erreur*; published 1786).

1787　*All on a Summer's Day* (never published); *Such Things Are* (published 1788); *The Midnight Hour* (adapted from M. Dumaniant, *Guerre Ouverte; ou, Ruse Contre Ruse*). Topham and Este launch successful newspaper, *The World and Fashionable Advertiser*. Inchbald contributes entries under the pseudonym, "The Muse."

1788　*The Child of Nature* (adapted from Mme. de Genlis's *Zelie, ou l'Ingenue*). *Animal Magnetism* (adapted from Dumaniant's *Le Medicin malgré tout le monde*; published 1789). Hastings Trial begins.

1789　*The Married Man* (adapted from Phillipe Destouches, *Le Philosophe Marie*; published 1789). Stops acting on the stage. Fall of Bastille.

1790　*The Contrast* ("from the French"). Translation of Rousseau's *Confessions*. Second Catholic Relief Act. Financial dispute ends collaboration between Topham and Este. William Godwin reads manuscript version of *A Simple Story*.

1791　First edition of *A Simple Story* published by Robinson in February. *Hue and Cry* (adapted from Dumaniant's *La*

Nuit aux aventures). Next Door Neighbors (adapted from Destouches, *Le dissipateur*, and Louis Sebastian Mercier, *L'indigent*; published 1791).
Second edition of *A Simple Story* published in March.

1792 *Young Men and Old Women* (adapted from Jean Baptiste Louis Gresset's *Le Mechant*; never published). Writes *The Massacre*, a response to the French Revolution (adapted from Mercier, *Jean Hennuer, Eveque de Lizieux*; never performed or published until Boaden includes it in his 1833 *Memoirs of Mrs. Inchbald*). Deborah Simpson (Inchbald's sister) dies. Mary Wollstonecraft publishes *A Vindication of the Rights of Woman.*

1793 *Everyone Has His Fault* (published 1793). Third edition of *A Simple Story* published. Louis XVI and Marie Antoinette executed in France. William Godwin publishes *Enquiry Concerning the Principles of Political Justice.*

1794 *The Wedding Day* (published 1794). Finishes *Nature and Art.* Godwin publishes *Caleb Williams.*

1795 Hastings acquitted. George Simpson (Inchbald's brother) killed in a duel.

1796 *Nature and Art* published. Meets Prince Hoare, publisher of *The Artist.*

1797 *Wives As They Were and Maids As They Are* (published 1797).Second edition of *Nature and Art* published. Godwin marries Wollstonecraft on March 29. Wollstonecraft dies on September 10 of complications following the birth of their daughter Mary.

1798 *Lovers' Vows* (adaptation of Kotzebue's *Das Kind der Liebe*; rehearsed by the Bertram family in Austen's *Mansfield Park*).

1799 *Wise Man of the East* (adaptation of Kotzebue's *Das Schreiberpult*); published 1799. Fourth edition of *A Simple Story* published.

1800 *Case of Conscience* (not performed or published until it is included in James Boaden's *Memoirs of Mrs. Inchbald*).

1801 George Robinson (Inchbald's friend and publisher) dies.

1805 *To Marry or not to Marry* (published 1805).

1806-08 Writes series of biographical and critical prefaces to popular plays, compiled and published in 1808 under the title *The British Theatre.*

1807 Letter "To the Artist" about the craft of novel-writing published in Prince Hoare's journal, *The Artist.*

1809 *Collection of Farces* published. (Seven volumes of plays selected by Inchbald, but not edited or prefaced.) Unsigned essay defending the theatre published in Prince Hoare's *The Artist.*

1810 Final edition of *A Simple Story* and third edition of *Nature and Art* published in Barbauld's *The British Novelists.*

1811 Inchbald's *Modern Theatre* published. (Ten-volume series of plays that she selected, but did not edit or preface.)

1819 At the advice of her confessor, burns her memoirs and all critiques of them.

1820 Fourth edition of *Nature and Art* published in *The British Novelists.* George III dies. His son becomes George IV.

1821 Dies on 1 August of inflammation of the intestines, at the age of 69, leaving an estate of more than 5,000£. Buried in Kensington churchyard and given all the rites and ceremonies of the Catholic Church. Two Catholic Priests attend the Church of England funeral service that follows the burial.

1833 *A Case of Conscience* and *The Massacre* published in James Boaden's *Memoirs of Mrs. Inchbald.*

A Note on the Text

After its initial publication, *A Simple Story* was revised four times: in March 1791 (only one month after its first publication), in 1793, in 1799, and again in 1810. This Broadview text is based on the first edition of February 1791. Readers prefer the first edition because they admire the spontaneity and force of Inchbald's prose, heightened by idiomatic vocabulary and informal phrasing. There is in the later editions a loss of energy and a diminished sense of Inchbald's unmediated and sometimes uncontrolled voice, even if the revisions erase a few grammatical idiosyncrasies or make certain scenes less startling or improbable. Inchbald's many corrections and emendations resulted in a more predictable and contrived prose style with a loss of the first edition's compelling vitality.

In this edition, I have retained Inchbald's original spelling and punctuation, and I have noted in footnotes and appendices significant changes Inchbald made for later editions. A few obvious typographical errors (such as an incorrect name or an inconsistent spelling of a name) have been corrected. These corrections are recorded in footnotes. Inchbald's errata, listed at the end of each volume of the first edition, have been integrated without note. With these few exceptions, every attempt has been made to preserve the spirit and details of the first edition text.

A SIMPLE STORY

A

SIMPLE STORY.

IN

FOUR VOLUMES.

By Mrs. INCHBALD.

VOL. I.

LONDON:

Printed for G. G. J. and J. ROBINSON,
Pater-noster Row.

M,DCC,XCI.

PREFACE[1]

IT is said, *a book should be read with the same spirit with which it has been written*.[2] In that case, fatal must be the reception of this—for the writer frankly avows, that during the time she has been writing it, she has suffered every quality and degree of weariness and lassitude, into which no other employment could have betrayed her.

It has been the destiny of the writer of this Story, to be occupied throughout her life, in what has the least suited either her inclination or capacity—with an invincible impediment in her speech, it was her lot for thirteen years to gain a subsistence by public speaking—and, with the utmost detestation to the fatigue of inventing, a constitution suffering under a sedentary life, and an education confined to the narrow boundaries prescribed her sex, it has been her fate to devote a tedious seven years to the unremitting labour of literary productions[3]—whilst a taste for authors of the first rank has been an additional punishment, forbidding her one moment of those self-approving reflections which are assuredly due to the industrious.—But, alas! in the exercise of the arts, industry scarce bears the name of merit.—What then is to be substituted in the place of genius? GOOD FORTUNE.—And if these volumes should be attended by the good fortune that has accompanied her other writings, to that divinity, and that alone, she shall attribute their success.

Yet, there is a *first cause* still, to whom I cannot here forbear to mention my obligations.

The Muses, I trust, will pardon me, that to them I do not feel myself obliged—for, in justice to their heavenly inspirations, I believe they have never yet favored me with one visitation; but sent in their disguise NECESSITY, who being the mother of

---

1 The Preface was omitted from the third, fourth, and fifth editions.
2 Compare to Pope's *An Essay on Criticism* (1711): "A perfect Judge will read each Work of Wit/With the same Spirit that its Author writ" (ll.233-34).
3 *Antient Law* (written in 1780) was the first play that Inchbald composed, but the reference here is probably to *A Mogul Tale* (performed in 1784 and published in 1786), the first of Inchbald's plays to be performed.

Invention,[1] gave me all mine—while FORTUNE kindly smiled, and was accessary to the cheat.

But this important secret I long wished, and endeavored to conceal; yet one unlucky moment candidly, though unwittingly, divulged it—I frankly owned, "That Fortune having chased away Necessity, there remained no other incitement to stimulate me to a labour I abhorred."—It happened to be in the power of the person to whom I confided this secret to send NECESSITY once more.[2]—Once more, then, bowing to its empire, I submit to the task it enjoins.

The case has something similar to the theatrical anecdote told (I think) by Colly Cibber:[3]

A performer of a very mean salary, played the Apothecary in Romeo and Juliet so exactly to the satisfaction of the audience, that this little part, independent of the other characters, drew immense houses whenever the play was performed—The manager in consequence, thought it but justice to advance the actor's salary; on which the poor man (who,

---

1   The axiom first appeared in Plato's *Republic* but was later used in several Restoration and eighteenth-century plays, including George Farquhar's *The Twin Rivals* (1702), William Wycherley's *Love in a Wood* (1671), and Sheridan's *The Critic*. Also compare to Samuel Richardson's *Clarissa* (1747-48) in which Clarissa states that "necessity may well be called the mother of invention—but calamity is the test of integrity" (1247). Inchbald's mother reportedly read this novel aloud to Elizabeth and her sisters. See Frances Phillips's transcription of the diary of Inchbald's sister, Ann Simpson Hunt. Folger M.s. Y.d. 592 (10), f. 1.

2   The necessity to which Inchbald refers may have been caused by the ending, in 1790, of the collaboration (begun in 1787) between Edward Topham, (1751-1820) and Charles Este (1753-1829) on the production of *The World and Fashionable Advertiser*. Inchbald contributed to the successful newspaper and may have been paid for her efforts, although her diary entries for 1788 do not contain the financial records that would verify this assumption. See Jenkins (245-348) for a discussion of Inchbald's contributions to *The World*.

3   Colley Cibber (1671-1757), dramatist, actor, manager for Drury Lane (1710-32), and poet laureate (1730-57). This story does not appear in his *Apology for the Life of Mr Colley Cibber, Comedian, with a Historical View of the Stage during his own Time* (1740) or in his *The Lives of the Poets of Great Britain and Ireland* (1753), although both works contain anecdotes about writers (including John Dryden and George Farquhar) who, like Inchbald, were driven by financial necessity to write. Farquhar (1678-1707), an Irish dramatist and actor, was forced to leave the stage and take up writing when he accidentally wounded another actor during a stage fight in a performance of John Dryden's *The Indian Emperor* (1665).

like the character, he represented, had been half starved before) began to live so comfortably, he became too plump for the part; and being of no importance in any thing else, the manager of course now wholly discharged him—and thus, actually reducing him to the want of a piece of bread, in a short time he became a proper figure for the part again.

Welcome, then, thou all-powerful principle, NECESSITY!—THOU, who art the instigator of so many bad authors and actors—but, to their shame, not of all:—THOU, who from my infancy seldom hast forsaken me, still abide with me.—I will not complain of any hardship thy commands require, so thou doest not urge my pen to prostitution.—In all thy rigour, oh! do not force my toil to libels—or, what is equally pernicious—panegyric on the unworthy!

— VOLUME I —

CHAPTER I

DORRIFORTH, bred at St. Omer's[1] in all the scholastic rigour of
that college, was by education, and the solemn vows of his order,
a Roman Catholic priest—but nicely discriminating between
the philosophical and the superstitious part of that character, and
adopting the former only, he possessed qualities not unworthy
the first professors of Christianity—every virtue which it was his
vocation to preach, it was his care to practise; nor was he in the
class of those of the religious, who, by secluding themselves from
the world, fly the merit they might have in reforming mankind.
He refused to shelter himself from the temptations of the layman
by the walls of a cloister, but sought for, and found that shelter
in the centre of London, where he dwelt, in his own prudence,
justice, fortitude, and temperance.[2]

He was about thirty, and had lived in the metropolis near five
years, when a gentleman, above his own age, but with whom he
had from his youth contracted a most sincere friendship, died,
and left him the sole guardian of his daughter, a young lady of
eighteen.

The deceased Mr. Milner,[3] on his approaching dissolution,
perfectly sensible of his state, thus reasoned to himself before he
made the nomination: "I have formed no intimate friendship
during my whole life, except one—I can be said to know the
heart of no man except the heart of Dorriforth—After knowing

---

1   Because the education of Catholics was prohibited in England, several colleges, in-
    cluding St. Omer, were established on the continent by English Catholics.
2   The four cardinal virtues of Christian theology, explained by St. Thomas Aquinas in
    his *Summa Theologica* and his Commentaries on the Nicomachean Ethics. These four
    virtues can also be found in Plato's *Symposium* and in the writings of Aristotle.
3   J.M.S. Tompkins has suggested that Mr. Milner's name might have been a refer-
    ence to Bishop Milner, a famous supporter of the English Catholic population. See
    Oxford edition of *A Simple Story* (6, note 1). Bishop Milner went to school with the
    actor John Philip Kemble and probably also knew Kemble's sister, the prominent
    actress, Sarah Siddons.

his, I never sought acquaintance with another—I did not wish to lessen the exalted estimation of human nature he had inspired. In this moment of trembling apprehension from every thought that darts across my mind, much more for every action which soon I must be called to answer for; all worldly views here thrown aside, I act as if that tribunal before which I every moment expect to appear, were now sitting in judgment upon my purpose.—The care of an only child is the great charge that in this tremendous crisis I have to execute—these earthly affections that bind me to her by custom, sympathy, or what I fondly call parental love, would direct me to study her present happiness, and leave her to the care of some of those she styles her dearest friends; but they are friends only in the sunshine of fortune; in the cold nipping frost of disappointment, sickness, or connubial strife, they will forsake the house of care, although the house which they themselves may have built."

Here the excruciating anguish of the father, overcame that of the dying man.

"In the moment of desertion," continued he, "which I now picture to myself, where will my child find comfort?—That heavenly aid religion gives, which now amidst these agonizing tortures, chears with the bright ray of consolation my frightened soul; that, she will be denied."

It is in this place proper to remark, that Mr. Milner was a member of the church of Rome, but on his marriage with a lady of Protestant tenets, they mutually agreed their sons should be educated in the religious opinion of their father, and their daughters in that of their mother.[1] One child only was the result of their union, the child whose future welfare now occupied the thoughts of her expiring father—from him the care of her education had been withheld, as he kept inviolate the promise made to her departed mother on the article of religion, and therefore consigned his daughter to a Protestant boarding-school, from whence she was sent with merely such sentiments of religion, as young ladies of fashion mostly imbibe. Her little heart employed in all the

---

1   A common practice among English Catholics. John Philip Kemble, for example, was Catholic, and his sister, Sarah Kemble Siddons, was Protestant.

endless pursuits of personal accomplishments, had left her mind without one ornament, except those which nature gave, and even they were not wholly preserved from the ravages made by its rival, *Art*.[1]

While her father was in health he beheld with the extreme of delight, his accomplished daughter without one fault with which taste or elegance could have reproached her, nor ever enquired what might be her other failings—Cast on a bed of sickness, and upon the point of leaving her to her future fate, those failings at once rushed on his memory—and all the pride, the fond enjoyment he had taken in beholding her open the ball, or delight her hearers with her sprightly wit, escaped his remembrance; or not escaping, were thought of with a sigh of contrition, or at best a contemptuous frown, at the frivolous qualification.

"Something more essential," said he to himself, "must be considered—something to prepare her for an hour like this I now experience—can I then leave her to the charge of those who themselves never remember such an hour will come?—Dorriforth is the only person I know, who, uniting every moral virtue to those of religion, and native honour to pious faith; will protect without controuling, instruct without tyrannizing, comfort without flattering, and perhaps in time make good by choice rather than by constraint, the dear object of his dying friend's sole care."

Dorriforth, who came post from London to visit Mr. Milner in his illness, received a few moments before his death all his injunctions, and promised to fulfil them—but in this last token of Mr. Milner's perfect esteem of his friend, he still restrained him from all authority to direct his ward in one religious opinion contrary to those her mother had professed, and in which she herself had been educated.

"Never perplex her mind with an idea that may disturb, but cannot reform"—were his latest words, and Dorriforth's reply gave him entire satisfaction.

Miss Milner was not with her father at this affecting period—

---

1   Compare to Inchbald's novel *Nature and Art* (1796), in which one brother is brought up on an African island away from the harmful influences of civilized society and another is educated in aristocratic society.

some delicately nervous friend, with whom she was on a visit at Bath, thought proper to conceal from her not only the danger of his death, but even his indisposition, lest it might alarm a mind she thought too susceptible. This refined tenderness gave poor Miss Milner the almost insupportable agony, of hearing her father was no more, even before she was told he was not in health. In the bitterest anguish she flew to pay her last duty to his remains, and performed it with the truest filial love, while Dorriforth, upon important business, was obliged to return to town.

CHAPTER II

DORRIFORTH returned to London heavily afflicted for the loss of his friend, and yet perhaps with his thoughts more engaged upon the trust that friend had reposed in him. He knew the life Miss Milner had been accustomed to lead; he dreaded the repulses his admonitions might possibly meet from her; and feared he had undertaken a task he was too weak to execute—the protection of a young woman of fashion.

Mr. Dorriforth was nearly related to one of our first catholic peers; his income was by no means confined, but approaching to affluence, yet his attention to those in poverty, and the moderation of his own desires were such, that he lived in all the careful plainness of œconomy—his habitation was in the house of a Mrs. Horton, an elderly lady, who had a maiden niece residing with her not many years younger than herself—But although Miss Woodley[1] was thirty,[2] and in person exceedingly plain, yet she possessed such an extreme chearfulness of temper, and such an inexhaustible fund of good nature, that she escaped not only the ridicule, but even the appellation of an old maid.

In this house Dorriforth had lived before the death of Mr. Horton, nor upon that event did he think it necessary, notwithstanding his religious vow of celibacy, to fly the roof of two such unseductive innocent females[3] as Mrs. Horton and her niece—on

---

1 Inchbald first submitted her play, *The Mogul Tale* (performed in 1784; published in 1786), under the pseudonym Mrs. Woodley.

2 In the second, third, fourth, and fifth editions, "thirty-five."

3 In the second, third, fourth, and fifth editions, "unseductive" is removed.

their part, they regarded him with all that respect and reverence the most religious flock regards its pastor; and his friendly society they not only esteemed a spiritual, but a temporal advantage, as the liberal stipend he allowed for his apartments and board enabled them to continue in the large and commodious house, where they had resided during the life of Mr. Horton.

Here, upon Mr. Dorriforth's return from his journey, preparations were made for the reception of his ward, her father having made it one of his requests that she might, for a time at least, dwell in the same house with her guardian, receive the same visits, and cultivate the acquaintance of his acquaintances and friends.

When the will of her father was made known to Miss Milner, she submitted without the smallest reluctance to all he had required—her mind, at that time impressed with the most poignant sorrow for his loss, made no distinction of happiness that was to come; and the day was appointed, with her silent acquiescence, when she was to arrive in London, and take up her abode at Mrs. Horton's, with all the retinue of a rich heiress.

Mrs. Horton was delighted with the addition this acquisition to her family was likely to make to her annual income, and to the style of her living.—The goodnatured Miss Woodley was overjoyed at the expectation of their new guest, yet she herself could not tell why—but the reason was, her kind heart wanted more ample field for its benevolence; and now her thoughts were all pleasingly employed how she should render, not only the lady herself, but even all her attendants, happy in their new situation.

The thoughts of Dorriforth were less agreeably engaged—Cares, doubts, fears, possessed his mind—so forcibly possessed it, that upon every occasion which offered, he would inquisitively try to gain intelligence of his ward's disposition before he saw her; for he was, as yet, a stranger not only to the real propensities of her mind, but even to her person; a constant round of visits having prevented his meeting her at her father's, the very few times he had been at his house, since her return from boarding-school. The first person whose opinion he, with all proper reserve, asked concerning Miss Milner was Lady Evans, the widow of a baronet who frequently visited at Mrs. Horton's.

But that the reader may be interested in what Dorriforth says and does, it is necessary to give some description of his person and manners. His figure was tall and elegant, but his face, except a pair of dark bright eyes, a set of white teeth, and a graceful fall in his clerical curls of dark brown hair, had not one feature to excite admiration—he possessed notwithstanding such a gleam of sensibility diffused over each, that many people mistook his face for handsome, and all were more or less attracted by it—in a word, the charm that is here meant to be described is a countenance—on his countenance you beheld the feelings of his heart—saw all its inmost workings—the quick pulses that beat with hope and fear, or the placid ones that were stationary with patient resignation.[1] On this countenance his thoughts were pictured, and as his mind was enriched with every virtue that could make it valuable, so was his honest face adorned with every emblem of those virtues—and they not only gave a lustre to his aspect, but added a harmonious sound to all he uttered; it was persuasive, it was perfect eloquence, whilst in his looks you behold his thoughts moving with his lips, and ever coinciding with what he said.

With one of those interesting looks which revealed the anxiety of his heart, and with that graceful restraint of all gesticulation, for which he was remarkable even in his most anxious concerns, he addressed lady Evans who had called on Mrs. Horton to hear and to tell the news of the day: "Your ladyship was at Bath last spring—you know the young lady to whom I have the honour of being appointed guardian.—Pray"—

He was earnestly intent upon asking a question, but was prevented by her ladyship.

"Dear Mr. Dorriforth, do not ask me any thing about the lady—when I saw her she was very young; though indeed that is but three months ago, and she can't be much older now."

"She is eighteen." Answered Dorriforth, colouring with regret at the doubts her ladyship had increased, but not inspired.

"And she is very beautiful, that I can assure you." Replied her ladyship.

"Which I call no qualification." Said Dorriforth, rising from his seat in evident uneasiness.

---

1   In the second, third, fourth, and fifth editions, "the gentle ones that moved in a more equal course of patience and resignation."

"But when there is nothing else," returned Lady Evans, "let me tell you, beauty is something."

"Much worse than nothing, in my opinion." Returned Dorriforth.

"But now, Mr. Dorriforth, do not from what I have said, frighten yourself, and imagine the young lady worse than she really is—all I know of her, is merely, that she's a young, idle, indiscreet, giddy girl, with half a dozen lovers in her suite; some coxcombs, some men of gallantry, some single, and some married."

Dorriforth started.—"For the first time of my life," cried he with a manly sorrow, "I wish I had never known her father."

"Nay," said Mrs. Horton, who expected every thing to happen just as she wished, (for neither an excellent education, the best company, or long experience had been able to cultivate or brighten this good lady's understanding.) "Nay," said she, "I am sure, Mr. Dorriforth, you will soon convert her from all her evil ways."

"Dear me," returned lady Evans, "I am sure I never meant to hint at any thing evil—and for what I have said, I will give you up my authors if you please; for they were not observations of my own; all I do is to mention them again."

The good natured Miss Woodley, who sat working at the window, an humble listener to this discourse, ventured on this to say exactly six words: "Then do'nt mention them any more."

"Let us change the subject," said Dorriforth.

"With all my heart," cried her ladyship, "and I am sure it will be to the young lady's advantage."

"Is she tall, or short?" asked Mrs. Horton, still wishing for farther information.

"Oh, tall enough of all conscience," returned lady Evans; "I tell you again there is no fault can be found with her person."

"But if her mind is defective"—exclaimed Dorriforth with a sigh—

"—That may be improved as well as the person." Cried Miss Woodley.

"No my dear," returned her ladyship, "I never heard of a pad to make strait an ill-shapen disposition."

"O yes, lady Evans," answered Miss Woodley, "good company,

good books, experience, and the misfortunes of others, may have more power to form the mind to virtue, than"—

Her ladyship would not suffer her to go on, but rising hastily from her seat, cried, "I must be gone—I have fifty people waiting for me at home—besides, were I inclined to hear a sermon, I should desire Mr. Dorriforth to preach, and not you."

Just then Mrs. Hillgrave was announced.—"And here is Mrs. Hillgrave."—Continued lady Evans—"I believe Mrs. Hillgrave you know Miss Milner, don't you? The young lady who has lately lost her father."

Mrs. Hillgrave was the wife of a merchant who had met with some severe losses, and as soon as the name of Miss Milner was uttered, she lifted up her hands, and the tears started in her eyes.

"There!" cried lady Evans, "I desire you will give your opinion of her, and I am sorry I cannot stay to hear it." Saying this, she courtesied and took her leave.

When Mrs. Hillgrave had been seated a few minutes, Mrs. Horton, who loved information equal to the most inquisitive of her sex, begged that lady,—"if she might be permitted to know, why, at the mention of Miss Milner, she had seemed so much affected?"

This question interesting the fears of Dorriforth, he turned anxiously round attentive to the reply.

"Miss Milner," answered she, "has been my benefactress, and the best I ever had." As she spoke, she took out her handkerchief and wiped away the tears that ran down her face.

"How so?" cried Dorriforth eagerly, with his eyes moistened with joy, nearly as much as her's were with gratitude.

"My husband, at the commencement of his distresses," replied Mrs. Hillgrave, "owed a sum of money to her father, and from repeated provocations, Mr. Milner was determined to seize upon all our effects—his daughter, however, procured us time in order to discharge the debt; and when she found that time was insufficient, and her father no longer to be dissuaded from his intention, she secretly sold some of her most valuable ornaments to satisfy his demand and screen us from its consequences."

Dorriforth, pleased at this recital, took Mrs. Hillgrave by the hand, and told her "she should never want a friend."

"Is Miss Milner tall, or short?" again asked Mrs. Horton, fearing from the sudden pause which had ensued the subject should be dropped.

"I don't know." Answered Mrs. Hillgrave.

"Is she handsome, or ugly?"

"I really can't tell."

"It is very strange you should not take notice!"

"I did take notice, but I cannot depend upon my own judgment—to me she appeared beautiful as an angel, but perhaps I was deceived by the beauties of her disposition."

CHAPTER III

THIS gentlewoman's visit inspired Mr. Dorriforth with some confidence in the principles and character of his ward.—The day arrived on which she was to leave her late father's seat, to take up her abode at Mrs. Horton's; and he, accompanied by Miss Woodley, went in his carriage to meet her, and waited at an inn on the road for her reception.

After many a sigh paid to the memory of her father, Miss Milner, upon the tenth of November, arrived at the place, half way on her journey to town, where Dorriforth and Miss Woodley were expecting her.—Besides attendants, she had with her a gentleman and a lady, distant relations of her mother's, who thought it but a proper testimony of their civility to attend her part of the way, but who so much envied her guardian the trust Mr. Milner had reposed in him, that as soon as they had delivered her safe into his care they returned.

When the carriage which brought Miss Milner stopped at the inn gate, and her name was announced to Dorriforth, he turned pale—something like a foreboding of disaster trembled at his heart, and consequently darted over all his face.[1]—Miss Woodley was even obliged to rouze him from the dejection into which he was cast, or he would have sunk beneath it—she was obliged also to be the first to welcome his lovely charge.—Lovely beyond description.

---

1 In the second, third, fourth, and fifth editions, "spread a gloom over all his face."

But the sprightly vivacity, the natural gaiety, which report had given to Miss Milner, were softened by her recent sorrow to a meek sadness—and that haughty display of charms, imputed to her manners, was changed to a pensive demeanor.—The instant Dorriforth was introduced to her by Miss Woodley as her "Guardian, and her deceased father's most beloved friend," she burst into a flood of tears, knelt down to him for a moment, and promised ever to obey him as her father.—He had his handkerchief to his face at the time, or she would have beheld the agitation of his heart—the remotest sensations of his soul.

This affecting introduction being over, and some minutes passed in general conversation, the carriages were again ordered, and, bidding farewell to the friends who had accompanied her, Miss Milner, her guardian, and Miss Woodley departed for town; the two ladies in Miss Milner's carriage, and Dorriforth in that in which he came.

Miss Woodley, as they rode along, made no attempts to ingratiate herself with Miss Milner; though, perhaps, it might constitute one of her first wishes—she behaved to her but as she constantly behaved to every other creature—that was sufficient to gain the esteem of one, possessed of an understanding equal to this young lady's—she had penetration to discover Miss Woodley's unaffected worth, and was soon induced to reward it with the warmest friendship.

CHAPTER IV

AFTER a night's rest in London, less strongly impressed with the loss of her father, reconciled, if not already attached to her new acquaintance, her thoughts pleasingly occupied with the reflection she was in that gay metropolis—a wild rapturous picture of which her active fancy had often formed—Miss Milner arose from a peaceful and refreshing sleep, with much of that vivacity, and all those airy charms, which for a while had yielded their transcendent power, to less potent sadness.[1]

---

[1] In the second, third, fourth, and fifth editions, "power to the weaker influence of her filial sorrow."

Beautiful as she had appeared to Miss Woodley and to Dorriforth the preceding day, when she joined them the next morning at breakfast, repossessed of her lively elegance and dignified simplicity, they gazed at her, and at each other alternately, with wonder![1]—and Mrs. Horton, as she sat at the head of her tea-table, felt herself but as a menial servant, such command has beauty if united with sense and with virtue.—In Miss Milner it was so united.—Yet let not our over-scrupulous readers be misled, and extend their idea of her virtue so as to magnify it beyond that which frail mortals commonly possess; nor must they cavil, if, on a nearer view, they find it less—but let them consider, that if Miss Milner had more faults than generally belong to others, she had likewise more temptations.

From her infancy she had been indulged in all her wishes to the extreme of folly, and habitually started at the unpleasant voice of controul—she was beautiful, she had been too frequently told the high value of that beauty, and thought those moments passed in wasteful idleness during which she was not gaining some new conquest—she had besides a quick sensibility, which too frequently discovered itself in the immediate resentment of injury or neglect—she had acquired also the dangerous character of a wit; but to which she had no real pretensions, although the most discerning critic, hearing her converse, might fall into this mistake.—Her replies had all the effect of repartee, not because she possessed those qualities which can properly be called wit, but that what she said was spoken with an energy, an instantaneous and powerful perception of what she said, joined with a real or well-counterfeited simplicity, a quick turn of the eye, and an arch smile of the countenance.—Her words were but the words of others, and, like those of others, put into common sentences; but the delivery made them pass for wit, as grace in an ill proportioned figure, will often make it pass for symmetry.

And now—leaving description—the reader must form a judgment of her by her actions; by all the round of great or trivial circumstances that shall be related.

---

1   In the second, third, fourth, and fifth editions, "with astonishment."

At breakfast, which was just begun at the beginning of this chapter, the conversation was lively on the part of Miss Milner, wise on the part of Dorriforth, good on the part of Miss Woodley, and an endeavour at all three on the part of Mrs. Horton.—The discourse at length drew from Mr. Dorriforth this observation.

"You have a greater resemblance of your father, Miss Milner, than I imagined you had from report: I did not expect to find you so like him."

"Nor did I, Mr. Dorriforth, expect to find you any thing like what you are."

"No?—pray, madam, what did you expect to find me?"

"I expected to find you an elderly man, and a plain man."

This was spoken in an artless manner, but in a tone which obviously declared she thought her guardian both young and handsome.—He replied, but not without some little embarrassment, "A plain man you shall find me in all my actions."

She returned, "Then your actions are to contradict your looks."

For in what she said, Miss Milner had the quality peculiar to wits, to speak the thought that first occurs, which thought has generally truth on its side.—On this he ventured to pay her a compliment in return.

"You, Miss Milner, I should suppose, must be a very bad judge of what is plain, and what is not."

"How so, Sir?"

"Because I am sure you will readily own you do not think yourself handsome; and allowing that, you instantly want judgment."

"And I would rather want judgment than beauty," she replied, "and so I give up the one for the other."

With a serious face, as if proposing a most serious question, Dorriforth continued, "And you really believe you are not handsome?"

"I should from my own opinion believe so, but in some respects I am like you Roman Catholics; I don't believe from my own understanding, but from what other people tell me."

"And let this be the criterion," replied Dorriforth, "that what we teach is truth; for you find you would be deceived did you not trust to persons who know better than yourself.—But, my dear Miss Milner, we will talk upon some other topic, and never resume this again—we differ in opinion, I dare say, on one subject only, and this difference I hope will never extend itself to any other.—Therefore, let not religion be named between us; for as I have resolved never to persecute you, in pity be grateful, and do not persecute me."

Miss Milner looked with surprise that any thing so lightly said, should be so seriously received.—The kind Miss Woodley ejaculated a short prayer to herself, that heaven would forgive her young friend the involuntary sin of ignorance[1]—while Mrs. Horton, unperceived as she imagined, made the sign of the cross upon her forehead to prevent the infectious taint of Heretical opinions. This, pious ceremony, Miss Milner, by chance, observed, and now shewed such an evident propensity to burst into a fit of laughter, that the good lady of the house could no longer contain her resentment, but exclaimed, "God forgive you." With a severity so far different from the idea the words conveyed, that the object of her anger was, on this, obliged freely to indulge that risibility which she had been struggling to smother; and without longer suffering under the agony of restraint, she gave way to her humour, and laughed with a liberty so uncontrouled, that in a short time left her in the room with none but the tender-hearted Miss Woodley a witness of her folly.

"My dear Miss Woodley," (then cried Miss Milner, after recovering herself,) "I am afraid you will not forgive me."

"No, indeed I will not." Returned Miss Woodley.

But how unimportant, how weak, how ineffectual are *words* in conversation—looks and manners alone express—for Miss Woodley, with her charitable face and mild accents, saying she would not forgive, implied only forgiveness—while Mrs. Horton, with her enraged voice and aspect, begging heaven to pardon the offender, palpably said, she thought her unworthy of all pardon.

---

1 In the second, third, fourth, and fifth editions, "the involuntary sin of religious ignorance."

CHAPTER V

Six weeks have now elapsed since Miss Milner has been in London, partaking with delight in all its pleasures, whilst Dorriforth has been sighing with apprehension, attending with precaution, and praying with the most zealous fervour for her safety.—Her own and her guardian's acquaintance, and the new friendships (to speak in the unmeaning language of the world) which she was continually forming, crowded so perpetually to the house, that seldom had Dorriforth even a moment left from her visits or visitors, to warn her of her danger—yet when a moment offered, he snatched it eagerly—pressed the necessity of "time not always passed in society; of reflection; of reading; of thoughts for a future state; and of virtues acquired to make old age supportable."—That forcible power of innate feeling, which directs the tongue to eloquence, had its effect while she listened to him, and she sometimes put on the looks and gesture of assent, and sometimes even spoke the language of conviction; but this, the first call of dissipation would change to ill-timed raillery, or peevish remonstrance at being limited in delights her birth and fortune entitled her to enjoy.

Among the many visitors who attended at her levees, and followed wherever she went, was one that seemed, even when absent, to share her thoughts.—This was Lord Frederick Lawnly, the son of a duke, and the avowed favourite of all the most discerning women of taste.

Lord Frederick was not more than twenty-three; sprightly, elegant, extremely handsome, and possessed of every accomplishment to captivate a heart less susceptible of love than Miss Milner's was supposed to be.—With these allurements, no wonder if she took a pleasure in his company—no wonder if she took a pride to have it known he was among the number of her most devoted admirers.—Dorriforth beheld the growing intimacy with alternate pain and pleasure—he wished to see Miss Milner married, to see his charge in the protection of another, rather than of himself; yet under the care of a young nobleman, immersed in all the vices of the town, without one moral excellence, but such as might result eventually from the influence of the moment—under such care he trembled for her happiness—yet trembled more lest her heart should be purloined, without even the authority of matrimonial views.

With these sentiments Dorriforth could never disguise his uneasiness at the sight of Lord Frederick, nor could his lordship but discern the suspicion of the guardian, and consequently each was embarrassed in the presence of the other.—Miss Milner observed, but observed with indifference, the sensations of both—there was but one passion which at present held a place in her heart, and that was vanity; vanity defined into all the species of pride, vain-glory, self-approbation—an inordinate desire of admiration, and an immoderate enjoyment of the art of pleasing, for her own individual happiness, and not for the happiness of others.—Still had she a heart inclined, and oftentimes affected by tendencies less unworthy; but those approaches to what was estimable, were generally arrested in their first impulse by some darling folly.

Miss Woodley (who could discover virtue, although of the most diminitive kind, and scarcely through the magnifying glass of calumny could ever perceive a fault) was Miss Milner's constant companion, and her advocate with Dorriforth, whenever, during her absence, she became the subject of discourse—he listened with hope to the praises of her friend, but saw with despair how little they were merited.—Sometimes he struggled to contain his anger, but oftener strove to suppress tears of pity for her hapless state.

By this time all her acquaintance had given Lord Frederick to her as a lover, the servants whispered it, and some of the public prints had even fixed the day of marriage;—but as no explanation had taken place on the part of his lordship, Dorriforth's uneasiness was encreased, and he seriously told his Ward he thought it prudent to entreat Lord Frederick to desist visiting her.—She smiled with ridicule at the caution, but finding it a second time repeated, and in a manner that favoured of authority, she promised to make, and to enforce the request.—The next time his lordship came she did so, assuring him it was by her guardian's desire; "who from motives of delicacy had permitted her rather to solicit as a favour, what he himself would make as a demand."—Lord Frederick reddened with anger—he loved Miss Milner, but he doubted whether (from the frequent proofs he had experienced of his own inconstancy) he should continue to love—and this interference of her guardian threatened an explanation or a dismission, before he became thoroughly acquainted with his own heart.—Alarmed, confounded, and provoked, he replied,

"By heaven I believe Mr. Dorriforth loves you himself, and it is jealousy makes him treat me thus."

"For shame, my lord!" cried Miss Woodley, who was present, and trembling with horror at the sacrilegious idea.

"Nay, shame for him if he be not in love"—answered his lordship, "for what but a savage could behold beauty like her's, and not own its power?"

"Habit," replied Miss Milner, "is every thing—and Mr. Dorriforth sees and converses with beauty, and from habit does not fall in love, as you, my lord, merely from habit do."

"Then you believe," cried he, "love is not in my nature?"

"No more of it, my lord, than habit could very soon extinguish."

"But I would not have it extinguished—I would rather it should mount to a flame, for I think it a crime to be insensible of the blessings love can bestow."

"Then your lordship indulges the passion to avoid a sin?—the very motive which deters Mr. Dorriforth."

"Which ought to deter him, madam, for the sake of his oaths—but monastick vows, like those of marriage, were made to be broken—and surely when your guardian looks on you, his wishes"—

"Are never less pure," returned Miss Milner eagerly, "than those which dwell in the bosom of my celestial guardian."

At that instant Dorriforth entered the room. The colour had mounted into Miss Milner's face from the warmth with which she had delivered her opinion, and his entering at the very moment this compliment had been paid in his absence, heightened the blush to a deep glow on every feature, and a confusion that trembled on her lips and shook through all her frame.

"What's the matter?" cried Dorriforth, looking with concern on her discomposure.

"A compliment paid by herself to you, Sir," replied his lordship, "has thus affected the lady."

"As if she blushed at the untruth." Said Dorriforth.

"Nay, that is unkind," cried Miss Woodley, "for if you had been here"—

"—I would not have said what I did," replied Miss Milner, "but left him to vindicate himself."

"Is it possible I can want vindication?" returned Dorriforth, "Who would think it worth their while to slander so unimportant a person as I am?"

"The man who has the charge of Miss Milner," replied lord Frederick, "derives a consequence from her."

"No ill consequence, I hope, my lord?" replied Dorriforth with a firmness in his voice, and an eye fixed so steadfastly, that his lordship hesitated for a moment in want of a reply—and Miss Milner softly whispering to him, as her guardian turned his head, to avoid an argument, he bowed acquiescence.—And then, as in compliment to her, he wished to change the subject, with a smile of ridicule he cried,

"I wish, Mr. Dorriforth, you would give me absolution of all my sins, for I confess they are many, and manifold."

"Hold, my Lord," exclaimed Dorriforth, "do not confess before the ladies, lest in order to excite their compassion, you should be tempted to accuse yourself of sins, you have never yet committed."

At this Miss Milner laughed, seemingly so well pleased, that lord Frederick with a sarcastic sneer, repeated,

> From Abelard it came,
> And Heloisa still must love the name.[1]

Whether from an inattention to the quotation, or from a consciousness it was wholly inapplicable, Dorriforth heard it without one emotion of shame or of anger—while Miss Milner seemed shocked at the implication; her pleasantry was immediately depressed, and she threw open the sash and held her head out

---

1 Misquoted from Pope's *Eloisa to Abelard* (1717), ll.7-8: "From Abelard it came,/And Eloisa yet must kiss the name." The poem is based on the actual love affair of Peter Abelard (1079-1142), a French academic, and his student Heloise (1101-64).

at the window to conceal the embarrassment these lines had occasioned.

The earl of Elmwood was at this juncture announced—a Catholic nobleman, just come of age, and on the eve of marriage—his Lordship's visit was to his cousin, Mr. Dorriforth, but as all ceremonious visits were alike received by Dorriforth, Miss Milner, and Mrs. Horton's family in one common apartment, lord Elmwood was ushered into this, and for the present directed the conversation to a different subject.

CHAPTER VI

In anxious desire that the affection, or acquaintance, between lord Frederick Lawnly and Miss Milner might be finally broken, her guardian received with the highest satisfaction, overtures from Sir Edward Ashton, in behalf of his passion for that young lady.—Sir Edward was not young or handsome; old or ugly; but immensely rich, and possessed of qualities that made him, in every sense, worthy the happiness to which he aspired.—He was the man Dorriforth would have chosen before any other for the husband of his Ward, and his wishes made him sometimes hope, against his reason, that Sir Edward would not be rejected—and he resolved to try the force of his own power in the strongest recommendation of him.

Notwithstanding that dissimilarity of opinion, which in almost every respect, subsisted between Miss Milner and her guardian, there was generally the most punctilious observance of good manners from each towards the other—on the part of Dorriforth more especially; for his politeness would sometimes appear even like the result of a system he had marked out for himself, as the only means to keep his Ward restrained within the same limitations.—Whenever he addressed her there was an unusual reserve upon his countenance, and more than usual gentleness in his tone of voice; which seemed the effect of sentiments her birth and situation inspired, joined to a studied mode of respect best suited to enforce the same from her.—The wished-for consequence was produced—for though there was an instinctive rectitude in the understanding of Miss Milner that would have taught her, without other instruction, what manners to observe towards her deputed father; yet, from some volatile thought, or some quick sense of feeling, she had not been accustomed to subdue, she was perpetually on the verge of treating him with levity; but he would immediately recall her recollection by a reserve too awful, and a gentleness too sacred for her to violate. The distinction which both required, was thus, by his skilful management alone, preserved.

One morning he took an opportunity, before her and Miss Woodley, to introduce and press the subject of Sir Edward Ashton's hopes. He first spoke warmly in his praise, then plainly told Miss Milner he believed she possessed the power to make so deserving a man happy to the summit of his wishes. A laugh of ridicule was the only answer,—but a sudden and expressive frown from Dorriforth having quickly put an end to it, he resumed his wonted politeness and said,

"I wish, Miss Milner, you would shew more good taste than thus pointedly to disapprove of Sir Edward."

"How, Mr. Dorriforth," replied she, "can you expect me to give proofs of a good taste, when Sir Edward, whom you consider with such high esteem, has given so bad an example of his, in approving of me?"

Dorriforth wished not to flatter her frailty by a compliment she seemed to have fought for, and for a moment hesitated what to say.

"Answer, Sir, that question," She cried.

"Why then, madam," replied he, "it is my opinion, that supposing what your humility has advanced to be just, yet Sir Edward will not suffer by the suggestion; for in cases where the heart is so immediately concerned, as I believe Sir Edward's to be, good taste, or rather reason, has not proper power to act."

"You are right, Mr. Dorriforth; this is a thorough justification of Sir Edward—and when I fall in love, I must beg you will make the same excuse for me."

"Then," returned he earnestly, "before your heart is in that state I have described, exert your reason."

"I shall," answered she, "and not consent to marry a man whom I could never love."

"Unless your heart is already given away, Miss Milner, what can make you speak with such a degree of certainty?"

He thought on Lord Frederick while he said this, and he fixed his eyes upon her as if he wished to penetrate her sentiments, and yet trembled for what he might find there.—she blushed, and her looks would have confirmed her guilty, had not a free and unembarrassed tone of voice, more than her words, preserved her from that sentence.

"No," she replied, "my heart is not given away, and yet I can venture to declare Sir Edward will never possess an atom of it."

"I am sorry, for both your sakes, these are your sentiments,"—he replied, "But as your heart is still your own," (and he seemed rejoiced to find it was) "permit me to warn you how you part with a thing so precious—the dangers, the sorrows you hazard in bestowing it, are greater than you may be aware of. The heart once gone, our thoughts, our actions, are no more our own, than that is."—He seemed *forcing* himself to utter all this, and yet to break off as if he could have said much more, had not the extreme delicacy of the subject prevented him.

When he left the room, and Miss Milner heard the door shut after him, she said with a thoughtful and inquisitive earnestness, "what can make good people so skilled in all the weaknesses of the bad? Mr. Dorriforth, with all those prudent admonitions, appears rather like a man who has passed his life in the gay world, experienced all its dangerous allurements, all its repentant sorrows, than like one who has lived his whole time secluded in a monastry or his own study.—Then he speaks with such exquisite sensibility on the subject of love, he commends the very thing he would decry.—I do not think my lord Frederick could make the passion appear in more pleasing colours by painting its delights, than Mr. Dorriforth can in describing its sorrows—and if he talks to me frequently in this manner, I shall certainly take pity on his lordship, for the sake of his enemy's eloquence."

Miss Woodley, who heard the conclusion of this speech with the tenderest concern, cried, "Alas! you then think seriously of lord Frederick!"

"Suppose I do, wherefore that *alas!* Miss Woodley?"

"Because I fear you will never be happy with him."

"That is plainly telling me he will not be happy with me."

"I cannot speak of marriage from experience," answered Miss Woodley, "but I think I can guess what it is."

"Nor can I speak of love from experience," replied Miss Milner, "but I think I can guess what it is."

"But do no fall in love, my dear Miss Milner," (cried Miss Woodley, with an earnestness as if she had been asking a favour that depended upon the will of the person entreated,) "do not fall in love without the approbation of your guardian."

Her young friend laughed at the inefficacious prayer, but promised to do "all she could to oblige her."

CHAPTER VII

SIR Edward, not wholly discouraged by the denial with which Dorriforth had, with delicacy, acquainted him, still hoped for a kinder reception, and was so frequently in the house of Mrs. Horton, that lord Frederick's jealousy was excited, and the tortures he suffered in consequence, convinced him beyond a doubt of the sincerity of his affection. He now, every time he beheld the object of his passion, (for he still continued his visits, tho' less frequently than before) pleaded his cause so ardently, that Miss Woodley, who was occasionally present, and ever compassionate, could scarce resist wishing him success. He now unequivocally offered marriage, and entreated to be suffered to lay his proposals before Mr. Dorriforth, but this Miss Milner positively forbid.

Her reluctance he imputed, however, more to the known partiality of her guardian to the addresses of Sir Edward, than to any motive which depended upon herself; and to Mr. Dorriforth his lordship conceived a greater dislike than ever; believing that through his interposition, in spite of his ward's attachment, he might yet be deprived of her—but Miss Milner declared both to him and to her friend, Love had, at present, gained no one influence over her mind.—Yet did the watchful Miss Woodley oftentimes hear a sigh burst forth, unknowing to herself, till she was reminded of it, and then a sudden blush of shame would instantly spread over her face.—This seeming struggle with her passion, endeared her more than ever to Miss Woodley, and she would even risk the displeasure of Dorriforth by her ready compliance in every new pursuit that might amuse the time, she else saw passed by her friend in heaviness of heart.

Balls, plays, incessant company, at length rouzed her guardian from that mildness with which he had been accustomed to treat her—night after night, his sleep had been disturbed by fears for her safety while abroad; morning after morning, it had been broken by the clamour of her return.—He therefore said to her one forenoon as he met her accidentally upon the stair case,

"I hope, Miss Milner, you pass this evening at home?"

Unprepared for the sudden question, she blushed and replied, "Yes." While she knew she was engaged to a brilliant assembly, for which she had been a whole week consulting her milliner in preparation.

She, however, flattered herself what she had said to Mr. Dorriforth might be excused as a slight mistake, the lapse of memory, or some other trifling fault, when he should know the truth—the truth was earlier divulged than she expected—for just as dinner was removed, her footman delivered a message to her from her milliner concerning a new dress for the evening—the *present evening* particularly marked.—Dorriforth looked astonished.

"I thought, Miss Milner, you gave me your word you would pass this evening at home?"

"I mistook then—for I had before given my word I should pass it abroad."

"Indeed?" cried he.

"Yes, indeed;" returned she, "and I believe it is right I should keep my first promise; is it not?"

"The promise you gave me then, you do not think of any consequence."

"Yes, certainly; if you do."

"I do."

"And mean, perhaps, to make it of much more consequence than it deserves, by being offended."

"Whether or not, I am offended—you shall find I am." And he looked so.

She caught his piercing, stedfast eye—her's were immediately cast down; and she trembled—either with shame or with resentment.

Mrs. Horton rose from her seat—moved the decanters and the fruit round the table—stirred the fire—and came back to her seat again, before another word was uttered.—Nor had this good woman's officious labours taken the least from the aukwardness of the silence, which as soon as the bustle she had made was over, returned in its full force.

At last, Miss Milner rising with alacrity, was preparing to go out of the room, when Dorriforth raised his voice, and in a tone of authority said,

"Miss Milner, you shall not leave the house this evening."

"Sir?"—she exclaimed with a kind of doubt of what she had heard—a surprise, which fixed her hand on the door she had half opened, but which now she shewed herself irresolute whether to open wide in defiance, or to shut submissive.—Before she could resolve, Dorriforth arose from his seat, and said with a degree of force and warmth she had never heard him speak with before.

"I command you to stay at home this evening."

And he walked immediately out of the apartment by the opposite door.—Her hand fell motionless from that she held—she appeared motionless herself for some time;—till Mrs. Horton, "beseeching her not to be uneasy at the treatment she had received," caused a flood of tears to flow, and her bosom to heave as if her heart was breaking.

Miss Woodley would have said something to comfort her, but she had caught the infection and could not utter a word—not from any real cause of grief did this lady weep; but there was a magnetic quality in tears, which always drew forth her's.

Mrs. Horton secretly enjoyed this scene, although the real well meaning of her heart, and ease of her conscience, did not tell her so—she, however, declared she had "long prognosticated it would come to this;" and she "now only thanked heaven it was no worse."

"What would you have worse, madam?" cried Miss Milner, "am not I disappointed of the ball?"

"You don't mean to go then?" said Mrs. Horton; "I commend your prudence; and I dare say it is more than your guardian gives you credit for."

"Do you think I would go," answered Miss Milner, with a

earnestness that for a time suppressed her tears, "in contradiction to his will?"

"It is not the first time, I believe, you have acted contrary to that, Miss Milner." Returned Mrs. Horton, and affected a tenderness of voice, to soften the harshness of her words.

"If that is the case, madam," replied Miss Milner, "I see nothing that should prevent me now." And she flung out of the room as if she had resolved to disobey him.—This alarmed poor Miss Woodley.

"Dear Aunt," she cried to Mrs. Horton, "follow and prevail upon Miss Milner to give up her design; she means to go to the ball in opposition to her guardian's will."

"Then," cried Mrs. Horton, "I'll not be an instrument in deterring her—if she does, it may be for the best; it may give Mr. Dorriforth a clearer knowledge what means are proper to use, to convert her from evil."

"But, dear madam, she must be prevented the evil of disobedience; and as you tempted, you will be the most likely to dissuade her—but if you will not, I must endeavour."

Miss Woodley was leaving the room to perform this good design, when Mrs Horton, in humble imitation of the example given her by Dorriforth, cried,

"Niece, I command you not to stir out of this room, this evening."

Miss Woodley obediently sat down—and though her thoughts and heart were in the chamber with her friend, she never shewed by one impertinent word, or by one line of her face, the restraint she suffered.

At the usual hour, Mr. Dorriforth and his ward were summoned to tea:—Dorriforth entered with a countenance which evinced the remains of anger; his eye gave testimony of his absent thoughts; and although he took up a pamphlet and affected to read, it was plain to discern he scarcely knew he held it in his hand.

Mrs. Horton began to make tea with a mind as wholly intent upon something else, as Dorriforth's—she was longing for the event of this misunderstanding, (for to age trivial matters are important,) and though she wished no ill to Miss Milner, yet with an inclination bent upon seeing something new—without the fatigue of going out of her own house—she was not over scrupulous what that novelty might be.—But for fear she should have the imprudence to speak a word upon the subject which employed her thoughts, or even look as if she thought of it at all; she pinched her lips close together, and cast her eyes on vacancy, lest their significant regards might detect her.—And for fear any noise should intercept even the sound of what might happen, she walked across the room more softly than usual, and more softly touched every thing she was obliged to lay her hand on.

Miss Woodley thought it her duty to be mute, and now the gentle gingle of a tea-spoon, was like a deep-toned bell, all was so quiet.

Mrs. Horton too, in the self-approving reflection that she herself was not in any quarrel, or altercation of any kind, felt at this moment remarkably peaceful, and charitable.—Miss Woodley did not recollect *herself* so, but was so in reality—in her peace and charity were instinctive virtues, accident could not encrease them.

The first cups of tea were scarcely poured out,[1] when a servant came with Miss Milner's compliments and she should drink none.—The book shook in Dorriforth's hand while this message was delivered—he believed her to be dressing for her evening's entertainment, and now studied in what manner to prevent, or to resent it.—He coughed—drank his tea—endeavoured to talk, but found it difficult—sometimes read—and in this manner near two hours were passed away, when Miss Milner came into the room.— Not drest for a ball, but as she rose from dinner.—Dorriforth read on, and seemed afraid to look up, lest he should behold what he could not have pardoned.—she drew a chair and sat down at the table by the side of Miss Woodley.[2]

After a few minutes pause, and some small embarrassment on the part of Mrs. Horton, at the disappointment she had to contend with from Miss Milner's unexpected obedience, she asked

---

1   In the second, third, and fourth editions, "the tea had scarce been made"; in the fifth edition, "the tea had scarcely been made."

2   In the second, third, fourth, and fifth editions, "by the side of her delighted friend."

that young lady "if she would now take tea?"—to which Miss Milner replied, "no, I thank you, ma'am," in a voice so languid, compared to her usual one, that Dorriforth lifted his eyes from the book; and seeing her in the same negligent dress she had worn all the day, cast them away again—not with a look of triumph, but of confusion.

And whatever he might have suffered had he beheld her decorated, and on the point of bidding defiance to his commands, yet even upon that trial, he had not endured half the painful sensations he now for a moment felt—he felt himself to blame.

He feared he had treated her with too much severity—he admired her condescension, accused himself for exacting it—he longed to ask her pardon, he did not know how.

A chearful reply from her, to a question of Miss Woodley's, embarrassed him still more—he wished she had been sullen, he then would have had a temptation, or a pretence, to have been so too.

With all these thoughts crowding fast on his mind he still read, or seemed to read, and to take no notice of what was passing; till a servant entered and asked Miss Milner what time she should want the chariot? to which she replied, "I don't go out to night."—He then laid the book out of his hand, and by the time the servant had left the room, thus began.

"Miss Milner, I give you, I fear, some unkind proofs of my regard—it is often the ungrateful task of a friend to be troublesome—sometimes unmannerly.—Forgive the duty of my office, and believe no one is half so much concerned if it robs you of any amusements, as I myself am."

What he said, he looked with so much sincerity, that had she been burning with rage at his behaviour, she must have forgiven him, for the regret he so forcibly exprest.—She was going to reply, but found she could not without accompanying her words with tears, therefore as soon as she attempted she desisted.

On this he rose from his seat, and going to her, said, "Once more shew your submission by obeying me a second time to day.—Keep your appointment, and be assured I shall issue my commands with greater circumspection for the future, as I find how strictly they are complied with."

Miss Milner, the gay, the proud, the haughty Miss Milner,[1] sunk underneath this kindness, and wept with a gentleness and patience, which did not give more surprise than it gave satisfaction to Dorriforth.—He was charmed to find her disposition so little untractable—foreboded the future prosperity of his guardianship, and her eternal, as well as temporal happiness from this specimen.

CHAPTER VIII

ALTHOUGH Dorriforth was that good man that has been described, there was in his nature shades of evil—there was an obstinacy; such as he himself, and his friends termed firmness of mind; but had not religion and some opposite virtues weighed heavy in the balance, it would frequently have degenerated into implacable stubbornness.

The child of a once beloved sister, who married a young officer against her brother's consent, was at the age of three years left an orphan, destitute of every support but from his uncle's generosity: but though Dorriforth mentioned, he would never see him. Miss Milner, whose heart was a receptacle for the unfortunate, no sooner was told the melancholy history of Mr. and Mrs. Rushbrook,[2] the parents of the child, than she longed to behold the innocent inheritor of her guardian's resentment, and took Miss Woodley with her to see the boy—he was at a farm house a few miles from town; and his extreme beauty and engaging manners, needed not the sorrows to which he had been born, to give him farther recommendation to the kindness of her, who had come to visit him. She beheld him with admiration and pity, and having endeared herself to him by the most affectionate words and caresses, on her bidding him farewell, he cried most sorrowfully to go along with her. Unused to resist temptations, whether to reprehensible, or to laudable actions, she yielded to his supplications, and having overcome a few scruples of Miss

---

1 In the second and third editions, "the gay, the proud, the dissipated, the haughty Miss Milner; in the fourth and fifth editions, "the gay, the vain, the dissipated, the haughty Miss Milner."
2 Rushbrook was the maiden name of Inchbald's mother.

Woodley's, determined to take young Rushbrook to town and present him to his uncle. This idea was no sooner formed than executed.—By making a present to the nurse, she readily gained her consent to part with him for a day or two, and the signs of joy the child denoted on being put into the carriage, seemed to repay her before-hand, for every reproof she might receive from her guardian, for the liberty she had taken.

"Besides," said she to Miss Woodley, who had still her apprehensions, "do you not wish his uncle should have some warmer interest in his care than duty?—it is that alone, which induces Mr. Dorriforth to provide for him, but it is proper, affection, should have some share in his benevolence—and how, hereafter, will he be so fit an object for that love, which compassion must excite, as his at present?"

Miss Woodley acquiesced.—But before they arrived at their own door it came to Miss Milner's remembrance, there was a grave sternness in the manners of her guardian when provoked; the recollection of which, made her something apprehensive for what she had done—Miss Woodley was more so.—They both became silent as they approached the street where they lived—for Miss Woodley having once represented her fears, and having suppressed them in resignation to Miss Milner's better judgment, would not repeat them—and Miss Milner would not confess they were now troubling her.

Just, however, as the coach stopt, she had the forecast and the humility to say, "we will not tell Mr. Dorriforth the child is his nephew, Miss Woodley, unless he should appear fond, and pleased with him, and then we may venture without any danger."

This was agreed, and when Dorriforth entered the room just before dinner, poor Harry Rushbrook was introduced to him as the son of a lady who frequently visited there. The deception passed—Dorriforth shook hands with him, and at length highly pleased with his engaging wiles, and applicable replies, took him on his knee, and kissed him with affection. Miss Milner could scarcely restrain the joy this gave her; but unluckily, Dorriforth said soon after the child, "and now tell me your name."

"Harry Rushbrook." Replied he with great force and clearness in his voice.

Dorriforth was holding him fondly round the waist as he stood with his feet upon his knees; and at this reply he did not throw him from him—but he removed his hands, which supported him, so suddenly, that the child to prevent falling to the floor, threw himself about his uncle's neck.—Miss Milner and Miss Woodley turned aside to conceal their tears. "I had liked to have been down."[1] Cried Harry, fearing no other danger.—But his uncle took hold of each hand that had twined around him, and placed him immediately on the ground; and dinner being that instant served, he gave no greater marks of his resentment than calling for his hat, and walking instantly out of the house.

Miss Milner cried for anger; yet she did not treat with less kindness the object of this vexatious circumstance: she held him in her arms all the while she sat at table, and repeatedly said to him, (though he had not the sense to thank her) "she would always be his friend."

The first emotions of resentment against Dorriforth being over, she was easily prevailed upon to return with poor Rushbrook to the farm house, before it was likely his uncle should come back; another instance of obedience which Miss Woodley was impatient her guardian should know; she therefore enquired where he was, and sent him a note to acquaint him with it, offering at the same time an apology for what had happened. He returned in the evening seemingly reconciled, nor was a word mentioned of the incident which had occurred during the day; yet there remained in the austere looks of Dorriforth a perfect remembrance of it, and not one trait of compassion for his helpless nephew.

CHAPTER IX

THERE are few things so mortifying to a proud spirit as to suffer by immediate comparison—men, can scarcely bear this humiliation, but to women the punishment is intolerable; and Miss Milner now laboured under the disadvantage to a degree, which gave her no small inquietude.

Miss Fenton, a young lady of the most delicate beauty, elegant

---

1   In the second, third, fourth, and fifth editions, "like to have been down."

manners, gentle disposition, and discreet conduct, was introduced to Miss Milner's acquaintance by her guardian; and frequently, sometimes inadvertently, held up by him as a pattern for her to follow—for when he did not say this in direct terms, it was insinuated by the warmth of his panegyrics on those virtues in which Miss Fenton excelled, and his ward was obviously deficient. Conscious of her inferiority in these subjects of her guardian's praise, Miss Milner, instead of being inspired to emulation, was provoked to envy.

Not to admire Miss Fenton was impossible—to find a fault in her person or sentiments was equally impossible—and yet to love her, was very unlikely.[1]

That serenity of mind which kept her features in a continual placid form, though enchanting at the first glance, upon a second, or third, fatigued the sight for a want of variety; and to have seen her distorted with rage, convulsed with mirth, or in deep dejection had been to her advantage.—But her superior soul appeared above those natural commotions of the mind, and there was more inducement to worship her as a saint, than to love her as a woman.—Yet Dorriforth, whose heart was not formed (at least not educated) for love; regarding her in the light of friendship, beheld her as the most perfect model for her sex, Lord Frederick on first seeing her was struck with her beauty, and Miss Milner apprehended she had introduced a rival; but he had not seen her three times, before he called her the most "insufferable of Heaven's creatures," and vowed there was more charming variation in the features of Miss Woodley.

Miss Milner had a heart affectionate to her sex, even where she saw them in the possession of charms superior to her own; but whether from the spirit of contradiction, whether from feeling herself more than ordinarily offended by her guardian's praise of this lady, or whether there was something in the reserve of Miss Fenton that did not accord with her own frank and ingenuous disposition so as to engage her esteem, it is certain she took infinite

---

1   Compare with Inchbald's discussion in *The British Theatre* (1808) of Nicholas Rowe's *Jane Grey*, where she complains about the heroine's insipid virtue: "it is scarcely possible to be heroical like Lady Jane."

satisfaction in hearing her beauty and her virtues depreciated, or turned to ridicule, particularly if Mr. Dorriforth was present. This was very painful to him upon many accounts; perhaps regard to Miss Milner's conduct was not among the least; and whenever the circumstance occurred, he could with difficulty restrain his anger. Miss Fenton was not only a young lady whose amiable qualities Dorriforth admired, but she was soon to be allied to him by her marriage with his nearest relation, lord Elmwood, a young nobleman whom he sincerely loved.

Lord Elmwood had discovered all that beauty in Miss Fenton which every common observer could not but see—the charms of her mind and her fortune had been pointed out to him by his Tutor; and the utility of their marriage in perfect submission to his precepts, his lordship never permitted himself to question.

This Preceptor, held with a magisterial power the government of his pupil's passions; nay, governed them so entirely, no one could perceive (nor did the young lord himself know) that he had any.

This rigid monitor and friend, was a Mr. Sandford, bred a jesuit in the same college where Dorriforth was educated, but before his time the order was compelled to take another name.[1]—Sandford had been the tutor of Dorriforth as well as of his cousin lord Elmwood, and by this double tie seemed now entailed upon the family.—As a jesuit, he was consequently a man of learning; possessed of steadiness to accomplish the end of any design once meditated, and of wisdom to direct the conduct of men more powerful, but less ingenious than himself. The young earl accustomed in his infancy to fear him as his master, in his youth and manhood received every new indulgence with which his preceptor favoured him with gratitude, and became at length to love him as his father—nor had Dorriforth as yet shook off similar sensations.

Mr. Sandford perfectly knew how to work upon the passions of all human nature, but yet had the conscience not to "draw all hearts towards him."[2]—There were of mankind, those, whose

---

1 In 1762, the Jesuit order was concealed in France, and the Jesuits were barred from the College of St. Omer.

2 Perhaps an ironic reference to John Milton, *Paradise Regained* (1671): "Many are in each region passing fair / As the noon sky, more like to goddesses / Than mortal creatures, graceful and discreet, / Expert in amorous arts, enchanting tongues /

hate he thought not unworthy his holy labour; and in that, he was more rapid in his success than even in procuring esteem. In this enterprize he succeeded with Miss Milner, even beyond his most sanguine wish.

She had been educated at an English boarding school, and had no idea of the superior, and subordinate state of a foreign seminary—besides, as a woman, she was privileged to say any thing she pleased; and as a beautiful woman, she had a right to expect whatever she pleased to say, should be admired.

Sandford knew the hearts of women, as well as those of men, notwithstanding he had passed but little of his time in their society—he saw Miss Milner's heart at the first view of her person; and beholding in that little circumference a weight of folly he wished to see eradicated, he began to toil in the vineyard, eager to draw upon him her detestation, in the hope he could also make her abominate herself. The mortifications of slight he was expert in, and being a man of talents, such as all companies, especially those Miss Milner often frequented, looked on with respect, he did not begin by wasting that reverence so highly valued upon ineffectual remonstrances, of which he could foresee the reception, but awakened the attention of the lady solely by his neglect of her. He spoke of her in her presence as of an indifferent person; sometimes forgot to name her when the subject required it; and then would ask her pardon and say he "did not recollect her," with such seeming sorrow for his fault, she could not think the offence intended, and of course felt the affront much more severely.

While, with every other person she was the principle, the first cause upon which a whole company depended for conversation, musick, cards, or dancing, with Mr. Sandford she found she was of no importance.—Sometimes she tried to consider this disregard of her as merely the effect of ill-breeding, but he was not an ill-bred man; he was a gentleman by birth, and one who had kept the best company; a man of sense and learning.—"And does such a man slight me without knowing it?" She cried—for she had not

---

Persuasive, virgin majesty with mild / And sweet allayed, yet terrible to approach, / Skilled to retire, and in retiring draw / Hearts after them tangled in amorous nets" (II, 159-160).

dived so deep into the powers of simulation, as to suspect such careless manners were the result of art.

This behaviour of Mr. Sandford's had its desired effect; it humbled Miss Milner in her own opinion, more than a thousand sermons would have done preached on the vanity of youth and beauty. She felt an inward nothingness she never knew before, and had been cured of all her pride, had she not possessed a degree of spirit beyond the generality of her sex, and such as even Mr. Sandford with all his penetration did not expect.—She determined to resent his treatment, and entering the list as his declared enemy, give reasons to the beholders why he did not, with them, acknowledge her sovereignty.

She now commenced hostilities on all his arguments, his learning, and his favourite axioms; and by a happy turn for ridicule, in want of other weapons, threw in the way of the holy Father as great trials for his patience, as any his order could have substituted in penance. Some things he bore like a martyr—at others, his fortitude would forsake him, and he would call on her guardian, his late pupil, to interpose with this authority; on which she would declare she only acted "to try the good man's temper," and had he combated with his fretfulness but a few minutes longer, she would have acknowledged his right to cannonization; but having yielded to the sallies of his anger, he must now go through numerous other probations."

If Miss Fenton was admired by Dorriforth, by Sandford she was adored—and instead of giving her as an example to Miss Milner, he spoke of her as of one, endowed beyond Miss Milner's power of imitation.—Often with a shake of his head and a sigh would he say,

"No, I am not so hard upon you as your guardian; I only desire you to love Miss Fenton; to resemble her, I believe, is above your ability."

This was something too much—and poor Miss Woodley, who was generally a witness of these controversies, suffered a degree of sorrow at every sentence that distrest Miss Milner.—Yet as she suffered for Mr. Sandford too, the joy of her friend's reply was abated by the uneasiness it gave to him. But Mrs. Horton felt for none but the right reverend priest; and often did she feel so violently interested in his cause, she could not refrain giving an answer herself in his behalf—thus, doing the duty of an adversary.

CHAPTER X

MR. Sandford finding his friend Dorriforth frequently perplexed in the management of his ward, and he himself thinking her incorrigible, gave his advice, that a proper match should be immediately sought out for her, and the care of so dangerous a person given into other hands. Dorriforth acknowledged the propriety of this counsel, but lamented the difficulty there was in pleasing his ward as to the quality of her lover, for she had refused, besides Sir Edward Ashton, many others of equal pretensions. "Depend upon it then," cried Mr. Sandford, "her affections are already engaged, and it is proper you should know to whom."—Dorriforth thought he did know, and mentioned lord Frederick Lawnly; but said he had no farther authority for the supposition, than what his observation had given him, for that every explanation both on his lordship's side, and on that of the lady's, were evaded.—"Take her then," cried Sandford, "into the country, and if his Lordship does not follow, there is an end to your suspicions."—"I shall not easily prevail upon Miss Milner to leave the town," replied Dorriforth, "while it is in its highest fashion; while all the gay world are resorted hither."—"You can but try," returned Sandford, "and if you should not succeed now; at least fix the time you mean to go during the Autumn, and keep to your determination."—"But in the Autumn," replied Dorriforth, "lord Frederick will of course be in the country, and as his uncle's estate is near to our residence, he will not then so evidently follow Miss Milner, as he would, could I induce her to go now."

It was agreed the attempt should be made—and instead of receiving the proposal with uneasiness, Miss Milner, to the surprise of every one present, immediately consented; and gave her guardian an opportunity of saying several of the kindest and politest things upon her ready compliance.

"A token of approbation from you, Mr. Dorriforth," returned she, "I always considered with the highest estimation—but your commendations are now become infinitely superior in value, by their scarcity; for I do not believe that since Miss Fenton and Mr. Sandford came to town, I have received one testimony of your friendship."

Had these words been uttered with pleasantry, they might have passed without observation; but at the conclusion of the period, resentment flew to Miss Milner's face, and she darted a piercing look at Mr. Sandford, which more pointedly expressed she was angry with him, than had she spoken volumes in her usual strain of raillery.—Dorriforth looked confused—but the concern which she had so plainly evinced for his good opinion throughout what she had said, silenced any rebuke he might else have been tempted to give her, for this unwarrantable charge against his friend.—Mrs. Horton was shocked at the irreverent manner in which Mr. Sandford was treated—while Miss Woodley turned to him with a smile upon her face, hoping to set him an example of the manner in which he should receive this reproach.—Her good wishes did not succeed—yet he was perfectly unruffled, and replied with coolness,

"The air of the country has affected the young lady already—but it is a comfortable thing," continued he, "that in the variety of humours some women are exposed to, they cannot be steadfast even in deceit."

"Deceit," cried Miss Milner, "in what am I deceitful? did I ever pretend Sir, I had an esteem for you?"

"That had not been deceit, madam, but merely good manners."

"I never, Mr. Sandford, sacrificed truth to politeness."

"Except when the country has been proposed and you thought it politeness to appear satisfied."

"And I was satisfied, till I recollected you might probably be of the party—then every grove was changed to a wilderness, every rivulet into a stagnated pool, and every singing bird into a croaking raven."

"A very poetical description." Returned he calmly.—"But, Miss Milner, you need not have had any apprehensions of my company in the country, for I understand the seat to which your guardian means to go, belongs to you; and depend upon it, madam, I shall never enter a house where you are the mistress."

"Nor any house I am certain, Mr. Sandford, but where you yourself are the master."

"What do you mean, madam? (and for the first time he elevated his voice,) am I the master here?"

"Your servants," replied she looking at the company, "will not tell you so, but I do."

"You condescend, Mr. Sandford," cried Mrs. Horton, "in talking so much to a young woman; but I know you do it for her good."

"Well, Miss Milner," cried Dorriforth, (and the most cutting thing he could say,) "since I find my proposal of the country has put you out of humour, I shall mention it no more."

With all that vast quantity of resentment, anger, or rage which sometimes boiled in the veins of Miss Milner, she was yet never wanting in that respect towards her guardian, which with-held her from uttering one angry sentence, immediately directed to him; and a severe word on his side, instead of exasperating, was sure to soften her. Such was the case at present—his words seemed to cut her to the heart, but she had not the asperity to reply to them as she thought they merited, and she burst into tears.—Dorriforth, instead of being concerned, as he usually was at seeing her uneasy, appeared on the present occasion provoked.—He thought her weeping was a new reproach to his friend Mr. Sandford, and to suffer himself to be moved by it, he considered would be a tacit condemnation of his friend's conduct.—She understood his thoughts, and getting the better of her tears, apologized for the weakness of which she had been guilty; adding,

"She could never bear with indifference an unjust accusation."

"To prove mine was such, madam," replied Dorriforth, "be prepared to quit London, without any marks of regret, within a few days."

She bowed assent; the necessary preparations were agreed upon; and while Miss Milner with apparent satisfaction adjusted the plan of her journey, (like those persons who behave well, not so much to please themselves as to vex their enemies,) she secretly triumphed in the mortification she supposed Mr. Sandford would receive, from her obedient behaviour.

The news of this intended journey was soon made public. There is a secret charm in being pitied, when the misfortune is but ideal, and Miss Milner found immense gratification in being told, "her's was a cruel case," and that it was "unjust and barbarous to force so much beauty to be concealed in the country, while London was filled with admirers; who, like her, would languish in consequence of the separation." These things, and a thousand such, a thousand times repeated, she still listened to with pleasure; yet preserved the constancy not to shrink from her resolution of submitting.

Those sighs, which Miss Woodley had long ago observed, became, however, more frequent still; and a tear half starting to her eye was an additional matter of her friend's observation. Yet though Miss Milner at those times was softened to melancholy, she by no means appeared unhappy. Miss Woodley was acquainted with the name of love only, yet she concluded from these encreased symptoms, what she before only suspected, that love *must* be their basis. "Her senses have been captivated by the person and accomplishments of Lord Frederick," said Miss Woodley to herself, "while her understanding beholds his faults, and reproaches her passion—and, oh!" cried she, "could her guardian and Mr. Sandford know of this conflict, how much more would they have to admire than to condemn!"

With these friendly thoughts, joined to the most perfect good intent, Miss Woodley did not fail to give both gentlemen cause to believe, a contention of this nature was the present state of Miss Milner's mind.—Dorriforth was affected at the description, and Sandford urged more than ever the necessity of the country expedition.—In a few days time they undertook it; Mrs. Horton, Miss Woodley, Miss Milner, and Mr. Dorriforth, accompanied by Miss Fenton, whom Miss Milner, as she knew it to be the wish of her guardian, invited to pass the three months previous to her marriage, at her country seat. Elmwood House, or rather Castle, the seat of lord Elmwood, was only a few miles from this residence, and his lordship was expected to pass a great part of the summer there with his tutor, Mr. Sandford.

In the neighbourhood was also an estate belonging to an uncle of lord Frederick's, and many of the company suspected they should soon see his lordship on a visit there, and to that expectation did they in great measure attribute Miss Milner's visible content.

CHAPTER XI

WITH this party Miss Milner arrived at her country house, and for near six weeks all around was the perfect picture of tranquillity;—her satisfaction was as evident as every other person's; and every severe reflection being at this time unnecessary, either to teize her to her duty, or to warn her against her follies, she was even in perfect good humour with Miss Fenton, and added to the hospitality of a host, the kindness of a friend.

Mr. Sandford, who came with lord Elmwood to the neighbouring seat about a week after the arrival of Miss Milner at her's, was so scrupulously exact in the observance of his word, *"never to enter a house of Miss Milner's,"* that he would not even call upon his friend Dorriforth there—but in their walks, and at lord Elmwood's, the two parties would occasionally join, and of course Sandford and she at those times met—yet so distant was the reserve on either side, that not a single word was upon any occasion, ever exchanged between them.

Miss Milner did not like Mr. Sandford; yet, as there was no real cause for inveterate rancour, admiring him too as a man who meant well, and being besides of a most forgiving temper, she frequently felt concerned that he did not speak to her, although it had been to find fault as usual—and one morning as they were all, after a long ramble, drawing towards her house, where lord Elmwood was invited to dine, she even burst into tears at seeing Sandford turn back and wish them a "good day."

But though she had generosity to forgive an affront, she had not the humility to make a concession; and she foresaw that nothing less than some very humble atonement on her part, would prevail upon the haughty priest to be reconciled. Dorriforth saw her concern upon this trifling occasion with a secret pleasure, and an admiration she had never before excited. She insinuated to him to be a mediator between them; but before any accommodation could take place, the peace and composure of their abode was disturbed by the arrival of Sir Edward Ashton at lord Elmwood's, where it appeared as if he had been invited in order to pursue his matrimonial plan.

At a dinner at lord Elmwood's Sir Edward was announced as an unexpected visiter; Miss Milner did not suppose him such, and turned pale when his name was uttered—Dorriforth fixed his eyes upon her with some tokens of compassion, while Sandford seemed to exult, and by his repeated "Welcomes" to the baronet, gave evident proofs how much he was rejoiced to see him. All the declining enmity of Miss Milner was renewed at this behaviour, and suspecting Sandford to be the instigator of his visit, she could not overcome her displeasure, but gave way to it in a manner she thought the most mortifying.—Sir Edward in the course of conversation, enquired "what neighbours were in the country;" and she with the highest appearance of satisfaction, named lord Frederick Lawnly, as one who was hourly expected at his uncle's. The colour spread over Sir Edward's face—Dorriforth looked confounded—and Mr. Sandford as if he could have struck her.[1]

"Did lord Frederick tell *you* he should be down?" Sandford asked of Dorriforth.

To which he replied, "No."

"But I hope, Mr. Sandford, you will permit me to know?" cried Miss Milner.—For as she now meant to torment him by what she said, she no longer constrained herself to silence—and as he harboured the same kind intent towards her, he had no longer any objection to make a reply, and therefore answered,

"No, madam, if it depended upon my permission, you should *not* know."

"Not *any thing*, Sir, I dare say;—you would keep me in utter ignorance."

"I would."

"From a self-interested motive, Mr. Sandford—that I might have a greater respect for you."

Some of the persons present laughed—Mrs. Horton coughed—Miss Woodley blushed—lord Elmwood sneered—Dorriforth frowned—and Miss Fenton, looked just as she did before.

---

1 In the second, third, fourth, and fifth editions, "Mr. Sandford looked enraged."

The conversation was changed as soon as possible, and early in the evening the company returned home.

Miss Milner had scarce left her dressing room, where she had been taking off some part of her dress, when Dorriforth's servant came to acquaint her his master was alone in his study, and begged to speak with her.—She felt herself tremble—she immediately experienced a consciousness she had not acted properly at lord Elmwood's; for she had a prescience her guardian was going to upbraid her, and her heart told her, he had never yet reproached her without a cause.

Miss Woodley just then entered the apartment, and she even found herself so much a coward, as to propose her going to Dorriforth along with her, and aiding her with a word or two occasionally in her excuse.

"What you, my dear," returned Miss Woodley, "who not two hours ago, had the courage to vindicate your own cause before a whole company, of whom many were your adversaries; do you want an advocate before your guardian only? and he, who has ever treated you with tenderness."

"It is that tenderness which frightens me, Miss Woodley; that intimidates, and strikes me dumb—is it possible I can return impertinence to the language and manners Mr. Dorriforth uses? and as I am debarred from that, what can I do but stand before him like a guilty creature, acknowledging my faults."

She again entreated Miss Woodley to go with her, but on a positive refusal, from the impropriety of such an intrusion, she was at length obliged to go by herself.

How much do different circumstances influence not only the manners, but even the persons of some people!—Miss Milner in the drawing room at lord Elmwood's surrounded by listeners, by admirers, (for even her enemies beheld her with admiration,) and warm with their approbation and applause—and Miss Milner, with no giddy observer to give a false eclat to her actions, left destitute of all but her own understanding, (which secretly condemns her,) and upon the point of receiving the censure of her guardian and friend, are two different beings.—Though still beautiful beyond description, she does not look even in person the same.—In the last mentioned situation, she was shorter in stature than in the former—she was paler—she was thinner—and a very different contour presided over her whole air, and all her features.

When she arrived at the study door, she opened it with a trepidation she could hardly account for, and entered to Dorriforth the altered woman she has been represented. His heart had taken the most decided part against her, and his face assumed the most severe aspect of reproach; when her appearance gave an instantaneous change to *his* whole mind, and countenance.

She halted, as if she feared to approach—he hesitated, as if he knew not how to speak.—Instead of the warmth with which he was prepared to begin, his voice involuntarily softened, and without knowing what he said, he began,

"My dear Miss Milner"—

She expected he was angry, and in her confusion his gentleness was lost upon her—she imagined what he said might be severe, and she continued to tremble, although he repeatedly assured her, he meant only to advise, not to upbraid her.

"For in respect to all those little disputes between Mr. Sandford and you," said he, "I should be partial if I blamed you more than him—indeed, when you take the liberty to censure him, his character makes the freedom appear in a more serious light than when he complains of you—yet, if he provokes your retorts, he alone must answer for them; nor will I undertake to decide betwixt you.—But I have a question to ask you, and to which I require a serious and unequivocal answer. —Do you expect lord Frederick in the country?"

Without hesitation she replied, "she did."

"I have one more question to ask, madam, and to which I expect a reply equally unreserved.—Is lord Frederick the man you approve for a husband?"

Upon this close interrogation she discovered an embarrassment, and a confusion beyond any she had ever before given proofs of; and in this situation she faintly replied,

"No, he is not."

"Your words tell me one thing," answered Dorriforth, "while your looks declare another—which am I to trust?"

"Which you please." She returned with an insulted dignity, that astonished, awed, yet did not convince him.

"But then why encourage him to follow you hither, Miss Milner?"

"Why commit a thousand follies (she replied in tears) every hour of my life?"

"You then promote the hopes of lord Frederick without one serious intention of completing them? This is a conduct which it is my duty to guard you against, and you shall no longer deceive either him or yourself. The moment he arrives it is my fixed resolution you refuse to see him, or agree to become his wife."

In answer to this, she appeared averse both to the one proposition and the other, yet came to no explanation why; but left her guardian at the conclusion of the conversation as much at a loss to decide upon her real sentiments, as he was before he had thus seriously requested to be informed of them; but having steadfastly taken the resolution which he had declared to her, he found that determination a certain relief to his mind.

CHAPTER XII

SIR Edward Ashton, though not invited by Miss Milner, yet frequently did himself the favour to come to her house; sometimes he accompanied lord Elmwood on a visit to her, at other times he came to see Dorriforth only, who generally introduced him to the ladies. But Sir Edward was either so unwilling to give pain to the object of his love, or so much intimidated by her frowns, that he seldom addressed a single word to her, except the common compliments at entering, and retiring.—This apprehension of offending, without one hope of pleasing, had the most awkward effect upon the manners of the worthy baronet, and his endeavours to insinuate himself into the affections of the woman he loved, merely by the means of not giving her offence either by speaking or looking at her, was a circumstance so whimsical, that it frequently forced a smile from Miss Milner, though the very name of Sir Edward was of power to throw a gloom over her face; for she looked upon him as the cause why she should be hurried to make an election of a lover, before her own mind could well direct her where to fix.—Besides, his pursuit was a trouble, while it was not the smallest triumph to her vanity, which by the addresses of lord Frederick, was in the highest manner gratified.

His lordship now arrives in the country, and calls at Miss Milner's; her guardian sees his chariot coming along the lawn and gives orders to the servants, to say their lady is not at home, but that Mr. Dorriforth is; lord Frederick leaves his compliments and goes away.

The ladies all saw his carriage and servants at the door; Miss Milner flew to the glass to adjust her dress, and in her looks expressed signs of palpitation—but in vain she keeps her eyes fixed upon the door of the apartment; he does not enter.

After some minutes expectation, the door opens and her guardian comes in; she was disappointed, he perceived she was, and he looked at her with a very serious face; she immediately called to mind the assurance he had given her, "that her acquaintance with lord Frederick in its present state should not continue," and between chagrin and confusion, she was at a loss how to behave.

Notwithstanding the ladies were all present, Dorriforth said to her, without the smallest reserve, "Perhaps, Miss Milner, you may think I have taken an unwarrantable liberty in giving orders to your servants to deny you to lord Frederick, but until his lordship and I have had a private conference, or you condescend to declare your sentiments more fully in regard to his visits, I think it my duty to put an end to them."

"You will always perform your duty, Mr. Dorriforth, I have no doubt, whether I concur or not."

"Yet believe me, madam, I should do it much more chearfully, could I hope it was sanctioned by your inclinations."

"I am not mistress of my inclinations, Sir, or they should conform to yours."

"Place them under my direction, madam, and I'll answer they will."

A servant entered.—"Lord Frederick is returned, Sir, and says he should be glad to see you."—"Shew him into the study." Cried Dorriforth hastily, and rising from his seat, left the room.

"I hope they won't quarrel." Said Mrs. Horton, meaning, she thought they would.

"I am sorry to see you so uneasy, Miss Milner." Said Miss Fenton, with the most perfect unconcern.

As the badness of the weather had prevented their usual morning's exercise, the ladies sat employed at their needles till the dinner bell called them away.—"Do you think lord Frederick is gone then?" whispered Miss Milner to Miss Woodley.—"I think not," returned Miss Woodley.—"Go ask of the servants, dear creature." And Miss Woodley went out of the room.—She soon returned and said, apart, "He is now getting into his chariot, I saw him pass hastily through the hall; he seemed to fly."

"Ladies, the dinner is waiting," cried Mrs. Horton, and they repaired to the dining room; where Dorriforth soon after came, and engrossed their whole attention by this disturbed looks, and unusual silence. Before dinner was over he was, however, more himself, but still he appeared thoughtful and dissatisfied. At the time of their evening walks he excused himself, and was seen in a distant field with Mr. Sandford in earnest conversation; for they frequently stopt on one spot for a quarter of an hour, as if the interest of the subject had so totally engaged them, they stood still without knowing it. Lord Elmwood, who had joined the ladies, walked home with them; Dorriforth entered soon after, in a much less gloomy humour than when he went out, and told his lordship he and the ladies would dine with him to-morrow if he was disengaged, and it was fixed they should.

Still Dorriforth was in some perturbation, but the immediate cause was concealed till the next day, when, about an hour before the company's departure from the Castle, Miss Milner and Miss Woodley were desired, by a servant, to walk into a separate apartment, where they found Dorriforth with Mr. Sandford waiting their coming. Her guardian made an apology to Miss Milner for the form, the ceremony, of which he was going to make use; but he trusted, the extreme weight with which his mind was oppressed, lest he should mistake the real sentiments of a lady whose happiness depended upon his being correct in the knowledge of them, he trusted, that would plead his excuse.

"I know, Miss Milner," continued he, "the world in general, allows to unmarried women great latitude in disguising their mind with respect to the man they love.—I too, am willing to pardon any little dissimulation that is but consistent with that modesty, becoming every woman on the subject of marriage. But to what point I may limit, or you may think proper to extend this kind of venial deceit, may so widely differ, that it is not impossible I remain wholly unacquainted with your sentiments, even after you have revealed them to me.—Under this consideration, I wish once more to hear your thoughts in regard to matrimony, and to hear them before one of your own sex, that I may be enabled to form my opinion by her constructions."

To all this serious oration, Miss Milner made no other reply than by turning to Mr. Sandford, and asking, "If he was the person of her own sex, to whose judgment her guardian meant to submit his own?"

"Madam," cried Sandford very angrily, "you are come hither upon serious business."

"Any business must be serious to me, Mr. Sandford, in which you are concerned; and if you had called it *sorrowful*, the epithet would have suited as well."

"Miss Milner," said her guardian, "I did not bring you here to contend with Mr. Sandford."

"Then why, Sir, bring him hither? For where he and I are, there must be contention."

"I brought him hither, madam, or rather brought you to this house, merely that he might be present on this occasion, and with his discernment relieve me from a suspicion, that my own judgment can neither suppress or confirm."

"Is there any more company you may wish to call in, Sir, to clear up your doubts of my veracity? if so, pray send for them before you begin your interrogations."

He shook his head—she continued. "The whole world is welcome to hear what I say, and every different judge welcome, if they please, to judge me differently."

"Dear Miss Milner—," cried Miss Woodley, with a tone of reproach for the vehemence with which she spoke.

"Perhaps, Miss Milner," said Dorriforth, "you will not now, reply to those questions I was going to put to you?"

"Did I ever refuse, Sir," returned she with a self-approving air, "to comply with any request you have seriously made me? Have

I ever refused to obey your commands whenever you thought proper to lay them upon me? if not, you have no right to suppose I will now."

He was going to reply, when Mr. Sandford sullenly interrupted him, and making towards the door, cried, "When you come to the point for which you brought me here, send for me again."

"Stay now," cried Dorriforth. "And Miss Milner," continued he, "I not only entreat, but command you to tell me.—Have you given your promises, your word, or your affections to lord Frederick Lawnley?"

The colour spread over her face, and she replied—"I thought confessions were only permitted in secrecy; however, as I am not a member of your church, I submit to the persecution of a heretick,[1] and answer—Lord Frederick has neither my word, my promise, nor any share in my affections."

Sandford, Dorriforth, and Miss Woodley all looked at each other with a surprise that was for some time dumb.—At length Dorriforth said, "And it is your firm intention never to become his wife?"

To which she answered—"At present it is."

"At present! do you suspect you shall change your sentiments?"

"Women, sometimes do."

"But before that change can take place, madam, your acquaintance will be broken off; for it is that, I shall next insist upon; and to which you can have no objection."

She replied, "I had rather it would continue."

"On what account?" cried Dorriforth.

"Because it entertains me."

"For shame, for shame!" returned he, "it endangers both your character and your happiness.—Yet again, do not suffer me to break with his lordship if you should like to become his wife; if in that respect it militates against your felicity?"

"By no means," she answered; "lord Frederick makes part of my amusement, but could never constitute my felicity."

---

1   Miss Milner alludes to a widespread fear that Protestants would be somehow forced or coerced into converting to Catholicism. See Haydon.

"Miss Woodley," said Dorriforth, "do you comprehend your friend in the same literal and unequivocal sense I do?"

"Certainly I do, Sir." Answered Miss Woodley.

"And pray, Miss Woodley," said he, "were those the sentiments which you have always entertained?"

Miss Woodley hesitated—he continued. "Or has the present conversation altered them?"

She hesitated again, then answered—"The present conversation has altered them."

"And yet you confide in it!" Cried Sandford, looking at her with contempt.

"Certainly I do." Replied Miss Woodley.

"Do not you then, Mr. Sandford?" asked Dorriforth.

"I would advise you to act the same as if I did." Replied Sandford.

"Then, Miss Milner," said Dorriforth, "you see lord Frederick no more—and I hope I have your permission to tell him so?"

"You have, Sir." She replied with a completely unembarrassed countenance and voice.

Miss Woodley looked hard at her, to discover some lurking wish adverse to all these protestations, but she could not discern one.— Sandford too fixed his penetrating eyes as if he would look through her soul, but finding it perfectly composed, he cried out,

"Why then not write his lordship's dismission herself, and save you, Mr. Dorriforth, the trouble of any farther contest with him?"

"Indeed, Miss Milner," said Dorriforth, "that would oblige me; for it is with the greatest reluctance I meet his lordship upon this subject—he was extremely impatient and importunate the last time he was with me—he took advantage of my ecclesiastic situation to treat me with a levity, and ill-breeding, I could ill have suffered upon any other consideration, than the complying with my duty to you."

"Dictate what you please, Mr. Dorriforth, and I will write it." Said she with a warmth like the most unaffected inclination.— "And while you, Sir," she continued, "are so indulgent as not to distress me with the importunities of any gentleman to whom I am averse, I think myself equally bound to rid you of the impertinence of every one, to whom you may have objection."

"But," answered he, "be assured I have no material objection to my lord Frederick, except from that dilemma, into which your acquaintance with him has involved us all; and the same I should conceive against any other man, where the same circumstance occurred.—As you have now, however, freely and politely consented to the manner in which it has been proposed, you shall break with him, I will not trouble you a moment longer upon a subject on which I have so frequently explained my wishes, but conclude it by assuring you, your ready acquiescence has given me the sincerest satisfaction."

"I hope, Mr. Sandford," said she, turning to him with a smile, "I have given you satisfaction likewise."

Sandford could not say yes, and was ashamed to say no; he, therefore, made no answer except by his looks, which were full of suspicion. She, notwithstanding, made him a very low courtesy.—Her guardian then handed her out of the apartment into her coach, which was waiting to take her, Miss Woodley, and himself home.

CHAPTER XIII

NOTWITHSTANDING the seeming readiness with which Miss Milner had resigned all farther acquaintance with lord Frederick, during the short ride home she appeared to have lost a great part of her wonted spirits; she was thoughtful, and once sighed most heavily. Dorriforth began to fear she had not only made a sacrifice of her affections, but of her varacity; yet, why she had done so, he could not comprehend.

As the carriage moved slowly thro' a lane between Elmwood Castle and her house, on casting her eyes out of the window, Miss Milner's countenance was brightened in an instant, and that instant lord Frederick on horse-back was at the coach door, and the coachman stopt.

"Oh, Miss Milner," cried he, (with a voice and manner that could give little suspicion of the truth of what he said) "I am over-joyed at the happiness of seeing you, even though it is but an accidental meeting."

She was evidently glad to see him, but the earnestness with

which he spoke, put her upon her guard not to express the like, and she said in a cool constrained manner, she "was glad to see his lordship."

The reserve with which she spoke, gave lord Frederick immediate suspicion who was in the coach with her, and turning his head quickly, he met the stern eye of Dorriforth; upon which, without the smallest salutation, he turned from him again abruptly and rudely. Miss Milner was confused, and Miss Woodley in torture at the palpable affront; to which Dorriforth alone appeared indifferent.

"Go on," said Miss Milner to the footman, "desire the coachman to drive on."

"No," cried lord Frederick, "not till you have told me when I shall see you again."

"I will write you word, my lord." Replied she, something alarmed; "You shall have a letter immediately after I get home."

As if he guessed what its contents were to be, he cried out with warmth, "Take care then, madam, how you treat me in that letter—and you, Mr. Dorriforth," turning to him, "do you take care what it contains, for if it is dictated by you, to you I shall send the answer."

Dorriforth, without making his lordship a reply, or casting a look at him, put his head out of the window on the opposite side, and called, in a very angry tone to the coachman, "How dare you not drive on, when your lady orders you?"

The sound of Dorriforth's voice in anger was to the servants so unusual, it acted like a stroke of electricity on the man, and he drove on at the instant so swiftly, that lord Frederick was in a moment left many yards behind. As soon, however, as he recovered from the surprise into which this sudden command had thrown him, he rode with speed after the carriage, and followed it till they all arrived at the door of Miss Milner's house; there his lordship, giving himself up to the rage of love, or to rage against Dorriforth for the contempt with which he had treated him, leapt from his horse as Miss Milner stept from her carriage, and seizing her hand, entreated her "Not to desert him, in compliance to the monastick precepts of hypocrisy."

Dorriforth heard this, standing silently by, with a manly scorn painted on his countenance.

Miss Milner struggled to loose her hand, saying, "Excuse me from replying to you now, my lord."

In return to which his lordship brought her hand to his lips, and began to devour it with kisses, when Dorriforth with an instantaneous impulse, rushed forward, and struck him a blow in the face.—Under the force with which this assault was given, and the astonishment it excited, his lordship staggered, and letting fall the hand of Miss Milner, her guardian immediately laid hold of it, and led her into the house.

She was terrified beyond description; and it was with difficulty Mr. Dorriforth could get her to her own chamber, without taking her in his arms.—When, with the assistance of her woman, he had placed her upon a sopha—all shame and confusion for what he had done, he dropped upon his knees before her, and earnestly "entreated her forgiveness for the indelicacy he had been guilty of in her presence."—And that he had alarmed her, and lost sight of the respect which he thought sacredly her due, seemed to be the only circumstance that dwelt upon his thoughts.

She felt the indecorum of the posture he had condescended to take, and was shocked—to see her guardian at her feet, struck her with the same impropriety as if she had beheld a parent there; and all agitation and emotion, she implored him to rise, and with a thousand protestations declared, "she thought the rashness of the act, was the highest proof of his regard for her."

Miss Woodley now entered; for her care being ever employed upon the unfortunate, lord Frederick on this occasion, had been the object of it; and she had waited by his side, and with every good purpose, preached patience to him, while he was smarting under the pain and shame of his chastisement.—At first, his fury threatened to retort upon the servants around him, and who refused his entrance into the house, the punishment he had received—But in the certainty of an honourable amends which must hereafter be made, he overcame the many temptations which the moment offered, and remounting his horse, rode from the place.

No sooner had Miss Woodley entered the room, and Dorriforth had resigned to her the care of his ward, than he flew to the spot where he had left his lordship, negligent what might have been the event had he still remained there.—After enquiring, and being told he was gone, Dorriforth returned to his own apartment; and with a bosom torn by more excruciating sensations far, than those he had given to his adversary.

The remorse that first struck him as he shut the door upon himself was—I have departed from my character—from the sacred character, and dignity of my profession and sentiments—I have departed from myself.—I am no longer the philosopher, but the ruffian—I have treated with an unpardonable insult a young nobleman, whose only crime was love, and a fond desire to insinuate himself into the favour of his mistress.—I must atone for this outrage in whatever manner he may choose, and the law of justice and equity (though in this one instance, contrary to the law of religion) enjoins, that if he demands my life, in satisfaction for his wounded honour, it is his due. "Alas," cried he, "that I could have laid it down this morning, unsullied with the cause, for which it will make but poor atonement."

He next reflected—I have offended, and filled with horror a beautiful young lady, whom it was my duty to have protected from the brutal manners, to which I myself have exposed her.

Again—I have drawn upon me the just reproaches of my faithful preceptor and friend; the man in whose judgment it was my delight to be approved—above all, I have drawn upon myself, the stings of my own conscience.

"Where shall I pass this sleepless night?" cried he, walking repeatedly across his chamber; "Can I go to the ladies? I am a brute, unworthy such society.—Shall I go and repose my disturbed mind on Sandford? I am ashamed to tell him the cause of my uneasiness.—Shall I go to lord Frederick, and humbling myself before him, beg his forgiveness? He would spurn me for a coward.— No"—(and he lifted his eyes to Heaven) "Thou all great, all wise, and all omnipotent being, whom I have above any other offended, to thee alone I apply in this hour of tribulation, and from thee alone I expect comfort.—And the confidence with which I now address myself to thee, encouraged by that long intercourse religion has effected, in this one moment pays me amply, for the many years of my past life wholly devoted to thy service."

CHAPTER XIV

ALTHOUGH Miss Milner had foreseen no fatal event from the indignity offered lord Frederick, yet she passed a night very different from those to which she had been accustomed. No sooner was she falling into a sleep, than a thousand vague, but distressing ideas darted across her imagination.—Her heart would at times whisper to her as she was half asleep, "lord Frederick is banished from you for ever."—She shakes off the uneasiness this idea brings along with it—she then starts, and beholds the blow still aimed at him by Dorriforth.—And no sooner has she driven away this painful image, than she is again awakened by seeing her guardian at her feet suing for pardon.—She sighs, she trembles, she is chilled with terror.

Relieved by a flood of tears; towards the morning she sinks into a refreshing slumber, but waking, finds the self-same images crowding all together upon her mind—she is doubtful to which to give the preference—one, however, rushes the foremost, and will continue so—she knows not the consequence of ruminating, nor why she dwells upon that, more than upon all the rest, and yet it will give place to none.

She rises in a languid and disordered state, and at breakfast adds fresh pain to Dorriforth by her altered appearance.

He had scarce left the breakfast room when an officer waited upon him charged with a challenge from lord Frederick. To the message delivered to him by this gentleman, Dorriforth replied,

"As a clergyman, more especially in the church of Rome, I know not whether I am not exempt from answering a claim of this kind;[1] but not having had forbearance to avoid an offence, I have no right to a privilege that would only indemnify me from making reparation."

"You will then meet his lordship, Sir, at the appointed time?" Said the officer.

---

1   The church forbade dueling, and, as a member of the clergy, Dorriforth risked excommunication by participating in the duel. See Appendix C2 for an essay by William Godwin on dueling.

"I will," answered Dorriforth, "and my immediate care shall be to procure a gentleman to accompany me."

The officer withdrew, and as soon as Dorriforth was once more alone, he was going once more to reflect, but he durst not—since yesterday, reflection, for the first time of his life, was become painful to him; and even as he rode the short way to lord Elmwood's immediately after, he found his own thoughts so insufferable, he was obliged to enter into conversation with his servant. Solitude, that he was formerly so charmed withal, at those moments had been worse than death.

At lord Elmwood's, he met Sandford in the hall, and the sight of him was no longer welcome, but displeasing—he knew how different the principles he had just adopted were to those of that reverend friend's, and without his complaining, or even suspecting what had happened, his presence was a sufficient reproach.— Dorriforth passed him as hastily as he could, and enquiring for lord Elmwood, disclosed to him his errand, which was to ask him to be his second; his lordship started, and wished to consult his tutor, but that his kinsman strictly forbid; and having urged his reasons with arguments, such as his lordship could not refute; he at length prevailed upon him to promise he would accompany him to the field, which was at a few miles distance only, and the parties were to be there at seven on the same evening.

As soon as his business with lord Elmwood was settled, Dorriforth returned home, to make some necessary preparations for the event which might ensue from this meeting—he wrote letters to several of his friends; and one to his ward, over which he shed tears.[1]

Sandford going into lord Elmwood's library soon after Dorriforth had left it, expressed his surprise at finding him gone; upon which that young nobleman, after answering a few questions, and giving a few significant tokens, that he was entrusted with a secret, frankly confessed, what he had promised to conceal.

Sandford, as much as a holy man could be, was enraged at

---

1 In the second, third, fourth, and fifth editions, "in writing which, he could with difficulty preserve the usual firmness of his mind."

Dorriforth for the cause of this challenge, but was still more enraged at him for his wickedness in accepting it—he applauded his pupil's virtue in making the discovery, and congratulated himself that he should be the instrument, of saving not only the blood of his friend, but of preventing the scandal of his being engaged in a duel.

In the ardour of his designs he went immediately to Miss Milner's—entered the house he had so long refused to enter, and at a time when he was on aggravated bad terms with its owner.

He asked for Dorriforth, went hastily into his apartment, and poured upon him a torrent of rebukes.—Dorriforth bore all he said with the patience of a devotee, but with the firmness of a man.—He owned his fault, but no eloquence could make him recall the promise he had given to repair the injury.—Unshaken by the arguments, persuasions, and menaces of Sandford, he gave a fresh proof of that inflexibility for which he has been described—and after two hours dispute they parted, neither of them the better for what either had advanced, but Dorriforth something the worse; his conscience gave testimony to Sandford's opinion, "that he was bound by ties more sacred than worldly honour," but while he owned, he would not yield to duty.

Sandford left him, determined, however, that lord Elmwood should not be accessary in his guilt, and this he declared, on which Dorriforth took the resolution of seeking another second.

In passing through the house on his return home, Sandford met, by accident, Mrs. Horton, Miss Milner, and the other two ladies returning from a saunter in the garden.—Surprised at the sight of Mr. Sandford in her house, Miss Milner would not express that surprise, but going up to him with all the friendly benevolence which generally played about her heart, she took hold of one of his hands, and pressed it with a kindness which told him he was welcome more forcibly, than if she had made the most elaborate speech to convince him of it.—He, however, seemed little touched with her behaviour, and as an excuse for breaking his word, cried,

"I beg your pardon, madam, but I was brought hither in my anxiety to prevent murder."

"Murder!" Exclaimed all the ladies.

"Yes," answered he, addressing himself to Miss Fenton, "your betrothed husband is a party concerned; he is going to be second to Mr. Dorriforth, who means this very evening to be killed by my lord Frederick, or to kill him, in addition to the blow he gave him last night."

Mrs. Horton exclaimed, "If Mr. Dorriforth dies, he dies a martyr."

Miss Woodley cried with fervour, "Heaven forbid!"

Miss Fenton cried, "Dear me!"

While Miss Milner, without uttering one word, sunk speechless on the floor.

They lifted her up and brought her to the door which entered the garden. She soon recovered; for the tumult of her mind would not suffer her to remain inactive, and she was rouzed, in spite of her weakness, to endeavour to ward off the present disaster.—In vain, however, she tried to walk to Dorriforth's apartment—in the trial she sunk as before, and was taken to a settee, while Miss Woodley was dispatched to bring her guardian to her.

Informed of the cause of her swoonings, he followed Miss Woodley with a tender anxiety for her health, and with grief and confusion that he had so carelessly endangered it.—On his entering the room Sandford beheld the inquietude of his mind, and cried, "here is your *guardian*," with a cruel emphasis on the word.

He was too much engaged by the indisposition of his ward to reply to Sandford.—He placed himself on the settee by her, and with the utmost tenderness, reverence, and pity, entreated her not to be concerned at an accident in which he, and he only, had been to blame; but which he had still no doubt would be accommodated in the most amicable manner.

"I have one favour to require of you, Mr. Dorriforth," said she, "and that is your promise, your solemn promise, which I know is sacred, that you will not fight with my lord Frederick."

He hesitated.

"Oh, madam," cried Sandford, "he is grown a libertine now, and I would not believe his word were he to give it you."

"Then, Sir," returned Dorriforth angrily, "you *may* believe my word, for I will keep that, I have passed to you.—I will give lord

Frederick all the restitution in my power.—But my dear Miss Milner, let not this alarm you; we may not find it convenient to meet this many a day; and most probably some fortunate explanation may yet take place and prevent our meeting at all. If not, reckon but among the many duels that are fought, how few are fatal; and even in that case, how small would be the loss to society"—He was proceeding.

"I should ever deplore the loss," cried Miss Milner, "I could not survive the death of either, in such a case."

"For my part," returned Dorriforth, "I look upon my life as much forfeited to his lordship, to whom I have given a high offence, as it might in other instances have been forfeited to the offended laws of the land. Honour, is the law of the polite part of the land; we know it; and when we transgress against it knowingly, we justly incur our punishment. —However, Miss Milner, this business is not to be settled immediately, and I have no doubt but all will be as you could wish.—Do you think I should appear thus easy," added he with a smile, "if I were going to be shot at by my lord Frederick?"

"Very well." Cried Sandford, with a look that demonstrated he knew better.

"You will stay within then, all this day?" said Miss Milner.

"I am engaged out to dinner," he replied, "it is unlucky—I am sorry for it—but I'll be at home early in the evening."

"Stained with human blood," cried Sandford, "or yourself a corpse."

The ladies all lifted up their hands, and Miss Milner rose from her seat and threw herself at her guardian's feet.

"You knelt to me last night, I now kneel to you," (she cried) "kneel, never desiring to rise more, if you persist in your intention.—I am weak, I am volatile, I am indiscreet, but I have a heart from whence some impressions can never be erased."

He endeavoured to raise her, she persisted to kneel—and here the trouble, the affright, the terror she endured, discovered to her for the first time her own sentiments—which, till that moment, she had doubted—and she continued,

"I no longer pretend to conceal my passion—I love lord Frederick Lawnly."

Her guardian started.

"Yes, to my shame I love him:" (cried she, all emotion) "I meant to have struggled with the weakness, because I supposed it would be displeasing to you—but apprehension for his safety takes away every power of restraint, and I beseech you to spare his life."

"This is exactly what I thought." Cried Sandford, triumphantly.

"Good heaven!" cried Miss Woodley.

"But it is very natural." Said Mrs. Horton.

"I own," said Dorriforth, (struck with amaze, and now taking her from his feet with a force she could not resist) "I own, Miss Milner, I am greatly affected at this contradiction in your character"—

"But did not I say so?" cried Sandford, interrupting him.

"However," continued he, "you may take my word, though you have deceived me in your's, that lord Frederick's life is secure.— For your sake, I would not endanger it for the universe.—But let this be a warning to you"—

He was proceeding with the most poignant language, and austere looks, when observing the shame, the terror, and the self-reproach which agitated her mind, he divested himself in great measure of his austerity, and said, mildly,

"Let this be a warning to you, how you deal in future with the friends who wish you well—you have hurried me into a mistake that might have cost me my life, or the life of the man you love; and thus exposed *you* to misery, more bitter than death."

"I am not worthy your friendship, Mr. Dorriforth," said she, sobbing with grief, "and from this moment forsake me."

"No, madam, not in the moment you first discover to me, how I can make you happy."

The conversation appearing now to become of that nature in which the rest of the company could have no share whatever; they all, except Mr. Sandford, were retiring; when Miss Milner called Miss Woodley back, saying, "Stay you with me; I was never so unfit to be left without your friendship."

"Perhaps for the present you can much easier dispense with mine?" said Dorriforth. She made no answer: he therefore having once more assured her lord Frederick's life was safe, was quitting the room; when he recollected in what a state of humiliation he had left her, and turning towards her as he opened the door, added,

"And be assured, madam, my esteem for you, shall be the same as ever."

Sandford, as he followed Dorriforth, bowed to Miss Milner too, and repeated the self-same words—"And, madam, be assured my esteem for you, shall be *the same as ever.*"

CHAPTER XV

THIS taunting reproof from Sandford made little impression upon Miss Milner, whose thoughts were all fixed on a subject of much more importance than the opinion he entertained of her.—She threw her arms about Miss Woodley as soon as they were left alone, and asked, with anxiety, "What she thought of her behaviour?" Miss Woodley, who could not approve of the duplicity her friend had betrayed, still wished to reconcile her as much as possible to her own conduct, and replied, she "highly commended the frankness with which she had, at last, acknowledged her sentiments."

"Frankness!" cried Miss Milner, starting. "Frankness, my dear Miss Woodley!—what you have just now heard me say, is all a falsehood."

"How, Miss Milner!"

"Oh, my dear Miss Woodley," returned she, sobbing upon her bosom, "pity the agonies of my heart, by nature sincere, when such are the fatal propensities it cherishes, I must submit to the grossest falsehoods rather than reveal the truth."

"What do you mean?" Cried Miss Woodley, with the strongest amazement painted on her face.

"Do you suppose I love lord Frederick?" Returned the other. "Do you suppose I *can* love him?—Oh fly, Miss Woodley, and prevent my guardian from telling him such an untruth."

"What do you mean?" repeated Miss Woodley; "I protest you frighten me:"—and this inconsistency in the behaviour of Miss Milner, really appeared as if her senses had been deranged.

"Only fly," resumed she, "and prevent the inevitable ill consequence which must ensue from lord Frederick's being told this falsehood.—It will involve us all in greater disquietude than we suffer at present."

"Then what has influenced you, my dear Miss Milner?"—

"That which impels my every action." Returned she; "An unsurmountable instinct—a fatality, that will ever render me the most miserable of human beings; and yet you, even you, my dear Miss Woodley, will not pity me."

Miss Woodley pressed her close in her arms and vowed, "That while she was unhappy, from whatever cause, she still would pity her."

"Go to Mr. Dorriforth then, and prevent him from imposing upon lord Frederick."

"But that imposition is the only means to prevent the duel." Replied Miss Woodley. "The moment I have told him you have no regard for his lordship, he will no longer refuse to fight with him."

"Then at all events I am undone," exclaimed Miss Milner, "for the duel is horrible, even beyond every thing else."

"How so?" returned Miss Woodley, "since you have declared you do not care for lord Frederick."

"But are you so blind," returned Miss Milner with a degree of madness in her looks, "to believe I do not care for Mr. Dorriforth? Oh, Miss Woodley! I love him with all the passion of a mistress, and with all the tenderness of a wife."

Miss Woodley at this sentence sat down—it was on a chair that was close to her—her feet could not have taken her to any other.—She trembled—she was white as ashes, and deprived of speech. Miss Milner, taking her by the hand, said,

"I know what you feel—I know what you think of me—and how much you hate and despise me.—But Heaven is witness to all my struggles—nor would I, even to myself, acknowledge the shameless prepossession, till forced by a sense of his danger"—

"Silence." Cried Miss Woodley, struck with horror.

"And even now," resumed Miss Milner, "have I not concealed it from all but you, by plunging myself into a new difficulty, from whence I know not how I shall be extricated?—And do I entertain a hope? No, Miss Woodley, nor ever will.—But suffer me to own my folly to you—to entreat your soothing friendship to free me from my weakness.—And, oh! give me your friendly advice to deliver me from the difficulties which surround me."

Miss Woodley was still pale, and still silent.

Education, is called second nature; in the strict (but not enlarged) education of Miss Woodley, it was more powerful than the first—and the violation of oaths, persons, or things consecrated to Heaven, was, in her opinion, if not the most enormous, the most horrid among the catalogue of crimes.

Miss Milner had lived too long in a family who had imbibed those opinions not to be convinced of their existence; nay, her own reason told her that solemn vows of whatever kind, ought to be binding; and the more she respected her guardian's understanding, the less she called in question his religious tenets—in esteeming him, she esteemed all his notions; and among the rest, even venerated those of his religion.—Yet that passion, which had unhappily taken possession of her whole soul, would not have been inspired, had there not subsisted an early difference, in their systems of divine faith—had she been early taught what were the sacred functions of a Roman ecclesiastick, though all her esteem, all her admiration, had been attracted by the qualities and accomplishments of her guardian; yet education would have given such a prohibition to her love, that she had been precluded from it, as by that barrier which divides a sister from a brother.

This, unfortunately, was not the case; and Miss Milner loved Dorriforth without one conscious check to tell her she was wrong, except that which convinced her, her love would be avoided by him, with detestation, with horror.

Miss Woodley, something recovered from her first surprise, and suffering—for never did her susceptible mind suffer so exquisitely—amidst all the grief and abhorrence she felt, pity was still predominant—and reconciled to the faults of Miss Milner by her misery, she once more looked at her with friendship, and asked, "what she could do, to render her less unhappy?"

"Make me forget," replied Miss Milner, "every moment of my past life since I first saw you—that moment was teeming with a weight of cares I must labour under till my death."

"And even in death," replied Miss Woodley, "do not be so presumptuous as to hope to shake them off—if unrepented in this world"—

She was proceeding—but the anxiety her friend endured, would not suffer her to be wholly free from the apprehension, that notwithstanding the positive assurance of her guardian, (should he and lord Frederick meet) the duel might still take place; she therefore rung the bell and enquired if Mr. Dorriforth was still at home?—the answer was—"He is rode out."—"You remember," said Miss Woodley, "he told her he should dine out."—This did not, however, dismiss her fears, and she dispatched two servants different ways in pursuit of him, acquainting them with her suspicions, and charging them to prevent his and lord Frederick's meeting. Sandford had also taken his precautions; but though he knew the time, he did not know the exact place of their appointment, for that, lord Elmwood had forgot to enquire.

The excessive alarm which Miss Milner discovered upon this occasion, was imputed by the servants, and others who were witness of it, to her affection for lord Frederick,[1] while none but Miss Woodley knew, or had the most distant suspicion of the real cause.

Mrs. Horton and Miss Fenton, who were sitting together expatiating on the duplicity of their own sex in the instance just before them, had, notwithstanding the interest of the discourse, a longing desire to break it off; for they were impatient to see this poor frail being whom they were loading with their innocent—as it was among friends—calumny. They longed to see if she would have the confidence to look them in the face: they, to whom she had so often protested, she had not the smallest attachment to lord Frederick but from motives of vanity.

These ladies heard with much satisfaction dinner was served, but met Miss Milner at table with a less degree of pleasure than they expected; for her mind was so totally abstracted from them, they could not discern a single blush, or confused glance, which their presence occasioned. No, Miss Milner had before them divulged nothing of which she was ashamed, she only was ashamed what

---

1   In the first edition, the name Edward was erroneously substituted for Frederick. See *The Critical Review*'s 1791 assessment of the first edition (Appendix B1).

she had said was not truth. In the bosom of Miss Woodley alone, was that secret entrusted which could call a blush into her face, and before her she *did* feel confusion—before the gentle friend, to whom she had till this time communicated all her faults without embarrassment, she now cast down her eyes in shame, and scarce durst lift them up to meet her's.

At table there was little talking, and less eating; Miss Milner did not attempt to eat; Miss Woodley endeavoured, but could not.

Soon after the dinner was removed, lord Elmwood entered; and that gallant nobleman declared—"Mr. Sandford had used him ill in not permitting him to accompany his relation; for he feared Dorriforth would now throw himself upon the sword of lord Frederick without a friend by to defend him."—A rebuke from the eye of Miss Woodley, which from this day forward had a command over Miss Milner, restrained her from expressing the affright she suffered from this supposition of his lordship's. Miss Fenton replied, "As to that, my lord, I see no reason why Mr. Dorriforth and lord Frederick should not now be friends.— "Certainly," said Mrs. Horton, "for as soon as my lord Frederick is made acquainted with Miss Milner's confession, all differences must be reconciled."—"What confession?" asked his lordship.

Miss Milner, to avoid hearing a repetition of that which gave her pain but to think of, arose in order to retire into her own apartment, but was obliged to sit down again—and received the assistance of her friend and lord Elmwood to lead her into her dressing room. Reclined upon a sopha there, a silence ensued between her and Miss Woodley for near half an hour; and when the conversation began, the name of Dorriforth was never uttered—they were both grown cool and considerate since the discovery, and both were equally ashamed and fearful of naming him.

The vanity of the world, the folly of riches, the pleasures of retirement, and such topics engaged their discourse, but not their thoughts, for near two hours; and the first time the word Dorriforth was spoken, a servant with alacrity opened the dressing room door, without previously rapping, and cried, "Mr. Dorriforth, madam."

Dorriforth immediately came in, and went eagerly to Miss Milner.—Miss Woodley beheld the glow of joy, and guilt upon her face, and did not rise to give him her seat, as was her custom if he came with intelligence to his ward, and she was sitting next her—he therefore stood while he repeated all that had happened in his interview with lord Frederick.

But with her gladness to see her guardian safe, Miss Milner had forgot to enquire for the safety of his lordship; the man whom she had pretended to love so passionately—even a smile of rapture was upon her face, though Dorriforth might be returned from putting him to death. This incongruity of behaviour Miss Woodley saw, and was confounded—but Dorriforth, in whose thoughts a suspicion either of her love to him, or want of love for lord Frederick, had not the smallest place, easily reconciled this inconsistency, and said,

"You see by my countenance all is well, and therefore you smile on me before I tell you what has passed."

This brought her to the recollection of her conduct, and now with a countenance constrained to some show of gravity, she tried to express alarm she did not feel.

"Nay, I have the pleasure to assure you Lord Frederick is safe," resumed Dorriforth, "and the disgrace of his blow washed entirely away, by a few drops of blood from this arm," and he laid his hand upon his left arm, which rested in his waistcoat as a sling.

She cast her eyes there, and seeing where the ball had entered the coat sleeve, she gave an involuntary scream, and sunk on the side of the sopha. Instead of that tender sympathy with which Miss Woodley used to attend her upon the slightest illness or affliction, she now addressed her in a sharp tone, and cried, "Miss Milner, you have heard lord Frederick is safe, you have then nothing to alarm you."—Nor did she run to offer a smelling bottle, or to raise her head. Her guardian seeing her near fainting, and without this assistance from her friend, was going to himself to give it; but on this, Miss Woodley interfered, and having taken her head upon her arm, assured him, "It was a trifling weakness to which Miss Milner was accustomed, and that she would ring for her woman, who knew how to relieve her instantly with a few drops."—Satisfied with this, Dorriforth left the room; and a surgeon being arrived to dress his wound, he retired into his own chamber.

CHAPTER XVI

THE power delegated to the keeper of our secrets, Miss Woodley was the last person on earth to abuse—but she was also the last, who, by her complacency would participate in the guilt of her friend—and there was no guilt, except that of murder, which she thought equal to the crime in question, provided it was ever perpetrated.—Adultery, her reason would perhaps have informed her, was a more pernicious evil to society; but to a religious mind, what sounds so horrible as sacrilege? Of vows made to God or to man, the former must weigh the heavier.—Moreover, the dreadful sin of infidelity in the marriage state, is much softened to a common understanding, by the frequency of the crime; whereas, of vows broken by a devotee she had scarce heard of any; or if any, they were generally followed by such examples of divine vengeance, such miraculous punishments in this world, (as well as eternal punishment in the other) that served to exaggerate their wickedness.

She, who could, and did pardon Miss Milner, was the person who saw her passion in the severest light, and resolved to take every method, however harsh, to root it from her heart—nor did she fear success, resting on the certain assurance, that however deep her love was fixed, it would never be returned. Yet this confidence did not prevent her taking every precaution, lest Dorriforth should come to the knowledge of it—she would not have his composed mind disturbed with such a thought—his steadfast principles so much as shook by the imagination—nor overwhelm him with those self-reproaches which his fatal attraction, unpremeditated as it was, would still have drawn upon him.

With this plan of concealment, in which the natural modesty of Miss Milner acquiesced, there was but one effort to make which that young lady was not prepared for; and that was an entire separation from her guardian.—She had, from the first, cherished her passion without the most distant prospect of a return—she was prepared to see Dorriforth without ever seeing him nearer to her than her guardian and friend, but not to see him at all—for that, she was not prepared.

But Miss Woodley reflected upon the inevitable necessity of this step before she made the proposal, and then made it with a firmness, that might have done honour to the inflexibility of Dorriforth himself.

During the few days that intervened between her open confession of love for lord Frederick, and this proposal, the most intricate incoherence appeared to the whole family, in the character of Miss Milner—and in order to evade a marriage with his lordship, and to conceal, at the same time, the shameful propensity which lurked in her breast, she was once, even on the point of declaring a passion for Sir Edward Ashton.

In the duel which had taken place between lord Frederick and Dorriforth, the latter had received his antagonist's fire, but positively refused to return it; by which he had kept his promise not to endanger his lordship's life, and had reconciled Sandford, in great measure, to his behaviour—and Sandford now (his resolution once broken) no longer refused entering Miss Milner's house, but came every time it was convenient, though he yet avoided its mistress as much as possible; or showed by every word and look, when she was present, that she was still less in his favour than she had ever been.

He visited Dorriforth on the evening after his engagement with lord Frederick, and again the next morning breakfasted with him in his own chamber; nor did Miss Milner see her guardian since his first return from that engagement till the following noon. She enquired, however, of the servant how his master did, and was rejoiced to hear his wound was but very slight—yet this enquiry she durst not make before Miss Woodley, but waited till she was absent.

When Dorriforth made his appearance the next day, it was evident he had thrown from his heart a load of cares; and though they had left a languor upon his face, there was content in his voice, his manners, in his every word and action.—Far from seeming to retain any resentment towards his ward, for the trouble and danger into which her imprudence had led him, he appeared rather to pity her weakness, and to wish to sooth the perturbation which the recollection of her own conduct had obviously raised in her mind—His endeavours were most successful—she was soothed every time he spoke to her; and had not the watchful eye of Miss Woodley stood guard over her inclinations, she had plainly evinced, she was enraptured with the joy of seeing him again himself, after the danger to which he had been exposed.

These emotions, which she laboured to subdue, passed, however, the bounds of her ineffectual resistance; when at the time of retiring after dinner, he said to her in a low voice, but such as it was meant to the company should hear, "Do me the favour, Miss Milner, to call at my study sometime in the evening; I have to speak to you upon business."

She answered, "I will, Sir." And her eyes swam with delight in expectation of the interview.

Let not the reader, nevertheless imagine, there was in that ardent expectation, one idea which the most spotless mind, in love, might not have indulged without reproach.—Sincere love, (at least among the delicate of the female sex) is often gratified by that degree of enjoyment, or rather forbearance, which would be torture in the pursuit of any other passion—real, delicate, and restrained love, like that of Miss Milner's, was indulged in the sight of the object only; and having bounded her wishes by her hopes, the height of her happiness was limited to a conversation in which no other but themselves partook a part.[1]

Miss Woodley was one who heard the appointment, but the only one who conceived with what sensation it was received.

While the ladies remained in the same room with Dorriforth, Miss Milner thought of little, except of him—as soon as they withdrew into another apartment, she remembered Miss Woodley, and turning her head suddenly, saw Miss Woodley's face imprinted with suspicion and displeasure—this at first was painful to her—but recollecting that in a couple of hours time she was to meet her guardian alone—speak to him, and hear him speak to herself only—every other thought was absorbed in that one, and she considered with indifference, the uneasiness, or the anger of her friend.

Miss Milner, to do justice to her heart, did not wish to beguile Dorriforth into the snares of love.—Could any supernatural power have endowed her with the means, and at the same time shewn to her the ills that must arise from such an effect of her

---

1 In the second, third, fourth, and fifth editions, "took a part."

charms, she had assuredly enough of virtue to have declined the conquest; but without enquiring of herself what she proposed? She never saw him without previously endeavouring to look more attractive than she would have desired, in any other company.—And now, without listening to the thousand exhortations that were speaking in every feature of Miss Woodley's face, she flew to a looking-glass, to adjust her dress in a manner that she thought most enchanting.

Time stole away, and the time to go to her guardian arrived. In this presence, unsupported by the presence of a third person, every grace she had practised, every look she had borrowed to set off her charms were annihilated, and she became a native beauty, with the artless arguments of reason, only for her aid.—Awed thus, by his power, from every thing but what she really was, she never was perhaps half so bewitching as in those timid, respectful, and embarrassed moments she passed alone with him.—He caught at those times her respect, her diffidence, nay, even her embarrassment; and never would one word of anger pass on either side.

On the present occasion, he first, expressed the highest satisfaction that she had at length, revealed to him the state of her mind.

"And taking every thing into consideration, Miss Milner," added he, "I rejoice that your sentiments happen to be such as you have owned—for although my lord Frederick is not the very man I could have wished for your perfect happiness, yet in the state of human perfection and human happiness, you might have fixed your affections with much less propriety; and yet, where my unwillingness to thwart your inclinations, might not have permitted me to contend with them."

Not a word of reply did this demand, or if it had, not a word could she have given.

"And now, madam, the reason of my desire to speak with you—is to know from yourself, the means you think most proper to pursue, in order to acquaint his lordship, that notwithstanding this late repulse, there are hopes of your partiality in his favour."

"Defer the explanation." Returned she, eagerly.

"I beg your pardon, Miss Milner, that cannot be—besides, how can you indulge a disposition thus unpitying?—even so ardently did I desire to render his lordship happy, though he came armed against my life, that had I not reflected, previous to our engagement it would appear like fear, and the means of bartering for his forgiveness; I should have revealed your sentiments the moment I had seen him. When the engagement was over, I was too impatient to acquaint you of his safety, to think then on gratifying him.—And indeed, the delicacy of the declaration, after the many denials you have no doubt given him should be considered—I therefore entreat your approbation of the manner in which it shall be made."

"Mr. Dorriforth, can you allow nothing to the moments of surprise? and that pity, which the fate impending inspired; and which might urge me to express myself of lord Frederick, in a manner my cooler thoughts will not warrant?"

"There was nothing in your expressions, my dear Miss Milner, the least equivocal—if you were off your guard, when you pleaded for lord Frederick, as I believe you were, you said more sincerely what you thought; and no discreet, or rather indiscreet retractions, can make me change my opinion."

"I am very sorry." She replied, confused, and trembling.

"Why sorry? Come, give me commission to reveal these sentiments.—I'll not be too hard upon you—a hint from me to his lordship will do—hope, is ever apt to interpret the slightest words to its own use, and a lover's hope, is beyond all others, sanguine."

"I never gave lord Frederick hope."

"But did you ever plunge him into despair?"

"His pursuit says I never have, but he has no other proof."

"However light and frivolous you have been upon frivolous subjects, yet I must own, Miss Milner, I expected, that when a case of this importance came seriously before you, you would have discovered a proper stability in your behaviour."

"I do, Sir; and it was only while I was affected with a weakness, which arose from accident, that I have ever shown an inconsistence."

"You then still assert you have no affection for my lord Frederick?"

"Not sufficient to become his wife."

"You are alarmed at marriage, and I do not wonder you should be so; it shews a prudent foresight that does you honour—but, my dear, are there no dangers in a single state?—if I may judge, Miss Milner, there are many more to a young lady of your accomplishments, than were you under the protection of a husband."

"My father, Mr. Dorriforth, thought your protection sufficient."

"But that protection was rather to direct your choice, than to be the cause of your not choosing at all.—Give me leave to point out an observation which, perhaps, I have too frequently done before, but upon this occasion I must intrude it once again.—Miss Fenton is its object—her fortune is inferior to your's, her personal attractions less."—

Here the strong glow of joy, and of gratitude, for an opinion so negligently, and yet so sincerely expressed, flew to Miss Milner's face, neck, and even to her hands and fingers; the blood mounted to every part of her skin that was visible, for not a fibre but felt the secret transport, that Dorriforth thought her more beautiful than the beautiful Miss Fenton.

If he observed her blushes, he was unsuspicious of the cause, and went on.

"There is, besides, in the temper of Miss Fenton, a sedateness that might with less hazard secure her safety in an unmarried life; and yet she very properly thinks it her duty, as she does not mean to seclude herself by any vows to the contrary, to become a wife—and in obedience to the counsel of her friends, will be married within a very few weeks."

"Miss Fenton may marry from obedience, I never will."

"You mean to say, Love shall alone induce you?"

"I do."

"If, madam, you would point out a subject upon which I am the least able to speak, and on which my sentiments, such as they are, are formed alone from theory (and even there instructed but with caution) it is the subject of love.—And yet, Miss Milner, even that little I know, tells me, without a doubt, that what you said to me yesterday, pleading for lord Frederick's life, was the result of the most violent and tender love."

"The *little you know* then, Mr. Dorriforth, has deceived you; had you *known more*, you would have judged otherwise."

"I submit to the merit of your reply; but without allowing me a judge at all, I will appeal to those who were present with me."

"Are Mrs. Horton and Mr. Sandford to be the connoisseurs?"

"No; I'll appeal to Miss Fenton and Miss Woodley."

"And yet, I believe," replied she with a smile, "I believe, theory, must only be the judge even there."

"Then from all you have said, madam, on this occasion, I am to conclude you still refuse to marry lord Frederick?'

"You are."

"And you submit never to see him again?"

"I do."

"All you then said to me, yesterday, was false?"

"I was not mistress of myself at the time."

"Therefore it was truth—for shame, for shame!"

At that moment the door opened, and Mr. Sandford walked in—he started back on seeing Miss Milner, and was going away again; but Dorriforth called to him to stay, and said with warmth,

"Tell me, Mr. Sandford, by what power, by what persuasion, I can prevail upon this lady to confide in me as her friend; to lay her heart open, and credit mine when I declare to her, I have no view in all the advice I give, but her immediate welfare?"

"Mr. Dorriforth, you know my opinion of the lady," replied Sandford, "it has been formed ever since my first acquaintance with her, and it still remains the same."

"But instruct me how I am to inspire her with confidence;" returned Dorriforth, "how I am to impress her with that which is for her advantage?"

"You can work no miracles," replied Sandford, "you are not holy enough."

"And yet Miss Milner," answered Dorriforth, "appears to be acquainted with that mystery; for what but the force of a miracle, can induce her to contradict to-day, what before you, and several other witnesses, she positively acknowledged yesterday?"

"Do you call that miraculous?" cried Sandford, "The miracle had been if she had not done so—for did she not yesterday, contradict what she acknowledged the day before?—and will she not to-morrow, disavow what she says to-day?"

"I wish she may." Replied Dorriforth mildly, for he beheld the tears flowing down her face at the rough and severe manner in which Sandford had spoken, and began to feel for her uneasiness.

"I beg pardon," cried Sandford, "for speaking so rudely to the mistress of the house—I have no business here, I know; but where you are, Mr. Dorriforth, unless I am turned out, I shall ever think it my duty to come."

Miss Milner courtesied, as much as to say he was welcome to come.—He continued,

"I was to blame, that on a nice punctilio, I left you so long without my visits, and without my counsel; in the time, you have run the hazard of being murdered, and what is worse, of being excommunicated; for had you been so rash as to have returned your opponent's fire, not all my interest at Rome would have obtained remission of the punishment."

Miss Milner, through all her tears, could not now restrain her laughter—on which he resumed;

"And here do I venture like a missionary among savages—but if I can only save you from the scalping knives of some of them; from the miseries which that lady is preparing for you, I am rewarded."

Sandford spoke this with great fervour, and the crime of her love never appeared to Miss Milner in so tremendous a point of view as thus, unknowingly alluded to by him.

"*The miseries that lady is preparing for you,*" hung upon her ears like the notes of a raven, and equally ominous.—The words "*murder*" *and* "*excommunication*" he had likewise uttered; all the fatal effects of sacrilegious love.—Frightful superstitions struck to her heart, and she could scarcely prevent falling down under their oppression.

Dorriforth beheld the difficulty she had in sustaining herself, and went with the utmost tenderness and supported her; saying, "I beg your pardon—I invited you hither with a far different view than your uneasiness."—

Sandford was beginning to speak.

"Hold, Mr. Sandford," resumed he, "the lady is under my protection, and I know not whether it is not necessary you should apologize to her, and to me, for what you have already said."

"You asked my opinion, or I had not given it you—would you have me, like her, speak what I do not think?"

"Say no more, Mr. Sandford." Cried Dorriforth—and leading her kindly to the door, as if to defend her from his malice, told her "He would take another opportunity to renew the subject."

CHAPTER XVII

WHEN Dorriforth was alone with Sandford, he explained to him what before, he had only hinted; and this learned jesuit frankly confessed, "That the mind of a woman was far above, or rather beneath, his comprehension."—It was so, indeed—for with all his penetration, and he had a great deal, he had not yet penetrated into the recesses of Miss Milner's heart.

Miss Woodley, to whom she repeated all that had passed between herself, her guardian, and Sandford, took this moment, during the alarm and agitation of her spirits, to alarm them still more by her prophetic insinuations; and at length represented to her here, for the first time, the necessity, "That Mr. Dorriforth and she should remain no longer under the same roof." This was like the stroke of sudden death to Miss Milner, and clinging to life, she endeavoured to avert the blow by prayers, and by promises—her friend loved her too sincerely, however, to be prevailed upon.

"But in what manner can I bring about the separation?" cried she, "for till I marry we are obliged, by my father's request, to live in the same house."

"Miss Milner," answered Miss Woodley, "much as I respect the will of a dying man, I regard your and Mr. Dorriforth's present, and eternal happiness much more; and it is my resolution you *shall part*—if you will not contrive the means, that duty falls on me, and without any invention, I see the measure at once."

"What is it?" Cried Miss Milner eagerly.

"To go and reveal to Mr. Dorriforth, without hesitation, the real state of your heart; which your present inconsistent conduct will but too readily confirm."

"You would not plunge me into so much shame, into so much anguish!" Cried she, distractedly.

"No," replied Miss Woodley, "not for the world, provided you will separate from him, by any method of your own—but that you *shall* separate is my determination; and in spite of all your sufferings, this shall be the means, unless you instantly agree to some other."

"Good Heaven, Miss Woodley! is this your friendship?"

"Yes—and the truest friendship I have to bestow.—Think what a task I undertake for your sake and his, and when I condemn myself to explain to him your weakness—what astonishment! what confusion! what remorse, do I foresee painted upon his face!—I hear him call you by the harshest names, and behold him fly from your sight for ever, as an object of his detestation."

"Oh spare the dreadful picture.—Fly from my sight for ever—detest my name. Oh! my dear Miss Woodley, let his friendship for me but still remain, and I will consent to any thing.—You may command me—I will go away from him directly—but let us part in friendship—Oh! without the friendship of Mr. Dorriforth, life would be a heavy burthen indeed."

Miss Woodley immediately began to plan schemes for their separation; and with all her invention alive on the subject, this was the only probable one she could form.

Miss Milner was to write to her distant relation at Bath, complaining of the melancholy of a country life, which she was to say her guardian imposed upon her, and entreat the lady to send a pressing invitation for her to pass a month or two with her; this invitation was to be shewn to Dorriforth for his approbation, and both Miss Woodley and Miss Milner were to enforce it, by expressing their earnest wishes for his consent. This plan properly regulated, the necessary letter was sent by Miss Milner to Bath, and Miss Woodley waited with patience, but with a watchful guard upon the conduct of her friend till the answer arrived.

During this interim a most tender and complaining epistle from lord Frederick was delivered Miss Milner; to which as he received no answer, his lordship prevailed upon his uncle, with whom he resided, to wait upon her, and obtain her verbal reply; for he still flattered himself, fear of her guardian's anger, or perhaps his interception of the letter he had sent, was the cause of her seeming contempt.

The old gentleman was introduced to Miss Milner, and after to Mr. Dorriforth, but received from each an answer so explicit, that left his nephew no longer in doubt but all farther pursuit was vain.

Sir Edward Ashton about this time also, submitted to a formal dismission, and had the mortification to reflect, he was bestowing upon the object of his affections the tenderest proof of his regard, by absenting himself wholly from her society.

Upon this serious and certain conclusion to the hopes of lord Frederick, Dorriforth was more astonished than he had ever yet been at the conduct of his ward—he had once thought her behaviour, in respect to his lordship, was ambiguous, but since her confession of a passion for him, he had no doubt but that in the end, she would become his wife.—He lamented to find himself mistaken, and now thought it proper to give some important marks of his condemnation of her pernicious caprice; and not merely in words, but by the general tenour of his behaviour. He consequently became much more reserved, and more austere than he had been, since his first acquaintance with her; for his manners, not from design, but unknowingly, were softened since his guardianship, by that tender respect he had never ceased to pay to the object of his protection.

Notwithstanding this severity he assumed, his ward in the prospect of parting from him grew melancholy; Miss Woodley's love to her friend rendered her little otherwise; and Dorriforth's peculiar gravity, oftentimes rigour, could not but make the whole party much less cheerful than they had been. Lord Elmwood too was lying dangerously ill of a fever; Miss Fenton of course was as much in sorrow as her nature would suffer her to be, and both Sandford and Dorriforth in extreme concern on his lordship's account.

In this state of affairs, the letter of invitation arrives from lady Luneham at Bath: it was shown to Dorriforth; and to prove to his ward he is so much offended, as no longer to feel that excessive interest in her concerns he once did, he gives his opinion on the subject with indifference—he desires "Miss Milner will do as she herself thinks proper."—Miss Woodley instantly accepts this permission, writes back, and appoints the day, her friend means to set off for the visit.

She is wounded to the heart by the cold and unkind manners of her guardian, but dares not take one method to retrieve his opinion.—Alone, and to Miss Woodley she sighs and weeps; he discovers her sorrow, and is doubtful whether the departure of lord Frederick from that part of the country, is not the cause.

When the day on which she was to set off for Bath, was within two days distance only; the behaviour of Dorriforth took, by degrees, its usual form; if not a greater share of polite and tender attention than ever.—It was the first time he had parted from Miss Milner since he became her guardian, and he felt upon the occasion, a reluctance.—He had been angry with her, he had shewn her he was so, and he now began to wish he had not.— She is not happy, (he considered within himself) every word and action declares she is not, and I may have been too severe, and added to her uneasiness.—"At least we will part on good terms."—Said he—"Indeed my regard for her is such, I cannot part otherwise."

She soon discerned his returning kindness, and it was a gentle tie that would have fastened her to the spot where she was, but for the firm resistance of Miss Woodley.

"What will a few months absence effect?" cried she, pleading her cause, "At the end of a few months at farthest, he will expect me back, and where will be the merit in this short separation?"

"In that time," replied Miss Woodley, "we may find some method to make it still longer."—To this she listened with a kind of despair, but uttered she "was resigned;" and accordingly prepared for her departure.

Dorriforth was all anxiety that every circumstance of her journey should be commodious; he was eager she should be happy, and he was eager she should see he entirely forgave her.—He would have gone part of the way with her, but for the extreme illness of lord Elmwood, in whose chamber he passed chief of the day, and slept in Elmwood House every night.

On the morning of her journey, when Dorriforth gave his hand and conducted Miss Milner to the carriage, all the way he led her she could not restrain a flood of tears; which encreased, as he parted from her, to convulsive sobs.—He was affected; and notwithstanding he had previously bid her farewell, he drew her gently on one side and said, with his eyes moistened from regard of the most laudable nature,

"My dear Miss Milner, we part friends?—I hope we do?—on my side, depend upon it, I regret nothing so much at this short separation, as having ever given you a moment's pain."

"I believe so." Was all she could say, for she hastened to break from him, lest his discerning eye should discover the cause of the weakness which thus overcame her.—But her apprehensions were groundless; the rectitude of his own heart was a bar to the suspicion of her's.—He once more kindly bade her adieu, and the carriage drove away.

Miss Fenton and Miss Woodley accompanied Miss Milner part of the journey, about thirty miles, where they were met by Sir Harry and lady Luneham.—Here was a parting nearly as affecting as that between her and her guardian. Miss Woodley, who for several weeks had treated her friend with a rigidness she herself hardly supposed was in her nature, now bewailed her own severity, begged her forgiveness, promised to correspond with her punctually, and to omit no opportunity of giving her every consolation short of cherishing her fatal passion; but in that, and that only, was the heart of Miss Milner to be consoled.

END OF THE FIRST VOLUME

— VOLUME II —

CHAPTER I

WHEN Miss Milner arrived at Bath, she thought it the most altered place she had ever seen—she was mistaken—it was she herself, who was changed.[1]

The walks were melancholy, the company insipid, the ball-room fatigueing—in fine, she had left behind, all that could charm or please her.

Though she found herself far less happy than when she was at Bath before, yet she felt, she would not, to enjoy all that past happiness, be again reduced to the being she was at that time. Thus, does the lover consider the extinction of his passion, with the same horror as the libertine looks upon annihilation; the one would rather live hereafter (though in all the tortures with which his future state is described) than cease to exist; so there are no tortures a lover would not suffer, rather than cease to love.

In the wide prospect of melancholy before her, Miss Milner's fancy caught hold of the only comfort which presented itself; and this, slender as it was, in the total absence of every other, her imagination pictured as excessive. The comfort was a letter from Miss Woodley—a letter wherein the subject of her love would most assuredly be mentioned, and in whatever terms, must still be the means of delight.

A letter arrived—she devoured it with her eyes.—The post mark on the outside denoting from whence it came, the name of "Milner Lodge" written on the top, were all sources of pleasure—and she read slowly every line it contained to procrastinate the pleasing expectation she enjoyed, till she should arrive at the name of Dorriforth. At last her impatient eye, caught the word three lines beyond the place she was reading—irresistibly, she skipped over those lines, and fixed on the point to which

---

1 Compare Satan's journey to Earth in Milton's *Paradise Lost*, Book IV, "horrour and doubt distract / His troubled thoughts, and from the bottom stir / The Hell within him" (18-20).

she was attracted. Miss Woodley was cautious in her indulgence; she made the slightest mention of Dorriforth, saying only, "He was extremely concerned, and even dejected, at the little hope there was of his cousin, lord Elmwood's, recovery."—Short and trivial as this passage was, it was still more important to Miss Milner than any other in the letter—she read it again and again, considered, and reflected upon it.—Dejected, thought she, what does that word exactly mean?—did I ever see Mr. Dorriforth dejected?—how I wonder does he look in that state?—Thus did she muse, while the cause of his dejection, though a most serious one, and pathetically described by Miss Woodley, scarce arrested her attention once.—She run over with haste the account of lord Elmwood's state of health; she certainly pitied him while she thought of him, but she did not think of him long. To die was a hard fate for a young nobleman just in possession of his immense fortune, and on the eve of marriage with a beautiful young woman; but Miss Milner thought Heaven might be still better than all this, and she had no doubt but his lordship would go there. The forlorn state of Miss Fenton ought to have been a subject for compassion, but she knew that lady had resignation to bear any lot with patience, and that a trial of her fortitude, might be more flattering to her vanity than to be countess of Elmwood: in a word, she saw nobody's misfortunes equal to her own, because she saw no one so little able to bear misfortune.

She replied to Miss Woodley's letter, and dwelt very long on that subject which Miss Woodley had taken care to pass over lightly; this was another indulgence; and to hear from, and to write to her friend, were now the only enjoyments she possessed. From Bath Miss Milner paid several festive visits with lady Luneham—all were alike tedious and melancholy.

But her guardian wrote to her, and though the subject was sorrowful, the letter gave her joy—the sentiments it expressed were but trite and common-place, yet she valued them as the dearest effusions of friendship and affection; and her hand trembled, and her heart beat with rapture while she wrote the answer, though she knew it would not be received with one emotion, such as those which she experienced. In her second letter to Miss Woodley she prayed like a person insane to be taken home from confinement, and like a lunatick protested, in sensible language, she "had no disorder." But her friend replied, "that very declaration proves its violence." And assured her that nothing less than placing her affections elsewhere, should induce her to believe, but that she was incurable.

Miss Woodley's third letter acquainted Miss Milner with the death of lord Elmwood—Miss Woodley was exceedingly affected by this event, and said little else on any other subject.—Miss Milner was shocked when she read the words "he is dead," and instantly thought, "How transient are all sublunary things!—within a few years *I* shall be dead—and how felicitous will it then be, if I have resisted every temptation to the delusive pleasures of this life!"—The happiness of a peaceful death occupied her contemplation for near an hour; but at length every virtuous and pious sentiment this meditation inspired, served but to remind her of the many sentences she had heard fall from her guardian's lips upon the same subject—her thoughts were again fixed on him, and she could think of nothing beside.

In a very short time after, her health became impaired from the indisposition of her mind; she languished, and was once in imminent danger. During a slight delirium of her fever, Miss Woodley's name and her guardian's were repeated incessantly; lady Luneham sent them immediate word of this, and they both hastened to Bath, and arrived there, just as her disorder had taken a most favourable turn. As soon as she became perfectly recollected, her first care was, knowing the frailty of her heart, to enquire what she had uttered while delirious.—Miss Woodley, who was by her bed-side, begged her not to be alarmed on that account, and assured her she knew, from all her attendants, that she had only spoken with a friendly remembrance (as was really the case) of those persons who were dear to her.

She wished to know whether her guardian was come to see her, but she had not the courage to ask before Miss Woodley; and her friend was afraid by the too sudden mention of his name to discompose her. Her woman, however, after some little time, entered the chamber and whispered to Miss Woodley. Miss Milner asked inquisitively "What she said?" and the woman going to her, replied softly, "Lord Elmwood, madam, would wish to come and see you for a few moments, if you will allow him?" Miss Milner turned her head, and stared wildly.

"I thought," said she, "I thought lord Elmwood had been dead—are my senses disordered still?"

"No, my dear," answered Miss Woodley, "it is the present lord Elmwood who wishes to see you; he whom you left ill when you came hither, *is* dead."

"And who is the present lord Elmwood?" She asked.

Miss Woodley after a short hesitation replied—"Your guardian."

"And so he is," cried Miss Milner, "he is the next heir—I had forgot.—But is it possible he is here?"

"Yes—" returned Miss Woodley with a grave voice and manner, to moderate that glow of satisfaction which for a moment sparkled even in her languid eye, and blushed over her pallid countenance—"Yes—as he heard you were ill, he thought it right to come and see you."

"He is very good." Answered she, and the tears started in her eyes.

"Would you please to admit his Lordship?" Asked her woman.

"Not yet, not yet," she replied, "let me recollect myself first." And she looked with a timid doubt upon her friend, to ask if it was proper.

Miss Woodley could scarce support this humble reference to her judgment from the wan face of the poor invalid, and taking her by the hand, whispered in tears, "You shall do what you please."—In a few minutes lord Elmwood was introduced.

To those who sincerely love, every change of situation or circumstances in the object beloved, appears an advantage.—So, the acquisition of a title and estate, was in Miss Milner's eye an immeasurable advantage to her guardian, not on the score of their real value, but any change instead of diminishing her passion would have served but to encrease it—even a change to the utmost poverty.

When he entered—the sight of him seemed to be too much for

her, and after the first glance she turned her head away—the sound of his voice encouraged her, however, to look once more—and now she riveted her eyes upon him.

"It is impossible, my dear Miss Milner," he gently whispered, "to say, the joy I feel that your disorder has subsided."

But though it was impossible to say, it was possible to *look* what he felt, and his looks expressed his feelings.—In the zeal of those sensations, he laid hold of her hand, and held it between his—this he himself did not know—but she did.

"You have prayed for me, my lord, I dare say?" Said she, with a smile of thanks for those prayers.

"Fervently, ardently!"—Returned he, and the fervency with which he prayed, spoke in every feature.

"But I am a protestant, my lord, and if I had died such, do you believe I should have gone to Heaven?"

"Most assuredly, that would not have prevented you."

"But Mr. Sandford does not think so."

"He must; for he means to go there himself."

To keep her guardian with her, Miss Milner seemed inclined to converse; but Miss Woodley perceived the temporal as well as the spiritual evil of this, and advised his lordship to retire.[1]

They had only one more interview before he left the place; at which Miss Milner was capable of sitting up—he was with her, however, but a very short time, some necessary concerns relative to the late lord Elmwood's affairs, calling him in haste to London. Miss Woodley continued with her friend till she saw her entirely reinstated in her health: during which time his lordship was frequently the subject of their private conversation; and upon those occasions Miss Milner has sometimes brought Miss Woodley to acknowledge, "That could Mr. Dorriforth have foreseen the early death of the late lord Elmwood, it had been for the greater honour of his religion (considering that ancient title would now after him become extinct), had he preferred marriage vows, to those of celibacy."

---

1 In the second, third, fourth, and fifth editions, "her solicitous friend gave Lord Elmwood a look, which implied that it might be injurious to her, and he retired."

CHAPTER II

WHEN time for Miss Woodley to depart arrived, Miss Milner entreated earnestly to accompany her home, and made the most solemn promises that she would guard not only her behaviour, but her very thoughts within the limitation her friend should prescribe. Miss Woodley at length yielded thus much, "That as soon as lord Elmwood was set out on his journey to Italy, where she had heard him say he should shortly be obliged to go, she would no longer deny her the pleasure of returning; and if (after the long absence which must consequently take place between him and her) she should then, positively affirm the suppression of her passion was the happy result, she would at that time take her word, and risk the danger of their once more residing together."

With this concession on the side of Miss Woodley they parted; and as winter was now far advanced, that lady returned to her aunt's house in town, from whence Mrs. Horton was, however, preparing to remove, in order to superintend lord Elmwood's house, (which had been occupied by the late earl,) in Grosvenor-square; and Miss Woodley was to accompany her.

If lord Elmwood was not desirous Miss Milner should conclude her visit and return to his protection, it was partly from the multiplicity of affairs in which he was at this time engaged, and partly from having Mr. Sandford now entirely placed with him as his chaplain; for he dreaded that living in the same house their natural antipathy might be encreased to aversion—upon this account he once thought of advising Mr. Sandford to take up his abode elsewhere; but the great pleasure his lordship took in his society, joined to the great mortification he knew such a proposal would be to his friend, would not suffer him to make it.

Miss Milner all this time was not thinking upon those she hated, but on those she loved.—Sandford never came into her thoughts, while the image of lord Elmwood never left them. One morning, as she sat talking to lady Luneham on various subjects, but thinking alone on him; Sir Harry, with another gentleman, a Mr. Fleetmond, came in, and the conversation turned upon the great improbability there was, during the present lord Elmwood's youth, that he should ever inherit the title and estate that had now fallen to him—and said Mr. Fleetmond, "Independent of the fortune, it must be matter of infinite joy to Dorriforth."—"No," answered Sir Harry, "independent of the fortune, it must be a motive of concern to him; for he must now regret, beyond measure, his folly in taking priest's orders—thus depriving himself of the hopes of an heir, by which the title, at his death, will be lost."

"By no means," replied Mr. Fleetmond, "he may yet have an heir, for he will certainly marry."

"Marry!" Cried Sir Harry.

"Yes," answered the other, "it was that I meant by the joy it might probably give him, beyond the possession of his estate and title."

"How be married?" said lady Luneham, "Has he not taken a vow never to marry?"

"Yes," answered Mr. Fleetmond, "but there are no religious vows, from which the great Pontiff of Rome cannot grant a dispensation—those commandments made by the church, the church has always the power to dispense withal; and when it is for the general good of religion, his holiness thinks it incumbent on him, to publish his bull to remit all pains and penalties for their non-observance; and certainly it is for the honour of the catholics, that this earldom should continue in a catholic family—In short, I'll lay a wager my lord Elmwood is married within the twelve-month."

Miss Milner, who listened with attention, feared she was in a dream, or deceived by the pretended knowledge of Mr. Fleetmond, who might know nothing—but on consideration, all that he had said was very probable; and to confirm its truth, he was himself a Roman Catholic, and must be well informed on the subject upon which he spoke.—If she had heard the direst news that ever sounded in the ears of the most susceptible of mortals, the agitation of her mind and person could not have been stronger—she felt, while every word was speaking, a chill through all her veins—it was a pleasure too exquisite, not to bear along with it the sensation of exquisite pain; of which she was so sensible, that for a few moments it caused her to wish she had not heard the intelligence; though, very soon after, she would not but have heard it for the world.

As soon as she had recovered from her first astonishment and joy, she wrote to Miss Woodley an exact account of what she had heard, and received this answer.

"I am sorry any body should have given you this piece of information, because it was a task, in the executing of which, I had promised myself the most extreme satisfaction—but the fear your health was not sufficiently returned to support, without danger, the burthen of hopes which I knew would, upon this occasion, press upon you, I deferred my pleasing communication, and have had it anticipated. Yet, as you seem in the utmost doubt as to the truth of what you have been told, perhaps this confirmation of it, may fall a little short of the first news; especially when it is strengthened by my entreating you to come to see us, as soon as you can with propriety leave lady Luneham."

"Come, my dear Miss Milner, and find in your once rigid monitor, a faithful confident—I will no longer threaten to disclose a secret you have trusted me with, but leave it to the wisdom and sensibility of his heart, (who is now to penetrate into the hearts of our sex, in search of one consonant to his own) to find it out.—I no longer condemn, but congratulate you on your passion; and will assist you with all my advice and earnest wishes, that you may obtain a return."

This letter was another of those excruciating pleasures, that nearly reduced Miss Milner to the grave—it took away from her all appetite to food, and from her eyes the power of being closed for several nights—she thought so much upon the prospect of accomplishing her wishes, that she could think of nothing beside; not even invent a probable excuse for leaving lady Luneham before the appointed time, which was yet two months to come. She wrote to Miss Woodley to beg her contrivance, to reproach her for keeping the secret so long from her, and to thank her for having revealed it to her in so kind a manner at last.—She begged also to be acquainted how Mr. Dorriforth (for still she called him by that name) spoke and thought of this sudden change in his destiny.

Miss Woodley's reply was a summons for her to town upon some pretended business, which she avoided explaining, but which entirely silenced her ladyship's entreaties for her stay.

To her question concerning lord Elmwood she answered, "It is a subject on which he seldom speaks—he appears just the same he ever did, nor could you by any part of his conduct, conceive that any such change had taken place." Miss Milner exclaimed to herself, "I am glad he is not altered—if his words, looks, or manners were anything different from what they formerly were, I should not like him so well." And just the reverse would have been the case, had Miss Woodley sent her word he was changed. The day for her leaving Bath was fixed; she expected it with rapture, but before its arrival sunk under the care of expectation; and when it came, was so much indisposed as to be forced to defer her journey for a week.

At length she found herself in London—in the house of her guardian—and that guardian no longer bound to a single life, but *enjoined* to marry. He appeared in her eyes, as in Miss Woodley's, the same as ever; or perhaps more endearing than ever, as it was the first time she had beheld him with hope.—Mr. Sandford did *not* appear the same; yet he was in reality as surly and as disrespectful in his behaviour to her as usual; but she did not observe, or she did not feel his morose temper as heretofore—he seemed amiable, mild, and gentle; at least such was the happy medium through which she saw him now;[1] for good humour, like the jaundice, makes every one of its own complexion.

CHAPTER III

LORD Elmwood was preparing to go abroad to receive in form, the dispensation from his vows; it was, however, a subject he seemed carefully to avoid speaking upon; and when by any accident he was obliged to mention it, it was without any marks either of satisfaction or concern.

Miss Milner's pride for the first time, began to take the

---

1   In the second, third, fourth, and fifth editions, "through which her self-complacent mind began to see him."

alarm—while he was Mr. Dorriforth, and confined to a single life, his indifference to her charms was rather an honourable, than a reproachful trait in his character, and in reality she admired him for the insensibility—but on the eve of being at liberty, and on the eve of making his choice, she was offended that choice was not immediately fixed upon her—She had been accustomed to receive the devotion of every man who saw her, and not to obtain it of the man from whom, of all others, she most wished it, was cruelly humiliating.—She complained to Miss Woodley, who advised her to have patience, but that was one of the virtues in which she was the least practised.

Encouraged, nevertheless, by her friend in the commendable desire of gaining the affections of him, who possessed all her's, she, however, left no means unattempted to make the conquest—but she began with too great certainty of success, not to be sensible of the deepest mortification in the disappointment—nay, she anticipated a disappointment, as she had before anticipated her success, and by turns felt the keenest emotions from hope and from despair.

As these passions alternately governed her, she was alternately in spirits or dejected; in good or in ill humour; and the frequent vicissitudes of her prospects, at length gave to her behaviour an air of capriciousness, which not all her follies had till now produced.—This was not the way to obtain the affections of lord Elmwood; she knew it was not; and before him she was under some restriction.—Sandford observed this, and added to her many other failings, hypocrisy. It was plain to see Mr. Sandford esteemed her less and less every day; and as he was the person who most of all influenced the opinion of her guardian, he became to her, very soon, an object not merely of dislike, but of abhorrence.

These sentiments for each other, were discoverable in every word and action while they were in each other's company, but still in his absence, Miss Milner's good nature, and little malice, never suffered her to utter a sentence injurious to his interest.—Sandford's charity did not extend thus far; and speaking of her with severity one evening while she was at the opera, "His meaning," as he said, "but to caution her guardian against her faults." Lord Elmwood replied,

"There is one fault, however, Mr. Sandford, I cannot lay to her charge."

"And what is that, my lord?" (cried Sandford, eagerly) "What is that one fault, which Miss Milner has not?"

"I never," replied his lordship, "heard Miss Milner, in your absence, utter a syllable to your disadvantage."

"She durst not, my lord, because she is in fear of you; and she knows you would not suffer it."

"She then," answered his lordship, "pays me a much higher compliment than you do; for you freely censure her, and yet imagine I will suffer it."

"My lord," replied Sandford, "I am undeceived now, and shall never take that liberty again."

As his lordship always treated Sandford with the utmost respect, he began to fear he had been deficient upon this occasion; and the disposition which had induced him to take his ward's part, was likely, in the end, to prove unfavourable to her; for perceiving Sandford was offended at what had passed, as the only means of retribution, his lordship began himself to lament her volatile and captious propensities; in which lamentation Sandford, now forgetting his affront, joined with the heartiest concurrence, adding,

"That you Sir having now other cares to employ your thoughts, ought to insist upon her marrying, or her retiring wholly into the country."

She returned home just as this conversation was finished, and Sandford the moment she entered rung for his candle to retire. Miss Woodley, who had been at the opera with Miss Milner, cried,

"Bless me, Mr. Sandford, are you not well; you are going to leave us so early?"

He replied, "No, I have a pain in my head."

Miss Milner, who never heard complaints without sympathy, rose immediately from her seat, saying,

"I think I never heard you, Mr. Sandford, complain of

indisposition before—will you accept of my specifick for the head-ach? indeed it is a certain relief—I'll fetch it instantly."[1]

She went hastily out of the room, and returned with a bottle, which, she assured him, "was a present from lady Luneham, and would certainly cure him."—And she pressed it upon him with such an anxious earnestness, that with all his churlishness he could not refuse taking it.

This was but a common-place civility, such as is paid by one enemy to another every day; but the *manner* was the material part—the unaffected concern, the attention, the good will, she demonstrated in this little incident, was that which was remarkable; and which immediately took from lord Elmwood the displeasure to which he had been just before excited, or rather transformed it into a degree of admiration. Even Sandford was not insensible to her behaviour, and in return, when he left the room, "wished her a good night."

To her and to Miss Woodley, who had not been witnesses of the preceding conversation, what she had done appeared of no merit, but to the mind of lord Elmwood it had much; and upon the departure of Sandford he began to be unusually cheerful. He first, reproached the ladies for not offering him a place in their box at the opera.

"Would you have gone, my lord?" Asked Miss Milner, highly delighted.

"Certainly," returned he, "had you invited me."

"Then from this day, my lord, I give you a general invitation: nor shall any other company be admitted, but such as you approve."

"I am very much obliged to you." Answered his lordship.

"And you," continued she, "who have been only accustomed to church-musick, will be more than any one, enchanted on hearing the soft, harmonious sounds of love."

"What ravishing pleasures are you preparing for me!" returned he, "I know not whether my weak senses will be able to support them."

---

1 Various kinds of remedies, usually opium and alcohol, were advertised for headaches.

She had her eyes upon him as he spoke this, and discovered in his, which were fixed upon her, a sensibility unexpected—a kind of fascination, which enticed her to look on, while her eyelids fell involuntarily before its mighty force; and a thousand blushes crowded over her face.—He was struck with these sudden signals; hastily recalled his former countenance, and stopt the conversation.

Miss Woodley, who had been a silent observer for some time, now thought a word or two from her, would be acceptable rather than troublesome.

"And pray, my lord," said she, "when do you go to France?"

"To Italy you mean,"—said he, "not at all—my superiors are very indulgent, for they dispense with all my duties.—I ought, and meant, to have gone abroad; but as variety of concerns[1] require my presence in England, every necessary ceremony has taken place here."

"Then your lordship is no longer in orders?" Said Miss Woodley.

"No, they have been resigned these five days."

"My lord, I give you joy." Said Miss Milner.

He thanked her, but added with a sigh, "If I have given up content in search of joy, I shall probably be a loser by the venture."—Soon after this, he wished the ladies good night, and retired.

Happy as Miss Milner found herself in his company, she saw him leave the room with infinite satisfaction, because her heart was impatient to give a loose to its hopes on the bosom of Miss Woodley.—She bad Mrs. Horton immediately good night, and in her friend's apartment gave way to all the language of the tenderest passion, warm with the confidence of meeting its return.—She described the sentiments she had read in lord Elmwood's looks, and though Miss Woodley had beheld them too, Miss Milner's fancy heightened every glance; and her construction became, by degrees, so extremely favourable to her own wishes, that had not her friend been present, and known in what measure to estimate those symptoms; she must infallibly have thought, by the joy to

---

1   In the second, third, fourth, and fifth editions, "as a variety of concerns."

which they gave birth, his lordship had openly avowed a passion for her.

Miss Woodley, therefore, thought it her duty to allay those ecstasies, and represented to her, she might be deceived in her hopes—or even supposing his lordship's inclinations tended towards her, there were yet great obstacles between them.—"Would Sandford, who governed, or at least directed his almost every thought and purpose, not be consulted upon this? and if he was; on what, but the most romantic affection on the part of lord Elmwood, had Miss Milner to depend? and his lordship was not a man to be suspected of submitting to the excess of any passion."—Thus did Miss Woodley argue, for fear her friend should be misled by her wishes, yet in her own mind she scarce harboured a doubt that any thing would thwart them.—The succeeding circumstance proved she was mistaken.

Another gentleman of family and fortune made overtures to Miss Milner; and her guardian, so far from having his thoughts inclined towards her on his own account, pleaded this lover's cause even with more zeal, than he had formerly pleaded for Sir Edward and lord Frederick; and thus at once destroyed all those plans of happiness poor Miss Milner had meditated.

In consequence, her melancholy humour was now predominant; and for several days she staid entirely at home, and yet was denied to all her visitants.—Whether this arose from pure melancholy, or the still lingering hope of making her conquest, by that sedateness of manners she knew her guardian admired, perhaps she herself did not know.—Be that as it may, lord Elmwood could not but observe this change, and one morning thought it fit to mention, and applaud it.

Miss Woodley and she were working together when he came into the room; and after sitting several minutes, and talking upon indifferent subjects; to which his ward replied with a dejection in her voice and manner—he said,

"Perhaps I am wrong, Miss Milner, but I have observed you are lately grown more thoughtful than usual."

She blushed, as she always did when the subject was herself.— He continued, "Your health appears perfectly restored, and yet you do not take delight in your former recreations."

"Are you sorry for that, my lord?"

"No, madam, I am extremely glad; and I was going to congratulate you upon the change—but give me leave to enquire, to what lucky accident we are to attribute this alteration?"

"Your lordship then thinks all my commendable deeds, arise from accident; and that I have no virtues of my own."

"Pardon me, Miss Milner, I think you have many." This he spoke emphatically; and the blood flowed to her face more than at first.

He resumed—"How can I doubt of a lady's virtues, when her countenance gives such evident proofs of them?—believe me, Miss Milner, that in the midst of your gayest follies; while you thus continue to blush, I shall reverence your internal sensations."

"Oh! my lord, did you know some of them, I am afraid you would think them unpardonable."

This was so much to the purpose, Miss Woodley found herself uneasy—but she needed not—Miss Milner loved too sincerely, to reveal it to the object.—His lordship answered,

"And did you, Miss Milner, know some of mine, you might think them equally unpardonable."

She turned pale, and could no longer guide her needle—in the fond transports of her heart she imagined, the sensations to which he alluded, was his love for her.—She was too much embarrassed to reply, and he continued,

"We have all a great deal to pardon in one another; and I know not whether the officious person who forces, even his good advice, is not as blameable as the obstinate one, who will not listen to it.—And now, having made a preface to excuse you, should you once more refuse mine, I will venture to give it."

"My lord," returned she, "I have never yet refused to follow your advice, but where my own peace of mind was so nearly concerned, as to have made me culpable, had I complied."

"Well, madam, I submit to your determinations; and shall never again oppose your inclination to remain single."

This sentence, as it excluded his ever soliciting for himself, gave her the utmost pain; and she cast a glance of her eye at him full of reproach.—He did not observe it, but went on.

"Continuing unmarried, it seems to have been your father's

intention, you should continue under my immediate care; but as I mean for the future to reside chiefly in the country—answer me candidly, do you think you could be happy there, for at least three parts of the year?"

After a short hesitation, she replied, —"I have no objection."

"I am glad to hear it," he returned eagerly, "for it is my earnest desire to have you with me—your welfare is dear to me as my own; and were we apart, continual apprehensions would prey upon my mind."

The tear started in her eye, at the earnestness with which this was spoken;—he saw it, and to soften her still more with the sense of this esteem for her, he encreased his earnestness while he said,

"If you will take the resolution to quit London for the time I mention, there shall be no means unemployed to make the country all you can wish—I shall insist upon Miss Woodley's accompanying you; and it will not only be *my* study to form such a society as you may approve, but I am certain it will be likewise the study of lady Elmwood—"

He was going on, but as if a poniard had thrust her heart, she writhed under this unexpected stroke.

He saw her countenance change—he looked at her steadfastly.

It was not a common change from joy to sorrow, from content to uneasiness, which Miss Milner discovered—she felt, and she expressed anguish.—Lord Elmwood was alarmed and shocked.—She did not weep, but she called Miss Woodley to come to her, with a voice that indicated a degree of agony.

"My lord," (cried Miss Woodley, seeing his consternation, and trembling lest he should guess the secret), "My lord, Miss Milner has again deceived you—you must not take her from London—it is that, which is the cause of her uneasiness."

He seemed more amazed still, and still more shocked at her duplicity than at her torture.—"Good Heaven," exclaimed he, "how am I to accomplish her wishes? what am I to do? how can I judge, while she will not confide in me, but thus grossly deceives me?"

She leaned, pale as death, on the shoulder of Miss Woodley, her eyes fixed, with a seeming insensibility to all that was said, while he continued,

"Heaven is my witness, if I knew—if I could conceive the means how to make her happy, I would sacrifice my own happiness to her's."

"My lord," cried Miss Woodley with a smile, "perhaps I may call upon you hereafter, to fulfil your word."

He was totally ignorant what she meant, nor had he leisure from the confusion of his thoughts to reflect upon her meaning; he nevertheless replied, with warmth, "Do—you will find I'll perform it.—Do—I will faithfully perform it."

Though Miss Milner was conscious this declaration could not, in delicacy, ever be brought against him; yet the fervent and solemn manner in which he made it, cheered her spirits; and as persons enjoy the reflection of having, in their possession some valuable gem, although they are determined never to use it, so she upon this, was comforted and grew better.—She now lifted up her head from Miss Woodley, and leaned it on her hand as she sat by the side of a table—still she did not speak, but seemed overcome with sorrow.— As her situation became, however, less alarming; her guardian's pity and affright began to take the colour of resentment; and though he did not say so, he was, and looked highly offended.

At this juncture Mr. Sandford entered.—On beholding the present party, it needed not his sagacity to see, at the first view, they were all uneasy; but instead of the sympathy this might have excited in some dispositions, Mr. Sandford, after casting a look at each of them, appeared in high spirits.

"You seem unhappy, my lord." Said he, with a smile.

"You do *not*—Mr. Sandford." Replied his lordship.

"No, my lord, nor would I, were I in your situation,"—returned he, "What should make a man of sense out of temper but a worthy object?"—And he looked at Miss Milner.

"There are no objects unworthy our care." Replied lord Elmwood.

"But there are objects on whom all care is fruitless, your lordship will allow."

"I never yet despaired of any one, Mr. Sandford."

"And yet there are persons, of whom it is presumption, to entertain hopes."—And he looked again at Miss Milner.

"Does your head ach, Miss Milner?" Asked Miss Woodley, seeing her hold it with her hand.

"Very much." Returned she.

"Mr. Sandford," said Miss Woodley, "Did you use all those drops Miss Milner gave you for a pain in the head?"

"Yes," answered he, "I did."—But the question at that moment somewhat embarrassed him.

"And I hope you found benefit from them." Said Miss Milner, with great kindness, as she rose from her seat, and walked slowly and despondently out of the room.

Though Miss Woodley followed her, so that Mr. Sandford was left alone with lord Elmwood, and might have continued his unkind insinuations without one restraint; yet his lips were closed for the present.—He looked down on the carpet—twitched himself upon his chair—and began to talk of the weather.

CHAPTER IV

As soon as the first transports of despair were over, Miss Milner suffered herself to be once more in hope—she found there were no other means to support her life; and to her no small joy, her friend, Miss Woodley, was much less severe on the present occasion than she expected.—No engagement between mortals, was, in Miss Woodley's opinion, binding like that entered into with heaven; and whatever vows lord Elmwood had made to another, she justly supposed, no woman's love for him, equalled Miss Milner's—it was prior to all others too, and that established a claim, at least to contend for success; and in a contention, what rival would not fall before her?

It was not difficult to guess who this rival was; or if they were a little time in suspense, Miss Woodley soon arrived at the certainty, by inquiring of Mr. Sandford; who, unsuspicious why she asked, readily informed her the intended lady Elmwood, was no other than Miss Fenton; and that her marriage with his lordship would be solemnized as soon as the mourning for the late lord Elmwood was expired.—This last intelligence made Miss Woodley shudder—however, she repeated it to Miss Milner, word for word.

"Happy! happy, woman!" exclaimed Miss Milner of Miss

Fenton; "she has received the first fond impulses of his heart, and has had the transcendent happiness of teaching him to love!"

"By no means," returned Miss Woodley, finding there was no other method to comfort her; "do not suppose lord Elmwood's marriage is the result of love—it is no more than a duty, a necessary piece of business, and this you may plainly see by the wife on whom he has fixed.—Miss Fenton was thought a proper match for his cousin, and this same propriety, you must perceive still exists."

It was easy to convince Miss Milner all her friend said was truth, for she wished it to be so. "And oh!" she exclaimed, "could I but stimulate passion, in the place of propriety—do you think my dear Miss Woodley," (and she looked with such begging eyes, it was impossible not to answer as she wished,) "do you think it would be unjust to Miss Fenton were I to inspire her destined husband with a passion which she may not have inspired, and which I believe she herself cannot feel?"

Miss Woodley paused a minute, and then answered, "No;"— but there was a hesitation in her manner of delivery—she did say, "No," but she looked as if she was afraid she ought to have said "Yes."—Miss Milner, however, did not wait to give her time to recall the word, or to alter its meaning by adding others to it, but run on eagerly, and declared, "As that was her opinion, she would abide by it, and do all she could to supplant her rival."—In order, nevertheless, to justify this determination, and satisfy the conscience of Miss Woodley, they both concluded, Miss Fenton's heart was not engaged in the intended marriage, and consequently she was indifferent whether it took place or not.

Since the death of the late earl, that young lady had not been in town; nor had the present lord been near the spot where she resided since the week her lover died; of course, nothing like love could be declared at so early a period; and if it had been made known since, it must only have been by letter, or by the deputation of Mr. Sandford, whom they knew had been once in the country to visit her; but how little he was qualified to enforce a tender passion, was a comfortable reflection.

Revived with these conjectures, of which some were true, and others false; the very next day a dark gloom overspread their bright prospects, on Mr. Sandford's saying, as he entered the breakfast room,

"Miss Fenton, ladies, desired me to present her compliments to you."

"Is she in town?" Asked Mrs. Horton.

"She came to town yesterday morning," returned Sandford, "and is at her brother's, in Ormond street; my lord and I supped there last night, and that made us so late home."

His lordship entered soon after, and confirmed what had been said, by bowing to his ward, and telling her, "Miss Fenton had charged him with her kindest respects."

"How does poor Miss Fenton look?" Mrs. Horton asked lord Elmwood.

To which question Sandford replied, "Beautiful—she looks beautifully."

"She has got over her uneasiness, I suppose then?" Said Mrs. Horton—not knowing she was asking the question before her new lover.

"Uneasy!" replied Sandford, "uneasy at any trial this world can send? that had been highly unworthy of her."

"But sometimes women do fret at such things." Replied Mrs. Horton innocently.

Lord Elmwood asked Miss Milner—"If she meant to ride, this charming day?"

While she was hesitating—

"There are very different kind of women," (answered Sandford, directing his discourse to Mrs. Horton,) "there is as much difference between some women, as between good and evil spirits."

Lord Elmwood asked Miss Milner again—if she took an airing?

She replied, "No."

"And beauty," continued Sandford, "when endowed upon spirits that are evil, is a mark of their greater, their more extreme wickedness.—Lucifer was the most beautiful of all the angels in paradise—"[1]

---

1 Compare to Milton's *Paradise Lost*, Book VII. Satan, called Lucifer (or light-bringer) before his fall, was "brighter once amidst the host / Of Angels, than that star the

"How do you know?" Said Miss Milner.

"But the beauty of Lucifer" (continued Sandford, in perfect neglect and contempt of her question,) "was an aggravation of his guilt; because it shewed a double share of ingratitude to the Divine Creator of that beauty."

"Now you talk of angels," said Miss Milner, "I wish I had wings; and I should like to fly through the park this morning."

"You would be taken for an angel in good earnest." said lord Elmwood.

Sandford was angry at this little compliment, and cried, "Then instead of the wings, I would advise the serpent's skin."[1]

"My lord," cried she, "does not Mrs. Sandford use me ill?"—Vext with other things, she felt herself extremely hurt at this, and made the appeal almost in tears.

"Indeed, I think he does." Answered his lordship, and he looked at Sandford as if he was displeased.

This was a triumph so agreeable to her, she immediately pardoned the offence; but the offender did not so easily pardon her.

"Good morning, ladies." Said his lordship, rising to go away.

"My lord," said Miss Woodley, "you promised Miss Milner to accompany her one evening to the opera; this is opera night."

"Will you go, my lord?" Asked Miss Milner, in a voice so soft, he seemed as if he wished, but could not resist it.

"I am to dine at Mr. Fenton's today," he replied, "and if he and his sister will go; and you will allow them part of your box, I will promise to come."

This was a condition that did not please her, but as she felt a strong desire to see him in the company of his intended bride, (for she fancied she could perceive his most secret sentiments, could she once see them together) she answered not ungraciously, "Yes,

---

stars among" (132-33). The name first appears in a version of *Isaiah* translated into Latin in the fourth century by St. Jerome (c. 347-419/420) and others.

1 In Milton's *Paradise Lost*, Book IX, Satan adopts the form of the serpent in order to deceive Eve. A kind of masquerader, Milton's Satan is an "inmate bad" (495) in the serpent's skin. In *Genesis*, the serpent itself is intrinsically malevolent and devious, "more subtle than any of the beasts of the earth" (3:1). As a Roman Catholic, Inchbald would have used the Rheims-Douay version of the *Bible* (New Testament 1582, Old Testament 1609-10), so all quotations from *The Bible* will be taken from this translation.

my compliments to Mr. and Miss Fenton, and I hope they will favour me with their company."

"Then, madam, if they come, you may expect me—else not." And he bowed and left the room.

All the day was passed in anxious expectation by Miss Milner, what would be the event of the evening; for upon the skill of her penetration that evening, all her future prospects she thought depended.—If she saw by his looks, his words, or assiduity, he loved Miss Fenton, she flattered herself she would never think of him again with hope; but if she observed him treat her with inattention or indifference, she meant to cherish from that moment the fondest expectations.—Against that short evening her toilet was consulted the whole day; and the alternate hope and fear which fluttered at her heart, gave a more than usual brilliancy to her eyes, and more than usual bloom to her complexion.—But in vain was her beauty; vain all the pains she had taken to decorate that beauty; vain the many looks she cast towards her box-door to see it open; lord Elmwood did not come.

The musick was discord—every thing she saw, was disgusting—in a word, she was miserable.

She longed impatiently for the curtain to drop, because she was uneasy where she was—yet she asked herself, "Shall I be less unhappy at home? yes, at home I shall see lord Elmwood, and that will be happiness—but he will behold me with neglect, and that will be misery.—Ungrateful man! I will no longer think of him." She said to herself.—Or could she have thought of him without joining in the same idea Miss Fenton, her anguish had been supportable; but while she pictured them as lovers, the tortures of the rack give but a few degrees more pain than she endured.

There are but few persons who ever felt the real passion of jealousy, because few have felt the real passion of love; but to those who have experienced them both, jealousy not only affects the mind, but every fibre of the frame is a victim to it; and Miss Milner's every limb ached, with agonizing torment, while Miss Fenton, courted and beloved by lord Elmwood, was present to her imagination.

The moment the opera was finished, she flew hastily down stairs, as if to fly from the sufferings she experienced.—She did not go into the coffee-room, though repeatedly persuaded by Miss Woodley, but waited at the door till her carriage drew up.

Piqued—heart-broken—full of resentment to the object of her uneasiness; as she stood inattentive to all that passed, a hand gently laid hold of her's, and the most humble and insinuating voice said, "Will you permit me to hand you to your carriage?" She was awaked from her reverie, and found lord Frederick Lawnly by her side.—Her heart, just then melting with tenderness to another, was perhaps more accessible than heretofore, or bursting with resentment, thought this the moment to retaliate. Whatever passion reigned that instant, it was favourable to the desires of lord Frederick, and she looked as if she was glad to see him; he beheld this with the rapture and the humility of a lover; and though she did not feel the slightest love in return, she felt a gratitude proportionate to the insensibility with which she had been treated by her guardian, and lord Frederick was not very erroneous if he mistook this gratitude for a latent spark of affection. The mistake, however, did not force from him his respect: he handed her to her carriage, bowed lowly, and disappeared. Miss Woodley wished to divert her thoughts from the object which could only make her wretched, and as they rode home, by many encomiums upon lord Frederick, endeavoured to incite her to a regard for him; Miss Milner was displeased at the attempt, and exclaimed,

"What, love a rake, a man of professed gallantry? impossible— To me, a common rake is as odious, as a common prostitute is to a man of the nicest feelings.—Where can be the pride of inspiring a passion, fifty others can equally inspire? or the transport of bestowing favours, where the appetite is already cloyed by fruition of the selfsame enjoyments?"

"Strange," cried Miss Woodley, "that you, who possess so many follies incident to your sex, should, in the disposal of your heart, have sentiments so contrary to women in general."

"My dear Miss Woodley," returned she, "put in competition the languid love of a debauchee, with the vivid affection of a sober man, and judge which has the dominion? Oh! in my calendar of love, a solemn lord chief justice, or a devout archbishop, ranks before a licentious king."

Miss Woodley smiled at an opinion which she knew half her

sex would laugh at; but by the air of sincerity with which it was delivered, she was convinced, her late behaviour to lord Frederick was but the mere effect of chance.

Lord Elmwood's carriage drove to his door just at the time her's did; Mr. Sandford was with him, and they were both come from passing the evening at Mr. Fenton's.

"So, my lord," said Miss Woodley, as soon as they met in the apartment, "you did not come to us."

"No," answered his lordship, "I was sorry; but I hope you did not expect me."

"Not expect you, my lord?" cried Miss Milner, "did not you say you would come?"

"If I had, I certainly should have come," returned he, "but I only said so conditionally."

"That I am witness to," cried Sandford, "for I was present at the time, and his lordship said it should depend upon Miss Fenton."

"And she, with her gloomy disposition," said Miss Milner, "chose to sit at home."

"Gloomy disposition?" repeated Sandford, "She is a young lady with a great share of sprightliness—and I think I never saw her in better spirits than she was this evening, my lord?"

Lord Elmwood did not speak.

"Bless me, Mr. Sandford," cried Miss Milner, "I meant no reflection upon Miss Fenton's disposition; I only meant to censure her taste for staying at home."

"I think," replied Sandford, "a much greater censure should be passed upon those, who prefer rambling abroad."

"But I hope, ladies, my not coming," said his lordship, "was no cause of inconvenience to you; you had still a gentleman with you, or I should certainly have come."

"Oh! yes, two gentlemen," Answered the young son of lady Evans, a lad from school, whom Miss Milner had taken along with her, and to whom his lordship had alluded.

"What two?" Asked lord Elmwood.

Neither Miss Milner or Miss Woodley answered.

"You know, madam," said young Evans, "that handsome gentleman who handed you into your carriage, and you called my lord."

"Oh! he means lord Frederick Lawnley." Said Miss Milner carelessly, but a blush of shame spread over her face.

"And did he hand you into your coach?" Asked his lordship, earnestly.

"By mere accident, my lord," Miss Woodley replied, "for the crowd was so great—"

"I think, my lord," said Sandford, "it was very lucky you were *not* there."

"Had lord Elmwood been with us, we should not have had occasion for the assistance of any other." Said Miss Milner.

"Lord Elmwood has been with you, madam," returned Sandford, "very frequently, and yet—"

"Mr. Sandford," said his lordship, interrupting him, "it is near bed-time, your conversation keeps the ladies from retiring."

"Your lordship's does not." Said Miss Milner, "for you say nothing."

"Because, madam, I am afraid to offend."

"But does not your lordship also hope to please? and without risking the one, it is impossible to arrive at the other."

"I think, at present, the risk of one would be too hazardous, and so I wish you a good night." And he went out of the room somewhat abruptly.

"Lord Elmwood," said Miss Milner, "is very grave—he does not look like a man who has been passing his evening with the woman he loves."

"Perhaps he is melancholy at parting from her." Said Miss Woodley.

"More likely offended," said Sandford, "at the manner at which that lady has spoken of her."

"Who, I?" cried Miss Milner, "I protest I said nothing but—"

"Nothing, madam? did not you say she was gloomy?"

"But, what I thought—I was going to add, Mr. Sandford."

"When you think unjustly, you should not express your thoughts."

"Then, perhaps, I should never speak."

"And it were better you did not, if what you say, is to give pain.—Do you know, madam, that my lord is going to be married to Miss Fenton?"

"Yes." Answered Miss Milner.

"Do you know that he loves her?"

"No." Answered Miss Milner.

"How, madam! do you suppose he does not?"

"I suppose he does, yet I don't know it."

"Then supposing he does, how can you have the imprudence to find fault with her before him?"

"I did not—to call her gloomy, was, I knew, to praise her both to him and to you, who admire such tempers."

"Whatever her temper is, *every one* admires it; and so far from its being what you have described, she has a great deal of vivacity; vivacity which proceeds from the heart."

"No, if it proceeded, I should admire it too; but it rests there, and no one is the better for it."

"Come, Miss Milner," said Miss Woodley, "it is time to retire; you and Mr. Sandford must finish your dispute in the morning."

"Dispute, madam!" said Sandford, "I never disputed with any one beneath a doctor of divinity in my life.—I was only cautioning your friend not to make light of virtues, which it would do her honour to possess.—Miss Fenton is a most amiable young woman, and worthy just such a husband as my Lord Elmwood will make her."

"I am sure," said Miss Woodley, "Miss Milner thinks so—she has a high opinion of Miss Fenton—she was at present only jesting."

"But, madam, jests are very pernicious things, when delivered with a malignant sneer.—I have known a jest destroy a lady's reputation[1]—I have known a jest give one person a distaste for another—I have known a jest break off a marriage."

"But I suppose there is no apprehension of that, in the present case?" Said Miss Woodley—wishing he might answer in the affirmative.

"Not that I can foresee." Replied he.—"No, Heaven forbid; for I look upon them to be formed for each other—their disposi-

---

1 Compare to Pope's *The Rape of the Lock*, Canto III, l. 16: "at ev'ry word a reputation dies."

tions, their pursuits, their inclinations the same.—Their passions for each other just the same—pure—white as snow."

"And I dare say, not warmer." Replied Miss Milner.

He looked provoked beyond measure.

"Dear Miss Milner," cried Miss Woodley, "how can you talk thus? I believe in my heart you are only envious my lord did not offer himself to you."

"To her!" said Sandford, affecting an air of the utmost surprise, "to her? Do you think his lordship received a dispensation from his vows to become the husband of a coquette—a—" he was going on.

"Nay, Mr. Sandford," cried Miss Milner, "I believe my greatest crime in your eyes, is being a heretick."

"By no means, madam—it is the only circumstance that can apologize for your faults; and had you not that excuse, there would be none for you."

"Then, at present, there is an excuse—I thank you, Mr. Sandford; this is the kindest thing you ever said to me. But I am vext to see you are sorry, you have said it."

"Angry at your being a heretick?" he resumed, "Indeed I should be much more concerned to see you a disgrace to our religion."

Miss Milner had not been in a good humour during the whole evening—she had been provoked to the full extent of her patience several times; but this harsh sentence hurried her beyond all bounds, and she arose from her seat in the most violent agitation, and exclaimed, "What have I done to be treated thus?"

Though Mr. Sandford was not a man easily intimidated, he was on this occasion evidently alarmed; and stared about him with so strong an expression of surprise, that it partook in some degree of fear.—Miss Woodley clasped her friend in her arms, and cried with the tenderest affection and pity, "My dear Miss Milner, be composed."

Miss Milner sat down, and was so for a minute; but her dead silence was nearly as alarming to Sandford as her rage had been; and he did not perfectly recover himself till he saw a flood of tears pouring down her face; he then heaved a sigh of content that it had so ended, but in his heart resolved never to forget the ridiculous affright into which he had been put.—He stole out of the room without uttering a syllable—But as he never retired to rest before he had repeated a long form of evening prayers, so when he came to that part which supplicates "Grace for the wicked," he named Miss Milner's name, with the most fervent devotion.

CHAPTER V

AMONG the many sleepless nights Miss Milner passed, the present was not one of them; it is true she had a weight of care upon her heart, even heavier than usual, but its burthen had overcome her strength; and wearied out with hopes, with fears, and at the end with disappointment and rage, she sunk into a profound slumber as soon as she was laid down—but the more forgetfulness had prevailed, the greater was the force of remembrance when she awoke—At first, so sound had her sleep been, she had a difficulty in calling to mind why she was unhappy; but that she was unhappy, she well recollected—and when the cause came to her memory, she would have slept again, but that was impossible.

Though her rest had been sound, it had not been refreshing; she was far from well, and sent word so as an apology for not being present at breakfast. Lord Elmwood looked concerned when the message was delivered; Mr. Sandford shook his head.

"Miss Milner's health is not good." Said Mrs. Horton a few minutes after.

Lord Elmwood laid down the newspaper to attend to her.

"To me there is something very extraordinary about her." Continued Mrs. Horton, finding she had caught his lordship's attention.

"So there is to me." Added Sandford, with a sarcastic sneer.

"And so there is to me." Said Miss Woodley, with a most serious face, and heartfelt sigh.

Lord Elmwood gazed by turns at each, as each delivered their sentiments—and when they were all silent, he looked bewildered, not knowing what judgment to form from any of these sentences.

Soon after breakfast, Mr. Sandford withdrew to his own apartments; Mrs. Horton in a little time went to her's, and lord

Elmwood and Miss Woodley were left alone.—His lordship immediately rose from his seat, and said,

"I think, Miss Woodley, Miss Milner was extremely to blame, though I did not choose to tell her so before Mr. Sandford, in giving my lord Frederick an opportunity of speaking to her; unless she means he shall renew his addresses."

"That, I am sure, my lord," replied Miss Woodley, "she does not mean—and I assure you, my lord, seriously, it was by mere accident she saw him yesterday evening; or permitted him to attend her to her carriage."

"I am glad to hear it;" he returned quickly; "for although I am not of a suspicious nature, yet in regard to her affection for him, I cannot but have my doubts."

"You need have none, my lord." Replied Miss Woodley, with a smile of confidence.

"And yet you must own her behaviour has warranted them— has it not been in this particular incoherent, undefinable, unaccountable!"

"The behaviour of a person in love, no doubt." Said Miss Woodley.

"Don't I say so?" replied he warmly, "And is not that a just reason for my suspicions?"

"But is there only one man in the world on whom these suspicions should fix?" Said Miss Woodley with the colour mounting into her face.

"Not that I know of—not one more that I know of." Returned he, with astonishment at what she had insinuated, and yet with a perfect assurance she was in the wrong.

"Perhaps I am mistaken." Replied she.

"Nay, that is impossible too—" returned he with anxiety, "You share her confidence; you are perpetually with her; and provided she did not confide in you, you must know, must be acquainted with her inclinations." "I believe I am *perfectly* acquainted with them." Replied Miss Woodley, with a significance in her voice and manner which convinced him there was some secret to learn.

After a hesitation;

"It is far from me," replied he, "to wish to be entrusted with the private sentiments of those who desire to withhold them from me, much less would I take any unfair means of being informed of them—to ask any more from you, I believe, would be unfair—yet I cannot but lament, that I am not as well informed as you are.—I wish to prove my friendship to Miss Milner, but she will not suffer me—and every step I take for her happiness, I take in the most perplexing uncertainty."

Miss Woodley sighed, but did not speak.—He seemed to wait for her reply, but as she made none, he proceeded.

"If ever a breach of confidence could be tolerated, I certainly know no occasion that would so justly authorise such a measure as the present.—I am not only proper from my character, but from my circumstances to be relied upon—my interest is so nearly connected with the interest, and my happiness with the happiness of my ward, that those principles as well as my honour, would protect her from every peril arising from my being trusted."

"Oh! my lord," cried Miss Woodley, with a most forcible accent, "*you* are the last person on earth, she would pardon me for intrusting."

"Why so?" (said he warmly,) "But that is the way—the person who is our friend we misdoubt—where a common interest is concerned, we are ashamed of drawing on a common danger—Afraid of advice, though that advice is to save us.—Miss Woodley," said he, (changing his voice with excess of earnestness) "do you believe that I would do anything to make Miss Milner happy?"

"Any thing in honour, my lord."

"She can desire nothing farther."—He replied in agitation—"Are her desires so unwarrantable I cannot grant them?"

Miss Woodley again did not speak—and he continued.

"Great as my friendship is, there are certainly bounds to it; bounds, that shall save her in spite of herself."—And he raised his voice.

"In the disposal of themselves," resumed he, with a less vehement tone, "that great, that terrifick disposal in marriage, (at which I have ever looked with affright and dismay) there is no accounting for the rashness of a woman's choice, or sometimes for the depravity of her taste.—But in such a case, Miss Milner's election of a husband shall not direct mine—if she does not know her own value, I do.—Independent of her fortune, she has beauty to captivate the heart of any man; and with all her follies, she has a frankness in her manner, an unaffected wisdom in her thoughts, a vivacity in her conversation, and withal, a softness in her demeanour, that might alone engage the affections of a man of the nicest sentiments, and the strongest understanding.—I will not see all these qualities and accomplishments debased. —It is my office to protect her from the consequences of a degraded choice, and I will."

"My lord, Miss Milner's taste is not a depraved one; it is but too much refined."

"What do you mean by that, Miss Woodley? you talk mysteriously.—Is she not afraid I will thwart her inclinations?"

"She is sure you will, my lord."

"Then must not the person be unworthy of her?"

Miss Woodley rose from her seat, the tears trinkled down her cheeks,[1] she clasped her hands, and every look, every gesture proved her alternate resolution, and irresolution of proceeding farther.—Lord Elmwood's attention was arrested before, but now it was fixed to a degree, which her manner could only occasion.

"My lord," said she, with a tremulous voice, "promise me, declare to me, swear to me, it shall ever remain a secret in your own breast, and I will reveal to you, on whom she has placed her affections."

This solemn preparation made lord Elmwood tremble; and he ran over instantly in his mind all the persons he could recollect, in order to arrive at the knowledge by thought, quicker than by words.—It was in vain he tried, and he once more turned his enquiring eyes upon Miss Woodley.—He saw her silent and covered with confusion.—Again he searched his own thoughts, nor ineffectually as before.—At the first glance the object was presented, and he beheld *himself*.

The rapid emotion of varying passions, which immediately darted over his features, informed Miss Woodley her secret was discovered—she hid her face, while the tears that fell down to her bosom, confirmed him in the truth of his suggestion beyond what

---

1 The phrase "the tears trinkled down her cheeks" is removed from the second, third, fourth, and fifth editions.

oaths could have done.—A short interval of silence followed, during which she suffered tortures for the manner in which he would speak to her—two seconds gave her his reply.

"For God's sake take care what you are doing—you are destroying my prospects of futurity—you are making this world too dear to me."

Her drooping head was then lifted up, and as she caught the eye of Dorriforth, she saw it beam expectation, amaze, joy, ardour, love.—Nay, there was a fire, a vehemence in the quick fascinating rays it sent forth, she never before had seen—it filled her with alarm—she wished him to love Miss Milner, but to love her with moderation.—Miss Woodley was too little versed in the subject to know, that, had been, not to love at all; at least not to the extent of breaking through engagements, and all the various obstacles, that still militated against their union.

Lord Elmwood was sensible of the embarrassment his presence gave Miss Woodley, and understood the reproaches which she seemed to vent upon herself in silence.—To relieve her from both, he laid his hand with force upon his heart, and said, "Do you believe me?"

"I do, my lord." She answered, trembling.

"I will make no unjust use of what I know." Returned he, with firmness.

"I believe you, my lord."

"But for what my passions now dictate," continued he, "I will not answer.—They are confused—they are triumphant at present.—I have never yet, however, been vanquished by them; and even upon this occasion, my reason shall combat to the last—that, shall fail me, before I do wrong."

He was going to leave the room—she followed him, and cried—"But my lord how shall I see again the unhappy object of my treachery?"

"See her," replied he, "as one to whom you meant no injury, and to whom you have done none."

"But she would account it such, my lord."

"We are not judges of what belongs to ourselves;"—he replied,—"I am transported at the tidings you have revealed, and yet, perhaps, I had better never have heard them."

Miss Woodley was going to say something farther, but as if incapable of attending to her, he hasted out of the room.

CHAPTER VI

MISS Woodley stood for some time to consider which way she was to go.—The first person she met would enquire, why she had been weeping to that excess her eyes were scarce discernible? and if Miss Milner was to ask the question, in what words could she tell, or in what manner deny the truth?—To avoid her, was her first caution, and she took the only method; she had a hackney-coach[1] ordered, rode several miles out of town, and returned to dinner with so little remains of her swoln eyes, that complaining of the head-ach was a sufficient excuse for them.

Miss Milner was enough recovered to be present at dinner, though she scarce tasted a morsel. Lord Elmwood did not dine at home, at which Miss Woodley rejoiced, but at which Mr. Sandford appeared highly disappointed.—He asked the servants, several times, what his lordship said when he went out? they replied, "nothing more than that he should not be at home to dinner."—"I can't imagine where he dines?" Said Sandford.—"Bless me, Mr. Sandford, can't you guess?" (cried Mrs. Horton, who by this time was made acquainted with his intended marriage), "he dines with Miss Fenton to be sure."—"No," replied Sandford, "he is not there; I came from thence just now, and they had not seen him all day."—Poor Miss Milner, on this, put a mouthful into her mouth; for where we hope for nothing, we receive small indulgences with joy.

Notwithstanding the anxiety and trouble under which Miss Woodley had laboured all the morning, her heart for many weeks had not felt so light as it did this day at dinner—The confidence she reposed in the promises of lord Elmwood—the firm reliance she had upon his delicacy and his justice—the unabated kindness with which her friend received her, while no one suspicious thought, she knew, had taken harbour in her bosom—and the

---

1 The *OED* defines a hackney coach as "a four-wheeled coach, drawn by two horses, and seated for six persons, kept for hire."

conscious integrity of her own intentions, however she might be misled by her judgment, all conspired to comfort her with the hope, she had done nothing she ought to wish recalled.—But although she felt thus tranquil, in respect to what she had divulged, yet she felt a great deal embarrassed with the dread of the next seeing lord Elmwood.

Miss Milner, not having spirits to go abroad, passed the evening at home—she read part of a new opera, played upon her guitar, mused, sighed, occasionally talked with Miss Woodley, and so passed the tedious hours till near ten, when Mrs. Horton asked Mr. Sandford to play a game at piquet, and on his excusing himself, Miss Milner offered in his stead, and was gladly accepted.—They had just begun to play when lord Elmwood came into the room—Miss Milner's countenance immediately brightened, and although she was in a negligent morning dress, and looked paler than usual, she did not look less beautiful—Miss Woodley was leaning on the back of her chair to observe the game, and Mr. Sandford sat reading one of the Greek Fathers at the other side of the fire place. Lord Elmwood as he advanced to the table bowed, not having seen the ladies since morning, or Miss Milner that day; they returned his salute, and he was going up to Miss Milner, (seemingly to enquire of her health) when Mr. Sandford, laying down his book, said,

"My lord, where have you been all day?"

"I have been very busy." Replied his lordship, and walking from the card-table went up to him.

Miss Milner began to make mistakes, and play one card for another.

"You have been at Mr. Fenton's this evening, I suppose?" Said Sandford.

"No, not at all to-day." Replied his lordship.

"How came that about, my lord?" Cried Sandford.

Miss Milner played the ace of diamonds, instead of the king of hearts.

"I shall call to-morrow." Answered his lordship, and going with a very ceremonious air up to Miss Milner, said, "He hoped she was perfectly recovered."

Mrs. Horton begged her "To mind what she was about."

She replied, "I am much better, Sir."

He then returned to Sandford again: but never, during all this time, did his eye once encounter Miss Woodley's, and she, with equal care, avoided his.

Some cold dishes were now brought up for supper—Miss Milner lost deal, and the game ended.

As they were arranging themselves at the supper-table, "Do, Miss Milner," said Mrs. Horton, "have something warm for your supper? a chicken boiled? or something of that kind? you have eat nothing all day."

With the feeling of humanity, and apparently no other sensation—but never did he feel philanthropy so forcibly—lord Elmwood said, "Let me beg of you, Miss Milner, to have something provided for you."

The earnestness and emphasis with which these few words were pronounced, were more flattering than the finest turned compliment had been; her gratitude was expressed by blushes, and by assuring his lordship she was now "so well as to be able to sup on what was before her."—She spoke, however, and had not made the trial; for the moment she carried a piece to her lips, she laid it on her plate again, and turned paler, from the vain endeavour to force her appetite. Lord Elmwood had ever been attentive to her, but now he watched her as he would a child; and when he saw by her struggles she could not eat, he took her plate from her; gave her something else; and all with a care and watchfulness in his looks, as if he had been a tender-hearted boy, and she his darling bird, the loss of which, would embitter all the joy of his holidays.

This attention had something about it so tender, so officious, and yet so sincere, that it brought the tears into Miss Woodley's eyes, attracted the notice of Mr. Sandford, and the observation of Mrs. Horton, while the heart of Miss Milner overflowed with a gratitude that gave place to no sentiment, except her love.

To relieve that anxiety her guardian expressed, she endeavoured to appear cheerful, and that anxiety, at length, really made her so.—He now pressed her to take one glass of wine with such solicitude, he seemed to say a thousand things beside—Sandford still made his observations, and being unused to conceal his thoughts before the present company, he said, bluntly,

"Miss Fenton was indisposed the other night, my lord, and yet you did not seem half so anxious about her health."

Had Sandford laid all lord Elmwood's estate at Miss Milner's feet, or presented her with that eternal bloom which adorns the face of a goddess, he would have done less to endear himself to her, than by that single sentence—she looked at him with the most benign countenance, and felt affliction that she had ever offended him.

"Miss Fenton," (lord Elmwood replied) "has a brother with her; her health and happiness are in his care, Miss Milner's are in mine."

"Mr. Sandford," said Miss Milner, "I am afraid I behaved very uncivilly to you last night; will you accept of an atonement?"

"No, madam," returned he, "I accept no expiation without amendment."

"Well, then," said she, smiling, "suppose I promise never to offend you again, what then?"

"Why then, you'll break your promise." Returned he, churlishly.

"Do not promise," said lord Elmwood, "for he means to provoke you to it."

In the like conversation the evening was passed, and Miss Milner retired to rest in far better spirits than the morning's prospect had given her to hope for. Miss Woodley too, had cause to be well pleased, but her pleasure was in a great measure eclipsed by the reflection, "there was such a person as Miss Fenton;" she could not but fear, that in doing Miss Milner a right, she had, perhaps, done that lady a wrong[1]—she wished she had been equally acquainted with her heart, as she was with Miss Milner's, and she would then have acted without injustice to either; but Miss Fenton had of late shunned their society, and even in their company she was of a temper too reserved to discover her mind; Miss Woodley was therefore obliged to act to the best of her judgment only, and leave all events to providence.

---

1 From "she could not" to "a wrong" is removed from the second, third, fourth, and fifth editions.

CHAPTER VII

WITHIN a few days, in the house of lord Elmwood, every thing, and every person wore a new face.—His lordship was the profest lover of Miss Milner—she, the happiest of human beings—Miss Woodley partaking in her joy—while Mr. Sandford was lamenting with the deepest concern, that Miss Fenton had been supplanted; and what added most poignantly to his sorrow was, that she had been supplanted by Miss Milner.—Though a church man, he bore his disappointment with the impatience of one of the laity; he could hardly speak to lord Elmwood; he would not look at Miss Milner, and was displeased with every body.—It was his intention when he first became acquainted with lord Elmwood's resolution, to quit his house; and as his lordship had, with the utmost degree of inflexibility, resisted all his good counsel, and advice upon this subject, he resolved, in quitting him, never to be his adviser or counsellor again.—But, in preparing to leave his friend, his pupil, his patron, and yet him, who, upon most occasions, implicitly obeyed his will, the spiritual got the better of the temporal man, and he determined to stay, lest in totally abandoning him to the pursuit of his own passions, he might make his punishment even greater than his offence.—"My lord," said he, "on the stormy sea, upon which you are embarked, though you will not shun the rocks, your faithful pilot would point out, he will, nevertheless, sail in your company, and lament over your watery grave. The more you slight my advice, the more you want it, and till you command me to leave your house, (as I suppose you will soon do, to oblige your lady) I will continue along with you."

Lord Elmwood liked him sincerely, and was glad he took this resolution; yet as soon as his lordship's reason and affections had once told him, he ought to break with Miss Fenton, and marry his ward, he became so decidedly of that opinion, Sandford's never had the most trivial weight upon the subject, nor would he flatter the supposed authority he possessed over him, by urging him to remain in his house a single day, contrary to his inclinations. Sandford beheld, with grief, this firmness, but finding it vain to contend, submitted—not, however, with a good grace.

Amidst all the persons affected by this change in lord Elmwood's marriage designs, Miss Fenton was, perhaps, the least—she would have been content to have married, she was contented to live single—Mr. Sandford was the first who made overtures to her on the part of lord Elmwood, and the first sent to ask her to dispense with the obligation—She received both these proposals with the same insipid smile of approbation, and the same cold indifference at the heart.

It was a perfect knowledge of this disposition in his intended wife, which had given to lord Elmwood's thoughts, on matrimony, the prospect of dreary winter; but the sensibility of Miss Milner had now reversed that prospect to perpetual spring; or the dearer variety of spring, summer, and autumn.

It was a knowledge also of this torpor in Miss Fenton's nature, from which he formed the purpose of breaking with her; for lord Elmwood still retained enough of the priest's sanctity, to have yielded up his own happiness, and even that of his beloved ward, rather than have plunged one heart into affliction by his perfidy. This, before he offered his hand to Miss Milner, he was perfectly convinced would not be the case—even Miss Fenton, herself, assured him, her thoughts were more inclined towards the joys of Heaven than earth; and as this circumstance would, she believed, induce her to retire to a convent, she thought it a happy, rather than an unhappy event.—Her brother, on whom her fortune devolved if she took this resolution, was exactly of her opinion.

Lost in the maze of happiness which surrounded her, Miss Milner oftentimes asked her heart, and her heart whispered like a flatterer, "Yes." Are not my charms even more invincible than I ever believed them to be? Dorriforth, the grave, the sanctified, the anchorite Dorriforth, by their force is animated to all the ardour of the most impassioned lover—while the proud priest, the austere guardian, is humbled, if I but frown, into the veriest slave of love.—She then asked, "Why did I not keep him longer in suspense? he could not have loved me more, I believe; but my power over him might have been greater still.—I am the happiest of women in that affection he has proved to me, but I wonder whether it would exist under ill treatment? if it would not, he still does not love me as I wish to be loved—if it would, my triumph, my felicity, would be enhanced."—These thoughts were mere phantoms of the brain, and never by system put into action; but repeatedly indulged, they were practised by casual occurrences; and the dear-bought experiment of being beloved in spite of her faults, (a glory proud women ever aspire to) was, at present, the ambition of Miss Milner.

Unthinking woman! she did not reflect, that to the searching eye of lord Elmwood she had faults, with her every care to conceal or overcome them, sufficient to try all his love, and all his patience. But what female is not fond of experiments? to which, how few are there, that do not fall a sacrifice!

Perfectly secure of the affections of the man she loved, her declining health no longer threatened her; her declining spirits returned as before; and the suspicions of her guardian being now changed to the liberal confidence of a doating lover, she now again professed all her former follies, all her fashionable levities, and indulged them with less restraint than she had ever done.

For a while, blinded by his passion, lord Elmwood encouraged and admired every new proof of her restored happiness; nor till sufferance had tempted her to proceed beyond her usual bounds, did he remonstrate.—But she, who as his ward, had been ever gentle, and (when he strenuously opposed) always obedient; he now found as a mistress, sometimes haughty; and to opposition, always insolent.—He was surprised, but the novelty pleased him.—And Miss Milner, whom he tenderly loved, could put on no change, nor appear in any new character that did not, for the time she adopted it, seem to become her.

Among the many causes of complaint she gave him, want of economy in the disposal of her income was one.—Bills and drafts came upon him without number, while the account, on her part, of money expended, amounted but to articles of dress she sometimes never wore; toys that were out of fashion before they were paid for; and charities directed by the force of whim.—Another complaint was, as usual, extreme late hours, and often-times company he did not approve.

She was charmed to see his love struggling with his censure—his politeness with his anxiety—and by the light, frivolous, or resentful manner, in which she treated his admonitions, she triumphed in shewing to Miss Woodley, and, more especially to Mr. Sandford, how much she dared upon the strength of his affections.

Everything in preparation for their marriage, which was to take place at Elmwood-House during the summer months, she resolved for the short time she had to remain in London, to let no occasion pass of tasting all those pleasures which were not likely ever to return; but which, eager as she was in their pursuit, she still placed in no kind of competition with those she hoped would succeed; those more sedate, and far greater joys she had in domestic contemplation—and often, merely to hasten on the tedious hours that intervened, she varied and diverted them with the many recreations her intended husband could not approve.

It so happened, and it was unfortunate it did, that a law-suit[1] and some other intricate affairs that came with his title and estate, frequently kept lord Elmwood from his house part of the day; sometimes the whole evening; and when at home, would often closet him for hours with his lawyers.—But while he was thus off his guard, Sandford never was—and had Miss Milner been the dearest thing on earth to him, he could not have watched her more narrowly; or had she been the frailest thing on earth, he could not have been more hard upon her, in all the accounts of her conduct he gave to lord Elmwood.—His lordship knew Sandford's failing was to think ill of Miss Milner, he pitied him for it, and he pitied her for it—and all the aggravation his representations gave to her real follies, affection for them both, in the heart of Dorriforth, stood between every other impression.

But facts are glaring; and he at length beheld those faults in their true colours, although previously pointed out by the prejudice of Mr. Sandford.

As soon as Sandford perceived his lordship's uneasiness, "There, my lord!" cried he, exultingly, "Did I not always say the marriage was an improper one?—but you would not be ruled—you would not see."

"Can you blame me for not seeing," replied his lordship, "when you yourself were blind?—Had you been dispassionate, had you

---

1   In the second, third, fourth, and fifth editions, "a lawsuit concerning some possessions in the West Indies."

seen Miss Milner's virtues as well as her faults, I should have believed, and been guided by you—but you saw her failings only, and therein have been equally deceived with me, who have only beheld her perfections."

"My observations, however, my lord, would have been of most use to you; for I have seen what to avoid."

"But mine have been the most charitable," replied his lordship, "for I have seen—what I must always love."

Sandford sighed, and lifted up his hands.

"Mr. Sandford," resumed his lordship, with a voice and manner such as he puts on when not all the power of Sandford, or any other, can change his fixed determination, "Mr. Sandford," resumed he, "my eyes are now open to every failing, as well as to every accomplishment; to every vice, as well as to every virtue of Miss Milner's; nor will I suffer myself to be again prepossessed in her favour by your prejudice against her—for I believe it was compassion at your unkind treatment of her, that first gained her my heart."

"I, my lord?" cried Sandford, "Do not load me with the burthen—with the mighty burthen of your love for her."

"Do not interrupt me." Said his lordship; "Whatever your meaning has been, the effect of your unkindness to her, is what I say.—Now, I will no longer," continued he, "have an enemy such as you have been, to heighten her charms, which are too transcendent in their native state. I will hear no more complaints against her, but I will watch her closely myself—and if I find her mind and heart (such as my suspicions have of late whispered) too frivolous for that substantial happiness I look for with an object so beloved; depend upon my word—the marriage shall yet be broken off."

"I depend upon your word, it *will* then." Replied Sandford, eagerly.

"You are unjust, Sir, in saying so before the trial," replied his lordship, "and your injustice shall make me more cautious, lest I follow your example."

"But, my lord—"

"My mind is made up, Mr. Sandford." Returned he, interrupting him, "I am no longer engaged to Miss Milner than she shall deserve I should—but in my observations I will take care not to wrong her as you have done."

"My lord, call my observations wrong, when you have reflected upon them as a man, and not as a lover—divest yourself of your passion, and meet me upon equal ground."

"I will meet no one—I will consult no one—my own judgment shall be the judge, and in a few months marry, or—*banish me from her for ever.*"

There was something in these last words, in the tone and firmness with which they were delivered, that the heart of Sandford rested upon with content—they bore the symptoms of a menace that would be executed; and he parted from his patron with congratulations upon his wisdom, and the warmest assurances of his firm reliance on his *word*.

Lord Elmwood having come to this resolution, was more composed than he had been for several days before; while the horror of domestick wrangles—a family without subordination—a house without economy—in a word, a wife without discretion, had been perpetually present to his mind.

Mr. Sandford, although he was a man of understandings, of learning, and a complete casuist; yet, all the faults he himself committed, were entirely—for want of knowing better.—He constantly reproved faults in others, and he was most assuredly too good a man not to have corrected and amended his own, had they been known to him—but they were not.—He had been for so long time[1] the superior of all with whom he lived, had been so busied with instructing others, he had not recollected he himself wanted instructions—and in such awe did his severity keep all about him, that notwithstanding he had many friends, not one told him of his failings—(except just now lord Elmwood, but who, in this instance, as a man in love, he would not credit)— Was there not then some reason for him to suppose he had no faults?—his enemies, indeed, hinted that he had, but enemies he never hearkened to; and thus, with all his good sense, wanted the sense to follow the rule, *Believe what your enemies say of you, rather than what is said by your friends*; this rule attended to, would

---

1   In the second, third, fourth, and fifth editions, "so long a time."

make many a one amiable that is now the reverse, and had made him, a perfect upright character.—For could an enemy, to whom he would have listened, whispered to Sandford as he left lord Elmwood's study, "Cruel, barbarous man! you go away with your heart satisfied, nay, even elated in the prospect, that Miss Milner's hopes, on which she alone exists; those hopes which keep her from the deepest affliction, and cherish her with joy and gladness, will all be disappointed—you flatter yourself it is for the sake of your friend lord Elmwood you rejoice; because he has escaped a danger—you wish him well, but there is another cause for your exultation which you will not seek to know—it is, that in his safety shall dwell the punishment of his ward.—For shame! for shame! forgive her faults, as this of yours needs forgiveness."

Had any one said this, to Sandford, whom he would have credited; or had his own heart suggested it, he was a man of that rectitude and conscientiousness, he would have returned immediately to lord Elmwood, and have endeavoured to strengthen all his favourable opinions of his intended wife—but having no such monitor as this, he walked on, highly contented, and meeting Miss Woodley, said, with an air of triumph,

"Where's your young lady?—where's lady Elmwood?"

Miss Woodley smiled, and answered—she was gone with such and such ladies to an auction.—"But why give her that title already, Mr. Sandford?"

"Because," answered he, "I think she will never have it."

"Bless me, Mr. Sandford!" said Miss Woodley, "you shock me!"

"I thought I should," replied he, "and that is why I tell it you."

"For Heaven's sake, what has happened?" Cried she.

"Nothing new—her indiscretions only."

"I know she is imprudent," said Miss Woodley; "I can see she is often to blame—but then my lord surely loves her, and love will overlook a great deal."

"He does love her—but he has understanding and resolution.—He loved his sister too, tenderly loved her, and yet when he had taken the resolution; passed his word he would never see her again; even upon her death-bed he would not retract it—no entreaties could prevail upon him.—And now, though he maintains, and I dare say loves her child, yet you remember when you brought him home he would not bear him in his sight."

"Poor Miss Milner!"—Said Miss Woodley in the most pitying accents.

"Nay," said Sandford, "lord Elmwood has not yet passed his word, that he will never see her more—he has only threatened to say so—but I know enough of him to know, his threats are generally the same as the action done."

"You are very good," said Miss Woodley, "to acquaint me of this in time: I may now warn Miss Milner of it, and she may behave with more circumspection."

"By no means,"—cried Sandford, hastily, "What would you warn her for?—it will do her no good—besides," added he, "I don't know whether his lordship does not expect secresy from me on this subject, and if he does—"

"But, with all deference to your opinion," said Miss Woodley, (and with all deference did she speak) "don't you think, Mr. Sandford, that secresy upon this occasion would be wicked? for consider the anguish it may cause my friend, and if by advising her we can save her from—" She was going on.

"You may call it wicked, madam, not to inform her of it," cried he, "but I call a breach of promise (if I did give my promise, which I don't say I did) much more sinful."[1]

"I suppose you are right; Sir," said Miss Woodley, with humility; "but if you have given *your* promise, I have not given mine, and therefore may divulge—"

"There now!" cried Sandford, "there is how you judge of this matter.—You judge of things as they are in reality, not what they are by construction; the only way to judge of any thing.—If I did make a promise to lord Elmwood—(which, I again say, I don't know that I did)—the promise was, that I would not communicate the secret; meaning, not to tell it to Miss Milner herself.—I have not; and therefore have kept my word—and in revealing it

---

1 In the second, third, fourth, and fifth editions, "a breach of confidence—if it was divulged to me in confidence—."

to you, I did it with a full persuasion you would conceal it; which confidence, on my part, binds you as much as the most solemn promise you could have given."

"The fault will be mine, then, not yours, if it comes to the knowledge of Miss Milner?"

"Certainly."

"Then, as it will be my fault, do not you, Sir, be uneasy about it."—[1]

He was going to explain again, but Miss Milner entered, and put an end to the discourse.—She had been passing the whole morning at an auction, and had laid out near two hundred pounds in different things she had no one use for; but bought them because they were said to be cheap.—Among the rest was a lot of books on chemistry, and some Latin authors.

"Why, madam," cried Sandford, looking over the catalogue, where her purchases were marked by a pencil, "do you know what you have done? you can't read a word of these books."

"Can't I, Mr. Sandford? but I assure you, you will be vastly pleased with them when you see how elegantly they are bound."

"My dear," said Mrs. Horton, "why have you bought china? you and lord Elmwood have more now, than you have places to put them in."

"Very true, Mrs. Horton—I forgot that—but then you know I can give these away."

Lord Elmwood was in the room at the conclusion of this conversation—he shook his head and sighed.

"My lord," said she, "I have had a very pleasant morning, but I wished for you—if you had been with me I should have bought a great many other things; but I did not like to appear unreasonable in your absence."

Sandford fixed his inquisitive eyes upon lord Elmwood, to observe his countenance—his lordship smiled, but appeared thoughtful.

"And, oh! my lord, I have bought you a present." Said she.

---

1   The entire exchange From "I suppose you are right, Sir" to "uneasy about it" is omitted from the second, third, fourth, and fifth editions.

"I do not wish for a present, Miss Milner."

"What, not from me?—very well."

"If you present me with yourself, madam, it is all I ask."

Sandford moved upon his chair as if he sat uneasy.

"Why then, Miss Woodley," said Miss Milner, "*you* shall have the present.—But then it won't suit you—it is for a gentleman.—I'll keep it and give it to my lord Frederick the first time I meet with him.—I saw him this morning, and he looked divinely; I longed to speak to him."

Miss Woodley cast, by stealth, an eye of apprehension upon lord Elmwood's face, and trembled to behold it red as scarlet.[1]

Sandford stared with both his eyes full upon him; then drew himself upright on his chair, and took a pinch of snuff upon the strength of his uneasiness.

A silence ensured.

After a short time.—"You all appear very melancholy," said Miss Milner; "I wish I had not come home yet."

Miss Woodley was in agony—she saw lord Elmwood's extreme displeasure, and dreaded lest he should express it by some words he could not recall, or she could not forgive—therefore, whispering to her she had something particular to say to her, she took her out of the room.

The moment she was gone, Mr. Sandford rose nimbly from his seat, rubbed his hands, walked briskly across the room, then asked his lordship, in a cheerful tone, "Whether he dined at home to-day?"

That which had given Sandford spirits to speak with cheerfulness, had depressed lord Elmwood's so much, that he sat silent and dejected.—At length he answered, in a faint voice, "No, I believe I shall *not* dine at home."

"Where is your lordship going to dine?" asked Mrs. Horton; "I thought we should have had your company today; Miss Milner dines at home, I believe."

"I have not yet determined where I shall dine." Replied he, taking no notice of the conclusion of her speech.

---

1   In the second, third, fourth, and fifth editions, "flushed with resentment."

"My lord, if you mean to go to the hotel, I'll go with you, if you please." Cried Sandford, officiously.

"With all my heart, Sandford." Replied his lordship, and they both went out together before Miss Milner returned to the apartment.

CHAPTER VIII

MISS Woodley, for the first time, disobeyed the will of Mr. Sandford; and as soon as Miss Milner and she were alone, informed her of all he had revealed to her; accompanying the recital with every testimony of sympathy and affection.—But had the genius of Sandford presided over this discovery, it could not have influenced the mind of Miss Milner to receive the intelligence, more exactly opposite to the intention of the informer. Instead of shuddering with fear at the menace lord Elmwood had uttered, she boldly said, she "Dared him to perform it." "He durst not." Repeated she.

"Why durst not?" Said Miss Woodley.

"Because he loves me too well—because his own happiness is too dear to him."

"I believe he loves you," replied Miss Woodley, "and yet there is a doubt if—"

"There shall be no longer a doubt."—Cried Miss Milner, "I'll put him to the proof."

"For shame, my dear! you talk inconsiderately—what do you mean by proof?"

"I mean, I will do something that any prudent man ought *not* to forgive; and yet, with that vast share of prudence he possesses, I will force him still to yield to his love."[1]

"But suppose you should be disappointed, and he should not yield?"[2] Said Miss Woodley.

---

1 In the second, third, fourth, and fifth editions, "with all his vast share of prudence, *he* shall forgive it, and make a sacrifice of just resentment to partial affection."

2 In the second, third, fourth, and fifth editions "yield?" becomes "make the sacrifice?"

"Then, I have only lost a man who had no regard for me."

"He may have a great regard for you, notwithstanding."

"But for the love I have, and do still bear my lord Elmwood, I will have something more than a *great regard* in return."

"You have his love, I am sure."

"But is it such as mine?—*I* could love *him* if he had a thousand faults.—And yet," said she, recollecting herself, "and yet, I believe, his being faultless, was the first cause of my passion."

Thus she talked on—sometimes in anger, sometimes apparently jesting—till her servant came to tell her dinner was served.— Upon entering the dining-room, and seeing his lordship's place at table vacant, she started back. She was disappointed of the pleasure she expected in dining with him; and his sudden absence so immediately after the intelligence she had received from Miss Woodley, encreased her uneasiness.—She drew her chair, and sat down with an indifference, that said she should not eat; and as soon as she was seated, she put her fingers sullenly to her lips, nor touched her knife and fork, or spoke a word in reply to any thing that was said to her during the whole dinner.—Miss Woodley and Mrs. Horton were both too well acquainted with the good disposition of her heart, to take offence, or any notice of this behaviour.—They dined, and wisely said nothing either to provoke or sooth her.—Just as the dinner was going to be removed, a loud rap came at the door—"Who is that?" Said Mrs. Horton.—One of the servants went to the window, and answered, "My lord and Mr. Sandford, madam."—"Come back to dinner, as I live." Cried Mrs. Horton.—

Miss Milner still continued her position and said nothing—but at the corners of her mouth, which her fingers did not entirely cover, there were discoverable a thousand dimpled graces like small convulsive fibres, which a restrained smile on lord Elmwood's return, had sent there.

His lordship and Sandford entered.

"I am glad you are returned, my lord," said Mrs. Horton, "for Miss Milner would not eat a morsel."

"It was because I had no appetite." Returned she, blushing like crimson.

"We should not have come back," said Sandford, "but at the place where we went to dine, all the rooms were filled with smoke."[1]

"It has been a very windy day indeed," said Mrs. Horton, "and one part of this house, is now in a smother."[2]

Lord Elmwood put the wing of a fowl on Miss Milner's plate, but without previously asking if she chose any; yet she condescended to eat—they spoke to each other too in the course of conversation, yet it was with a reserve that appeared as if they had been quarrelling, and so felt to themselves, though no such circumstance had happened.

About two weeks passed away in this kind of distant behaviour on both sides; without either venturing a direct quarrel, and without either expressing (except inadvertently) their strong affection for each other.

During this time they were once, however, nearly becoming the dearest friends in expressions, as well as in sentiments.—This arose from a favour he granted in compliance to what he knew was her earnest desire; and, as a favour which he had refused to the repeated requests of many friends, she could not but esteem the high value of the obligation.

She and Miss Woodley had taken an airing to see the poor child, young Rushbrook; and on their return, his lordship inquiring of the ladies how they had passed their morning, Miss Milner frankly told him; and added, "What pain it gave her to leave the child behind, as he still cried to come away with her."

"Go for him then to-morrow," said his lordship, "and bring him home."

"Home!" She repeated, with surprise.

"Yes," replied he, "if you desire it, this shall be his home—you shall be a mother, and I will, henceforward, be a father to him."

Sandford, who was present, looked unusually sour at this high token of his lordship's regard to Miss Milner; yet, with resentment on his face, he wiped a tear of joy from his eye, for the boy's

---

1   In the second, third, fourth, and fifth editions "smoke" becomes "company."
2   This paragraph is omitted from the second, third, fourth, and fifth editions.

sake—his frown was the force of prejudice, his tear the force of nature.

Rushbrook was brought home; and whenever lord Elmwood wished to shew a kindness to Miss Milner, without directing it immediately to her, he took his nephew upon his knee, talked to him, and told him, he "Was glad they had become acquainted."

In the various, though delicate, struggles for power between Miss Milner and her guardian, there was not one person witness to these incidents, who did not suppose, all would at last end in wedlock—for the most common observer perceived, ardent love was the foundation of every discontent, as well, as of every joy they experienced.—One great incident, however, totally reversed the prospect of all future accommodation.

The fashionable Mrs. G—— gave a masked ball;[1] tickets were presented to persons of the first quality, and among the rest, three were sent to Miss Milner.—She had never been at a masquerade, and received them with extacy—more especially as the masque being at the house of a woman of fashion, she did not conceive there could be any objection to her going.—She was mistaken— the moment she mentioned it to lord Elmwood, he desired her, somewhat sternly, "Not to think of being there."—She was vext at the prohibition, but more at the manner in which it was delivered, and flatly said, "She should certainly go."

She expected a severe rebuke for this, but what alarmed her much more, he never replied a word; but looked with a resignation which foreboded her more sorrow, than the severest reproaches would have done.—She sat for a minute reflecting how to rouse him from this composure—she first thought of attacking him with upbraidings; then she thought of soothing him; and at last of laughing at him.—This was the least supportable of all, and yet this she ventured upon.

---

1   Masquerades were popular forms of entertainment, but were often considered dangerous because the disguises concealed or distorted categories of social class and even gender. Because of the masquerade's potential ambiguity, it was a common device in novels and plays, including Aphra Behn's *The Rover* (1677) Hannah Cowley's *The Belle's Stratagem* (1780) and Henry Fielding's *Amelia* (1751). Boaden relates an anecdote about Inchbald's own attendance, dressed as a man, at a masquerade (I, 141), although Jenkins argues that this biographical detail has been overemphasized by Boaden and later critics. See Appendix C4 for sample essays on the masquerade.

"I am sure your lordship," said she, "with all your saintliness, can have no objection to my being present at the masquerade, provided I go as a Nun."

He made no reply.

"That is a habit," continued she, "which covers a multitude of faults—and, for that evening, I may have the chance of making a conquest even of you, my lord—nay, I question not, if under that inviting attire, even the pious Mr. Sandford would not ogle me."

"Hush."—Said Miss Woodley.

"Why hush?" cried Miss Milner, aloud, though Miss Woodley had spoken in a whisper, "I am sure," continued she, "I am only repeating what I have read in books about nuns, and their confessors."[1]

"Your conduct, Miss Milner," replied lord Elmwood, "gives evident proofs what authors you have read; you may spare yourself the trouble of quoting them."

Her pride was hurt at this, beyond bearing; and as she could not, like him, govern her anger, it flushed in her face, and almost forced the tears.

"My lord," said Miss Woodley, (in a voice so soft and peaceful, it ought to have calmed the resentment of both,) "my lord, suppose you were to accompany Miss Milner? there are tickets for three, and you can then have no objection."

Miss Milner's brow was immediately smoothed; her eye beamed hope;[2] and she fetched a sigh in anxious expectation he would consent.

"I go, Miss Woodley?" he replied, with astonishment, "Do you imagine I would play the buffoon at a masquerade?"

Miss Milner's face changed to its former state.

"I have seen many grave characters there, my lord." Said Miss Woodley.

"Dear Miss Woodley," cried Miss Milner, "why persuade lord Elmwood to put on a mask, just at the time he has laid it aside?"

His patience seemed now to be tempted to its height, and

---

1 Miss Milner refers to the popular anti-Catholic "nunnery tales," which depicted members of the clergy in sensational terms.

2 The phrase "her eye beamed hope" is omitted from the second, third, fourth, and fifth editions.

he answered, "If you suspect it, madam, you shall find me changed."

Pleased, she had been able at last to irritate him, she smiled with a degree of triumph, and in that humour was going to reply; but before she could speak four words, and before she thought of it, he abruptly left the room.

She was highly offended at this insult, and declared, "From that moment she banished him her heart for ever." And to prove she set both his love and anger at defiance, she immediately ordered her chariot, and said, she "was going to some of her acquaintance, whom she knew had tickets, and with whom she would fix upon the dress she meant to appear in at the masquerade; for nothing, unless she was locked up, should alter the resolution she had taken, of being there." To remonstrate at that moment, Miss Woodley knew would be in vain; the chariot came to the door, and she drove away.

She did not return to dinner, nor till late in the evening; lord Elmwood was at home, but never once mentioned her name.

She came home, after he had retired to bed, and in great spirits; the first time she ever appeared careless what he might think of her behaviour:—but her whole thoughts were occupied upon the business she had been about, and her dress engrossed all her conversation as soon as Miss Woodley and she were alone.—She told Miss Woodley, she had been shewn the greatest variety of beautiful and becoming dresses she had ever beheld,[1] and yet, said she, "I have fixed upon a very plain one; but one I look so well in, you will hardly know me when I have it on."

"You are seriously then resolved to go," said Miss Woodley, "provided you hear no more on the subject from your guardian?"

"Whether I do or not, Miss Woodley, I am equally resolved to go."

"But you know, my dear, he has desired you not—and you used always to obey his commands."

"As my guardian, I certainly did obey him; and I could obey him as a husband; but as a lover, I will not."

"Yet that is the means, never to have him for a husband."

---

1 See Appendix C4 for sample advertisements for masquerade costumes.

"As he pleases—for if he will not submit to be my lover, I will not submit to be his wife—nor has he the affection I require in a husband."

Thus, the old sentiments were repeated as heretofore, and prevented a separation till towards morning.

Miss Milner, for that night, dreamt less of her guardian than of the masquerade. On the evening of the next day it was to be; she was up early, breakfasted in her dressing-room, and remained there most of the day, busied in all the thousand preparations for the night; one of which, was to take every particle of powder out of her hair,[1] and have it curled all over in falling ringlets.[2]—Her next care was, that her dress should exactly fit, and display her fine person to the best advantage—it did so.—Miss Woodley entered as it was trying on, and was struck with astonishment at the elegance of the habit, and the beautiful effect it had upon her graceful person; but most of all, she was astonished at her venturing on such a character—for although it was the representative of the goddess of Chastity,[3] yet from the buskins, and the petticoat made to festoon far above the ankle, it had, on the first glance, the appearance of a female much less virtuous.—Miss Woodley admired the dress, yet objected to it; but as she admired first, her objections after had no weight.

"Where is lord Elmwood?" Said Miss Milner, "he must not see me."

"No, for heaven's sake," cried Miss Woodley, "I would not have him see you for the universe."

"And yet," returned the other, with a sigh, "Why am I then thus pleased with this dress? for I had rather he should admire me then all the world beside, and yet he is not to see me in it."

---

1   A popular fashion in the 1790s. Beginning in 1788, Inchbald herself insisted on acting on the stage without powder in her Auburn hair.

2   Compare to Milton's description of Eve's hair in *Paradise Lost*, Book IV: "Dissheveld, but in wanton ringlets waved / As the vine curls her tendrils" (306-07). Also compare Pope's description of Belinda in *The Rape of the Lock*. Belinda's locks are "well conspir'd to deck / With shining ringlets the smooth iv'ry neck" (21-22).

3   Diana or Artemis (Greek) was the protector of female chastity and also the goddess of the hunt. See Appendix C4 for Eliza Haywood's description of another masquerader who wore the habit of Diana.

"But he would not admire you thus." Said Miss Woodley.

"How shall I contrive to avoid him," said Miss Milner, "if he should offer to hand me into my carriage?—but I believe he will not be in good humour enough for that."

"You had better dress at the ladies' house with whom you go." Said Miss Woodley; and this was agreed upon.

At dinner they learnt, his lordship was to go that evening to Windsor, in order to be in readiness for the king's hunt, early in the morning; and this intelligence having dispersed Miss Milner's fears, she concluded to dress at home.

Lord Elmwood appeared at dinner in an even, but not in a good temper;—the subject of the masquerade was never brought up, or indeed was once in his thoughts; for though he was offended at his ward's behaviour on the occasion, and thought she committed a fault in telling him, "She would go," yet he never suspected she meant to do so, not even at the time she said it, much less that she would persist, coolly and deliberately in so direct a contradiction to his will.—She, for her part, flattered herself his going to Windsor, was intended in order to give her an opportunity of passing the evening as she pleased, without his being obliged to know of it, and consequently to complain.—Miss Woodley, who was willing to hope as she wished, began to be of the same opinion; and, without reluctance, drest herself as a wood-nymph, to accompany her friend.

CHAPTER IX

At half after eleven, Miss Milner's chair, and another with Miss Woodley, took them from lord Elmwood's house to call upon the party (a group of wood-nymphs and huntresses) which were to accompany them, and make up the suit of Diana.

They had not left the house two minutes, when a thundering rap came at the door—it was lord Elmwood in a post chaise.— Upon some occasion the next day's hunt was put off: he had been made acquainted with it, and came from Windsor at that late hour.—After his lordship had told Mrs. Horton and Mr. Sandford, who were sitting together, the cause of his sudden return, and some supper was ordered for him, he inquired, "What company had just left the house?"

"We have been alone the whole evening, my lord." Replied Mrs. Horton.

"Nay," returned he, "I saw two chairs, with several servants, come out of the door as I drove up; but what livery I could not discern."

"We have had no creature here." Repeated Mrs. Horton.

"Nor has Miss Milner?" Asked he.

This brought Mrs. Horton to her recollection, and she cried, "Oh! now I know."—And then checked herself, as if she knew too much.

"What do you know, madam?" Said his lordship, sharply.

"Nothing"—said Mrs. Horton, "I know nothing." And she lifted up her hands and shook her head.

"So all people say, who know a great deal," cried Sandford, "and I suspect, that is at present your case."

"Then I know more than I wish to know, I am sure, Mr. Sandford." Returned she, shrugging up her shoulders.

Lord Elmwood was all impatience. "Explain, madam, explain." Cried he.

"Dear my lord," said she, "if your lordship will recollect, you may just have the same knowledge that I have."

"Recollect what?" Said he, sternly.

"The quarrel you and your ward had about the masquerade."

"What of that? she is not gone there?" He cried.

"I am not sure she is," returned Mrs. Horton, "but if your lordship saw two sedan chairs going out of this house, I cannot but suspect it must be Miss Milner, and my niece going to the masquerade."

His lordship made no answer, but rung the bell violently.—A servant entered.—"Send Miss Milner's woman hither," said he, "immediately."—The man withdrew.

"Nay, my lord," cried Mrs. Horton, "any of the other servants could tell you just as well, whether Miss Milner is at home, or gone out."

"Perhaps not." Replied he.

The maid entered.

"Where is your lady?" Said he.

The woman had received no orders to conceal where her lady was gone, and yet some secret influence which governs the replies of all waiting women and chamber maids, whispered to her, she ought not to tell the truth.

"Where is your lady?" Repeated lord Elmwood, in a louder voice than before.

"Gone out, my lord." She replied.

"Where?"

"My lady did not tell me."

"And don't you know?"

"No, my lord." She answered, and without blushing.

"Is this the night of the masquerade?" Said he.

"I don't know, my lord, upon my word; but, I believe, my lord, it is not."

Sandford, as soon as lord Elmwood had asked the last question, run hastily to the table, at the other side of the room, snatched something from it, and returned to his place again—and as soon as the maid said, "It was not the night of the masquerade," he exclaimed, "But it is, my lord, it is—yes, it is." And showing a news-paper he held in his hand, pointed to the paragraph which contained the information.

"Leave the room," said lord Elmwood to the woman, "I have done with you."—She withdrew.

"Yes, yes, here it is." Repeated Sandford, with the paper in his hand.—He then read the paragraph: "*The masquerade at the honourable Mrs. G—'s this evening—*" "This evening, my lord, you find:" "*it is expected will be the most brilliant, of any thing of the kind, for these many years past.*"

"They should not put such things in the papers," said Mrs. Horton, "to tempt young women to their ruin."

The word ruin, seemed to grate upon his lordship's ear, and he said to the servant who came to wait on him, while he supped, "Take the supper away."—He had not attempted to eat, or even to sit down; and he now walked backwards and forwards in the room, lost in thought and care.

A little time after, one of Miss Milner's footmen came in upon some occasion, and Mr. Sandford said to him, "Pray did you attend your lady to the masquerade?"

"Yes, Sir." Replied the man.

Lord Elmwood stopt himself short in his walk, and said to the servant, "You did?"

"Yes, my lord." Replied he.

His lordship walked again.

"I should like to know what she was drest in." Said Mrs. Horton; and turning to the servant, "Do you know what your lady had on?"

"Yes, madam," replied the man, "she was in mens cloaths."

"How?" cried lord Elmwood.

"You tell a story to be sure." Said Mrs. Horton to the servant.

"No," cried Sandford, "I am sure he does not; for he is an honest good young man, and would not tell a lie upon any account,—would you?"

Lord Elmwood ordered Miss Milner's woman to be again sent up.—She came.

"In what dress did your lady go to the masquerade?" Asked his lordship, and with a look so extremely morose, it seemed to command her to answer in a word, and to answer truly.

A mind, with a spark of sensibility more than she possessed, could not have equivocated with such an interrogator, but her reply was, "She went in her own dress, my lord."

"Was it a man's, or a woman's dress?" Asked his lordship with the same commanding look.

"Ha, ha, my lord," (half laughing and half crying,) "a woman's dress to be sure, my lord."

On which Sandford cried,

"Call the footman up, and let him confront her."

He was called; but lord Elmwood, now disgusted with the scene, sat down at the farther end of the room, and left Sandford to question them.

With all the authority and consequence of a country magistrate, Sandford, with his back to the fire and the witnesses before him, began with the footman.

"In what dress do you say, you saw your lady, when you attended, and went along with her, to the masquerade?"

"In mens cloaths." Replied the man, boldly and firmly as before.

"Bless my soul, George, how can you say such a thing?" Cried the woman.

"In what dress, do *you* say she went in?" Cried Sandford to her.

"In women's cloaths, indeed, Sir."

"This is very odd!" said Mrs. Horton.

"Had she on, or had she not on, a Coat?" Asked Sandford.

"Yes, Sir, a petticoat." Replied the woman.

"Do *you* say she had on a petticoat?" Said Sandford to the man.

"I can't answer exactly for that," replied he, "but I know she had boots on."

"They were not boots," replied the maid, with vehemence, "indeed, Sir, (turning to Sandford) they were only half boots."

"My girl," said Sandford, kindly to her, "your own evidence convicts her.—What has a woman to do with *any* boots?"

Impatient at this mummery, lord Elmwood rose from his seat, and ordered the servants out of the room; and then looking at his watch, found it was near one. "At what time am I to expect her at home?" Said he.

"Perhaps not till three in the morning." Answered Mrs. Horton.

"Three! six, more likely." Cried Sandford.

"I can't wait with patience till that time." Answered his lordship with a most anxious sigh.

"You had better go to bed, my lord," said Mrs. Horton, "and by sleeping, the time will pass away unperceived."

"If I *could* sleep, madam." Returned he.

"Will you play a game of cards, my lord?" said Sandford, "for I will not leave you till she comes home; and though I am not used to sit up all night—"

"All night," repeated his lordship, "she durst not stay all night."

"And yet, after going," said Sandford, "in defiance to your commands, I should suppose she dares?"

"She is in good company, at least, my lord." Said Mrs. Horton.

"She does not know herself, what company she is in." Replied his lordship.

"How should she?" cried Sandford, "where every one hides his face."

Till five o'clock in the morning, in such conversation as this, the hours passed away.—Mrs. Horton, indeed, retired to her chamber at two; and left the gentlemen to a graver discourse, but a discourse still less advantageous to poor Miss Milner.

She, during this time, was at the scene of pleasure she had pictured to herself, and all the pleasure it gave her was, that she was sure she should never desire to go to a masquerade again.— The crowd and bustle fatigued her—the freedom offended her delicacy—and though she perceived she was the first object of admiration in the place, yet there was one person still wanting to admire; and the remorse at having transgressed his injunctions for so trivial an entertainment, weighed upon her spirits, and added to its weariness.—She would have come away sooner than she did, but she could not, with any degree of good manners, leave the company with whom she went, and not till half after four were they prevailed on to return.

Day-light just peeped through the shutters of the room where his lordship and Sandford were sitting, when the sound of her carriage, and its sudden stop at the door, caused lord Elmwood as suddenly to start from his seat.—He trembled extremely, and looked pale.—Sandford was ashamed to seem to notice it, yet he could not help asking him, "To take a glass of wine."—He took it—and for once evinced he was reduced so low, as to be *glad* of such a resource.

What passion thus agitated lord Elmwood at this crisis, it is hard to define.—Perhaps it was indignation at Miss Milner's imprudence, and the satisfaction he felt at being on the point of revenge—perhaps his emotion arose from joy, to find she was safe—perhaps it was perturbation at the regret he felt that he must upbraid her—perhaps it was one alone of these sensations, but most probably, it was them all combined.

She, wearied out with the tedious night's dissipation, and less joyous than melancholy, had fallen asleep as she rode home, and when the carriage stopt, came half asleep out of it.—"Light me to my bed-chamber instantly." Said she to her woman, who waited in the hall to receive her.—But one of lord Elmwood's valets went up to her, and answered, "Madam, my lord desires to see you before you go to bed."

"Your lord, man?" cried she, "Is he not out of town?"

"No, madam, my lord has been at home ever since you went out, and has been sitting up with Mr. Sandford, waiting for your return."

She was wide awake instantly.—The heaviness was removed from her eyes, but fear, grief, and shame, seized upon her heart.— She leaned against her woman, as if unable to support herself under those feelings, and said to Miss Woodley,

"Make my excuse—I can't see him to night—I am unfit—indeed I cannot."

Miss Woodley was alarmed at the thought of going to him by herself, and thus perhaps aggravating him still more; she therefore said, "He has sent for you; for heaven's sake, do not disobey him a second time."

"No, dear madam," cried her woman, "for he is like a lion—he has been scolding me."

"Good God!" exclaimed Miss Milner, (and in a tone that seemed prophetic) "Then he is not to be my husband, after all."

"Yes," cried Miss Woodley, "if you will only be humble, and appear sorry.—You know your power over him, and all may yet be well."

She turned her speaking eyes upon her friend, the tears starting from them, her lips trembling; "Do I not appear sorry?" She cried.

The bell at that moment rung furiously, and they mended their pace to the door of the apartment where his lordship was.

"No, this is only fright,"—replied Miss Woodley, "Say to him you are sorry, and beg his pardon."

"I cannot," said she, "if Mr. Sandford is with him."

The servant opened the door, and she and Miss Woodley went in.—Lord Elmwood by this time was composed, and received her with a slight inclination of his head; she bowed to him in return, and said, with some marks of humility,

"I suppose, my lord, I have done wrong."

"You have indeed, Miss Milner;" answered he, "but do not suppose, I mean to upbraid you; I am, moreover, going to release you from any such apprehension *for the future*."

Those last three words he spoke with a countenance so serious and so determined, with an accent so firm and so decided, they pierced through her heart.—She did not however weep, or even sigh; but her friend, Miss Woodley, knowing what she felt, exclaimed, "Oh!" as if for her.

She herself strove with her anguish, and replied, (but with a faltering voice) "I expected as much, my lord."

"Then, madam, you may perhaps expect all that I intend?"

"In regard to myself," she replied, "I suppose I do."

"Then," said he, "you may expect in a few days we shall part."

"I am prepared for it, my lord." She answered, and while she said so, sunk upon a chair.

"My lord, what you have to say farther," said Miss Woodley, in tears, "defer till the morning; Miss Milner, you see, is not able to bear it now."

"I have nothing to say farther," replied he, coolly, "I have now only to act."

"Lord Elmwood," cried Miss Milner, divided between grief and anger, "you think to frighten me by your menaces, but I can part with you; heaven knows I can—your late behaviour has reconciled me to a separation."

On this he was going out of the room—but Miss Woodley, catching hold of him, cried, "Oh! my lord, do not leave her in this sorrow—pity her weakness, and forgive it."—She was proceeding, and he seemed inclined to listen to her, when Sandford called out in so sharp a tone,

"Miss Woodley, what do you mean?" she gave a start, and desisted.

His lordship turned to Sandford and said, "Nay, Mr. Sandford, you need entertain no doubts of me; I have judged, and have deter—"

He was going to say determined; but Miss Milner, who dreaded to hear the word, interrupted the period, and exclaimed, "Oh! could my poor father know the grief, the days of sorrow, I have experienced since his death, how would he repent his fatal choice in a protector!"

This sentence, wherein his friend's memory was recalled, with the additional allusion to her long, and secret affection for himself, affected lord Elmwood much—he was moved, but ashamed of being so, and as soon as possible, conquered the propensity.—Yet, for a short interval, he did not know whether to go out of the room, or to remain in it, whether to speak, or to be silent.—At length he turned towards her and said,

"Appeal to your father in some other form, in that (pointing to her dress) he will not know you.—Reflect upon him too in your moments of dissipation, and let his idea controul your indiscretions—not merely in an hour of contradiction call peevishly upon his name, only to wound the dearest friend you have."

There was a degree of truth, and a degree of feeling, in the conclusion of this speech, that alarmed Sandford, and he caught up one of the candles, and laying hold of his lordship's elbow, drew him out of the room, crying, "Come, my lord, come to your bedchamber, it is very late—it is morning—it is time to rise." And by a continual repetition of these words, in a very loud voice, drowned whatever his lordship, or any other person, might have wished to have spoken, or heard.—In this manner, lord Elmwood was taken out of the apartment, and the evening's entertainment concluded.

CHAPTER X

Two whole days passed in the bitterest suspense on the part of Miss Milner, while neither one word or look from lord Elmwood, denoted the most trivial change of those sentiments he had declared on the night of the masquerade.—Still those sentiments, or intentions, were not explicitly delivered; they were more like intimations, than solemn declarations—for though he had said, "He would never reproach her *for the future*," and that "she might expect they should part," he had not positively said they should; and upon this doubtful meaning of his words, she hung with the strongest agitation of hope, and of fear.

Miss Woodley seeing the distress of her mind, (much as she endeavoured to conceal it) entreated, nay implored, of her, to permit her to be a mediator; to suffer her to ask for a private interview with lord Elmwood, and provided she found him inflexible, behave with a proper degree of spirit in return; but if he appeared not absolutely averse to a reconciliation, to offer it to him in so cautious a manner, it might take place without farther uneasiness on either side. But Miss Milner peremptorily forbad this, and acknowledging to her friend every weakness she felt on the occasion, yet concluded with solemnly declaring, "That after what had passed between her and lord Elmwood, *he* must be the first to make a concession, before she herself would condescend to be reconciled."

"I believe, I know lord Elmwood's temper," replied Miss Woodley, "and I do not think he will be easily induced to beg pardon for a fault, which he thinks you have committed."

"Then he does not love me."

"Pshaw! Miss Milner, this is the old argument.—He may love you too well to spoil you—consider, he is your guardian as well as your lover, he means also to become your husband; and he is a man of such nice honour, he will not give you a specimen of that power before marriage, which he does not intend to submit to hereafter."

"But tenderness, affection, the politeness due from a lover to his mistress, demands this submission; and as I now despair of enticing, I will oblige him to it—at least I'll make the trial, and know my fate at once."

"What do you mean to do?"

"Invite my lord Frederick to the house, and ask my guardian's consent for our immediate union; you will then see, what effect that has upon his pride."

"But you will then make it too late for him to be humble.—If you resolve on this, my dear Miss Milner, you are undone at once—you may thus hurry yourself into a marriage with a man you do not love, and the misery of your whole future life may be the result.—Or, would you force Mr. Dorriforth (I mean lord Elmwood) to another duel with my lord Frederick?"

"No, call him Dorriforth—" answered she, with the tears stealing from her eyes, "I thank you for calling him so; for by that name alone, is he dear to me."

"Nay, Miss Milner, with what rapture did you not receive his love, as lord Elmwood."

"But under that title he has been barbarous; under the first, he was all friendship and tenderness."

Notwithstanding Miss Milner indulged herself in all those soft bewailings to her friend—before lord Elmwood she maintained a degree of pride and steadiness which surprised even him, who had perhaps ever thought less of her love for him, than any other person.—She now began to fear she had gone too far in discovering her affection, and resolved to make trial of a contrary method.—She determined to retrieve that haughty character which had inspired so many of her admirers with passion, and take the chance of the effect upon this only one, to whom she ever acknowledged a mutual love.—But, although she acted this character well—so well, that every one but Miss Woodley thought her in earnest—yet, with the nicest and most attentive anxiety, did she watch even the slightest circumstance, that might revive her hopes, or confirm her despair. Lord Elmwood's behaviour was calculated to produce the latter—he was cold, polite, and perfectly indifferent.—Yet, whatever his manners now were, they did not remove from her recollection what they had been—she recalled, with delight, the ardour with which he had first declared his passion to her, and the thousand proofs he had since given of its reality.—From the constancy of his disposition, she depended a great deal, that those sentiments were not totally eradicated; and from the extreme desire, which Mr. Sandford now, more than ever, discovered to depreciate her in his patron's esteem—from the now, more than common earnestness, with which he never failed to take lord Elmwood from her company, whenever he had it in his power, she was led to believe, that while his friend entertained such strong fears of his lordship relapsing into love, she had reason to indulge the strongest hopes that he would.

But the reserve, and even indifference she had so well assumed for a few days, and which might perhaps have effected her designs, she had not the patience to persevere in, without calling levity to their aid.—She visited repeatedly without saying where, or with whom—kept later hours than usual—appeared in the highest spirits; sung, laugh'd, and never heaved a sigh, but when she was alone.

Still, lord Elmwood protracted a resolution, he was determined not to break when once taken.

Miss Woodley was extremely uneasy, and with cause; she saw her friend was providing herself with a weight of cares, she would soon find too much for her strength to bear—she would have reasoned with her, but all her arguments had long since proved unavailing.—She strongly wished to speak to lord Elmwood upon the subject, and (unknowing to her) plead her excuse; but he apprehended Miss Woodley's intention and evidently shunned her.—Mr. Sandford was now the only person to whom she could speak of Miss Milner, and the delight he took to expatiate on her faults, was more sorrow to her friend, than not to speak of her at all. She, therefore, sat a silent spectator, waiting with dread for that time, when she, who now scorned her advice, would fly to her in vain for comfort.

Sandford had, however, said one thing to Miss Woodley, which gave her a ray of hope. During their conversation on this subject (not by way of consolation to her, but as a reproach to lord Elmwood), he one day angrily exclaimed, "And yet, notwithstanding all this provocation, he has not come to the determination to think no more of her—he lingers and hesitates—I never saw him so weak upon any occasion before."

This was joyful hearing to Miss Woodley; still, she could not but reflect, the longer he was in coming to this determination, the more irrevocable it would be, when once taken; and every moment she passed, she trembled lest that should be the moment, in which lord Elmwood resolved to banish Miss Milner from his heart.

Among the unpardonable indiscretions, she was guilty of during this trial upon the temper of her guardian, was the frequent mention of many gentlemen, who had been her profest admirers, and mentioning them with partiality.—Teased, if not tortured by this, lord Elmwood still behaved with a manly evenness of temper, and neither appeared provoked on the subject, or insolently careless.—In a single instance, however, this calmness had nearly deserted him.

Entering the drawing-room, one evening, he suddenly started, on seeing lord Frederick Lawnly there, in earnest conversation with Miss Milner.

Mrs. Horton and Miss Woodley were both indeed present, and lord Frederick was talking in an audible voice, and upon some indifferent subjects; but with that impressive manner, in which a man never fails to speak to the woman he loves, be the subject what it will.—The moment lord Elmwood started, which was the moment he entered, lord Frederick arose.

"I beg your pardon, my lord," said lord Elmwood, "I protest I did not know you."

"I ought to entreat your lordship's pardon," returned lord Frederick, "for this intrusion, which an accident alone has occasioned. Miss Milner has been nearly overturned, by the carelessness of a lady's coachman, in whose carriage she was, and therefore suffered me to bring her home in mine."

"I hope you are not hurt." Said lord Elmwood to Miss Milner, but his voice was so much affected, by what he felt, he could scarcely articulate the words.—Not with the apprehension she was hurt, was he thus agitated, for the gaiety of her manners convinced him that could not be the case, nor did he indeed suppose any accident, such as was mentioned, had occurred; but the circumstance of unexpectedly seeing lord Frederick had taken him off his guard, and being totally unprepared, he could not conquer those signs of surprise, and the shock it had given him.

Lord Frederick, who had heard nothing of his intended union with his ward, (for it was even kept a secret, at present, from every servant in the house) imputed this discomposure, to the personal resentment his lordship might bear him, in consequence of their duel; for, notwithstanding lord Elmwood had assured the uncle of lord Frederick, (who once waited upon him on the subject of Miss Milner) that all resentment was, on his part, entirely at an end; and that he was willing to consent to the ladies marriage with his nephew, if she herself would concur, yet lord Frederick doubted the sincerity of this, and would still have had the delicacy not to have entered his house, but, encouraged by Miss Milner, and emboldened by his love. Personal resentment was then the construction he put upon lord Elmwood's emotion on entering the room, but Miss Milner and Miss Woodley knew his agitation to arise from a far different cause.

After his entrance, lord Frederick did not attempt to resume his seat, but bowing most respectfully to all present, took his leave; while Miss Milner followed him, as far as the door, repeating her thanks and gratitude for his protection.

Lord Elmwood was hurt beyond measure; but he had a second concern, and that was, he had not the power to conceal how much he was affected.—He trembled—when he attempted to speak, he stammered—he perceived his face burning with the blood that had flushed to it from confusion, and thus one confusion gave birth to another, till his state was pitiable.

Miss Milner, with all her assumed gaiety and real insolence, had not, however, the insolence to seem to observe his situation; she had only the confidence to observe it by stealth.—And Mrs. Horton and Miss Woodley, having opportunely begun a discourse upon some trivial occurrences, gave him time to recover himself by degrees—yet, still it was merely by degrees, for the impression this incident had made, was deep, and not easily to be erased.—The entrance of Mr. Sandford, who knew nothing of what had happened, was also some relief, and his lordship and he entered into a conversation, which they very soon retired into the library to terminate.—Miss Milner, taking Miss Woodley with her, went directly to her own apartment, and there exclaimed to her friend, in rapture,

"He is mine—he loves me—and he is mine for ever."

Miss Woodley congratulated her upon believing so, but confessed, she herself, "had her fears."

"What fears?" cried Miss Milner, "don't you perceive he loves me?"

"I do," said Miss Woodley, "but that, I always supposed; and, I think, if he loves you now, he has still the good sense to know, he has cause to hate you."

"What has good sense to do with love?" returned Miss Milner, "If a lover of mine suffers his understanding to get the better of his affection—"

And the same arguments were again going to be repeated, but Miss Woodley interrupted her, by requiring an explanation of her conduct, not in respect to her guardian, but to lord Frederick; whom, at least, she must allow, she was treating with cruelty, if she only made use of his affection, to stimulate that of lord Elmwood's.

"By no means, my dear Miss Woodley."—Returned she—"I have, indeed, done with my lord Frederick from this day; and he has certainly given me the proof I wanted of lord Elmwood's love; but then, I did not engage him to this, by the smallest degree of hope.—No, do not suspect me of that, while my heart was another's.—And I assure you, seriously, it was from the circumstance we described, that he came with me home—yet, I must own, that had I not had this design upon lord Elmwood's jealousy in idea, I would have walked on foot through the streets, rather than have suffered his rival's civilities.—But he pressed his services so violently, and my lady Evans (in whose chariot I was, when the accident happened) pressed me so violently to accept them, that he cannot expect any farther meaning from my acquiescence, than my own convenience."

Miss Woodley was going to reply, when she resumed,

"Nay, if you intend to say I have done wrong, still I am not sorry for it, while it has given me such convincing proofs of lord Elmwood's love.—Did you see him? I am afraid you did not see how he trembled?—and that manly, firm voice faltered, as mine does some times—his proud heart was humbled too; as mine is some times.—Oh! Miss Woodley, I have been counterfeiting indifference to *him*; I now find all *his* indifference has been counterfeit too, and we not only love, but we love equally."

"Supposing this, all as you hope; I yet think it highly necessary, your guardian should be informed, seriously informed, that it was mere accident, (for, at present, that plea seems but as a subterfuge) which brought lord Frederick hither."

"No, that will be destroying the work so successfully began.—I will not suffer any explanation to take place, but let my lord Elmwood act just as his love shall dictate; and now I have no longer a doubt of its excess, instead of stooping to him, I wait in the certain expectation, of his submission to me."

CHAPTER XI

IN vain, for three long days, did Miss Milner wait impatiently for this submission; not a sign, not a symptom appeared—nay, lord Elmwood had, since the evening of lord Frederick's visit, (which, at the time it happened, seemed to affect him so exceedingly) become just the same man, he was before the circumstance occurred; except, indeed, something less thoughtful, and now and then cheerful; but without the smallest appearance, that his cheerfulness was affected.—Miss Milner was vext; she was alarmed; but was ashamed to confess those humiliating sensations, even to Miss Woodley—she assumed, therefore, the vivacity she had so long assumed, but gave way, when alone, to a still greater degree of melancholy than usual. She no longer applauded her scheme of bringing lord Frederick to the house, and trembled, lest, on some pretence, he should dare to call again. But as these were feelings her pride would not suffer her to disclose to her friend, who would have condoled along with her, their effects were doubly poignant.

Sitting in her dressing-room, one forenoon with Miss Woodley, and burthened with a load of grief, she blushed to acknowledge; while her companion was charged with apprehensions she was as loath to disclose; one of lord Elmwood's valets tapped gently at the door, and delivered a letter to Miss Milner.—By the person who brought it, as well as by the address, she knew it came from lord Elmwood, and laid it down upon her toilet, as if fearful to unfold it.

"What is that?" Said Miss Woodley.

"A letter from my guardian." Replied Miss Milner.

"Good Heaven!" Exclaimed Miss Woodley.

"Nay," returned she, "it is, I have no doubt, to beg my pardon." But her reluctance to open it, plainly evinced she did not think so.

"Do not read it yet." Said Miss Woodley.

"I do not intend." Replied she, trembling extremely.

"Will you dine first?" Said Miss Woodley.

"No—for not knowing its contents, I shall not know how to conduct myself towards him."

Here a silence ensued—during this silence, Miss Milner took up the letter—looked earnestly at the hand-writing on the out side—at the seal—inspected into its folds—and seemed to wish, by some equivocal method, to guess at the contents, without daring to come at the certain knowledge of them.

Curiosity, at length, got the better of her fears; she opened the letter, and scarce able to hold it while she read, read the following words:

"Madam,

"While I considered you only as my Ward, my friendship for you was unbounded—when I looked upon you as a woman formed to grace a fashionable circle, my admiration equalled my friendship—and when fate permitted me to behold you in the tender light of my betrothed wife, my soaring love left those humbler passions at a distance.

"That you have still my friendship, my admiration, and even my love, I will not attempt to deceive either myself or you, by disavowing; but still, with a firm assurance, I declare, Prudence outweighs them all, and I have not, from henceforward, a wish to be regarded by you in any other respect, than as one 'who wishes you well.'—That you ever beheld me in the endearing quality of a destined, and an affectionate husband, (such as I would have proved) my hopes, my vanity, own the deception, and are humiliated—but I entreat you to spare their farther trial, and for a single week, do not insult me with the open preference of another.—In the space of that time, I shall have taken my leave of you *for ever.*

"I shall visit Italy, and some other countries for a few years, till I[1] become once more reconciled to the change of state I am enjoined; a change, I now most fervently wish could be entirely dispensed with.

"The occasion of my remaining in England a week longer, is to settle some necessary affairs, but chiefly that of delivering to a friend, a man of worth and tenderness, all those writings, which

---

1   In the second, third, fourth, and fifth editions, "some other parts of the continent; from whence I propose passing to the West Indies, in order to inspect my possessions there:—nor shall I return to England till after a few years absence; in which time I hope to."

have invested me with the power of my guardianship—he will, the day after my departure (without one upbraiding word), resign them to you in my name; and even your father, could he behold the resignation, would concur in its propriety.

"And now, my dear Miss Milner, let not affected resentment, contempt or levity, oppose that serenity, which, for the week to come, I wish to enjoy.—By complying with this request, give me to believe, that since you have been under my care, you think I have, at least, faithfully discharged some part of my duty.—And wherever I have been inadequate to your wishes, attribute my demerits to some infirmity of mind, rather than to a negligence of your happiness.—Yet, be the cause what it will, since these faults have existed, I acknowledge them, and beg your pardon.

"However, time, and succession of objects, may eradicate more tender sentiments; I am sure *never* to lose the liveliest anxiety for your welfare—and with all that solicitude, which I cannot describe, I entreat for your own sake, for mine—when we shall be far asunder—and for the sake of your dead father's memory, *call upon every important occasion, your serious judgment to direct you.*

"I am, Madam,

"Your sincerest friend,

"Elmwood."

After reading every syllable of this letter, it dropped from Miss Milner's hands; but she uttered not a word.—There was, however, a paleness in her face, a deadness in her eye, and a kind of palsy over her frame, which Miss Woodley, who had seen her in every stage of her uneasiness, never had seen before.

"I do not want to read the letter," said Miss Woodley, "your looks tell me its contents."

"They will then discover to lord Elmwood," replied she, "what I feel; but heaven forbid—that would sink me even lower than I am."

Scarce able to crawl, she rose, and looked in the glass, as if to arrange her features, so as to impose upon him: alas! this was of no avail; a serenity of mind, could, alone, effect what she desired.

"You must endeavour," said Miss Woodley, "to feel that disposition, you wish to make appear."

"I will," replied she, "I will feel a proper pride—and a proper scorn of this treatment."

And so desirous was she to attain the appearance of these sentiments, she made the strongest efforts to calm her thoughts, in order to acquire it.

"I have but a few days to remain with him," she said to herself, "and we part for ever—in those few days, it is not only my duty to obey his commands, or rather comply with his request, but it is also my wish to leave upon his mind, an impression, which may not add to the ill opinion he has formed of me, but, perhaps, serve to diminish it.—If, in every other instance, my conduct has been blameable, he shall, at least in this, acknowledge its merit.—The fate I have drawn upon myself, he shall find I can be resigned to; and he shall be convinced, that the woman, of whose weakness he has had so many fatal proofs, is yet in possession of some fortitude—fortitude to bid him farewell without discovering one affected, or one real pang, though her death should be the immediate consequence."

Thus she resolved, and thus she acted.—The severest judge could not have arraigned her conduct from the day she received lord Elmwood's letter, to the day of his departure.—She had, indeed, involuntary weaknesses, but none with which she did not struggle, and in general her struggles were victorious.

The first time she saw him after the receipt of his letter, was on the evening of the same day—she had a little concert of amateurs in musick, and was, herself, singing and playing when he entered the room; the connoisseurs immediately perceived she lost the tune, but lord Elmwood was no connoisseur in the art, and did not observe it.

They occasionally spoke to each other during the evening, but the subjects were general—and though their manners every time they spoke were perfectly polite, they were not tinctured with the smallest degree of familiarity.—To describe his behaviour exactly, it was the same as his letter, polite, friendly, composed, and resolved.—Some of the company staid supper, which prevented the embarrassment that must unavoidably have arisen, had the family been by themselves.

The next morning each breakfasted in their separate apartments—more company dined with them, and in the evening, and at supper, lord Elmwood was from home.

Thus all passed on as peaceably as he had requested, and Miss Milner had not betrayed one particle of frailty; when, the third day at dinner, some gentlemen of his acquaintance being at table, one of them said,

"And so, my lord, you absolutely set off on Tuesday morning?"

This was Friday.

Sandford and he both replied at the same time, "Yes." And Sandford, but not lord Elmwood, looked at Miss Milner when he spoke.—Her knife and fork gave a sudden spring in her hand, but no other emotion witnessed what she felt.

"Ay, Elmwood," cried another gentleman at table, "you'll bring home, I am afraid, a foreign wife, and that I shan't forgive."

"It is his errand abroad, I make no doubt." Said another visitor.

Before his lordship could return an answer, Sandford cried, "And what objection to a foreigner for a wife? do not crowned heads all marry foreigners? and who happier in the marriage state than some kings?"

Lord Elmwood directed his eyes to the side of the table, opposite to that where Miss Milner sat.

"Nay," (answered one of the guests, who was a country gentleman) "what do you say, ladies—do you think my lord ought to go out of his own nation for a wife?" And he looked at Miss Milner, for the reply.

Miss Woodley, uneasy at her friend's being thus forced to give an opinion upon so delicate a subject, endeavoured to satisfy the gentleman, by answering to the question herself: "Whoever my lord Elmwood marries, Sir," said Miss Woodley, "he, no doubt, will be happy."

"But what say you, young lady?" Asked the gentleman, still keeping his eyes on Miss Milner.

"That whoever his lordship marries, he *deserves* to be happy." Returned she, with the utmost command of her voice and looks; for Miss Woodley, by replying first, had given her time to collect herself.

The colour flew to lord Elmwood's face, as she delivered this short sentence; and Miss Woodley flattered herself, she saw a tear start in his eye.

Miss Milner did not look that way.

In an instant his lordship found means to change the subject, but that of his journey, still employed the conversation; and what horses, servants, and carriage he took with him, was minutely asked, and so accurately answered either by himself or by Mr. Sandford, that Miss Milner, although she had beheld her doom before, till now had received no circumstantial account of it—and as circumstances add to, or diminish all we feel, hearing these things told, encreased the bitterness of their truth.

Soon after dinner, the ladies retired, and from that time, though Miss Milner's behaviour still continued the same, yet her looks and her voice were totally altered—for the world, she could not have looked cheerfully; for the world, she could not have spoken with a sprightly accent; she frequently began in one, but not three words could she utter, before her tones sunk into the flattest dejection.—Not only her colour, but her features became changed; her eyes lost their brilliancy, her lips seemed to hang without the power of motion, her head drooped, and her dress was wholly neglected.—Conscious of this distrest appearance, and conscious of the weakness from whence it arose, it was her desire to hide herself from the only object she could have wished to have charmed.—Accordingly, she sat alone, or with Miss Woodley in her own apartment, as much as was consistent with that civility her guardian had requested, and which forbade her from totally absenting herself.

Miss Woodley felt so acutely the torments of her friend, that had not her reason told her the inflexible mind of lord Elmwood was fixed beyond her power to shake, she had cast herself at his feet, and implored the return of his affection and tenderness as the only means to save his once beloved ward from an untimely grave. But her understanding—her knowledge of his lordship's firm and immoveable temper; and all his grievous provocations—her knowledge of his word, long since given to Sandford, "That if once resolved, he would not recall his resolution."—The certainty of the many plans that had been arranged for his travels, all agreed to convince her, that by any interference, she only exposed Miss Milner's tenderest love and delicacy to a contemptuous rejection.

If the conversation did not every day turn upon the subject of lord Elmwood's departure—a conversation he evidently avoided himself—yet every day some new preparation for his journey, struck the ear or the eye of Miss Milner—and had she beheld a frightful spectre, she could not have shuddered with more horror, than when she unexpectedly passed his large trunks in the hall, nailed and corded, ready to be sent off to meet him at Venice.—At the sight, she flew from the company that happened to be along with her, and stole to the first lonely corner of the house to conceal her tears—she reclined her head upon her hands, and bedewed them with the sudden anguish that had overcome her.—She heard a footstep advancing towards the spot where she hoped to have been concealed; she lifted up her eyes, and beheld his lordship.—Pride was the first emotion his presence inspired—pride, which arose from the humility into which she was plunged.

She instantly stifled her tears, and looked at him earnestly, as if to imply, "What now, my lord?"

He only answered with a bow, which expressed these words alone: "I beg your pardon." And immediately withdrew.

Thus each understood the other's language, without either uttering a word.

The just construction, which she put upon his looks and behaviour upon this occasion, kept up her spirits for some little time; and she blessed heaven, repeatedly, for the singular favour of shewing to her, clearly, by this accident, his negligence of her sorrows, his total indifference.

The next day was the eve of that, on which he was to depart—and the one on which she was to bid adieu to Dorriforth, to her guardian, to lord Elmwood; to all her hopes at once.

The moment she awoke on Monday morning, the recollection, that this was, perhaps, the last day she was ever again to see him, softened all the resentment his yesterday's conduct had given birth to, and forgetting his austerity, and all she once termed, cruelties; she now only remembered his friendship, his anxious tenderness, and his love.—She was impatient to behold him, and promised to herself, for this last day, to neglect no one opportunity of being with him. For that purpose she did not breakfast in her own room, as she had done for several mornings before, but went into the breakfast-room, where all the family generally met.—She was rejoiced on hearing his voice as she opened the door, yet the sound made her tremble so much, she could scarcely totter to the table.

Miss Woodley looked at her as she entered, and was never so much shocked at seeing her; for never had she yet seen her look so ill.—As she approached, she made an inclination of her head to Mrs. Horton, and then to her guardian, as was her custom, when she first saw them in a morning—his lordship looked in her face as he bowed, then turned his eyes upon the fire place, rubbed his forehead, and began talking with Mr. Sandford.

Sandford, during breakfast, by accident, cast his eyes upon Miss Milner; his attention was caught by her deathly countenance, and he looked earnestly.—He then turned to lord Elmwood to see if he was observing her appearance—he was not—and so much were her thoughts engaged on him alone, she did not once perceive Sandford gazing at her.

Mrs. Horton after a little while observed, "It was a beautiful morning."

Lord Elmwood said, "He thought he heard it rain in the night."

Sandford cried, "For his part he slept too well to know." And then (unasked) held a plate with biscuits to Miss Milner—it was the first civility he had ever in his life offered her; she smiled at the whimsicality of the circumstance, but took one in return for his attention.—He looked grave beyond his usual gravity, and yet not with his usual ill temper. She did not eat what she had so politely taken, but laid it down soon after.

Lord Elmwood was the first who rose from breakfast, and did not return to dinner.

At dinner, Mrs. Horton said, "She hoped his lordship would, however, favour them with his company at supper."

To which Sandford replied, "No doubt, for you will hardly any of you see him in the morning; as we shall be off by six, or soon after."

Sandford was not going abroad with lord Elmwood, but was to go with him as far as Dover.

These words of his—"*not see lord Elmwood in the morning*"—(never again to see him after this evening,) were like the knell of death to Miss Milner.—She felt the symptoms of fainting, and eagerly snatched a glass of wine,[1] which the servant was holding to Sandford, (who had called for wine) and drank a part of it.—As she returned the glass to the servant, she began to apologize to Mr. Sandford for her seeming rudeness, but before she could utter what she meant, he said, good-naturedly, "Never mind—you are very welcome—I am glad you took it."—She looked at him to observe, whether he had really spoken kindly, or ironically; but before his countenance could satisfy her, her thoughts were away from that trivial circumstance, and again fixed upon lord Elmwood.

The moments seemed tedious till he came home to supper, and yet, when she reflected for how short a time the rest of the evening would continue, she wished to defer the hour of his return, for months.—At ten o'clock he arrived, and at half after ten the family, without any visitor, met at supper.

Miss Milner had considered, that the period for her to counterfeit appearances, was diminished now to a very short one; and she rigourously enjoined herself not to shrink from that little which remained.—The certain end, that would be so soon put to this painful deception, encouraged her to struggle through it with redoubled zeal; and this was but necessary, as her weakness encreased.—She therefore listened, she talked, and even smiled with the rest of the company, nor did their vivacity seem to arise from a much less compulsive source than her own.

It was past twelve, when lord Elmwood looked at his watch, and rising from his seat, went up to Mrs. Horton, and taking her hand, said, "Till I see you again, madam, I sincerely wish you every happiness."

Miss Milner fixed her eyes upon the table before her.

"My lord," replied Mrs. Horton, "I sincerely wish you health and happiness likewise."

---

1   In the second, third, fourth, and fifth editions, "water."

He then went to Miss Woodley, and taking her hand, repeated much the same, as he had said to Mrs. Horton.

Miss Milner now trembled beyond all power of concealment.

"My lord," replied Miss Woodley, a good deal affected, "I sincerely hope my prayers for your happiness may be heard."

She and Mrs. Horton were both standing as well as his lordship; but Miss Milner kept her seat, till his eye was turned upon her, and he moved slowly towards her; she then rose—and every one who was present attentive to what he would now say, and how she would receive what he said, cast their eyes upon them, and listened with impatience.—They were all disappointed—he did not utter a syllable.—Yet he took her hand, and held it closely between his.—He then bowed most respectfully, and left her.

No, "I wish you well;—I wish you health and happiness." No "Prayers for blessings on her."—Not even the word "farewell," escaped his lips—perhaps, to have attempted any of these, might have choked his utterance.

She had behaved with fortitude the whole evening, and she continued to do so, till the moment he turned away from her.— Her eyes then overflowed with tears, and in the agony of her mind, not knowing what she did, she laid her cold hand upon the person next to her—it happened to be Sandford; but not observing it was him, she grasped his hand with violence—yet he did not snatch it away, nor look at her with his wonted severity.—And thus she stood, silent, and motionless, while his lordship lighted a candle,[1] he took from the side-board, bowed once more to all the company, and retired.

Sandford had still Miss Milner's hand fixed upon his; and when the door was shut after lord Elmwood, he turned his head to look in her face, and turned it with some marks of apprehension for the grief he might find there.—She strove to overcome that grief, and after a heavy sigh, sat down, as if resigned to the fate to which she was decreed.

Instead of following lord Elmwood, as usual, Sandford poured out a glass of wine, and drank it.—A general silence ensued for

---

1   In the second and third editions, "Lord Elmwood"; in the fourth and fifth editions, "Lord Elmwood, now at the door."

near three minutes.—At last turning himself round on his seat, towards Miss Milner, who sat like a statue of despair at his side. "Will you breakfast with us to-morrow?" Said he.

She made no answer.

"We shan't breakfast before half after six," continued he, "I dare say; and if you can rise so early—why do."

"Miss Milner," said Miss Woodley, (for she caught, eagerly, at the hope of her passing this night in less unhappiness than she had foreboded) "pray rise at that hour to breakfast; Mr. Sandford would not invite you, if he thought it would displease his lordship."

"Not I." Replied Sandford, churlishly.

"Then desire her woman to call her." Said Mrs. Horton to Miss Woodley.

"Nay, she will be awake, I have no doubt." Returned her niece.

"No;" replied Miss Milner, "since lord Elmwood has thought proper to take his leave of me, without even speaking a word; by my own design, never will I see him again." And here a flood of tears burst forth, as if her heart burst at the same time.

"Why did not *you* speak to *him*?" cried Sandford—"pray did you bid *him* farewell?—and I don't see why one is not as much to be blamed, in that respect, as the other."

"I was too weak to say, I wished him happy;" cried Miss Milner, "but, heaven is my witness, I do wish him so from my soul."

"And do you imagine, he does not wish you so too?" cried Sandford.—"You should judge him by your own heart; and what you feel for him, imagine he feels for you, my dear."

Though "*my dear*" is a trivial phrase, yet from certain people, and upon certain occasions, it is a phrase of infinite comfort and assurance.—Mr. Sandford seldom said "my dear" to any one; to Miss Milner never; and upon this occasion, and from him, it was an expression most precious.

She turned to him with a look of gratitude; but as she only looked, and did not speak, he rose up, and soon after said, with a friendly tone he had seldom spoken with in her presence, "I sincerely wish you a good night."

As soon as he was gone, Miss Milner exclaimed, "However

my fate may have been precipitated by the unkindness of Mr. Sandford, yet, for that particle of concern he has shown for me this night, I will always be grateful to him."

"Ay," cried Mrs. Horton, "good Mr. Sandford may show his kindness now, without any danger from its consequences.—Now his lordship is going away for ever, he is not afraid of your seeing him once again." And she thought she praised him by this suggestion.

CHAPTER XII

WHEN Miss Milner retired to her bed-chamber, Miss Woodley went with her, nor would leave her the whole night—but in vain did she persuade her to go to rest, she absolutely refused; and declared she would never, from that hour, indulge the smallest repose.—"The part I undertook to perform," cried she, "is over; I will now, for my whole life, appear in my own character, and give a loose to the anguish I endure."

As day light showed itself, "And yet I might see him once again." Said she. "I might see him within these two hours, if I pleased, for Mr. Sandford invited me."

"If you think, my dear Miss Milner," said Miss Woodley, "that a second parting from lord Elmwood, would but give you a second agony, in the name of heaven do not see him any more—but, if you think your mind would be easier, were you to bid each other adieu in a more direct manner than you did last night, let us go down and breakfast with him.—I'll go before, to prepare him for your reception—you shall not unexpectedly surprise him—and I will let him know, it is by Mr. Sandford's invitation you are coming."

She listened with a smile to this proposal, yet objected to the indelicacy of her wishing to see him, after he had taken his leave—but as Miss Woodley, nevertheless, perceived she was inclined to infringe this delicacy, of which she had so proper a sense, she easily persuaded her, it was impossible for the most suspicious person (and lord Elmwood was far from such a character) to suppose, that by paying him a visit at that period of time, could be with the most distant idea of regaining his heart, or of altering one resolution he had taken.

In this opinion, Miss Milner acquiesced, yet she had not the courage to come to the determination she would go.

Day light now no longer peeped, but stared broad upon them.—Miss Milner went to the looking-glass, breathed upon her hands and rubbed them on her eyes; put some powder into her hair; yet said, after all, "I dare not see him again."

"You may do as you please," said Miss Woodley, "but I will. I that have lived for so many years under the same roof with him, and on the most friendly terms, and he going away, perhaps for these ten years, perhaps for ever; I should think it a disrespect not to see him to the last moment of his remaining in the house."

"Then do you go," said Miss Milner, eagerly, "and if he should ask for me, I will gladly come, you know; but if he does not ask for me, I will not—and pray do not deceive me."

Miss Woodley gave her word not to deceive her; and soon after, as they heard the servants pass about the house, and the clock had struck six, Miss Woodley went to the breakfast-room.

She found lord Elmwood there in his travelling dress, standing pensively by the fire place—and, as he did not dream of seeing her, he started when she entered, and with an appearance of alarm said, "Dear Miss Woodley, what's the matter?"—She replied, "Nothing, my lord; but I could not be satisfied without seeing your lordship once again, while I had it in my power."

"I thank you." He returned with a sigh, and the heaviest and most intelligent sigh, she ever heard him condescend to give.— She imagined, also, he looked as if he wished to ask how Miss Milner did, but would not allow himself the indulgence.—She was half inclined to mention her to him, and debating in her mind whether she should or not, Mr. Sandford came into the room; saying as he entered,

"For heaven's sake, my lord, where did you sleep last night?"

"Why do you ask?" Said his lordship.

"Because," replied Sandford, "I went into your bed-chamber but now, and I found your bed made.—You have not slept there to-night."

"I have slept no where;" answered his lordship, "I could not sleep—and having some papers to look over, and to rise early, I thought I might as well not go to bed at all."

Miss Woodley was pleased at the frank manner in which he made this confession, and could not resist the strong impulse to say, "You have done just then, my lord, like Miss Milner, for she has not been in bed the whole night."

Miss Woodley spoke this in a negligent manner, and yet, lord Elmwood echoed back the words with solicitude and tenderness, "Has not Miss Milner been in bed the whole night?"

"If she is up, why does not she come and take some coffee?" Said Sandford, as he began to pour it out.

"If she thought it would be agreeable," returned Miss Woodley, "I dare say she would." And she looked at lord Elmwood while she spoke, though she did not absolutely address him; but he made no reply.

"Agreeable!" returned Sandford, angrily, "Has she then a quarrel with any body here? Or does she suppose any body here bears enmity to *her*?—Is she not in peace and charity?"

"Yes," replied Miss Woodley, "that I am sure she is."

"Then bring her hither," (said he) "directly.—Would she have the wickedness to imagine we are not all friends with her?"

Miss Woodley left the room, and found Miss Milner almost in despair, lest she should hear lord Elmwood's carriage drive off before her friend's return.

"Did he send for me?" were the words she uttered as soon as she saw her.

"Mr. Sandford did, in his presence," returned Miss Woodley, "and you may go with the utmost decorum, or I would not tell you so."

She required no protestations of this, but readily followed her beloved adviser, whose kindness never appeared in half the amiable light as at that moment.

On entering the room, through all the dead white of her present complexion, she blushed to a crimson.—Lord Elmwood rose from his seat, and brought a chair for her to sit down.

Sandford looked at her inquisitively, then sipped his tea, and said, "He never made tea to his own liking."

Miss Milner took a cup, but had scarce strength to hold it.

It seemed but a very short time they were at breakfast, when the carriage, that was to take his lordship away, drove to the door.—Miss Milner started at the sound; so did he; but she had nearly dropped her cup and saucer: on which Sandford took them out of her hand, saying,

"Perhaps you had better rather have coffee?"

Her lips moved, but he could not hear what she said.

A servant came in, and told lord Elmwood, "The carriage was at the door."

He replied, "Very well." But though he had breakfasted, he did not attempt to move.

At last, rising briskly from his seat, as if it was necessary to go in haste, when he did go; he took up his hat, which he had brought with him into the room, and was turning to Miss Woodley to take his leave, when Sandford cried, "My lord, you are in a great hurry."—And then, as if he wished to give poor Miss Milner every moment he could, added, (looking about) "I don't know where I have laid my gloves."

His lordship, after repeating to Miss Woodley his last night's farewell, now went up to Miss Milner, and taking one of her hands, again held it between his, but still without speaking— while she, unable to suppress her tears as heretofore, suffered them to fall in torrents.

"What is all this?" Cried Sandford, going up to them in anger.

They neither of them replied, or changed their situation.

"Separate this moment."—Cried Sandford—"Or resolve never to be separated but by death."

The commanding, and awful manner in which he spoke this sentence, made them both turn to him in amazement! and almost petrified with the sensation his words had caused.

He left them for a moment, and going to a small bookcase in one corner of the room, took out of it a book, and returning with it in his hand, said,

"Lord Elmwood, do you love this woman?"

"More than my life." Replied his lordship, with the most heartfelt accents.

He then turned to Miss Milner—"Can you say the same by him?"

She spread her hands over her eyes, and cried, "Oh, heavens!"

"I believe you *can* say so;" returned Sandford, "and in the name of God, and your own happiness, since this is the case, let me put it out of your power to part."

Lord Elmwood gazed at him with wonder! and yet, as if enraptured by the sudden appearance of a change in his prospects.

She, sighed with a trembling kind of ecstasy; while Sandford, with all the pomp and dignity of a clergyman in his official character, delivered these words:

"My lord, while I thought my counsel might save you from the worst of misfortunes, conjugal strife, I importuned you hourly; and set forth your danger in the light it appeared to me.—But though old, and a priest, I can submit to think I have been in an error; and now I firmly believe, it is for the welfare of you both, to become man and wife.—My lord, take this woman's marriage vows; you can ask no fairer promises of her reform; she can give you none half so sacred, half so binding; and I see by her looks she will mean to keep them.—And my dear," continued he, addressing himself to her, "act but under the dominion of those vows, to a husband of sense and virtue, like him, and you will be all that I, himself, or even heaven can desire.—Now then, lord Elmwood, this moment give her up for ever; or this moment constrain her by such ties from offending you, she shall not *dare* to violate."

Lord Elmwood struck his forehead in doubt and agitation; but still holding her hand, he cried, "I cannot part from her."— Then feeling this reply was equivocal, he fell upon his knees, and cried, "Will you pardon my hesitation?—and will you, in marriage, show me that tender love you have not shown me yet?—will you, in possessing all my affections, bear with all my infirmities?"

She raised him from her feet, and by the expression of her face, the tears with which she bathed his hands, gave him confidence.

He turned to Sandford—then placing her by his own side, as the form of matrimony requires, gave this as a sign for Sandford to begin the ceremony.—On which, he opened his book, and— married them.

While with a countenance—manner—and voice, so serious, and so fervent, did he perform these rites, that the idea of jest, or even of lightness, was far from the mind of every one present.

Miss Milner, covered with shame, sunk on the bosom of Miss Woodley.

When the ring was wanting, lord Elmwood supplied it with one from his own hand, but throughout all the rest of the ceremony, appeared lost in zealous devotion to heaven.—Yet, no sooner was it finished; than his thoughts seemed to descend to this world.—He embraced his bride with all the transport of the fondest, happiest bridegroom, and in raptures called her by the endearing name of, "wife."

"But still, my lord," cried Sandford, "you are only married by your own church and conscience, not by your wife's; or by the law of the land; and let me advise you not to defer that marriage long, lest in the time you disagree, and she yet refuse to become your legal spouse."

"I think there is danger," returned his lordship, "and therefore our second marriage must take place to-morrow."[1]

To this the ladies objected, and it was left to Sandford to fix their second wedding-day, as he had done their first.—He, after consideration, gave four days interval.

Miss Woodley then recollected (for every one else had forgot it) that the carriage was still at the door to convey lord Elmwood abroad.—It was of course dismissed—and one of those great incidents of delight Miss Milner that morning tasted, was to look out of the window, and see this very carriage drive from the door unoccupied.

Never was there a more rapid change from despair to happiness—to happiness most supreme—than was that, which Miss Milner, and lord Elmwood experienced within one single hour.

The few days that intervened between this and their legal marriage, were passed in the delightful care of preparing for that happy day—yet, with all its delights inferior to the first; when every joy was doubled by the expected sorrow.

Nevertheless, on that first wedding-day, that joyful day, which restored her lost lover to her hopes again; even on that *very* day,

---

1 Inchbald herself was married twice—first in a Catholic ceremony and then (the next day) in a Church of England ceremony.

after the sacred ceremony was over, Miss Milner—(with all the fears, the tremors, the superstition of her sex)—felt an excruciating shock; when, looking on the ring lord Elmwood had put upon her finger, in haste, when he married her, she perceived it was a—MOURNING RING.

END OF THE SECOND VOLUME

— VOLUME III. —

CHAPTER I

THROUGHOUT life, there cannot happen an event to arrest the reflection of a thoughtful mind more powerfully, or to leave so lasting an impression, as that of returning to a place after a few years absence, and observing an entire alteration in respect to all the persons who once formed the neighbourhood—To find some, who but a few years before were left in the bloom of youth and health, dead—to find children left at school, married, with children of their own—some persons who were in riches, reduced to poverty—others who were in poverty, become rich—those, once renowned for virtue, now detested for their vice—roving husbands, grown constant—constant ones, become rovers—the firmest friends, changed to the most implacable enemies—beauty faded.—In a word, every change to demonstrate "All is transitory on this side of the grave."[1]

Actuated by a wish, that the reflective reader may experience the sensation, which an attention to circumstances such as these, must cause; he is desired to imagine seventeen years elapsed, since he has seen or heard of any of those persons, who in the foregoing volumes have been introduced to his acquaintance—and now, supposing himself at the period of those seventeen years, follow the sequel of their history.

To begin with the first female object of this story.—The beautiful, the beloved Miss Milner—she is no longer beautiful—no longer beloved—no longer—tremble while you read it!—no longer—virtuous.

---

1   Compare to chapter 32, "The Conclusion," of Oliver Goldsmith's *The Vicar of Wakefield* (1766): "I had nothing now on this side of the grave to wish for, all my cares were over, my pleasure was unspeakable." Also compare to *Ecclesiastes*, 3:19: "Therefore the death of man, and of beasts is one, and the condition of them both is equal: as man dieth, so they also die: all things breathe alike, and man hath nothing more than beast: all things are subject to vanity."

Dorriforth, the pious, the good, the tender Dorriforth, is become a hard-hearted tyrant. The compassionate, the feeling, the just Lord Elmwood, an example of implacable rigour and injustice.

Miss Woodley is grown old, but less with years than grief. The child Rushbrook is become a man, and the apparent heir of Lord Elmwood's fortune;[1] while his own daughter, his only child by his once adored Miss Milner, he refuses ever to see again, in vengeance to her mother's crimes.

The least wonderful change, is the death of Mrs. Horton. Except Sandford, who remains, much the same as heretofore.

We left Lady Elmwood in the last volume at the summit of human happiness; a loving and beloved bride.—We begin this volume, and find her upon her death bed.

At thirty-five, her "Course was run"—a course full of perils, of hopes, of fears, of joys, and at the end of sorrows; all exquisite of their kind, for exquisite were the feelings of her susceptible heart.

At the commencement of this story, her father is described in the last moments of his life, with all his cares fixed upon her, his only child—how vain these cares! how vain every precaution that was taken for her welfare! She knows, she reflects upon this; and yet, torn by that instinctive power which a parent feels, Lady Elmwood on her dying day has no worldly thought, but that of the future happiness of *her* only child.—To every other prospect before her, "Thy will be done"[2] is her continual exclamation; but where the misery of her daughter presents itself, the dying penitent would there, combat the will of heaven.

To state the progression by which vice gains a predominance in the heart, may be a useful lesson; but it is one so little to the satisfaction of most readers, that it is not meant to be related here, all the degrees of frailty by which Lady Elmwood fell; but instead

---

1   Uncontestable, legal heir.

2   Compare to Matthew 6:10: "Thy kingdom come. Thy will be done on earth as it is in heaven"; Luke 11:2, "And he said to them: When you pray, say: Father, hallowed be thy name. Thy kingdom come"; Matthew 26:42: "Again the second time, he went and prayed, saying: My Father, if this chalice may not pass away, but I must drink it, thy will be done."

of picturing every occasion of her fall, come briefly to the events that followed.

There are, nevertheless, some articles under the former class, which ought not to be entirely omitted.

Lord Elmwood, after four years passed in the most perfect enjoyment of happiness, the marriage state could give; after seeing himself the father of a beautiful daughter, whom he loved with a tenderness nearly equal to his love for her mother, Lord Elmwood was then under the indispensable necessity of leaving them both for a time, in order to save from the depredation of his steward, a very large estate in the West Indies. His voyage was tedious; his residence there, from various accidents, prolonged from time to time, till near three years had at length passed away.[1]—Lady Elmwood, at first only unhappy, became at last provoked; and giving way to that impatient, irritable disposition she had so seldom governed, resolved, in spite of his injunctions, to divert the melancholy hours his absence caused, by mixing in the gaiest circles of London. His Lordship at this time, and for many months before, had been detained abroad by a severe and dangerous illness, which a too cautious fear of her uneasiness had prompted him to conceal; and she received his frequent apologies for not returning, with a suspicion and resentment they were calculated, but not intended, to inspire.

To violent anger, succeeded a degree of indifference still more fatal—Lady Elmwood's heart was never formed for such a state— there, where all the passions tumultuous strove by turns, one among them soon found the means to occupy all vacancies—that one was love.[2] The dear object of her fondest, truest, affections was away; and those affections painted the time so irksome that

---

1 The patriarch's extended absence and subsequent return to find an unexpectedly changed situation occurs in several later novels, including Jane Austen's *Mansfield Park* (1814), in which the father, Sir Thomas, returns from an extended stay in the West Indies to discover his children acting in a private production of August Von Kotzebue's *Lovers' Vows* (adapted by Inchbald for the English stage). Also, in Mary Elizabeth Braddon's *Lady Audley's Secret* (1862), a husband returns from a three and a half year absence in Australia to discover that his wife has married another man and taken on another identity.

2 In the second, third, fourth, and fifth editions, "a passion, commencing innocently, but terminating in guilt."

was past; so wearisome that, which was still to come; she flew from the present tedious solitude, to the dangerous society of one, whose every care to charm her,[1] could not repay her for a moment's loss of him, whose absence he supplied.—Or if the delirium gave her a moment's recompense, what were her sufferings and remorse, when she was awakened from the fleeting joy by the unexpected arrival of her husband?—How happy, how transporting, had been that arrival a few months before!—As it had then been felicitous, it was now bitter—this word, however, weakly expresses—Language affords none, to describe Lady Elmwood's sensations on being told her Lord was arrived, and that necessity only had so long delayed his return.

Guilty, but not hardened in her guilt, her pangs, her shame were the more excessive. She fled the place at his approach; fled his house, never again to return to a habitation where he was the master.—She did not, however, escape with her paramour, but eloped to shelter herself in the most dreary retreat; where she partook of no one comfort from society, or from life, but the still unremitting friendship of Miss Woodley.—Even her infant daughter she left behind, nor would allow herself the consolation of her innocent, but reproachful smiles—she left her in her father's house that she might be under his protection; parted with her, as she thought for ever, with all the agonies that mothers part from their infant children: and yet even a mother scarcely can conceive how much more sharp those agonies were, on beholding the child sent after her, as the perpetual outcast of its father.

Lord Elmwood's love to his lady had been extravagant—the effect of his hate was extravagant likewise. Beholding himself separated from her by a barrier never to be removed, he vowed in the deep torments of his revenge, not to be reminded of her by one individual object; much less by one so nearly allied to her as her child. To bestow upon that[2] his affections, would be, he imagined, still in some sort, to divide them with the mother.— Firm in his resolution, the beautiful Matilda was, at the age of six

---

1   In the second and third editions, "whose mind and heart, depraved by fashionable vices"; in the fourth and fifth editions, "whose mind, depraved by fashionable vices."

2   In the second, third, fourth, and fifth editions, "bestow upon that child."

years, sent out of her father's house, and received by her mother with the tenderness, but with the anguish, of those parents, who behold their offspring visited with the punishment due only to their own offences.

During this transaction, which was performed by his Lordship's agents at his command, he himself was engaged in an affair of still weightier importance—that of life or death:—he determined upon his own death, or the death of the man who had wounded his honour and his happiness. A duel with his old antagonist was the result of this determination; nor was the Duke of Avon (before the decease of his father and eldest brother, Lord Frederick Lawnly) backward to render all the satisfaction that was required.—For it was no other than he, whose love for Lady Elmwood had still subsisted, and whose art and industry left no means unessayed to perfect his designs;—No other than he, (who, next to Lord Elmwood, was ever of all her lovers most prevalent in her heart,) to whom Lady Elmwood yielded her own and her husband's future peace, and gave to his vanity a prouder triumph, than if she had never given her hand in preference to another. This triumph however was but short—a month only, after the return of Lord Elmwood, his Grace was called upon to answer for his conduct, and was left upon the spot where they met, so maimed, and defaced with scars, as never again to endanger the honour of a husband. As Lord Elmwood was inexorable to all accommodation; their engagement lasted for some space of time; nor any thing but the steadfast assurance his opponent was slain, could at last have torn his Lordship from the field, though he himself was mortally wounded.

Yet even during that period of his danger, while for days he laid in the continual expectation of his own death, not all the entreaties of his dearest, most intimate, and most respected friends could prevail upon him to pronounce forgiveness to his wife, or suffer them to bring his daughter to him for his last blessing.

Lady Elmwood, who was made acquainted with the minutest circumstance as it passed, appeared to wait the news of her Lord's decease with patience; but upon her brow, and in every lineament of her face it was marked, his death was an event she would not for a day survive—and she had left her child an orphan, to have followed Lord Elmwood to the grave.—She was prevented the trial; he recovered; and from the ample and distinguished vengeance he had obtained upon the irresistible person of the Duke, in a short time seemed to regain his usual tranquillity.

He recovered, while Lady Elmwood fell sick and lingered—possessed of youth and a good constitution, she lingered till ten years decline, brought her to that period, with which the reader is now going to be presented.

CHAPTER II

In a lonely country on the borders of Scotland, a single house by the side of a dreary heath, was the residence of the once gay, volatile Miss Milner—In a large gloomy apartment of this solitary habitation (the windows of which scarce rendered the light accessible) was laid upon her death-bed, the once lovely Lady Elmwood—pale, half suffocated with the loss of breath; yet her senses perfectly clear and collected, which served but to sharpen the anguish of the dying.

In one corner of the room, by the side of an old-fashioned stool, kneels Miss Woodley, praying most devoutly for her still beloved friend, but in vain endeavouring to pray composedly—floods of tears pour down her furrowed cheeks, and frequent sobs of sorrow break through each pious ejaculation.

Close by her mother's side, one hand supporting her head, the other wiping from her face the damp dew of death, behold Lady Elmwood's daughter—Lord Elmwood's daughter too—yet he far away, negligent of what either suffers.—Lady Elmwood turns to her often and attempts an embrace, but her feeble arms forbid, and they fall motionless.—The daughter perceiving those ineffectual efforts, has her whole face convulsed with sorrow; kisses her mother; holds her to her bosom; and hangs upon her neck, as if she wished to cling there, and the grave not to part them.

On the other side the bed sits Sandford—his hair grown white—his face wrinkled with age—his heart the same as ever—The reprover, the enemy of the vain, idle, and wicked; but the friend, the comforter of the forlorn and miserable.

Upon those features where sarcasm, reproach, and anger dwelt to threaten and alarm the sinner; mildness, tenderness, and pity beamed, to support and console the penitent. Compassion changed his language, and softened all those harsh tones that used to denounce resentment.

"In the name of God," said he to Lady Elmwood, "that God who suffered for you, and, suffering, knew and pitied all our weaknesses—By him, who has given his word to *take compassion on the sinner's tears*, I bid you hope for mercy.—By that innocence in which you once lived, be comforted—By the sorrows you have known since your degradation, hope, in some degree, to have atoned—By that sincerity which shone upon your youthful face when I joined your hands; those thousand virtues you have at times given proof of, you were not born to die *the death of the wicked*."[1]

As he spoke these words of consolation, her trembling hand clasped his—her dying eyes darted a ray of brightness—but her failing voice endeavoured, in vain, to articulate.—At length, her eyes fixing upon her daughter as their last dear object, she was just understood to utter the word "Father."

"I understand you," replied Sandford, "and by all that influence I ever had over him, by my prayers, my tears," (and they flowed at the word) "I will implore him to own his child."

She could now only smile, in thanks.

"And if I should fail," continued he, "yet while I live, she shall not want a friend or protector—all an old man like me can answer for"—here his tears interrupted him.

Lady Elmwood was sufficiently sensible of his words and their import, to make a sign as if she wished to embrace him; but finding her life leaving her fast, she reserved this last token of love for her daughter—With a struggle she lifted herself from her pillow, clung to her child—and died in her arms.

---

1 Ezekiel 33:11: "Say to them: As I live, saith the Lord God, I desire not the death of the wicked, but that the wicked turn from his way, and live. Turn ye, turn ye from your evil ways: and why will you die, O house of Israel?"

CHAPTER III

LORD Elmwood was by nature, and more from education, of a serious, thinking, and philosophic turn of mind. His religious studies had completely taught him to consider this world but as a passage to another; to enjoy with gratitude what Heaven in its bounty should bestow, and to bear with submission, all which in its vengeance it might inflict—In a greater degree than most people he practised this doctrine; and as soon as the first shock he received from Lady Elmwood's conduct was abated, an entire calmness and resignation ensued; but still of that sensible and feeling kind, which could never force him to forget the happiness he had lost; and it was this sensibility, which urged him to fly from its more keen recollection as much as possible—this he alledged as the reason he would never suffer Lady Elmwood, or even her child, to be named in his hearing. But this injunction (which all his friends, and even the servants in the house who attended his person, had received) was, by many people, suspected rather to proceed from his resentment, than his tenderness; nor did he himself deny, that resentment mingled with his prudence; for prudence he called it not to remind himself of happiness he could never taste again, and of ingratitude that might impel him to hatred; and prudence he called it, not to form another attachment near to his heart; more especially so near as a parent's, which might a second time expose him to all the torments of ingratitude, from one whom he affectionately loved.

Upon these principles he formed the unshaken resolution, never to acknowledge Lady Matilda as his child—or acknowledging her as such—never to see, hear of, or take one concern whatever in her fate and fortune. The death of her mother appeared a favourable time, had he been so inclined, to have recalled this declaration which he had solemnly and repeatedly made—she was now destitute of the protection of her other parent, and it became his duty, at least to provide her a guardian, if he did not choose to take that tender title upon himself.—But to mention either the mother or child to Lord Elmwood was an equal offence, and prohibited in the strongest terms to all his friends and household: and as he was an excellent good master, a sincere friend, and a most generous patron, not one of his acquaintance or dependants, were hardy enough to draw upon themselves his certain displeasure, which was violent in the extreme, by even the official intelligence of Lady Elmwood's death.

Sandford himself, intimidated through age, or by the austere, and even morose, manners Lord Elmwood had of late years adopted; Sandford wished, if possible, some other would undertake the dangerous task of recalling to his Lordship's memory, there ever was such a person as his wife. He advised Miss Woodley to indite a proper letter to him on the subject; but she reminded him, such a step was still more perilous in her, than any other person, as she was the most destitute being on earth, without the benevolence of Lord Elmwood. The death of her aunt, Mrs. Horton, had left her sole reliance on Lady Elmwood; and now her death, had left her totally dependant upon the earl—for her Ladyship, long before her decease, had declared it was not her intention, to leave a single sentence behind her in the form of a will—She had no will, she said, but what she would wholly submit to Lord Elmwood's; and, if it were even his will, her child should live in poverty, as well as banishment, it should be so.—But, perhaps, in this implicit submission to his Lordship, there was a distant hope that the necessitous situation of his daughter might plead more forcibly than his parental love; and that knowing her abandoned of every support but through himself, that idea might form some little tie between them; and be at least a token of the relationship.

But as Lady Elmwood anxiously wished this principle upon which she acted, should be concealed from his Lordship's suspicion, she included her friend, Miss Woodley, in the same fate; and thus, the only persons dear to her, she left, but at Lord Elmwood's pleasure, to be preserved from perishing in want.—Her child was too young to advise her on this subject, her friend too disinterested; and at this moment they were both without the smallest means of support, except through the justice or compassion of his Lordship.—Sandford had, indeed, promised his protection to the daughter; but his liberality had no other source than from his patron, with whom he still lived as usual, except during the winter when his Lordship resided in town, he then mostly stole a visit to Lady Elmwood—On this last visit, he staid to see her buried.

After some mature deliberations, Sandford was now preparing to go to Lord Elmwood at his house in town, and there to deliver himself the news that must sooner or later be told; and he meant also to venture, at the same time, to keep the promise he had made to his dying Lady—but the news reached Lord Elmwood before Sandford arrived; it was announced in the public papers, and by that means came first to his knowledge.

He was breakfasting by himself, when the newspaper that first gave the intelligence of Lady Elmwood's death, was laid before him—the paragraph contained these words:

On Wednesday last died, at Dring Park, a village in Northumberland, the right honourable Countess Elmwood—This lady, who has not been heard of for many years in the fashionable world, was a rich heiress, and of extreme beauty; but although she received overtures from many men of the first rank, she preferred her guardian, the present Lord Elmwood (then the humble Mr. Dorriforth) to them all—and it is said, they enjoyed an uncommon share of felicity, till his Lordship going abroad, and remaining there some time, the consequences (to a most captivating young woman left without a protector) were such, as to cause a separation on his return.—Her Ladyship has left one child, a daughter, about fifteen.

Lord Elmwood had so much feeling upon reading this, as to lay down the paper, and not take it up again for several minutes—nor did he taste his chocolate during this interval, but leaned his elbow on the table and rested his head upon his hand.—He then rose up—walked two or three times across the room—sat down again—took up the paper—and read as usual.—Nor let the vociferous mourner, or the perpetual weeper, here complain of his want of sensibility—but let them remember Lord Elmwood was a man—a man of understanding—of courage—of fortitude—with all, a man of the nicest feelings—and who shall say, but that at the time he leaned his head upon his hand, and rose to walk away the sense of what he felt, he might not feel as much as Lady Elmwood did in her last moments.

Be this as it may, his Lordship's susceptibility on the occasion was not suspected by any one—he passed that day the same as usual; the next day too, and the day after.—On the morning of the fourth day, he sent for his steward to his study, and after talking of other business, said to him,

"Is it true that Lady Elmwood is dead?"

"It is, my Lord." replied the man.

His Lordship looked unusually grave, and at this reply, fetched an involuntary sigh.

"Mr. Sandford, my lord," continued the steward, "sent me word of the news, but left it to my own discretion, whether I made your Lordship acquainted with it or not."

"Where is Sandford?" asked Lord Elmwood.

"He was with my Lady." replied the steward.

"When she died?" asked his Lordship.

"Yes, my Lord."

"I am glad of it—he will see every thing she desired done.— Sandford is a good man, and would be a friend to every body."

"He is a very good man indeed, my Lord."

There was now a silence.—Mr. Giffard then bowing, said, "Has your Lordship any farther commands?"

"Write to Sandford," said Lord Elmwood, hesitating as he spoke, "and tell him to have every thing performed as she desired.—And whoever she may have selected for the guardian of her child, has my consent to act as such.—Nor in one instance, where I myself am not concerned, will I contradict her will."— The tears rushed to his eyes as he said this, and caused them to start in the steward's—observing which, he sternly resumed,

"Do not suppose from this conversation, that any of those resolutions I have long since taken are, or will be, changed—they are the same; and shall continue the same:—and your interdiction, Sir, (as well as every other person's) remains just the same as formerly; never to mention this subject to me in future."[1]

---

1. In the second, third, fourth, and fifth editions, "'continue to be inflexible.' 'I understand you my lord,' replied Mr Giffard, 'your express orders, to me, as well as to every other person, remain just the same as formerly, never to mention this subject to you again.' 'They do, sir.'"

"My Lord, I always obeyed you," replied Mr. Giffard, "and hope I always shall."

"I hope so too." replied his Lordship, in a threatening accent—"Write to Sandford," continued he, "to let him know my pleasure, and that is all you have to do."

The steward bowed and withdrew.

But before his letter arrived to Sandford, Sandford arrived in town; and Mr. Giffard related to him word for word what had passed between him and his Lord.—Upon every occasion, and upon every topic, except that of Lady Elmwood and her child, Sandford was just as free with Lord Elmwood as he had ever been; and as usual (after his interview with the steward) went into his Lordship's apartment without any previous notice. His Lordship shaked him by the hand as upon all other meetings; and yet, whether his fears suggested it or not, Sandford thought he appeared more cool and reserved with him than common.

During the whole day, the slightest mention of Lady Elmwood, or of her child, was cautiously avoided—and not till the evening (after Sandford had rung for his candle to retire to rest, it was brought, and he had wished his Lordship good night) did he dare to mention the subject.—He then, after taking leave, and going to the door—turned back and said, "My Lord,"—

It was easy to guess on what he was preparing to speak—his voice failed, the tears began to trickle down his cheeks, he took out his handkerchief, and could proceed no farther.

"I thought," said Lord Elmwood, angrily, "I thought I had given my orders upon this subject—did not my steward write them to you?"

"He did, my Lord," said Sandford, humbly, "but I was set out before they arrived."

"Has he not *told* you my mind then?" cried his Lordship, more angrily still.

"He has;" replied Sandford,—"But"—

"But what, Sir?"—cried Lord Elmwood.

"Your Lordship," continued Sandford, "was mistaken in supposing Lady Elmwood left a will; she left none."

"No will? no will at all?"—Said his Lordship, surprised.

"No, my Lord," answered Sandford, "she wished every thing to be as you willed."

"She left me all the trouble, then, you mean?"

"No great trouble, Sir; for except two persons, her Ladyship has not left any one else to hope for your protection."

"And who are those two?" cried he hastily.

"One, my Lord, I need not name—the other is Miss Woodley."

There was a delicacy and an humility, in the manner in which Sandford delivered this reply, that Lord Elmwood could *not* resent, and he only returned,

"Miss Woodley, is she yet living?"

"She is—I left her at the house I came from."

"Well, then," answered his Lordship, "you must see that my steward provides for those two persons.—That care I leave to you—and should there be any complaints, on you they fall."

Sandford bowed and was going.

"And now," resumed his Lordship, in a stern and exalted voice, "let me *never* hear again on this subject.—You have full power to act in regard to the persons you have mentioned; and upon you their situation, their care, their whole management depend—but be sure, you never let them be named before me, from this moment."

"Then," said Sandford, "as this must be the last time they are mentioned, I must now take the opportunity to disburthen my mind of a charge"—

"What charge?"—cried his Lordship, morosely interrupting him.

"Though Lady Elmwood, my Lord, left no will behind, she left a request."

"Request"—said his Lordship, starting—"If it is for me to see her daughter, I tell you now before you ask, I will not grant it—for by heaven (and he spoke and looked most solemnly) though I have no resentment to the innocent child, and wish her happy, yet I will never see her.—Never, for her mother's sake, suffer my heart to be again softened by an object I might doat on.—Therefore, Sir, if that is the request, it is already answered; my will is fixed."

"The request, my Lord," replied Sandford, (taking out a pocket book from whence he drew several papers) "is contained in this letter; nor do I rightly know what its contents are."—And he held it out to him.

"Is it Lady Elmwood's writing?" cried his Lordship, extremely discomposed.

"It is, my Lord—She called for ink and paper and wrote it a few days before she died, and enjoined me to deliver it to you, with my own hands."

"I refuse to read it."—cried he, putting it from him—and trembling while he did so.

"She desired me," said Sandford, (still presenting the letter) "to conjure you to read it, *for her father's sake.*"

Lord Elmwood took it instantly.—But as soon as it was in his hand, he seemed distressed to know what he should do with it—in what place, to go to read it—or how fortify himself against its contents.—He appeared ashamed too, that he had been so far prevailed upon, and said, by way of excuse,

"For Mr. Milner's sake I would do much—nay, any thing, but that to which, I have just now sworn never to consent.—For his sake I have borne a great deal—for his sake alone, his daughter died my wife.—You know, no other motive than respect for him, prevented my divorcing her.—Pray (and he hesitated) was she buried with him?"

"No, my Lord—she expressed no such desire; and as that was the case, I did not think it necessary to carry the corpse so far."

At the word corpse, Lord Elmwood shrunk, and looked shocked beyond measure—but recovering himself, said, "I am sorry for it;—for he loved *her* sincerely, if she did not love him—and I wish they had been buried together."

"It is not then too late," said Sandford, and was going on—but his Lordship interrupted him.

"No, no—we will have no disturbing of the dead."

"Read her letter then," said Sandford, "and bid her rest in peace."

"If it is in my power," returned his Lordship, "to grant what she asks I will—but if her demand is what I apprehend, I cannot, I will not, bid her rest by complying—You know my resolution, and my disposition, and take care how you provoke me.—You may do an injury to the very person you are seeking to befriend—the very maintenance I mean to allow her daughter I can withdraw."

Poor Sandford, all alarm at this menace, replied with energy, "My Lord, unless you begin the subject, I never will presume to mention it again."

"I take you at your word,"—returned his Lordship, "and in consequence of that, and that alone, we are friends.—Good night Sir."

Sandford bowed with all humility, and they went to their separate bedchambers.

CHAPTER IV

AFTER Lord Elmwood had retired into his chamber, it was some time before he read the letter Sandford had given him. He first walked backwards and forwards in the room—he then began to take off some part of his dress, but did it slowly. At length he dismissed his valet, and sitting down, took the letter from his pocket.—He looked at the seal, but not at the direction; for he seemed to dread to see Lady Elmwood's hand writing.—He then laid it on the table, and began again to undress. He did not proceed, but taking up the letter quickly, (with a kind of effort in making the resolution) broke it open. These were its contents:

"My Lord,

"Who writes this letter I well know—I well know also to whom it is addressed—I feel with the most powerful force both our situations;—nor should I dare to offer you even this humble petition, but that at the time you receive it, there will be no such person as I am in existance.

"For myself, then, all concern will be over—but there is a care that pursues me to the grave, and threatens my want of repose even there.

"I leave a child—I will not call her mine, that has undone her—I will not call her yours, that will be of no avail.—I present her before you as the granddaughter of Mr. Milner.—Oh! do not refuse an assylum even in your own house, to the destitute offspring of your friend; the last, and only remaining branch of his family.

"Receive her into your household, be her condition there ever so abject.—I cannot write distinctly what I would—my senses are not impaired, but the powers of expression are.—The unfortunate child in the scripture (a lesson I have studied)[1] his complaint, has made this wish cling so fast to my heart, that without the distant hope of its being fulfilled, death would have more terrors than my weak mind could support.

"I will go to my father; how many servants live in my father's house, and are fed with plenty, while I starve in a foreign land?"[2]

"I do not ask a parent's festive rejoicing at her approach—I do not even ask her father to behold her;—but let her live under his protection.—For her grandfather's sake do not refuse this—to the child of his child whom he trusted to your care, do not refuse it.

"Be her host; I remit the tie of being her parent.—Never see her—but let her sometimes live under the same roof with you.

"It is Miss Milner your ward, to whom you never refused a request, suplicates you—not now for your nephew Rushbrook, but for one so much more dear, that a denial—she dares not suffer her thoughts to glance that way—She will hope—and in that hope, bids you farewell, with all the love she ever bore you.

"Farewell Lord Elmwood[3]—and before you throw this letter from you with contempt or anger, cast your imagination into the grave where I am lying.—Reflect upon all the days of my past life—the anxious moments I have known, and what has been their end.—Behold *me*, also—in my altered face there is no anxiety—no joy or sorrow—all is over.—My whole frame is motionless—my heart beats no more.—Look at my horrid habitation, too,—and ask yourself—whether I am an object of resentment?"

---

1 In the second, third, fourth, and fifth editions, "The complaint of the unfortunate child in the scriptures (a lesson I have studied)."

2 Compare to Luke: 15, 17, 19: "And returning to himself, he said: How many hired servants in my father's house abound with bread, and I here perish with hunger! I will arise and will go to my father and say to him: Father, I have sinned against heaven and before thee. I am not worthy to be called thy son: make me as one of thy hired servants."

3 In the second, third, fourth, and fifth editions, "Farewell Dorriforth—farewell Lord Elmwood."

While Lord Elmwood read this letter, it trembled in his hand: he once or twice wiped the tears from his eyes as he read, and once laid the letter down for a few minutes. At its conclusion the tears flowed fast down his face; but he seemed both ashamed and angry they did, and was going to throw the paper upon the fire; he however suddenly checked his hand, and putting it hastily into his pocket, went to bed.

CHAPTER V

THE next morning, when Lord Elmwood and Sandford met at breakfast, Sandford was pale with fear for the success of Lady Elmwood's letter—his Lordship was pale too, but there was beside upon his face something which evidently marked he was displeased—Sandford observed it, and was all humbleness, both in his words and looks, in order to soften him.

As soon as the breakfast was removed, his Lordship drew Lady Elmwood's letter from his pocket, and holding it towards Sandford, said,

"That may be of more value to you, than it is to me, therefore I give it you."

Sandford called up a look of surprise, as if he did not know the letter again.

"'Tis Lady Elmwood's letter," said his Lordship, "and I give it to you for two reasons."

Sandford took it, and putting it up, asked fearfully "What those two reasons were?"

"First," said Lord Elmwood, "because I think it is a relick you may like to preserve—my second reason is, that you may show it to her daughter, and let her know why, and on what conditions I grant her mother's request."

"You do then grant it?" cried Sandford joyfully; "I thank you—you are kind—you are considerate."

"Be not too hasty in your gratitude," returned his Lordship, "you may have cause to recall it."

"I know what you have said," replied Sandford, "You have said you grant Lady Elmwood's request—you cannot recall these words, nor I my gratitude."

"Do you know what her request is?" said Lord Elmwood.

"Not exactly, my Lord—I told you before, I did not; but it is no doubt something in favour of her child."

"I think not." replied his Lordship, "Such as it is, however, I grant it.—But in the strictest sense of the word—no farther;—and one neglect of my commands, releases my promise totally."

"We will take care, Sir, not to disobey them."

"Then listen to what they are—and to you I give the charge of delivering them again.—Lady Elmwood has petitioned me in the name of her father, (a name I reverence) to give his grandchild the sanction of my protection.—In the litteral sense, to suffer her to reside occasionally at one of my seats; dispensing at the same time with my ever seeing her."

"And you will comply?"

"I will, till she encroaches on this concession, and dare to ask for a greater.—I will, while she avoids my sight, or the giving me any remembrance of her.—But whether[1] by design or by accident, I ever see or hear from her; that moment my compliance to her mother's supplication ceases, and I abandon her once more."

Sandford sighed.—His Lordship continued.

"I am glad her request stopped where it did.—I would rather comply with her desires than not; and I rejoice they are such as I can grant with ease and honour to myself. I am seldom now at Elmwood house; let her daughter go there;—the few weeks or months I am down in the summer she may easily in that extensive house avoid me—while she does, she lives in security—when she does not, you know my resolution."

Sandford bowed—his Lordship resumed.

"Nor can it be a hardship to obey this command—she cannot lament the separation from a parent whom she never knew—" Sandford was going eagerly to prove the error of that assertion, but his Lordship prevented him saying, "In a word—without farther argument—if she obeys me in this, I certainly provide for her as my daughter during my life, and leave her a fortune at my death—but if she dares—"

Sandford interrupted the menace he saw prepared for utterance,

---

1 In the second, third, fourth, and fifth editions, "but, if, whether."

saying, "And you still mean, I suppose, to make Mr. Rushbrook your heir?"

"Have you not heard me say so? And do you imagine I have changed my determination? I am not given to alter my resolutions, Mr. Sandford; and I thought you knew I was not;—besides, will not my title be extinct, whoever I make my heir?—Could any thing but a son have preserved my title?"

"Then it is yet possible—"

"By marrying again, you mean?—No—no—I have had enough of marriage—and Henry Rushbrook I leave my heir. Therefore, Sir—"

"My Lord, I do not presume—"

"Do not, Sandford, and we may still be friends.—But I am not to be controlled as formerly; my temper is changed of late; changed to what it was originally; till your scholastic and religious rules reformed it. You may remember, how troublesome it was, to conquer my stubborn disposition in my youth; then, indeed you did; but in my manhood you will find the task more difficult."

Sandford again repeated "He should not presume—"

To which his Lordship again made answer, "Do not, Sandford;" and added, "For I have a sincere regard for you, and should be loath at these years to quarrel with you seriously."

Sandford turned away his head to hide his tears.[1]

"Nay, if we do quarrel," resumed his Lordship, "You know it must be your own fault;—and as this is a theme the most likely of any (indeed the only one on which we can have a difference such as we cannot forgive) take care never from this day to resume it;—indeed that of itself, is an offence I will not pardon.—I have been clear and explicit in all I have said; there can be no fear of mistaking my meaning, therefore all future explanation is unnecessary—nor will I permit a word, or a hint on the subject from any one, without showing my resentment to the hour of my death." He was going out of the room.

"But before we bid adieu to the subject for ever, my Lord—there was another person whom I named to you—"

"Do you mean Miss Woodley?—Oh, by all means let her live

---

1 In the second, third, fourth, and fifth editions, "to conceal his feelings."

at Elmwood House too.—On consideration, I have no objection to see Miss Woodley at any time—I shall be glad to see her.—do not let *her* be frightened at me—to her I shall be the same, I have always been."

"She is a good woman, my Lord," cried Sandford, pleased.

"You need not tell me that, Mr. Sandford; I know her worth."—And his Lordship left the room.

Sandford, to relieve Miss Woodley and her lovely charge from the suspense in which he had left them, set off for their habitation the next day; in order himself to conduct them from thence to Elmwood House, and appoint some retired part of it for Lady Matilda, against the annual visit her father paid there. But before he left London, Giffard, the steward, took an opportunity to wait upon him, and let him know, that his Lord had acquainted him, with the consent he had given for his daughter to be admitted at Elmwood Castle; and upon what restrictions; likewise that he had denounced the most severe threats, should these restrictions be broken. Sandford thanked Giffard for his friendly information, which served him as a second warning of the circumspection that was necessary; and having taken leave of his Lordship under the pretence "he could not live in the smoke of London," he set out for the north.

It is unnecessary to say with what delight Sandford was received by Miss Woodley, and the hapless daughter of Lady Elmwood, even before he told his errand. They both loved him sincerely; more especially Lady Matilda; whose forlorn state, and innocent sufferings, had ever excited his compassion in the extremest degree, and had caused him ever to treat her with the utmost affection, tenderness, and respect. She knew, too, how much he had been her mother's friend; for that she also loved him; and being honoured with the friendship of her father, she looked up to him with reverence and awe. For Matilda (with an excellent understanding, a sedateness above her years, and early accustomed to the most private converse between Lady Elmwood and Miss Woodley) was perfectly acquainted with the whole fatal history of her mother; and was by her taught, that respect and admiration of her father's virtues which they justly merited.

Notwithstanding the joy of beholding Mr. Sandford, once

more to cheer by his presence their solitary dwelling; no sooner were the first kind greetings over, than the dread of what he might have to inform them, possessed both poor Matilda and Miss Woodley so powerfully, their gladness was changed into affright.—Their apprehensions were far more forcible than their curiosity;—they durst not ask a question, and even began to wish he would continue silent upon the subject, on which they feared to listen.—For near two hours he was so.—At length, after a short interval from speaking, (during which they waited with anxiety for what he might next say) he turned to Lady Matilda, and said,

"You don't ask for your father, my dear."

"I did not know it was proper," she replied timidly.

"It is always proper," answered Sandford, "for *you* to think of him, though he should never think on you."

She burst into tears, saying, she "*did* think of him, but she felt an apprehension at mentioning his name."—and she wept bitterly while she spoke.

"Nay, do not think I reproved you," said Sandford; "I but told you what was right."

"Nay," said Miss Woodley, "it is not for that she cries thus—she fears her father has not complied with her mother's request.—Perhaps not even read her letter?"

"Yes, he has read it," returned Sandford.

"Oh Heavens!" exclaimed Matilda, clasping her hands together, and the tears falling faster still.

"Do not be so much alarmed, my dear," said Miss Woodley; "you know we are prepared for the worst; and you know you promised your mother, whatever your fate was, to submit with patience."

"Yes," replied Matilda, "and I am prepared for every thing, but my father's refusal to my dear mother."

"Your father has not refused your mother's request," replied Sandford.

She was leaping from her seat in ecstasy.

"But," continued he, "do you know what her request was?"

"Not entirely," replied Matilda, "and since it is granted I am careless.—But she told me her letter concerned none but me."

To explain perfectly to Matilda Lady Elmwood's letter, and

that she might perfectly understand upon what terms she was admitted into Elmwood House, Sandford now read the letter to her; and repeated, as nearly as he could remember, the whole of the conversation that passed between Lord Elmwood and himself; not even sparing, with an erroneous delicacy, any of those threats her father had denounced, should she dare to break through the limits he prescribed—nor did he try to soften, in one instance, a word his Lordship uttered. She listened sometimes with tears, sometimes with hope, but always with awe, and terror, to every sentence wherein her father was concerned. Once she called him cruel—then exclaimed "he was kind," but at the end of Sandford's intelligence, concluded she was happy and grateful for the boon bestowed.—Even her mother had not a more exalted and transcendent idea of Lord Elmwood's worth, than his daughter had formed; and this little bounty just obtained, had not been greater in her mother's estimation, than it was now in her's.—Miss Woodley, too, smiled at the prospect before her—she esteemed Lord Elmwood beyond any mortal living—she was proud to hear what he had said in her praise, and overjoyed at the prospect she should be once again in his company; picturing, at the same time, a thousand of the brightest hopes, from watching every emotion of his soul, and catching every proper occasion to excite, or increase, his paternal sentiments.—Yet she had the prudence to conceal those vague hopes from his child, lest a disappointment might prove fatal; and assuming a behaviour not too much elated or depressed, she advised they should hope for the best, but yet, as usual, expect and prepare for the worst.—After taking measures for quitting their melancholy abode; within the fortnight they all departed for Elmwood Castle.—Matilda, Miss Woodley, and even Sandford, first visiting Lady Elmwood's grave, and bedewing it with their tears.

CHAPTER VI

It was on a dark evening in the month of March, that Lady Matilda, accompanied by Sandford and Miss Woodley, arrived at Elmwood Castle, the magnificent seat of her father.—Sandford chose the evening; rather to steal into the House privately, than by any appearance of parade, suffer Lord Elmwood to be reminded of it by the public prints, or by any other accident.—Nor would he give the neighbours or servants the slightest reason to suppose, the daughter of their Lord was admitted into his house in any other situation than, that, which she really was.[1]

As the Porter opened the gates of the avenue to the carriage that brought them, Matilda felt an awful, and yet a gladsome sensation no terms can describe.—As she entered the door of the house this sensation increased—and as she passed along the spacious hall, the splendid staircase, and many stately apartments, wonder! With a crowd of the tenderest, yet most afflicting, sentiments rushed to her heart.—She gazed with astonishment!—she reflected with more.

"And is *my father* the master of this house?" she cried—"And was my mother once the mistress of this house?"—Here a flood of tears relieved her from a part of that burthen, which was before insupportable.

"Yes." replied Sandford, "And you are the mistress of it now, till your father arrives."

"Good God!" exclaimed she, "and will he ever arrive? And shall I live to sleep under the same roof with my father?"

"My dear," replied Miss Woodley, "have not you been told so?"

"Yes," said she, "but though I heard it with extreme pleasure, yet the idea never so forcibly affected me as at this moment.—I now feel, as the reality approaches, this has been kindness sufficient—I do not ask for more—I am now convinced, from what this trial makes me feel, that to see my father, would cause a sensation, a feeling, I could not survive."

The next morning gave to Matilda more objects still of admiration and wonder, as she walked over the extensive gardens, groves, and other pleasure grounds belonging to the house. She, who had never been beyond the dreary, ruinate place where her deceased mother had chosen her residence, was naturally struck with amazement and delight at the grandeur of a seat, which

---

1   In the second, third, fourth, and fifth editions, "that, in which she really was permitted to be there."

travellers have come for miles to see, and not thought their time misspent.

There was one object, however, among all she saw, which attracted her attention above the rest, and she would stand for hours to look at it—This was a full length portrait of Lord Elmwood, esteemed a very capital picture, and a great likeness—to this picture she would sigh and weep; though when it was first pointed out to her, she shrunk back with fear, and it was some time before she dared venture to cast her eyes completely upon it. In the features of her father she was proud to discern the exact moulds in which her own appeared to have been modelled; yet Matilda's person, shape, and complection were so extremely like what her mother's once were, that at the first glance she appeared to have a still greater resemblance of her, than of her father—but her mind and manners were all Lord Elmwood's; softened by the delicacy of her sex, the extreme tenderness of her heart, and the melancholy of her situation.

She was now in her seventeenth year—of the same age, within a year and a few months, of her mother when she became the ward of Dorriforth.—She was just three years old when her father went abroad, and remembered something of bidding him farewell; but more of taking cherries from his hand as he pulled them from the tree to give to her.

Educated in the school of adversity,[1] and inured to retirement from her infancy, she had acquired a taste for all those amusements which a recluse life affords—She was fond of walking and riding—was accomplished in the arts of music and drawing, by the most careful instructions of her mother—and as a scholar she excelled most of her sex, from the great pains Sandford had taken

---

1 Mary Wollstonecraft (1759-97) refers to this phrase in her review of *A Simple Story* (*Analytical Review* 10 [May 1791]): "Educated in the school of adversity, she should have learned (to prove that a cultivated mind is not advantage) how to bear, nay, rise above her misfortunes, instead of suffering her health to be undermined by the trials of her patience, which ought to have strengthened her understanding." (See Appendix B1.) Also compare to William Godwin's *Political Justice* III (1793): "Elizabeth of England and Frederic of Prussia were educated in the school of adversity. The way in which they profited by this discipline was by finding resources in their own minds, enabling them to regard, with an unconquered spirit, the violence employed against them."

with that part of her education, and the great abilities he possessed for the task.

In devoting certain hours of the day to study with him, others to music, riding, and such recreations, Matilda's time never appeared tedious at Elmwood House, although she neither received nor paid one visit—for it was soon divulged in the neighbourhood upon what stipulation she resided at her father's, and intimated, that the most prudent and friendly behaviour of the friends both of her father and of herself, would be, to take no notice whatever that she lived among them: and as Lord Elmwood's will was a law all around, such was the consequence, of his will being known or supposed.

Neither did Miss Woodley regret the want of visiters, but found herself far more satisfied in her present situation, than her most sanguine hopes could have formed—She had a companion whom she loved with an equal fondness, with which she had loved her deceased mother; and frequently in this charming mansion, where she had so often beheld Lady Elmwood, her imagination pictured Matilda as her risen from the grave in her former youth, health, and exquisite beauty.

In peace, in content, though far from happiness, the days and weeks passed away till about the middle of August, when preparations began to be made for the arrival of Lord Elmwood.—The week in which he was to come was at length fixed, and some part of his retinue was arrived before him.—When this was told to Matilda she started, and looked just as her mother at her age often times had done, when, in spite of her love, she was conscious she had offended him, and was terrified at his approach. Sandford observing this, put out his hand, and taking hers shook it kindly; and bade her (but it was not in a cheerful tone) "not be afraid." This gave her no confidence; and she began, before his Lordship's arrival, to seclude herself in those apartments which were allotted for her during the time of his stay; and in the timorous expectation of his coming, her appetite declined and she lost all her colour.—Even Miss Woodley, whose spirits had been for some time elated with the hopes she had formed, on drawing near to the test, found those hopes vanished; and though she endeavoured to conceal it, she was replete with apprehensions.—Sandford, had certainly fewer fears than either; yet upon the eve of the day on which his patron was to arrive, he was evidently cast down.

Lady Matilda once asked him—"Are you certain, Mr. Sandford, you made no mistake in respect to what Lord Elmwood said, when he granted my mother's request? Are you sure he *did* grant it?—Was there nothing equivocal on which he may ground his displeasure should he hear I am here?—Oh! do not let me hazard being once again turned out of his house!—Oh! save me from provoking him perhaps to curse me."—And here she clasped her hands together with the most fervent petition, in the dread of what might happen.

"If you doubt my word or my senses," said Sandford, "call Giffard, and let him inform you;—my Lord repeated the same words to him he did to me."

Though from her reason Matilda could not doubt of any mistake from Mr. Sandford, yet her fears suggested a thousand scruples; and this reference to the steward she received with the utmost satisfaction, (though she did not think it necessary to apply to him) as it perfectly convinced her of the folly of those suspicions she had entertained.

"And yet, Mr. Sandford," said she, "if it is so, why are you less cheerful than you were? I cannot help thinking but it must be the expectation of Lord Elmwood here, which has caused in you this change."

"I don't know;" replied Sandford, carelessly, "but I believe I am grown afraid of your father.—His temper is a great deal altered from what it once was—he exalts his voice, and uses harsh expressions upon the least provocation—his eyes flash lightning, and his face is distorted with anger on the slightest motives—he turns away his old servants at a moment's warning, and no concession can make their peace.—In a word, I am more at my ease when I am away from him—and I really believe," added he with a smile, but with a tear at the same time, "I really believe I am more afraid of him in my age, than he was of me when he was a boy."

Miss Woodley was present; she and Matilda looked at one another; and each saw the other turn pale, at this description.

The day at length came on which Lord Elmwood was expected to dinner.—It had been a high gratification to his daughter to have gone to the topmost window of the house, to have only beheld his chariot enter the avenue; but it was a gratification which her fears, her tremor, her extreme sensibility would not permit her to enjoy.

Miss Woodley and she sat down that day to dinner in their retired apartments; which were detached from the other part of the house by a gallery; and of the door leading to the gallery they had a key to impede any one from passing that way, without first ringing a bell; to answer which, was the sole employment of a servant who was placed there during his Lordship's residence, lest by any accident he might chance to come near that unfrequented part of the house; on which occasion the man was to give immediate notice to his Lady.

Miss Woodley and she sat down to dinner, but did not dine.—Sandford ate, as usual, with Lord Elmwood.—When the servant brought up tea, Miss Woodley asked him if he had seen his Lord—The man answered, "Yes, Madam; and he looks vastly well."—Matilda wept with joy to hear it.

About nine in the evening Sandford rung at the bell, and was admitted—and never was he so welcome—Matilda hung upon him, as if his recent society with her father had endeared him to her more than ever; and staring anxiously in his face, seemed to ask him to tell her something of Lord Elmwood, and something that should not alarm her.

"Well—how do you find yourself?" said he to her.

"How are you, Mr. Sandford?" she returned, with a sigh.

"Oh! very well," replied he.

"Is my Lord in a good temper?" asked Miss Woodley.

"Yes; very well." replied Sandford, with indifference.

"Did he seem glad to see you?" asked Matilda.

"He shook me by the hand." replied Sandford.

"That was a sign he was glad to see you, was it not?" said Matilda.

"Yes; but he could not do less."

"Nor more." replied she.

"He looks very well, our servant tells us." said Miss Woodley.

"Extremely well indeed," answered Sandford: "and, to tell the truth, I never saw him in better spirits."

"That is well:" said Matilda, and sighed a weight of fears from her heart.

"Where is he now, Mr. Sandford?"

"Gone to take a walk about his grounds, and so I stole here the time."

"What was your conversation during dinner?"

"Horses, hay, farming, and politics."

"Won't you sup with him?"

"I shall see him again before I go to bed."

"And again to-morrow!" cried Matilda, "what happiness!"

"He has visiters to-morrow," said Sandford, "coming for a week or two."

"Thank heaven!" said Miss Woodley, "he will then be diverted from thinking on us."

"Do you know," returned Sandford, "it is my firm opinion, that his thinking of ye at present, is the cause of his good spirits."

"Oh, heavens!" cried Matilda, lifting up her hands with rapture.

"Nay, do not mistake me;" said Sandford; "I would not have you build a foundation for joy upon this; for if he is in spirits that you are in this house—so near him—positively under his protection—yet he will not allow himself to think that, is the cause of his content—and the sentiments he has adopted, and are now become natural to him, will remain the same as ever; nay, perhaps with greater force, while he suspects his weakness (as he calls it) acting in opposition."

"If he does but think of me with tenderness," cried Matilda, "I am recompensed."

"And what recompense would his kind thoughts be to you," said Sandford, "were he to turn you out to beggary?"

"A great deal—a great deal." she replied.

"But how are you to know he has these kind thoughts, while he gives you no proof of them?"

"No, Mr. Sandford; but *supposing* we could know them without the proof."

"But as that is impossible," answered he, "I shall suppose, till the proof appears, I am mistaken."

Matilda looked deeply concerned that the argument should

conclude in her disappointment; for to have believed herself thought of with tenderness by her father, would have alone constituted her happiness.

When the servant came up with something by way of supper, he told Mr. Sandford his Lordship was returned from his walk and had enquired for him; Sandford immediately bade his companions good night, and left them.

"How strange is this!" cried Matilda, when Miss Woodley and she were alone, "My father within a few rooms of me, and yet I am debarred from seeing him!—Only by walking a few paces I might be at his feet, and perhaps receive his blessing."

"You make me shudder," said Miss Woodley; "but some spirits less fearful than mine, might perhaps advise you to try the experiment."

"Not for worlds," returned Matilda; "no counsel could tempt me to such temerity; and yet to entertain the thought, that it is possible I could do this, is a source of great comfort."

This conversation lasted till bed time, and later; for they sat up beyond their usual hour to indulge it.

Miss Woodley slept little, but Matilda less—she awaked repeatedly during the night, and every time sighed to herself, "I sleep in the same house with my father! Blessed spirit of my mother, look down and rejoice."

CHAPTER VII

THE next day the whole Castle appeared to Lady Matilda (though she was in some degree retired from it) all tumult and bustle; as was usually the case while his Lordship was there. She saw from her windows servants running across the yards and park, horses and carriages driving with fury, all the suit of a nobleman; and it seemed sometimes to elate, at other times to depress her.

These impressions however, and others of fear and anxiety, which her father's first arrival had excited, by degrees wore away; and after some short time, she was in the same tranquil state she enjoyed before he came.

He had visitors, to stay a week or two; he paid some visits himself for several days; and thus the time passed, till it was about four weeks since he arrived; during which, Sandford, with all his penetration, could never clearly discover whether he had once called to mind his daughter was living in the same house. He had not named her (that was not extraordinary) consequently no one durst name her to him; but he had not even mentioned Miss Woodley, of whom he had so lately spoken in the kindest terms, and said, "He should take pleasure in seeing her again." From these contradictions in Lord Elmwood's behaviour in respect to her, it was Miss Woodley's plan neither to throw herself in his way, or avoid him. She therefore frequently walked about the house while he was in it, not indeed wholly without restraint, but at least with the show of liberty. This freedom, indulged for some time without peril, became at last less cautious; and no ill consequences arising from its practice, her scruples gradually ceased.

One morning, however, as she was crossing the large hall, thoughtless of danger, a footstep at a distance alarmed her almost without knowing why—She stopped for a moment, thinking to return; the steps approached quicker, and before she could retreat she beheld Lord Elmwood at the other end of the hall, and perceived that he saw her.—It was now too late to hesitate what was to be done; she could not go back, and had not courage to go on; she therefore stood still.—Disconcerted, and much affected at his sight, (their former intimacy coming to her mind, together with the many years, and many sad occurrences passed, since she last saw him) all her intentions, all her meditated plans how to conduct herself on such an occasion, gave way to a sudden shock—and to make the meeting yet more distressing, her very fright she knew must serve to recall more powerfully to his mind, the subject she most wished him to forget. The steward was with his Lordship, and as they came up close by her side, Giffard observing him look at her earnestly, said softly, but so as she heard him, "My Lord, it is Miss Woodley." Lord Elmwood's hat was off immediately, and coming to her with alacrity, he took her by the hand and said, "Indeed Miss Woodley, I did not know you—I am very glad to see you." and while he spoke, shook her hand with a cordiality her tender heart could not bear—and never did she feel so hard a struggle as to restrain her tears. But the thought of Matilda's fate—the idea of awaking in his mind a sentiment that might irritate him against his child, wrought more forcibly than every other effort; and though she could not reply distinctly, she replied without weeping.—Whether he saw her embarrassment, and wished to release her from it, or was in haste to conceal his own; he left her almost instantly; but not till he had entreated she would dine that very day with him and Mr. Sandford, who were to dine without other company.—She curtsied assent, and flew to tell Matilda what had occurred.—After listening with anxiety and joy to all she told, Matilda laid hold of that hand she said Lord Elmwood had held, and pressed it to her lips with love and reverence.

When Miss Woodley made her appearance at dinner, Sandford, (who had not seen her since the invitation, and did not know of it) looked amazed!—on which his Lordship said, "Do you know, Sandford, I met Miss Woodley this morning, and had it not been for Giffard I should have passed her without knowing her—but Miss Woodley, if I am not so much altered but that you knew me, I take it unkind you did not speak first."—She was unable to speak even now—he saw it, and changed the conversation; which Sandford was happy to join, for in the present discourse he did not feel himself very comfortable.

As they advanced in their dinner, Miss Woodley's and Sandford's embarrassment diminished; while Lord Elmwood in his turn became, not embarrassed, but absent and melancholy.—He now and then sighed heavily—and called for wine much oftener than he was accustomed.

When Miss Woodley took her leave, his Lordship invited her to dine with him and Sandford whenever it was convenient to her;—and said many things, too, of the same kind, and all with the utmost civility, yet not with that warmth with which he had spoken in the morning—into that he had been surprised, while this coolness was the effect of reflection.

When she came to Lady Matilda, and Sandford had joined them, they talked and deliberated on what had passed.—

"You acknowledge, Mr. Sandford," said Miss Woodley, "that you think my presence affected Lord Elmwood so as to make him much more thoughtful than usual; if you imagine these thoughts were upon Lady Elmwood, I will never intrude again, but if you suppose I caused him to think upon his daughter, I cannot go too often."

"I don't see how he can divide those two objects in his mind," replied Sandford, "and therefore you must e'en visit him on, and take your chance, what reflections you may inspire—but, be they what they will, time, will take away from you that power of affecting him."

She concurred in the opinion, and occasionally walked into his Lordship's apartments, dined, or took coffee with him, as the accident suited; and observed according to Sandford's prescience, that time, wore off that impression her visits first made.—Lord Elmwood now became just the same before her, as before others.—She easily discerned, too, through all that politeness which he assumed—he was no longer the considerate, the forbearing character he formally was; but haughty, impatient, imperious, and more than ever, implacable.

CHAPTER VIII

WHEN Lord Elmwood had been at his country seat about six weeks, Mr. Rushbrook, his nephew, and his adopted child, the friendless boy whom poor Lady Elmwood first introduced into his uncle's house, and by her kindness preserved there—arrived from his travels, and was received by his Lordship with all that affectionate warmth due to the man he thought worthy to make his heir. Rushbrook had been a beautiful boy, and was now an extremely handsome young man; he had made an unusual progress in his studies, had completed the tour of Italy and Germany, and returned home with the air and address of a perfect man of fashion—there was, beside, an elegance and persuasion in his manner almost irresistible.—Yet with all those accomplishments, when he was introduced to Sandford, and put out his hand to take his, Sandford, with evident reluctance, gave it to him; and when Lord Elmwood asked him, in the young man's presence, "if he did not think his nephew greatly improved?" He looked at him from head to foot, and muttered "he could not say he observed it." The colour heightened in Mr. Rushbrook's face upon this occasion, but he was too well bred not to be still in perfect good humour.

Sandford saw this young man treated in the house of Lord Elmwood with the same respect and attention as if he had been his Lordship's son; and it was but probable the old priest should make a comparison between the situation of him, and of Lady Matilda Elmwood.—Before her, it was Sandford's meaning to have concealed his thoughts upon the subject, and never to have mentioned it but with composure; that was, however, impossible—unused to conceal his feelings; at the name of Rushbrook his countenance would always change, and a sarcastic sneer, and sometimes a frown of resentment, force their way in spite of his resolution.—Miss Woodley, too, with all her boundless charity and good will, was, upon this occasion, induced to limit their excess; and they did not extend so far as to reach poor Rushbrook—She even, and in *reality*, did not think him handsome or engaging in his manners—she thought his gaiety frivolousness, his complaisance affectation, and his good humour impertinence.—It was impossible to conceal those unfavourable sentiments entirely from Matilda; for when the subject arose, as it frequently did, Miss Woodley's undisguised heart, and Sandford's undisguised countenance, told them instantly.—Matilda had the understanding to imagine, she was, perhaps, the object who had thus deformed Mr. Rushbrook, and frequently (though he was a stranger to her, and one who had caused her many a jealous heartache) frequently she would speak in his vindication.

"You are very good," said Sandford one day to her; "you like him because you know your father loves him."

This was a hard sentence to the daughter of Lord Elmwood, to whom her father's love would have been more precious than any other blessing—She, however, checked the assault of envy, and kindly replied,

"My mother loved him, too, Mr. Sandford."

"Yes," answered Sandford, "he has been a grateful man to your poor mother—She did not suppose when she took him into the house, when she intreated your father to take him, and through her caresses and officious praises of him to his uncle, first gave him that power he now possesses over him; she little foresaw, at that time, his ingratitude, and its effects."

"Very true." said Miss Woodley, with a heavy sigh.

"What ingratitude?" said Matilda; "do you suppose Mr. Rushbrook is the cause my father will not see me? Oh do not pay Lord Elmwood's motives so ill a compliment."

"I do not say he is the absolute cause," returned Sandford; "but if a parent's heart is void, I would have it remain so, till stored by its lawful owner—a usurper I detest."

"No one can take Lord Elmwood's heart by force," replied his daughter, "it must, I believe, be a free gift to the possessor; and as such, whoever has it, has a right to it."

In this manner she would plead the young man's excuse—perhaps but to hear what could be said in his disfavour, for secretly his name was bitter to her—and once she exclaimed in vexation, on Sandford's saying Lord Elmwood and Mr. Rushbrook were gone out shooting together,

"All that pleasure is now eclipsed which I used to take in listening to the report of my father's gun, for I cannot now distinguish his, from his parasite's."

Sandford, much as he disliked Rushbrook—for this expression which comprised her father in the reflection, turned to Matilda in extreme anger; but as he saw the colour mount to her face, for what, in the strong feelings of her heart, had escaped her lips, he did not say a word—and by a flood of tears that followed after, he rejoiced to see how much she reproved herself.

Miss Woodley, vext to the heart, and provoked every time she saw Lord Elmwood and Rushbrook together, and saw the familiar terms on which this young man lived with his benefactor, now made her visits to his Lordship very seldom.—If Lord Elmwood observed this, he did not appear to observe it; and though he received her very politely when she did pay him a visit, it was always very coldly; nor did she suppose if she never went, he would ever ask for her. For his daughter's sake, however, she thought it right sometimes to show herself before him; for she knew it must be impossible that, with all his seeming indifference, Lord Elmwood could ever see her without thinking for a moment on his child;

and what one fortunate thought might sometime bring about, was an object too serious for her to slight.—She therefore, after remaining confined to her apartments near three weeks, (excepting those short and anxious walks she and Matilda stole, while Lord Elmwood dined, or before he rose in a morning) went one forenoon into his Lordship's apartments, where as usual, she found him, Mr. Sandford, and Mr. Rushbrook.—After she had sat about half an hour, conversing with them all, though but very little with the latter, his Lordship was called out of the room upon some business; presently after Sandford; and now, not much pleased with the companion with whom she was left, she rose and was going likewise, when Rushbrook fixed his speaking eyes upon her, and cried,

"Miss Woodley, will you pardon me what I am going to say?"

"Certainly, Sir—You can, I am sure, say nothing but what I must forgive."—But she made this reply with a distance and a reserve, very unlike the usual manners of Miss Woodley.

He looked at her earnestly and cried, "Ah! Miss Woodley, you don't behave so kindly to me as you used to do!"

"I do not understand you, Sir,"—she replied, very gravely;—"Times are changed, Mr. Rushbrook, since you were last here—you were then but a child."

"Yet I love all those persons now, I loved then;" replied he; "and so I shall for ever."

"But you mistake, Mr. Rushbrook; I was not even then so very much the object of your affections—there were other ladies you loved better.—Perhaps you don't remember Lady Elmwood?"

"Don't I?"—cried he, "Oh!" (clasping his hands and lifting up is eyes to heaven) "shall I ever forget her?"

That moment Lord Elmwood opened the door; the conversation of course that moment ended; but confusion at the sudden surprise was on the face of both parties—his Lordship saw it, and looked at each by turns, with a sternness that made poor Miss Woodley ready to faint; while Rushbrook, with the most natural and happy laugh that ever was affected, cried, "No, don't tell my Lord, pray, Miss Woodley."—She was more confused than before; and his Lordship turning to him, asked what the subject was.—By this time he had invented one, and continuing his laugh, said, "Miss Woodley, my Lord, will to this day protest she saw my apparition when I was a boy; and she says it is a sign I shall die young, and is really much affected at it."

Lord Elmwood turned away before this ridiculous speech was concluded; yet so well had it been acted, he did not for an instant doubt its truth.

Miss Woodley felt herself greatly relieved; and yet so little is it in the power of those we dislike to do any thing to please us, that from this very circumstance, she formed a still more unfavourable opinion of Mr. Rushbrook than she had done before.—She saw in this little incident the art of dissimulation, cunning, and duplicity in its most glaring shape; and detested the method by which they had each escaped Lord Elmwood's suspicion, and perhaps anger, the more, because it was so dexterously managed.

Lady Matilda and Sandford were both in their turns informed of this trait in Mr. Rushbrook's character; and although Miss Woodley had the best of dispositions, and upon every occasion spoke the strictest truth, yet in relating this occurrence, she did not speak all the truth; for every circumstance that would have told to the young man's advantage, *literally* slipped her memory.

The twenty ninth of October arrived; on which a dinner, a ball, and supper, was given by Lord Elmwood to all the neighbouring gentry—the peasants also dined in the park off a roasted bullock; several casks of ale were distributed, and the bells of the village rung.—Matilda, who heard and saw some part of this festivity from her windows, inquired the cause, but even the servant who waited upon her had too much sensibility to tell her, and answered, "he did not know." Miss Woodley however soon learnt the reason, and groaning with the painful secret, informed her, "Mr. Rushbrook, on that day was come of age."

"My birth day was last week." replied Matilda; but not a word beside.

In their retired apartments, the day passed away not only soberly, but almost silently; for to speak upon any subject that did not engage their thoughts had been difficult, and to speak upon the only one that did, had been afflictive.

Just as they were sitting down to dinner their bell gently rung, and in walked Sandford.

"Why are not you among the revellers, Mr. Sandford?" cried

Miss Woodley, with an ironical sneer—(the first her features ever wore)—"Pray, were not you invited to dine with the company?"

"Yes," replied Sandford; "but my head aked; and so I had rather come and take a bit with you."

Matilda, as if she had beheld his heart as he spoke, clung round his neck and sobbed on his bosom: he put her peevishly away, crying, "Nonsense, nonsense—eat your dinner." But he did not eat himself.

CHAPTER IX

ABOUT a week after this, Lord Elmwood went out two days for a visit; consequently Rushbrook was for that time master of the house. The first morning he went a shooting, and returning about noon, enquired of Sandford, who was sitting in the room, if he had taken up a volume of plays left upon the table.—

"I read no such things." replied Sandford, and quitted the room abruptly. Rushbrook then rung for his servant, and desired him to look for the book, asking him angrily, "Who had been in the apartment? for he was sure he had left it there when he went out."—The servant withdrew to enquire, and presently returned with the volume in his hand, and "Miss Woodley's compliments, she begs your pardon, Sir, she did not know the book was yours, and hopes you will excuse the liberty she took."

"Miss Woodley!" cried Rushbrook with surprize, "she comes so seldom into these apartments, I did not suppose it was her who had it—take it back to her instantly, with my respects, and I beg she will keep it."

The man went; but returned with the book again, and laying it on the table without speaking, was going away; when Rushbrook, hurt at receiving no second message, said, "I am afraid, Sir, you did very wrong in taking this book from Miss Woodley."

"It was not from her I took it, Sir," replied the man, "it was from Lady Matilda."

Since he had entered the house, Rushbrook had never before heard her name—he was shocked—confounded more than ever—and to conceal what he felt, instantly ordered the man out of the room.

In the mean time, Miss Woodley and Matilda were talking over this trifling occurrence; and frivolous as it was, drew from it strong conclusions of Rushbrook's insolence and power.—In spite of her pride, the daughter of Lord Elmwood even wept at the insult she had received on this insignificant occasion; for the volume being merely taken from her at Mr. Rushbrook's command, she felt an insult; and the manner in which it was done by the servant, might contribute to the offence.

While Miss Woodley and she were upon this conversation, a note came from Rushbrook to Miss Woodley, wherein he entreated he might be permitted to see her.—She sent a verbal answer, "She was engaged." He sent again, begging she would name her own time. But certain of a second denial, he followed the servant who took the last message, and as Miss Woodley came out of her apartment into the gallery to speak to him, Rushbrook presented himself, and told the man to retire.

"Mr. Rushbrook," said Miss Woodley, "this intrusion is insupportable;—and destitute as you may think me of the friendship of Lord Elmwood"—

In the ardour with which Rushbrook was waiting to express himself, he interrupted her, and caught hold of her hand.

She immediately snatched it from him, and withdrew into her chamber.

He followed, saying in a low voice, "Dear Miss Woodley hear me."

At that juncture Lady Matilda, who was in an inner room, came out of it into Miss Woodley's.—Perceiving a gentleman, she stopped short at the door.

Rushbrook cast his eyes upon her, and stood motionless—his lips only moved.

"Do not depart, Madam," said he, "without hearing my apology for being here."

Though Matilda had never seen him since her infancy, there was no cause to tell her who it was that addressed her—his elegant and youthful person, joined to the incident which had just occurred, convinced her it was Rushbrook; and she looked at him with an air of surprise, but with still more, of dignity.

"Miss Woodley is severe upon me, Madam," continued he,

"she judges me unkindly; and I am afraid she will prepossess you with the same unfavourable sentiments."

Still Matilda did not speak, but looked at him with the same air of dignity.

"If, Lady Matilda," resumed he, "I have offended you, and must quit you without pardon, I am more unhappy than I should be with the loss of your father's protection—more forlorn, than when an orphan boy, your mother first took pity on me."

At this last sentence, Matilda turned her eyes on Miss Woodley, and seemed in doubt what reply she was to give.

Rushbrook immediately fell upon his knees—"Oh! Lady Matilda," cried he, "if you knew the sensations of my heart, you would not treat me with this disdain."

"We can only judge of those sensations, Mr. Rushbrook," said Miss Woodley, "by the effect they have upon your conduct; and while you insult Lord and Lady Elmwood's daughter by an intrusion like this, and then ridicule her abject state by mockery, such as the present"—

He flew from his knees instantly, and interrupted her, crying "What can I do?—What am I to say, to make you change your opinion of me?—While Lord Elmwood has been at home I have kept at an awful distance; and though every moment I breathed was a wish to cast myself at his daughter's feet, yet as I feared, Miss Woodley, you were incensed against me, by what means was I to procure an interview but by stratagem or force?—This accident has given a third method, and I had not strength, I had not courage, to let it pass.—Lord Elmwood will soon return, and we may both be hurried to town immediately;—then how for a tedious winter could I sustain the thought that I was despised, nay perhaps considered as an object of ingratitude, by the only child of my deceased benefactress."

Matilda replied with all her father's haughtiness, "Depend upon it, Sir, if you should ever enter my thoughts, it will only be as an object of envy."

"Suffer me then, Madam," said he, "as an earnest you do not think worse of me than I merit, suffer me to be sometimes admitted into your presence."

She scarcely permitted him to finish the period, before she

replied, "This is the last time, Sir, we shall ever meet, depend upon it—unless, indeed, Lord Elmwood should delegate to you the control of me—his commands I never dispute." And here she burst into a flood of tears.

Rushbrook walked to the window, and did not speak for a short time—then turning himself to make a reply, both Matilda and Miss Woodley were somewhat surprised to see, he had shed tears too.—Having conquered them, he said, "I will not offend you, Madam, by staying one moment longer; and I give my honour, that, upon no pretence whatever, will I presume to intrude here again.—Professions, I find, have no weight, and only by this obedience to your orders can I give a proof of that respect which you inspire;—and let the agitation I now feel, convince you, Lady Matilda, that, with all my seeming good fortune, I am not happier than yourself."—And so much was he agitated while he delivered this, it was with difficulty he came to the conclusion.—When he did, he bowed with reverence, as if he had left the presence of a deity, and went away.

Matilda immediately entered the chamber she had come from, and without casting a single look at Miss Woodley, by which she might guess of the opinion she had formed of Mr. Rushbrook's conduct.—The next time they met they did not even mention his name; for they were ashamed to own any partiality in his favour, and were too just to bring any serious accusation against him.

But Miss Woodley the day following communicated the intelligence of this visit to Mr. Sandford, who not being present, and a witness of those marks of humility and respect which were conspicuous in the deportment of Mr. Rushbrook, was highly offended at his presumption; and threatened if he ever dared to force his company there again, he would acquaint Lord Elmwood with his arrogance, whatever might be the event.—Miss Woodley however, assured him, she believed he would have no cause for such a complaint, as the young man had made the most solemn promise never to commit the like offence; and she thought it her duty to enjoin Sandford, till he did repeat it, not to mention the circumstance, even to Rushbrook himself.

Matilda could not but feel a regard towards her father's heir in return for that which he had so fervently declared for her; yet the more favourable her opinion of his mind and manners, the more he became a proper object of her jealousy for the affections of Lord Elmwood, and was now consequently an object of greater sorrow to her, than when she believed him less worthy.—This, was the reverse on his part towards her—no jealousy intervened to bar his admiration and esteem, and the beauty of her person, and grandeur of her mien, not only confirmed, but improved, the exalted idea he had formed of her previous to their meeting, and which his affection to both her parents had inspired.—The next time he saw his benefactor, he began to feel a new esteem and regard for him, for his daughter's sake; as he had at first an esteem for her on the foundation of his love for Lord and Lady Elmwood—He gazed with wonder at his uncle's insensibility to his own happiness, and longed to lead him to the jewel he cast away, though even his own expulsion should be the fatal consequence.—Such was the youthful, warm, generous, grateful, but unthinking mind of Rushbrook.

CHAPTER X

AFTER this incident, Miss Woodley left her own apartments less frequently than before—she was afraid, though till now mistrust had been a stranger to her heart, she was afraid duplicity might be concealed under the apparent friendship of Rushbrook; it did not indeed appear so from any part of his behaviour, but she was apprehensive for the fate of Matilda; she disliked him also, and therefore she suspected him.—For near three weeks she had not now paid a visit to Lord Elmwood, and though to herself every visit was a pain, yet as Matilda took a delight in hearing of her father, what he said, what he did, what his attention seemed most employed on, and a thousand other circumstantial informations, in the detail of which, Sandford would scorn to be half so particular, it was a deprivation to her, Miss Woodley did not go oftener.—Now too the middle of November had arrived, and it was expected his Lordship would shortly quit the country.

Partly therefore to indulge her hapless companion, and partly because it was a necessary duty, Miss Woodley paid his Lordship a morning visit, and staid dinner.—Rushbrook was officiously polite to her, (for that was the epithet she gave his attention in relating it to Lady Matilda) yet she owned he had not that forward impertinence she had formerly discovered in him, but appeared much more grave and sedate.

"But tell me of my father." said Matilda.

"I was going, my dear—but don't be concerned—don't let it vex you."

"What? what?" cried Matilda, frightened by the preface.

"Why, on my observing that I thought Mr. Rushbrook looked paler than usual, and appeared not to be in perfect health, (which was really the case) your father expressed the greatest anxiety imaginable; he said he could not bear to see him look so ill, begged him with all the tenderness of a parent to take the advice of a physician, and added a thousand other affectionate things."

"I detest Mr. Rushbrook."—said Matilda, with her eyes flashing indignation.

"Nay, for shame," returned Miss Woodley: "do you suppose I told you this, to make you hate him?"

"No, there was no occasion for that," replied Matilda; "my sentiments (though I have never before avowed them) were long ago formed; he was always an object which added to my unhappiness; but since his daring intrusion into my apartments, he has been an object of my hatred."

"But now perhaps I may tell you something to please you." cried Miss Woodley.

"And what is that?" said Matilda, with indifference; for the first intelligence had hurt her spirits too much to suffer her to listen with pleasure to any other.

"Mr. Rushbrook," continued Miss Woodley, "replied to your father, his indisposition was but a slight nervous fever, and he would defer a physician's advice till he went to London— on which his Lordship said, "And when do you expect to be there?"—he replied, "Within a week or two, I suppose, my Lord." But your father answered, "I do not mean to go myself till after Christmas."—"No indeed, my Lord!" said Mr. Sandford, with surprise: "you have not passed your Christmas here," continued he, "these many a year."—"No," returned his Lordship; "but I think I feel myself more attached to this house at present, than ever I did in my life."

"You imagine then, my father thought of me, when he said that?" cried Matilda eagerly.

"But I may be mistaken," replied Miss Woodley.—"I leave you to judge.—But I am sure Mr. Sandford imagined he thought of you, for I saw a smile over his whole face immediately."

"Did you, Miss Woodley?"

"Yes; it appeared on every feature except his lips; those he closed fast together, for fear Lord Elmwood should perceive it."

Miss Woodley, with all her minute intelligence, did not however acquaint Matilda that Rushbrook followed her to the window while his Lordship was out of the room, and Sandford half asleep at the other end of it, and inquired respectfully and anxiously for her Ladyship; adding, "It is my concern for Lady Matilda which makes me thus indisposed: I suffer more than her, but I am not permitted to tell her so, nor can I hope, Miss Woodley, you will."—She replied, "You are right, Sir." Nor did she reveal this conversation, while not a sentence that passed except that, was omitted.

When Christmas arrived Lord Elmwood had many convivial days at Elmwood House, but the name of Matilda was never mentioned by one of his guests, and most probably never thought of.—During all those holidays she was unusually melancholy, but sunk into the deepest dejection when she was told the day was fixed on which her father was to depart for the season.—On the morning of that day she wept incessantly; and all her consolation was, "She would go to the chamber window which was fronting the door he was to pass through to his carriage, and for the first time, and most likely for the last time of her life, behold him."

This design was soon forgot in another:—"She would rush boldly into the apartment where he was, and at his feet take leave of him for ever—She would lay hold of his hands, clasp his knees, provoke him to spurn her, which would be joy in comparison to this cruel indifference."—In the bitterness of her grief, she once called upon her mother, and reproached her memory—but the moment she recollected the offence, (which was almost instantaneously) she became all mildness and resignation. "What have I said?" cried she; "Dear, dear saint, forgive me, and behold for your sake I will bear all with patience—I will not groan, I will not even sigh again—this task I set myself to atone for what I have dared to utter."

While Lady Matilda laboured under these variety of sensations, Miss Woodley was occupied in bewailing and endeavouring to calm her sorrows—and Lord Elmwood, with Rushbrook, was prepared ready to set off.—His Lordship, however, loitered, and did not once seem in haste to be gone.—When at last he got up to depart, Sandford thought he pressed his hand, and shook it with more warmth than ever he had done in his life.—Encouraged by this supposition, Sandford, with the tears starting in his eyes,[1] said, "my Lord, won't you condescend to take your leave of Miss Woodley?"—"Certainly, Sandford." replied his Lordship, and seemed glad of an excuse to sit down again.

Impressed with the idea of the state in which she had left his only child, Miss Woodley, when she came before Lord Elmwood to bid him farewell, was pale, trembling, and in tears.—Sandford, notwithstanding his Lordship's apparent kind humour, was shocked at the construction he must put upon her appearance, and cried, "What, Miss Woodley, are you not recovered of your illness yet." Lord Elmwood, however, took no notice of her looks, but after wishing her health and happiness, walked slowly out of the house; turning back frequently and speaking to Sandford or some other person who was behind him, as if part of his thoughts were left behind, and he went with reluctance.

When he had quitted the room where Miss Woodley was; Rushbrook, timid before her, as she had been before her benefactor, went up to her all humility, and said, "Miss Woodley, we ought to be friends; our concern, our devotion is paid to the same objects, and one common interest should teach us to be friendly."

She made no reply.—"Will you permit me to write to you when I am away?" said he; "You may wish to hear of Lord

---

1 The phrase "with the tears starting in his eyes" is removed from the second, third, fourth, and fifth editions.

Elmwood's health, and of what changes may take place in his resolutions—Will you permit me?"—At that moment a servant came and said, "Sir, my Lord is in his carriage and waiting for you." He hasted away, and Miss Woodley was relieved from the pain of giving him a denial.

No sooner was the chariot,[1] with all its attendants, out of sight, than Lady Matilda was conducted by Miss Woodley from her lonely retreat into that part of the house from whence her father had just departed—and she visited every spot where he had so long resided, with a pleasing curiosity that for a while diverted her grief.—In the breakfast and dining rooms she leaned over those seats with a kind of filial piety, on which she was told he had been accustomed to sit. And in the library she took up with filial delight, the pen with which he had been writing; and looked with the most curious attention into those books that were laid upon his reading desk.—But a hat, lying on one of the tables, gave her a sensation beyond any other she experienced on this occasion—in that trifling article of his dress, she thought she saw he himself, and held it in her hand with pious reverence.

In the mean time, Lord Elmwood and Rushbrook were proceeding on their road with hearts not less heavy than those which they had left at Elmwood House, though neither of them could so well as Matilda tell the cause of the weight.

CHAPTER XI

YOUNG as Lady Matilda was during the life of her mother, neither her youth, nor the recluse state in which she lived, had precluded her from the notice and solicitations of a nobleman who had professed himself her lover. Viscount Margrave had an estate not far distant from the retreat Lady Elmwood had chosen, and being devoted to the sports of the country, he seldom quitted it for any of those joys which the town offered.—He was a young man, of a handsome person, and was what his neighbours stiled "A man of spirit."—He was an excellent fox-hunter, and as

---

1   In the second, third, and fourth editions, "chaise"; in the fifth edition, "traveling carriage."

excellent a companion over his bottle at the end of the chace—he was prodigal of his fortune in all cases where his pleasures were concerned, and as those pleasures were mostly social, his sporting companions and his mistresses (for these were also of the plural number) partook largely of his wealth.[1]

Two months previous to Lady Elmwood's death, Miss Woodley and Lady Matilda were taking their usual walk in some fields and lanes near to their house, when chance threw Lord Margrave in their way, during a thunder storm in which they were suddenly caught; and he had the satisfaction to convey his new acquaintances to their home in his carriage, safe from the fury of the elements.—Grateful for the service his Lordship had rendered them, Miss Woodley and her charge permitted him to enquire occasionally of their healths, and would sometimes see him.— The story of Lady Elmwood was known to Lord Margrave, and as he beheld her daughter with a passion such as he had been unused to overcome, he indulged it with the probable hope, that on the death of the mother Lord Elmwood would receive his child, and perhaps accept him as his son-in-law.—Wedlock was not the plan which Lord Margrave had ever proposed to himself for happiness; but the excess of his love on this new occasion, subdued every resolution he had taken against the marriage state, and not daring to hope for the consummation of his wishes by any other means, he suffered himself to look forward to that, as his only resource.—No sooner was the long-expected death of Lady Elmwood arrived, than his Lordship waited with impatience to hear Lady Matilda was sent for and acknowledged by her father; for he meant to be the first to lay before Lord Elmwood his pretensions as a suitor.—But those pretensions were founded on the vague hopes of a lover only; and Miss Woodley, to whom he first declared them, said every thing possible to convince him of their falaciousness.—As to the object of his passion, she was not only insensible, but totally inattentive to all that was said to her on the subject.—Lady Elmwood died without ever being disturbed

---

[1] Margrave's character is reminiscent of the prodigal country gentlemen in several eighteenth-century novels. Compare, for example, to Squire Western in Fielding's *Tom Jones*.

with it; for her daughter did not even remember his proposals so as to repeat them again, and Miss Woodley thought it prudent to conceal from her friend, every new incident which might give her cause for fresh anxieties.

When Sandford and the ladies left the north and came to Elmwood House, so much were their thoughts employed with other ideas, Lord Margrave did not occupy a place; and during the whole time they had been at their new abode, they had never once heard of him.—He had, nevertheless, his whole mind fixed upon Lady Matilda, and placed spies in the neighbourhood to inform him of every circumstance in her situation.—Having imbibed an aversion to matrimony, he heard with but little regret, that there was no prospect of her ever becoming her father's heir; while such an information gave him the hope of obtaining her, upon the illegal terms of a mistress.[1]

Lord Elmwood's departure to town forwarded this hope, and flattering himself that the humiliating situation in which Matilda must feel herself in the house of her father, might gladly induce her to take shelter under any other protection, he boldly advanced as soon as the Earl was gone, to make such overtures as his wishes and his vanity told him, could not be rejected.

Inquiring for Miss Woodley, he easily gained admittance; but at the sight of so much modesty and dignity in the person of Matilda, so much good will, and yet such circumspection in her companion; and the good sense and proper spirit which were always apparent in the manners of Sandford, his Lordship fell once more into the despondency, of becoming to Lady Matilda nothing more important to his reputation, than a husband.

Even that humble hope was, however, sometimes denied him, while Sandford set forth the impropriety of troubling Lord Elmwood on such a subject at present; and while the Viscount's penetration, small as it was, discovered in his fair one much more to discourage than to favour his wishes.—Plunged, however, too deep in his passion to emerge from it in haste, he meant still to visit, and wait for a change to happier circumstances, when he

---

1   In the second, third, and fourth editions, "terms of a mistress"; in the fifth edition, "terms of a traveling companion."

was peremptorily desired by Mr. Sandford to desist from ever coming again.

"Wherefore, Mr. Sandford?" cried his Lordship.

"For two reasons, my Lord;—in the first place, your visits might be displeasing to Lord Elmwood;—and in the next place, I know they are so to his daughter."

Unaccustomed to be spoken to so plainly, particularly in a case where his heart was interested, his Lordship nevertheless submitted with patience; but in his own mind determined how long this patience should continue—no longer than it served as the means to prove his obedience, and by that artifice, secure his better reception at some future period.

On his return home, cheered with the huzzas of his jovial companions, he began to consult those friends, what scheme was best to be adopted for the accomplishment of his desires.—Some, boldly advised application to the father, in defiance to the old priest; but that was the very last method his Lordship himself approved, as marriage must inevitably have followed Lord Elmwood's consent; besides, though a Peer, Lord Margrave was unused to rank with Peers; and even the necessary formality of an interview with one of his equals, carried along with it a terror, or at least a fatigue, to a rustic Baron.—Others, of his companions advised seduction; but happily his Lordship possessed no arts of this kind to affect a heart appendant to such a mind as Matilda's.—There were not wanting among his most favourite counsellors some, who painted the triumph and gratification of force; those assured him there was nothing to apprehend under this head; as from the behaviour of Lord Elmwood to his child, it was more than probable he would be utterly indifferent to any violence that might be offered her.—This last advice seemed inspired by the aid of wine; and no sooner had the wine freely circulated, than this was always the scheme which appeared by far the best.

While Lord Margrave alternately cherished his hopes and his fears in the country, Rushbrook in town gave way to his fears only—every day of his life made him more acquainted with the firm, unshaken temper of Lord Elmwood, and every day whispered more forcibly to his own heart, that pity, gratitude, and friendship, strong and affectionate as these passions are, are weak and cold to that, which had gained the possession of him—he doubted, but he did not long doubt, that which he felt was love.—

"And yet," said he to himself, "it is love of that kind, which arising from causes independent of the object itself, can scarcely deserve this sacred title.—Did I not love Lady Matilda before I beheld her?—for her mother's sake I loved her—and even for her father's.—Should I have felt the same affection for her, had she been the child of other parents?—no. Or should I have felt that sympathetic tenderness which now preys upon my health, had not her misfortunes excited it?—no."—Yet the love which is the result of gratitude and pity only, he thought had little claim to rank with his; and after the most deliberate and deep reflection, he concluded with this decisive opinion—He had loved Lady Matilda, in *whatever state*, in *whatever circumstances*; and that the tenderness he felt towards her, and the anxiety for her happiness before he knew her, extreme as they were, were yet cool and dispassionate sensations, compared to that which her person and demeanour had incited—and though he acknowledged, that by those preceding sentiments his heart was softened, prepared, and moulded, as it were, to receive this last impression, yet the violence of his passion told him genuine love, if not the basis on which it was founded, had been the certain consequence.—With a strict scrutiny into his heart he sought this knowledge, but arrived at it with a regret that amounted to despair.

To shield him from despondency, he formed in his mind a thousand projects, depicting the joys of his union with Lady Matilda; but her father's implacability stood foremost and confounded them all.—His Lordship was a man who made but few resolutions—those were the effect of deliberation; and as he was not the least capricious or inconstant in his temper, they were resolutions which no probable event could shake.—Love, that produces wonders, that seduces and subdues the most determined and rigid spirits, had in two instances overcome the inflexibility of Lord Elmwood; he married Lady Elmwood contrary to his determination, because he loved; and for the sake of this beloved object, he had, contrary to his resolution, taken under his immediate care young Rushbrook; but the magic which once enchanted away this spirit of immutability was no more—Lady Elmwood was no more, and the charm was broken.

As Miss Woodley was deprived the opportunity of desiring Rushbrook not to write when he asked her the permission, he passed one whole morning in the gratification of forming and writing a letter to her, which he thought might possibly be shewn to Matilda.—As he durst not touch upon any of those circumstances in which he was the most interested, that, joined to the respect he wished to pay the lady to whom he wrote, limited his letter to about twenty lines; yet the studious manner with which these lines were dictated, the hope and fear they might, or might not, be seen and regarded by Lady Matilda, rendered the task an anxiety so pleasing, he could have wished it to have lasted for a year; and in all this magnifying of trifles was discoverable, the never-failing symptom of ardent love.

A reply to this formal address was a reward he wished for with impatience, but he wished in vain; and in the midst of his chagrin at the disappointment, a sorrow, little thought of, occurred, and gave him a perturbation of mind he had never before experienced.—Lord Elmwood proposed a wife to him; and in a way so assured of his acquiescence, that if Rushbrook's life had depended upon his daring to dispute his benefactor's will, he would not have had the courage to have done so. There was, however, in his reply, and his embarrassment, something which his Lordship discerned from a free concurrence; and looking steadfastly at him, he said, in that stern manner which he now almost constantly adopted,

"You have no engagements, I suppose? Have made no previous promises?"

"None on earth, my Lord." replied Rushbrook candidly.

"Nor have you disposed of your heart?"

"No, my Lord." replied he; but not candidly,—nor with the appearance of candour: for though he spoke hastily, it was rather like a man frightened than assured.—He hurried to tell the falsehood he thought himself obliged to tell, that the pain and shame might be over; but there Rushbrook was deceived; the lie once told was as troublesome as in the conception, and added to his first confusion, an encreasing one.

Lord Elmwood now fixed his eyes upon him with a sullen contempt, and rising from his seat, said, "Rushbrook, if you have been so inconsiderate as to give away your heart, tell me so at once, and tell me the object."

Rushbrook shuddered at the thought.

"I here," continued his Lordship, "tolerate the first untruth you ever told me, as the false assertion of a lover; and give you an opportunity to recall it—but after this moment, it is a lie between man and man—a lie to your friend and father, and I will not forgive it."

Rushbrook stood silent, confused, alarmed, and bewildered in his thoughts.—His Lordship resumed,

"Name the person, if there is any such, on whom you have bestowed your heart; and though I do not give you the smallest hope I shall not censure your folly, I will at least not reproach you for having at first denied it."

To repeat these words in writing, the reader must condemn the young man that he could hesitate to own he loved, if he was even afraid to name the object of his passion; but his Lordship in his question had made the two answers inseparable, and all evasions of the second, Rushbrook knew would be fruitless, after having avowed the first—and how could he confess the latter? The absolute orders he received from the steward on his first return from his travels, were, "Never to mention his daughter, any more than his late wife, before Lord Elmwood."—The fault of having rudely intruded into Lady Matilda's presence, rushed too upon his mind; for he did not even dare to say, by what means he had beheld her.—But more than all, the threatening manner in which his Lordship uttered this rational and seeming conciliating speech, the menaces, the severity which sat upon his countenance while he delivered those moderate words, might have intimidated a man wholly independent, and less used to fear him than his nephew had been.

"You make no answer, Sir." said his Lordship, after waiting a few moments for his reply.

"I have only to say, my Lord," returned Rushbrook, "that although my heart may be totally disengaged, I may yet be disinclined to the prospect of marriage."

"May! May! Your heart *may* be disengaged," repeated his Lordship. "Do you dare to reply to me equivocally, when I have asked a positive answer?"

"Perhaps I am not positive myself, my Lord; but I will inquire the state of my mind, and make you acquainted with it very soon."

As the angry demeanour of his uncle affected Rushbrook with fear, so that fear, powerfully (but with the proper manliness) expressed, again softened the displeasure of Lord Elmwood; and seeing and pitying his nephew's sensibility, he now changed his austere voice, and said mildly, but firmly,

"I give you a week to consult with yourself; at the expiration of that time I shall talk with you again, and I command you to be then prepared to speak, not only without deceit, but without hesitation." He left the room at these words, and left Rushbrook released from a fate, which his apprehensions had beheld impending that moment.

He had now a week to call his thoughts together, to weigh every circumstance, and to determine whether implicitly to submit to his Lordship's recommendation for a wife, or revolt from it, and see some other more subservient to his will, appointed his heir.

Undetermined how to act upon this great trial which was to decide his future destiny, Rushbrook suffered so poignant an uncertainty, that he became at length ill, and before the end of the week which his uncle had allotted him for his reply, he was confined to his bed in a high fever.—His Lordship was extremely affected at his indisposition; he gave him every care he could bestow, and even a great deal of his personal attendance.—This last favour had a claim upon the young man's gratitude, superior to every other obligation which since his infancy his benefactor had conferred; and he was at times so moved by those marks of kindness he received from Lord Elmwood, he would form the intention of tearing from his heart every trace Lady Matilda had left there, and as soon as his health permitted him, obey to the utmost of his views every wish his uncle had conceived.—Yet again, Matilda's pitiable situation presented itself to his compassion, and her beautious person to his love.—Divided between the claims of obligation to the father, and tender attachment to the daughter, his sickness was increased by the tortures of his mind, and he once sincerely wished for that death, of which he was in danger, to free him from the dilemma into which his affections had involved him.

At the time his illness was at its height, and he lay complaining of the violence of his fever, Lord Elmwood, taking his hand, asked him, "If there was any thing he could do for him?"

"Yes, yes, my Lord, a great deal." he replied eagerly.

"What is it, Harry?" asked his Lordship kindly.

"Oh! my Lord," replied he, "that is what I must not tell you."

"Defer it then till you are well." said his Lordship, fearful of being surprised, or affected by the state of his health, into any promises which he might hereafter find the impropriety of granting.

"And when I recover, my Lord, you give me leave to reveal to you, that which I wish you to comply with, let it be what it will?"

His Lordship hesitated—but seeing an anxiety for the answer, by this raising himself upon his elbow in the bed and staring wildly, Lord Elmwood at last said,

"Certainly—Yes, yes." as a child is answered for its quiet.

That Lord Elmwood could have no idea what the real petition which Rushbrook meant to present him is certain; but it is certain he expected he had some request to make, with which it might be wrong for him to comply, and therefore he avoided hearing what it was; for great as his compassion for him in his present state, it was not of force to urge him to give a promise he did not mean to perform.—Rushbrook on his part was pleased with the assurance he might speak when he was restored to health, but no sooner was his fever abated, and his senses perfectly recovered from the slight derangement his malady had caused, than the lively remembrance of what he had hinted alarmed him, and he was even afraid to look his kind, but awful relation in the face.—Lord Elmwood's cheerfulness, however, on his returning health, and his undiminished attention, soon convinced him he had nothing to fear—But, alas! he found too, he had nothing to hope.—As his health re-established his wishes re-established also, and with his wishes his despair.

Convinced now that his nephew had something on his mind which he feared to reveal, his Lordship no longer doubted but some youthful attachment had armed his heart against any marriage he should propose; but he had so much pity for his present weak state, to delay that farther inquiry which he had threatened before his sickness, to a time when he should be wholly restored.

It was the end of May before Rushbrook was able to be present and partake in the usual routine of the day—the country was now prescribed him as the means of entire restoration; and as Lord Elmwood designed to leave London some time in June, he advised him to go to Elmwood House a week or two before him;—this advice was received with delight, and a letter was sent to Mr. Sandford to prepare for Mr. Rushbrook's arrival.

CHAPTER XII

DURING the illness of Rushbrook, news had been sent of his danger from the servants in town to those at Elmwood House, and Lady Matilda expressed compassion when she was told of it—she began to conceive the instant she thought he would soon die, that his visit to her had some merit rather than impertinence in its design, and that he might possibly be a more deserving man than she had supposed him to be. Even Sandford and Miss Woodley began to recollect qualifications he possessed, which they never had reflected on before, and Miss Woodley in particular reproached herself that she had been so severe and inattentive to him.—Notwithstanding the prospects his death pointed out to her, it was with infinite joy she heard he was recovered; nor was Sandford less satisfied; for he had treated the young man too unkindly not to dread, lest any ill should befall him;—but although he was glad to hear of his restored health, when he was informed he was coming down to Elmwood House for a few weeks in the style of its master, Sandford, with all his religious and humane principles, could not help thinking, "that provided the lad had been properly prepared, he had been as well out of the world as in it."

He was still less his friend when he saw him arrive with his usual florid appearance: had he come pale and sickly, Sandford had been kind to him; but in apparent good health and spirits, he could not form his mouth to tell him he was "glad to see him."

On his arrival, Matilda, who for five months had been at large, secluded herself as she would have done upon the arrival of Lord Elmwood; but with far different sensations.—Notwithstanding her restriction on the latter occasion, the residence of her father in that house had been a source of pleasure, rather than of sorrow to her; but from the abode of Rushbrook she derived punishment alone.

When, from inquiries made to his own servant, who inquired again, Rushbrook found that on his approach Matilda had retired to her own confined apartments, the thought was torture to him; it was the hope of seeing and conversing with her, of being admitted at all to her society as the mistress of the house, that had raised his spirits, and effected his perfect cure, beyond any other cause; and he was hurt to the greatest degree at this respect, or rather contempt, shown to him by her retreat.

It was, nevertheless, a subject too delicate to touch upon in any one sense—an invitation for her company on his part, might carry the appearance of superior authority, and an affected condescension, which he justly considered as the worst of all insults.—And yet, how could he support the idea that his visit had placed the daughter of his benefactor as a dependant stranger in that house, where in reality he was the dependant, and she the lawful heir.—For two or three days he suffered the torments of these reflections, hoping to come to an explanation of all he felt by a fortunate meeting with Miss Woodley; but when that meeting occurred, although he observed she talked to him with less reserve than she had formerly done, and even gave some proofs of the goodness of her disposition, yet she scrupulously avoided naming Lady Matilda; and when he diffidently enquired of her Ladyship's health, a cold restraint spread over Miss Woodley's face, and she left him instantly.—To Sandford it was still more difficult to apply; for though they were frequently together, they were never sociable; and as Sandford seldom disguised his feelings, to Rushbrook he was always extremely severe, and sometimes unmannerly.

In this perplexed situation, the country air was rather of detriment than service to the invalid; and had he not, like a true lover, held fast to hope, while he could perceive nothing but despair; he had returned to town, rather than by his stay placed in a subordinate state the object of his adoration.—But still persisting in his hopes, he one morning met Miss Woodley in the garden, and engaging her a longer time than usual in conversation, at last obtained her promise "She would that day dine with him and Mr. Sandford."— But no sooner had she parted from him than she repented of her consent, and upon communicating it to Matilda, that young lady, for the first time in her life, darted upon her kind companion, a look of the most cutting reproach and haughty resentment.—Miss Woodley's own sentiments had upbraided her before; but she was not prepared to receive so pointed a mark of disapprobation from her young friend, till now, duteous and humble to her as to a mother, and not less affectionate. Her heart was too susceptible to bear this disrespectful and contumelious frown from the object of her long-devoted care and concern; the tears instantly covered her face, and she laid her hands upon her heart, as if she thought it would break.—Matilda was moved, but she possessed too much of the manly resentment of her father, to discover what she felt for the first few minutes.—Miss Woodley, who had given so many tears to her sorrows, but never till now, one to her anger, had a still deeper sense of this indifference, than of the anger itself, and to conceal what she suffered, left the room.—Matilda, who had been till this time working at her needle, seemingly composed, now let her work drop from her hand, and sat for a little while in a deep reverie.—At length she rose up, and followed Miss Woodley to the other apartment.—She entered grave, majestic, and apparently serene, while her poor heart fluttered with a thousand distressing sensations.—She approached Miss Woodley (who was still in tears) with a sullen silence; and awed by her manners the faithful friend of her deceased mother exclaimed, "Dear Lady Matilda, think no more on what I have done—do not resent it any longer, and on my knees I'll beg your pardon." Miss Woodley rose as she uttered these last words; but Matilda laid fast hold of her to prevent the posture she offered to take, and instantly assumed it herself. "Oh, let this be my atonement!" she cried with the most earnest supplication.

They interchanged forgiveness; and as this reconciliation was sincere, they each without reserve gave their opinion upon the subject which had caused the misunderstanding; and it was agreed that an apology should be sent to Mr. Rushbrook, "That Miss Woodley had been suddenly indisposed." nor could this be said to differ from the truth, for since what had passed she was unfit to pay a visit.

Rushbrook, who had been all the morning elated with the advance he supposed he had made in that lady's favour, was highly disappointed, vext, and angry when this apology was delivered to him; nor did he, nor perhaps could he, conceal what he felt, although his severe observer, Mr. Sandford, was present.

"I am a very unfortunate man." said he, as soon as the servant was gone who brought the message.

Sandford cast his eyes upon him with a look of surprise and contempt.

"A very unfortunate man indeed, Mr. Sandford," repeated he, "although you treat my complaint contemptuously."

Sandford made no reply, and seemed above making one.

They sat down to dinner;—Rushbrook eat scarce any thing, but drank frequently; Sandford took no notice of either, but had a book (which was his custom when he dined with persons whose conversation was not interesting to him) laid by the side of his plate, which he occasionally looked into, as the dishes were re-moving, or other opportunities served.

Rushbrook, just now more hopeless than ever of forming an acquaintance with Lady Matilda, began to give way to the symp-toms of despair; and they made their first attack by urging him to treat on the same level of familiarity that he himself was treated, Mr. Sandford, to whom he had till now ever behaved with the most profound tokens of respect.

"Come," said he to him as soon as the dinner was removed, "Lay aside your book and be good company."

Sandford lifted up his eyes upon him—stared in his face—and cast them on the book again.

"I say," continued Rushbrook, "I want a companion; and as Miss Woodley has disappointed me, I must have your company."

Sandford now laid down his book upon the table, but still hold-ing his fingers in the pages he was reading, said, "And why are you disappointed of Miss Woodley's company?—When people expect what they have no right to hope for, they have yet the assurance to complain they are disappointed."

"I had a right to expect she would come," answered Rushbrook, "for she promised she would."

"But what right had you to ask her?"

"The right every one has, to make his time pass as agreeably as he can."

"But not at the expence of another."

"I believe, Mr. Sandford, it would be a heavy expence to you, to see me happy; I believe it would cost you even your own happiness."

"That is a price I have not now to give." replied Sandford, and he began reading again.

"What, you have already paid it away? No wonder that at your time of life it should be gone.—But what do you think of my having already squandered mine?"

"I don't think about you." returned Sandford, without taking his eyes from the book.

"Can you look me in the face and say that, Mr. Sandford?—No, you cannot—for you know you *do* think of me, and you know you hate me."—Here he drank two glasses of wine one after another; "And I can tell you why you hate me." continued he: "It is from a cause for which I often hate myself."

Sandford read on.

"It is on Lady Matilda's account you hate me, and use me thus."

Sandford put down his book hastily, and put both his hands by his side.

"Yes," resumed Rushbrook, "you think I am wronging her."

"I think you grossly insult her," exclaimed Sandford, "by this rude mention of her name; and I command you at your peril to desist."

"At my peril! Mr. Sandford? Do you assume the authority of Lord Elmwood?"

"I do on this occasion; and if you dare to give your tongue a freedom"—

Rushbrook interrupted him—"Why then I boldly say, (and as her friend you ought rather to applaud than resent it) I boldly say, my heart suffers so much for her situation, I am regardless of my own.—I love her father—I loved her mother more—but she herself beyond either."

"Hold your licentious tongue," cried Sandford, "or quit the room."

"Licentious? Oh! the pure thoughts that dwell in her innocent mind, are not less sensual than mine towards her.—Do you upbraid me with my respect, my pity for her? These are the sensations which impel me to speak thus undisguised, even to you, my open—no, even worse—my secret enemy!"

"Insult *me* as you please, Mr. Rushbrook,—but beware how you mention Lord Elmwood's daughter."

"Can it be to her dishonour that I pity her? that I would quit the house this moment never to return, so she supplied the place I withhold from her."

"Go, then." cried Sandford.

"It would be of no use to her, or I would.—But come, Mr. Sandford, I will dare do as much as you.—Only second me, and I will entreat Lord Elmwood to be reconciled—to see and own her."

"Your vanity would be equal to your rashness.—You entreat?—She must greatly esteem those parental favours which your entreaties gained her!—Do you forget, young man, how short a time it is, since you were entreated for?"

"I prove I do not, while this anxiety for Lady Matilda, arises, from what I feel on that account."

"Remove your anxiety, then, from her to yourself; for were I to let Lord Elmwood know what has passed now"—

"It is for your own sake, not for mine, if you don't."

"You shall not dare me to it, Mr. Rushbrook,"—And he rose from his seat: "You shall not dare me to do you an injury.—But to avoid the temptation, I will never again come into your company, unless my friend Lord Elmwood is present, to protect me and his child from your insults."

Rushbrook rose in yet more warmth than Sandford. "Have you the injustice to say I have insulted Lady Matilda?"

"To speak of her at all, is in you an insult.—But you have done more—You have dared to visit her—to force into her presence and shock her with your offers of services which she scorns; and of your compassion which she is far above."

"Did she complain to you?"

"She, or her friend did."

"I rather suppose, Mr. Sandford, you have bribed some of the servants to reveal this."

"The suspicion becomes Lord Elmwood's heir."

"It becomes the man, who lives in a house with you."

"I thank you, Mr. Rushbrook, for what has passed this day—it has taken a weight off my mind.—I thought my disinclination to you, might perhaps arise from prejudice—this conversation has relieved me from those fears, and I thank you."—Saying this he calmly walked out of the room, and left Rushbrook to reflect on what he had been doing.

Heated with the wine he had drank, (and which Sandford engaged on his book had not observed) no sooner was he alone, than he became at once cool and repentant.—"What had he done?" was the first question to himself—"He had offended Sandford"—The man whom reason as well as prudence had ever taught him to treat with respect and even reverence.—He had grossly offended the firm friend of Lady Matilda, and even by the unreserved, the wanton use of her name.—All the retorts he had uttered came now to his memory; with a total forgetfulness of all Sandford had said to provoke them.

He once thought to follow him and Beg his pardon; but the contempt with which he had been treated, more than all the anger, withheld him.

As he sat forming plans how to retrieve the opinion, ill as it was, which Sandford formerly entertained of him, he received a letter from Lord Elmwood, kindly enquiring after his health, and saying he should be down early in the following week.—Never were the friendly expressions of his Lordship half so welcome to him; for they served to sooth his imagination, racked with Sandford's wrath and his own displeasure.

CHAPTER XIII

WHEN Sandford acted deliberately he always acted up to his duty; it was his duty to forgive Rushbrook and he did so—but he had declared he would never "be again in his company unless Lord Elmwood was present;"—and with all his forgiveness, he found an unforgiving gratification, in the duty, of being obliged to keep his word.

The next day Rushbrook dined alone, while Sandford gave his company to the ladies.—Rushbrook was too proud to seek to Sandford with abject concessions, but he endeavoured to meet him as by accident, and try what, in such a case, a submissive apology might effect.—For a day or two, all the schemes he formed on that head proved fruitless; he could never procure even a sight of him.—But on the evening of the third day, taking a lonely walk, he turned the corner of a grove, and saw in the very path he was going, Sandford accompanied by Miss Woodley; and, what agitated him much more, Lady Matilda was with them.—He knew not whether to proceed, or to quit the path and palpably shun them—To one who seemed to put an unkind construction upon all he said and did, he knew to do either, would be to do wrong.—In spite of the propensity he felt to pass so near to Lady Matilda, could he have known what conduct would have been deemed the most respectful, whatever painful denial it had cost him, that, he would have adopted.—But undetermined whether to go forward, or to cross to another path, he still walked on till he came too nigh to recede; he then, with a diffidence not affected, but felt in the most powerful degree, pulled off his hat; and without bowing, stood silently while the company passed.—Sandford walked on some paces before, and took no farther notice as he went by him, than just touching the fore part of his hat with his finger.—Miss Woodley curtsied as she followed.—But Lady Matilda made a full stop, and said, in the gentlest accents, "I hope, Mr. Rushbrook, you are perfectly recovered."

It was the sweetest music he ever listened to; and he returned with the most respectful bow, "I am better a great deal, Ma'am." and pursued his way as if he did not dare to utter another syllable.

Sandford seldom found fault with Lady Matilda; not because he loved her, but because she seldom did wrong—upon this occasion, however, he was half inclined to reprimand her; but yet he did not know what to say—the subsequent humility of Rushbrook had taken from the indiscretion of her speaking to him, and the event could by no means justify his censure.—On hearing her begin to speak Sandford had stopped; and as Rushbrook after replying, walked away, Sandford called to her crossly, "Come, come along." But at the same time he put out his elbow for her to take hold of his arm.

She hastened her steps, and did so—then turning to Miss Woodley, she said, "I expected you would have spoken to Mr. Rushbrook; it might have prevented me."

Miss Woodley replied, "I was at a loss what to do;—when we met formerly, he always spoke first."

"And ought now." cried Sandford angrily—and then added, with a sarcastic smile, "It is certainly the duty of the superior, to be the first who speaks."

"He did not look as if he thought himself our superior." replied Matilda.

"No," returned Sandford, "some people can put on what looks they please."

"Then while he looks so pale," replied Matilda, "and so dejected, I can never forbear speaking to him when we meet, whatever he may think of it."

"And were he and I to meet a hundred, nay a thousand times," replied Sandford, "I don't think I shall ever speak to him again."

"Bless me! what for, Mr. Sandford?" cried Matilda—for Sandford, who was not a man that repeated little incidents, had never mentioned the circumstance of their quarrel.

"I have taken such a resolution,"—answered he, "yet I bear him no enmity."

As this short reply indicated he meant to say no more, no more was asked; and the subject dropped.

In the mean time, Rushbrook, happier than he had been for months; intoxicated with joy at that voluntary mark of civility he had received from Lady Matilda, felt his heart so joyous, so free from every particle of malice, that he resolved in the humblest manner, to make atonement for the breach of decorum he had lately been guilty of to Mr. Sandford.

Too happy at this time to suffer a mortification from any treatment he might receive, he sent his servant to him into his study, as soon as he was returned home, to beg to know "If he might be permitted to wait upon him, with a message he had to deliver from Lord Elmwood."

The servant returned—"Mr. Sandford desired he would send the message by him, or the house steward." This was highly affronting; but Rushbrook was not in a humour to be offended, and he sent again, begging he would admit him;—but the answer was, "He was busy." Thus defeated in his hopes of reconciliation, his new transports felt an allay, and the few days that remained before Lord Elmwood came, he passed in solitary musing, and ineffectual walks and looks towards that path where he had met Matilda—she came that way no more—nor indeed scarce quitted her apartment, in the practice of that confinement she had to experience on the arrival of her father.

All her former agitations now returned.—On the day he arrived she wept—all the night she did not sleep—and the name of Rushbrook again became hateful to her.—His Lordship came in extreme good health and spirits, but appeared concerned to find Rushbrook less well than when he went from town.—Sandford was now under the necessity of being in Rushbrook's company, yet he took care never to speak to him but when he was obliged; or to look at him but when he could not help it.—Lord Elmwood observed this conduct, yet he neither wondered, or was offended at it—he had always perceived what little esteem Sandford showed his nephew from his first return; but he forgave in Sandford's humour a thousand faults he would forgive in no other; nor did he deem this one of his greatest faults, knowing the claim to his partiality from another object.

Miss Woodley waited on Lord Elmwood as formerly; dined with him, and as heretofore related to the attentive Matilda all that passed.

About this time Lord Margrave, deprived by the season of all the sports of the field, felt his love for Matilda (which had been extreme while divided with the love of hunting) too violent to be subdued; and he resolved, though reluctantly, to apply to her father for his consent to their union;—but writing to Sandford this resolution, he was once more repulsed, and charged as a man of honour, to forbear to disturb the tranquility of the family by any application of the kind.—To this Sandford received no answer; for his Lordship, highly incensed at his mistress's repugnance to him, determined more firmly than ever, to consult his own happiness alone; and as that depended merely upon his obtaining her, he cared not by what method it was effected.

About a fortnight after Lord Elmwood came into the country, as he was riding one morning, his horse fell with him, and crushed his leg in so unfortunate a manner, as to be pronounced of dangerous consequence.—He was brought home in a post chaise, and Matilda heard of the accident with more grief than would, on such an occasion, appertain to the most fondled child.

In consequence of the pain he suffered his fever was one night very high; and Sandford, who seldom quitted his apartment, went frequently to his bed side; every time with the secret hope he should hear him ask to see his daughter—he was every time disappointed—yet he saw him shake with a cordial friendship the hand of Rushbrook, as if he delighted in seeing those he loved.

The danger in which Lord Elmwood was supposed to be, was but of short duration, and his sudden recovery succeeded.—Matilda who had wept, moaned, and watched during the crisis of his illness, when she heard he was amending, exclaimed (with a kind of surprise at the novelty of the sensation) "And this is joy that I feel!—Oh! I never till now knew, what those persons felt that experienced joy."

Nor did she repine, like Mr. Sandford and Miss Woodley, at her father's inattention to her during his malady, for she did not hope like them—she did not hope he would behold her, even in dying.

But notwithstanding his Lordship's seeming indifference while his indisposition continued, no sooner was he recovered so as to receive the congratulations of his friends, than there was no one person he evidently showed so much satisfaction at seeing, as Miss Woodley.—She waited upon him timorously, and with more than ordinary distaste at his late conduct; when he put out his hand with the utmost warmth to receive her, drew her to him, saluted her, (an honour he had never in his life conferred before) and all with signs of the sincerest friendship and affection.—Sandford was present, and ever associating the idea of Matilda with Miss Woodley, felt his heart bound with a triumph it had not enjoyed for many a day.

Matilda listened with delight to the recital Miss Woodley gave on her return, and many times while it lasted exclaimed "She was happy." But poor Matilda's sudden transports of joy, which she termed happiness, were not made for long continuance; and if she ever found cause for gladness, she far oftener had motives for grief.

As Mr. Sandford was sitting with her and Miss Woodley one evening about a week after, a person rung at the bell and enquired for him; on being told of it by the servant, he went to the door of the apartment and cried "Oh! is it you? Come in."—An elderly man entered, who had been for many years the head gardener at Elmwood House; a man of honesty and sobriety, and with a large indigent family of aged parents, children, and other relatives, who subsisted wholly on the income arising from his place—The ladies, as well as Sandford, knew him well, and they all, almost at once, asked "What was the matter?" for his looks told them something distressful had befallen him.

"Oh, Sir!" said he to Sandford, "I come to entreat your interest."

"In what, Edwards?" said Sandford with a mild voice; for when his assistance was supplicated in distress, his rough tones always took a plaintive key.

"My Lord has discharged me from his service,"—(returned Edwards trembling, and the tears starting in his eyes)[1] "I am undone, Mr. Sandford, unless you plead for me."

"I will," said Sandford, "I will."

"And yet I am almost afraid of your success," replied the man, "for my Lord has ordered me out of his house this moment; and though I knelt down to him to be heard, he had no pity."

---

1   The phrase "tears starting in his eyes" is removed from the second, third, fourth, and fifth editions.

Matilda sighed from the bottom of her heart, and yet she envied this poor man who had been kneeling to her father.

"What was your offence?" cried Sandford.

The man hesitated; then looking at Matilda, said, "I'll tell you, Sir, some other time."

"Did you name me, before Lord Elmwood?" cried she eagerly, and terrified.

"No, Madam," replied he, "but I unthinkingly spoke of my poor Lady that is dead and gone."

Matilda burst into tears.

"How came you to do so mad a thing?" cried Sandford, with the encouragement his looks had once given him, now fled from his face.

"It was unthinkingly," repeated Edwards; "I was showing my Lord some plans for the new walks, and told him, among other things, that her Ladyship had many years ago approved of them.— 'Who?' cried he.—Still I did not call to mind, but repeated 'Lady Elmwood, Sir, while you were abroad'—As soon as these words were delivered I saw my doom in his looks, and he commanded me to quit his house and service that instant."

"I am afraid," said Sandford, sitting down, "I can do nothing for you."

"Yes, Sir, you know you have more power over my Lord than any body—and perhaps you may be able to save me and all mine from misery."

"I would if I could." replied Sandford quickly.

"You can but try, Sir."

Matilda was all this while drowned in tears; nor Miss Woodley much less affected—Lady Elmwood was before their eyes— Matilda beheld her in her dying moments; Miss Woodley saw her, as the gay ward of Dorriforth.

"Ask Mr. Rushbrook," said Sandford, "prevail on him to speak; he has more power than I have."

"He has not enough, then," replied Edwards, "for he was in the room with my Lord when what I have told you happened."

"And did he say nothing?" asked Sandford.

"Yes, Sir; he offered to speak in my behalf, but my Lord

interrupted him, and ordered him out of the room—he instantly went."

Sandford now observing the effect which this narration had on the two ladies, led the man to his own apartments, and there assured him he durst not undertake his cause; but that if time or chance should happily make an alteration in his Lordship's disposition, he would be the first to try to replace him.—Edwards was obliged to submit; and before the next day at noon, his pleasant house by the side of the park, his garden, and his orchard, which he had occupied above twenty years, were cleared of their old inhabitant, and all his wretched family.

CHAPTER XIV

THIS melancholy incident perhaps affected Matilda and all the friends of the deceased Lady Elmwood, beyond any other that had occurred since her death.—A few days after this circumstance, Miss Woodley, in order to divert the disconsolate mind of Lady Matilda, (and perhaps bring her some little anecdotes, to console her for that which had given her so much pain) waited upon Lord Elmwood in his library, and borrowed some books out of it.—He was now perfectly well from his fall, and received her with the same politeness as usual, but, of course, not with that particular warmth he had received her just after his illness.—Rushbrook was in the library at the same time; he shewed to her several beautiful prints which his Lordship had just received from London, and appeared anxious to entertain, and give tokens of his esteem and respect for her.—But what gave her pleasure beyond any other attention was, that after she had taken (by the aid of Rushbrook) about a dozen volumes from different shelves, and had laid them together, saying she would send her servant to fetch them, Lord Elmwood went eagerly to the place where they were, and taking up each book, examined attentively what it was.—One author he complained was too light, another too depressing, and put them on the shelves again; another was erroneous and he changed it for a better; and thus he warned her against some, and selected other authors; as the most cautious preceptor culls for his pupil, or a fond father for his darling child.—She thanked him for his attention to her, but her heart thanked him for his attention to his daughter.—For as she herself had never received such a proof of his care since all their long acquaintance, she reasonably supposed Matilda's reading, and not hers, was the object of his solicitude.

Having in these books store of comfort for poor Matilda, she eagerly returned with them; and in reciting every particular circumstance, made her consider the volumes almost like presents from her father.

The month of September was now arrived, and Lord Elmwood, accompanied by Rushbrook, went to a small shooting seat, about twenty miles distant from Elmwood Castle, for a week's particular sport.—Matilda was once more at large; and one beautiful forenoon, about eleven o'clock, seeing Miss Woodley walking on the lawn before the house, she hastily took her hat to join her; and not waiting to put it on, went nimbly down the great staircase with it hanging on her arm.—When she had descended a few stairs, she heard a footstep walking slowly up; and, (from what emotion she could not tell,) she stopt short, half resolved to return back.—She hesitated a single instant which to do—then went a few steps farther till she came to the second landing place; when, by the sudden winding of the staircase,—Lord Elmwood was immediately before her!

She had felt something like affright before she saw him—but her reason told her she had nothing to fear, as he was far away.— But now the appearance of a stranger whom she had never before seen; an air of authority in his looks as well as in the sound of his steps; a resemblance to the portrait she had seen of him; a start of astonishment which he gave on beholding her; but above all—her *fears* confirmed her it was him.—She gave a scream of terror—put out her trembling hands to catch the balustrades on the stairs for support—missed them—and fell motionless into her father's arms.

He caught her, as by that impulse he would have caught any other person falling for want of aid.—Yet when he found her in his arms, he still held her there—gazed on her attentively—and once pressed her to his bosom.

At length, trying to escape the snare into which he had been led, he was going to leave her on the spot where she fell, when her eyes opened and she uttered, "Save me."—Her voice unmanned him.—His long-restrained tears now burst forth—and seeing her relapsing into the swoon again, he cried out eagerly to recall her.—Her name did not however come to his recollection—nor any name but this—"Miss Milner—Dear Miss Milner."

That sound did not awake her; and now again he wished to leave her in this senseless state, that not remembering what had passed, she might escape the punishment.

But at this instant Giffard, with another servant, passed by the foot of the stairs; on which, Lord Elmwood called to them—and into Giffard's hands delivered his apparently dead child; without one command respecting her, or one word of any kind; while his face was agitated with shame, with pity, with anger, with paternal tenderness.

As Giffard stood trembling, while he relieved his Lord from this hapless burthen, his Lordship had to unloose her hand from the side of his coat, which she had caught fast hold of as she fell, and grasped so closely, it was with difficulty released.—On taking the hand away his Lordship trembled—faltered—then bade Giffard do it.

"Who, I, my Lord, I separate you?" cried he.—But recollecting himself, "My Lord, I will obey your commands whatever they are." And seizing her hand, pulled it with violence—it fell—and her father went away.

Matilda was carried to her own apartments, laid upon the bed, and Miss Woodley called to attend her, after listening to the recital of what had passed.

When Lady Elmwood's old and affectionate friend entered the room, and saw her youthful charge lying pale and speechless, yet no father by to comfort or sooth her, she lifted up her hands to heaven exclaiming, with a flood of tears, "And is this the end of thee, my poor child?—Is this the end of all our hopes?—of thy own fearful hopes—and of thy mother's supplications?—Oh! Lord Elmwood! Lord Elmwood!"

At that name Matilda started, and cried, "Where is he?—Is it a dream, or have I seen him?"

"It is all a dream, my dear." said Miss Woodley.

"And yet I thought he held me in his arms," she replied—"I thought I felt his hands press mine—Let me sleep and dream it again."

Now thinking it best to undeceive her, "It is no dream, my dear." returned Miss Woodley.

"Is it not?" cried she, starting up and leaning on her elbow—"Then I suppose I must go away—go for ever away."—

Sandford now entered.—Having been told the news he came to condole—But at the sight of him Matilda was terrified, and cried, "Do not reproach me, do not upbraid me—I know I have done wrong—I know I had but one command from my father, and that I have disobeyed."

Sandford could not reproach her, for he could not speak;—he therefore only walked to the window and concealed his tears.

That whole day and night was passed in sympathetic grief, in alarm at every sound, lest it should be a messenger to pronounce Matilda's destiny.

Lord Elmwood did not stay upon this visit above three hours at Elmwood House; he then set off again for the seat he had left; where Rushbrook still remained, and from whence his Lordship had merely come by accident, to look over some writings he wanted dispatched to town.

During his short continuance here, Sandford cautiously avoided his presence; for he thought, in a case like this, what nature would not of herself do, no art, no arguments of his could effect—and to nature and to providence he left the whole.—What these two powerful principles brought about, the reader must judge, on perusing the following letter, received early the next morning by Miss Woodley.

END OF THE THIRD VOLUME

— VOLUME IV —

CHAPTER I

A letter from Giffard, Lord Elmwood's House Steward, to Miss Woodley.

"Madam,

"MY Lord, above a twelvemonth ago, acquainted me he had permitted his daughter to reside in his house; but at the same time he informed me, the grant was under a certain restriction, which if ever broken, I was to see his then determination (of which he also acquainted me) put in execution. In consequence of Lady Matilda's indisposition, Madam, I have ventured to delay this notice till morning—I need not say with what concern I now give it, or mention to you I believe, what is forfeited.—My Lord staid but a few hours yesterday after the unhappy circumstance on which I write, took place; nor did I see him after, till he was in his carriage; he then sent for me to the carriage door, and told me he should be back in two days time, and added "Remember your duty." That duty, I hope, Madam, you will not require I should mention in more direct terms.—As soon as my Lord returns, I have no doubt but he will ask me if it is fulfilled, and I shall be under the greatest apprehension should his commands not be obeyed.

"If there is any thing wanting for the convenience of your and Lady Matilda's departure, you have but to order it, and it is at your service—I mean likewise any cash you may have occasion for. I should presume to add my opinion where you might best take up your abode; but with such advice as you will have from Mr. Sandford, mine would be but assuming.

"I would also have waited upon you, Madam, and have delivered myself the substance of this letter; but I am an old man, and the changes I have been witness to in my Lord's house since I first lived in it, has encreased my age many years; and I have not the strength to see you upon this occasion.—I loved my deceased

Lady—I love my Lord—and I love their child—nay, so I am sure does my Lord himself; but there is no accounting for his resolutions, or for the alteration his disposition has lately undergone.

"I beg pardon, Madam, for this long intrusion, and am, and ever will be (while you and my Lord's daughter are so) your afflicted humble servant,

"ROBERT GIFFARD.

"Elmwood House,
"Sept. 12.

When this letter was brought to Miss Woodley, she knew what it contained before she opened it, and therefore took it with an air of resignation—yet though she guessed the momentous part of its contents, she dreaded in what words it might be related; and having now no great good to hope for, hope, that will never totally expire, clung at this crisis to little circumstances, and she hoped most fervently the terms of the letter might not be harsh, but that Lord Elmwood had delivered his commands in gentle language.—The event proved he had; and lost to every important comfort, she felt grateful to him for this small one.

Matilda, too, was cheared by this letter, because she expected something worse; and the last line where Giffard said he knew "his Lordship loved her." She thought repaid her for the purport of the other part.

Sandford was not so easily resigned or comforted—he walked about the room when the letter was shewn to him—called it cruel—stifled his tears, and wished to show his resentment only—but the former burst through all his endeavours, and he sunk into grief.

Nor was the fortitude of Matilda, which came to her assistance on the first onset of this trial, sufficient to arm her, when the moment came she was to quit the house—her father's house—never to see that, or him again.

When word was brought that the carriage was at the door, which was to convey her from all she held so dear, and she saw before her the prospect of a long youthful and healthful life, in which misery and despair were all she could discern; that despair seized her at once, and gaining courage from it, she cried,

"What have I to fear if I disobey my father's commands once more?—he cannot use me worse.—I'll stay here till he returns—again throw myself in his way, and then I will not faint, but plead for mercy.—Perhaps were I to kneel to him—kneel, like other children, and beg his blessing; he would not refuse it me."

"You must not try." said Sandford mildly.

"Who?" cried she, "shall prevent my flying to my father?—have I another friend on earth to go to?—have I one relation in the world but him?—This is the second time I have been commanded out of the house.—In my infant state my cruel father turned me out; but then he sent me to a mother—now I have none; and I will stay with him."

Again the steward sent to let them know the coach was waiting.

Sandford now, with a determined countenance, went coolly up to Lady Matilda, and taking her hand, seemed resolved to lead her to the carriage.

Accustomed to be awed by every serious look of his, she yet resisted this; and cried "Would *you* be the minister of my father's cruelty?"

"Then," said Sandford solemnly to her, "farewell—from this moment you and I part.—I will take my leave, and do you remain where you are—at least till you are forced away.—But I'll not stay to be turned out—for it is impossible your father will suffer any friend of yours to continue here, after this disobedience.—Adieu."

"I'll go this moment." said she, and rose hastily.

Miss Woodley took her at her word and hurried her immediately out of the room.

Sandford followed slow behind, with the same spirits as if he had followed at her funeral.

When she came to that spot on the stairs where she had met her father, she started back; and scarcely knew how to pass it.—When she had—"There he held me," said she, "and I thought I felt him press me to his heart, but I now find I was mistaken."

As Sandford came forward to hand her into the coach, "Now you behave well;" said he, "by this behaviour, you do not entirely close all prospect of reconciliation with your father."

"Do you think it is not yet impossible?" cried she, clasping his hand. "Giffard says he loves me," continued she, "and do you think he might yet be brought to forgive me?"

"Forgive you?" cried Sandford.

"Suppose I was to write to him, and entreat his forgiveness."

"Do not write yet." said Sandford with no chearing accent.

The carriage drove off—and as it went, Matilda leaned her head from the window, to survey Elmwood House from the roof to the bottom.—She cast her eyes upon the gardens too—upon the fishponds—the coach houses even, and all the offices adjoining—which as objects she should never see again—she gazed at, as objects of importance.

CHAPTER II

RUSHBROOK, who at twenty miles distance, could have no conjecture what had passed at Elmwood House, (during the short visit Lord Elmwood made there) went that way with his dogs and gun in order to meet his Lordship's charriot on its return and ride with him back—he did so—and getting into the carriage, told my Lord eagerly the sport he had had during the day; laughed at an accident that had befallen one of his dogs, and for some time did not perceive but that his Lordship was perfectly attentive.—At length, observing he answered more negligently than usual to what he said, Rushbrook turned his eyes quickly upon him and cried,

"My Lord, are you not well?"

"Yes; perfectly well, I thank you, Rushbrook." replied his Lordship, and leaned back against the carriage.

"I thought, Sir," returned Rushbrook, "you spoke languidly; I beg your pardon."

"I have the head-ake a little." answered he;—Then taking off his hat, brushed the powder from it, and as he put it on again, fetched a most heavy sigh; which no sooner had escaped him, than, to drown its sound, he said briskly,

"And so you tell me you have had good sport to-day?"

"No, my Lord, I said but indifferent."

"True, so you did.—Bid the man drive faster—it will be dark before we get home."

"You will shoot to-morrow, my Lord?"

"Certainly."

"How does Mr. Sandford do, Sir?"

"I did not see him."

"Not see Mr. Sandford, my Lord?—but he was out, I suppose—for they did not expect you at Elmwood House."

"No, they did not."

In such conversation Rushbrook and his uncle continued till the end of their journey.—Dinner was then immediately served, and his Lordship now appeared much in his usual spirits; at least not suspecting any cause for their abatement, Rushbrook did not observe any alteration.

Lord Elmwood went however earlier to bed than ordinary, or rather to his bedchamber; for though he retired some time before his nephew, when Rushbrook passed his chamber door it was open; and he not in bed, but sitting in a musing posture as if he had forgot to shut it.

When Rushbrook's valet came to attend his master, he said to him,

"I suppose, Sir, you do not know what has happened at Elmwood House."

"For heaven's sake what?" cried Rushbrook.

"My Lord has met Lady Matilda." replied the man.

"How? Where? What's the consequence?"

"We don't know yet, Sir; but all the servants suppose, her Ladyship will not be suffered to remain there any longer."

"They all suppose wrong," returned Rushbrook hastily; "my Lord loves her I am certain, and this event may be the happy means, of his treating her as his child, from this day."

The servant smiled and shook his head.

"Why, what more do you know?"

"Nothing more than I have told you, Sir; except that his Lordship took no kind notice of her Ladyship, that appeared like love."

Rushbrook was all uneasiness and anxiety to know the particulars of what had passed; and now Lord Elmwood's inquietude, which he had but slightly noticed before, came full to his observation.—He was going to ask more questions, but he recollected

Lady Matilda's misfortunes were too sacred, to be talked of thus familiarly by the servants of the family;—besides, it was evident this man thought, and but naturally, it might not be for his master's interest the father and the daughter should be united; and therefore would certainly give to all he said the opposite colouring.

In spite of his prudence, however, and his delicacy towards Matilda, Rushbrook could not let his valet leave him till he had inquired, and learnt all the circumstantial account of what had happened; except, indeed, the order received by Giffard; which being given after his Lordship was in his carriage, and in concise terms, the domestics who attended him (and from whom this man had gained his intelligence) were of that unacquainted.

When the valet had left Rushbrook alone, the perturbation of his mind was so great, that he was at length undetermined whether to go to bed, or to rush into his uncle's apartment, and at his feet beg for that compassion upon his daughter, which he feared he had denied her.—But then again, to what dangers did he not expose himself by such a step? Nay, he might perhaps even injure her whom he wished to serve; for if his Lordship was at present unresolved whether to forgive or to resent this disobedience to his commands, another's interference might enrage, and determine him on the latter.

This consideration was so weighty it resigned Rushbrook to the suspense he must endure till the morning; when he flattered himself, that by watching every look and motion of Lord Elmwood's, his penetration would be able to discover that state of his heart, and how he meant to act.

But the morning came, and he found all his prying curiosity was of no avail; his Lordship did not use one word, one look, or action that was not customary.

On first seeing him, Rushbrook blushed at the secret with which he was entrusted; then contemplated the joy he ought to have known in clasping in his arms a child like Matilda—whose tenderness, reverence, and duty had deprived her of all sensation at his sight; which was in Rushbrook's mind an honour, that rendered him superior to what he was before.

They were in the fields all day as usual; Lord Elmwood now chearful, and complaining no more of the head-ake.—Yet once being separated from his nephew, Rushbrook crossed over a stile into another field, and found him sitting by the side of a bank, his gun laying by him, and he lost in thought. He rose on seeing him, and proceeded to the sport as before.

At dinner, he said he should not go to Elmwood House the next day, as he had appointed, but stay where he was, three or four days longer.—From these two small occurrences, Rushbrook would fain have extracted something by which to judge the state of his mind; but upon the test, that was impossible—he had caught him musing many a time before; and as to his prolonging his stay, that might arise from the sport—or, indeed, had any thing more material swayed him, who could penetrate whether it was the effect of the lenity, or the severity, he had dealt towards his child? whether his continuance there was to shun here, or to shun the house from whence he had turned her?

The three or four days for their abode where they were, being passed, they both returned together to Elmwood House.— Rushbrook thought he saw his uncle's countenance change as they entered the avenue, yet he did not appear less in spirits; and when Sandford joined them at dinner, his Lordship went with his usual chearfulness to him, and (as was his custom after any separation) put out his hand chearfully to take his.—Sandford said, "How do you do, my Lord?" chearfully in return; but put both his hands into his bosom, and walked to the other side of the room.—Lord Elmwood did not seem to observe this affront—nor was it done as an affront—it was merely what poor Sandford felt; and he felt he could *not* shake hands with him.

Rushbrook soon learnt the news that Matilda was gone, and Elmwood House was to him a desert—he saw about it no real friend of hers, except poor Sandford, and to him Rushbrook knew himself now, more displeasing than ever; and all the overtures he made to him to be friends, he at this time, found more and more ineffectual.—Matilda was banished; and her supposed triumphant rival was, to Sandford, more odious than he ever had been.

In alleviation of their banishment, Miss Woodley with her charge had not returned to their old retreat; but were gone to a large farm house, no more than about thirty miles from Lord Elmwood's: here Sandford with little inconvenience visited them;

nor did his Lordship ever take any notice of his occasional absence; for as he had before given his daughter, in some measure, to his charge, so honour, delicacy, and the common ties of duty, made him approve rather than condemn his attention to her.

Though Sandford's frequent visits soothed Matilda, they could not comfort her; for he had no consolation to bestow suited to her mind—her father had given no one token of regret for what he had done. He had even inquired sternly of Giffard on his returning home,

"If Miss Woodley had left the house?"

The steward guessing the whole of his meaning, answered, "Yes, my Lord; and *all* your commands in that respect have been obeyed."

He replied, "I am satisfied." and, to the grief of the old man, appeared really so.

To the farm house, the place of Matilda's residence, there came, besides Sandford, another visitor far less welcome; Viscount Margrave.—He had heard with surprise, and still greater joy, that Lord Elmwood had once more shut his doors against his daughter.—In this her discarded state, his Lordship no longer burthened his lively imagination with the dull thoughts of Marriage, but once more formed the brutal idea of making her his mistress.

Ignorant of a certain decorum which attended all Lord Elmwood's actions, he suspected his child might be in want; and an acquaintance with the worst part of her sex informed him, relief from poverty was the sure bargain for his success.—With these hopes, he again paid Miss Woodley and her a visit; but the coldness with which he was still received by the first, and the haughtiness with which the last, still kept him at a distance, again made him fear to give one allusion of his purpose: but he returned home resolved to write what he durst not speak—he did so—he offered his services, his purse, his house; they were rejected with contempt, and a still stronger prohibition given to his visits.

CHAPTER III

LORD Elmwood had now allowed Rushbrook a long vacation, in respect to his answer upon the subject of marriage; and the young man vainly imagined, his Lordship's intentions upon that subject were entirely given up.—One morning however, as he was attending him in the library,

"Henry"—said his Lordship, with a pause at the beginning of his speech, which indicated he was going to say something of importance, "Henry—you have not forgot the discourse I had with you, a little time previous to your illness?"

Henry hesitated—for he wished to have forgotten it—but it was too strongly impressed upon his mind. His uncle resumed:

"What, equivocating again, Sir?—Do you remember it, or do you not?"—

"Yes, my Lord, I do."

"And are you prepared to give me an answer?"

Rushbrook paused again.

"In our former conversation," his Lordship continued, "I gave you but a week to determine—there is, I think, elapsed since that time, half a year."

"About as much, Sir."

"Then surely you have now made up your mind?"

"I had done that, at first, my Lord—provided it had met with your concurrence."

"You wished to lead a bachelor's life, I think you said."

Rushbrook bowed.

"Contrary to my will?"

"No, my Lord, I wished to have your approbation."

"And you wished for my approbation of the very opposite thing to that I proposed?—But I am not surprised—such is the gratitude of the world—and such is yours."

"My Lord, if you doubt my gratitude"—

"Give me a proof of it, Harry, and I will doubt of it no longer."

"Upon every other subject but this, my Lord, heaven is my witness your happiness"—

His Lordship interrupted him. "I understand you—upon every other subject, but the only one, my content requires, you are ready to obey me.—I thank you."

"My Lord, do not torture me with this suspicion; it is so contrary to my deserts, I cannot bear it."

"Suspicion of your ingratitude!—you judge too favourably of my opinion;—it amounts to certainty."

"Then to convince you, Sir, I am not ungrateful,—tell me who the lady is you have chosen for me, and here I give you my word, I will sacrifice all my future prospects of happiness—all, for which I would wish to live—and become her husband, as soon as you shall appoint."

This was spoken with a tone so expressive of despair, that Lord Elmwood replied,

"And while you obey me, you take care to let me know, it will cost you your future happiness.—This is, I suppose, to enhance the merit of the obligation—but I shall not accept your acquiescence on these terms."

"Then in dispensing with it, I hope Sir, for your pardon!"

"Do you suppose, Rushbrook, I can pardon an offence, the sole foundation of which, arises from a spirit of disobedience?—for you have declared to me your affections are disengaged.—In our last conversation did you not say so?"

"At first I did, my Lord—but you permitted me to consult my heart more closely; and I have found I was mistaken."

"You then own you at first told me a falsehood, and yet have all this time, kept me in suspense without confessing it."

"I waited, Sir, till you should enquire"—

"You have then Sir, waited too long." And the fire flashed from his eyes.

Rushbrook now found himself in that perilous state, that admitted of no medium of resentment, but by such dastardly conduct on his part, as would wound both his truth and courage;—and thus animated by his danger, he was resolved to plunge boldly at once into the depth of his patron's anger.

"My Lord," said he, (but he did not undertake this task without sustaining the trembling and convulsion of his whole frame) "My Lord—waving for a moment the subject of my marriage—permit me to remind you, that when I was upon my sick bed, you promised, that on my recovery, you would listen to a petition I had to offer you."

"Let me recollect."—said his Lordship. "Yes—I remember something of it.—But I said nothing to warrant any improper petition."

"Its impropriety was not named, my Lord."

"No matter—that, you yourself must judge of, and answer for the consequences."

"I would answer with my life, willingly—but I own I shrink from your anger."

"Then do not provoke it."

"I have already gone too far to recede—and you would of course demand an explanation, if I attempted to stop here."

"I should."

"Then, my Lord, I am bound to speak—but do not interrupt me—hear me out, before you banish me from your sight for ever."

"I will, Sir." replied his Lordship, prepared to hear something that would displease him, and yet determined to hear with patience to the conclusion.

"Then, my Lord"—(cried Rushbrook in the greatest agitation both of mind and body) "Your daughter"—

The resolution his Lordship had taken (and on which he had given his word to his nephew not to interrupt him) immediately gave way.—The colour rose in his face—his eyes darted lightning—and his hand was lifted up with the emotion, that word had created.

"You promised to hear me, my Lord;" cried Rushbrook, "and I claim your promise."

His Lordship now suddenly overcame his violence of passion, and stood silent and resigned to hear him; but with a determined look, expressive of the vengeance that should ensue.

"Lady Matilda," resumed Rushbrook, "is an object that wrests from me the enjoyment of every blessing your kindness bestows.—I cannot but feel myself as her adversary—as one who has supplanted her in your affections—who supplies her place, while she is exiled, a wanderer, and an orphan."

His Lordship took off his eyes from Rushbrook, during this last sentence, and cast them on the floor.

"If I feel gratitude towards you, my Lord," continued he, "gratitude is innate in my heart, and I must also feel it towards her, who first introduced me to your protection."

Again the colour flew to Lord Elmwood's face; and again he could hardly restrain himself from uttering his indignation.

"It was the mother of Lady Matilda;" continued Rushbrook, "who was this friend to me; nor will I ever think of marriage, or any other joyful prospect, while you abandon the only child of my beloved patroness, and load me with the rights, which belong to her."

Here Rushbrook stopped—and Lord Elmwood was silent too, for near half a minute; but still his countenance continued fixed, with his unvaried resolves.

After this long pause, his Lordship said composedly, but firmly, "Have you finished, Mr. Rushbrook?"

"All that I dare to utter, my Lord, and I fear, already too much."

Rushbrook now trembled more than ever, and looked pale as death; for the ardour of speaking being over, he waited his sentence, with less constancy of mind than he expected he should.

"You disapprove my conduct, it seems;" said Lord Elmwood, "and in that, you are but like the rest of the world—and yet, among all my acquaintance, you are the only one who has dared to insult me with your opinion.—And this you have not done inadvertently; moreover knowingly, willingly, and deliberately.—But as it has been my fate to be used ill, and severed from all those persons to whom my soul has been most attached; with less regret I can part from you, than was this my first trial."

There was a truth and a pathetic sound in the utterance of these words that struck Rushbrook to the heart—and he beheld himself as a barbarian, who had treated his benevolent and only friend, with an insufferable liberty; void of respect for those gnawing sorrows which had imbittered so many years of his life, and in open violation of his most strict commands.—He felt he deserved all he was going to suffer, and he fell upon his knees, not so much to deprecate the doom he saw impending, as thus humbly to acknowledge it was his due.

Lord Elmwood, irritated by this posture, as a sign of the presumptuous hopes he might be forgiven, suffered now his anger to break through all bounds; and raising his voice, he cried in rage,

"Leave my house, Sir,—Leave my house instantly, and seek some other home."

Just as these words were begun, Sandford opened the library door; was witness to them, and to the imploring situation of Rushbrook.—He stood silent with amaze!

Rushbrook arose, and feeling in his mind a presage, that he might never from that hour, behold his benefactor more; as he bowed to him in token of obedience to his commands, a shower of tears covered his face;—but Lord Elmwood, unmoved, fixed his eyes upon him which pursued him with their enraged looks to the end of the room.—Here he had to pass Sandford; who, for the first time in his life, took hold of him by the hand, and said to Lord Elmwood, "My Lord, what's the matter?"

"That ungrateful villain," cried his Lordship, "has dared to insult me.—Leave my house this moment, Sir."

Rushbrook made an effort to go, but Sandford still held his hand; and said to Lord Elmwood,

"He is but a boy, my Lord, and do not give him the punishment of a man."

Rushbrook now snatched his hand from Sandford's, and threw it with himself upon his neck; where he indeed sobbed like a boy.

"You are both in league." exclaimed Lord Elmwood.

"Do you suspect me of partiality to Mr. Rushbrook?" said Sandford, advancing nearer to his Lordship.

Rushbrook had now gained the point of remaining in the room; but the hope that privilege inspired (while he still harboured all the just apprehensions for his fate) gave birth, perhaps, to a more exquisite sensation of pain, than despair would have done.—He stood silent—confounded—hoping he was forgiven—fearing he was not.

As Sandford approached still nearer to Lord Elmwood, he

continued, "No, my Lord, I know you do not suspect me, of partiality to Mr. Rushbrook—has any part of my behaviour ever discovered it?"

"You now then," replied his Lordship, "only interfere to provoke me."

"If that were the case," returned Sandford, "there have been occasions, when I might have done it more effectually—when my own heart-strings were breaking, because I would not provoke, or add to what you suffered."

"I am obliged to you, Mr. Sandford." said his Lordship mildly.

"And if, my Lord, I have proved any merit in a late forbearance, reward me for it now; and take this young man from the depth of despair in which I see he is sunk, and say you pardon him."

Lord Elmwood made no answer—and Rushbrook drawing strong inferences of hope from his silence, lifted up his eyes from the ground, and ventured to look in his face; he found it composed to what it had been, but still strongly marked with agitation.—He cast his eyes away again, in confusion.

On which his Lordship said to him—"I shall postpone your complying with my orders, till you think fit once more to provoke them—and then, not even Sandford, shall dare to plead your excuse."

Rushbrook bowed.

"Go, leave the room, Sir."

He instantly obeyed.

While Sandford, turning to Lord Elmwood, shook him by the hand, and cried, "My Lord, I thank you—I thank you very kindly, my Lord—I shall now begin to think I have some weight with you."

"You might indeed think so, did you know how much I have pardoned."

"What was his offence, my Lord?"

"Such as I would not have forgiven you, or any earthly being besides himself—but while you were speaking in his behalf, I recollected there was a gratitude so extraordinary in the hazards he ran, that almost made him pardonable."

"I guess the subject then," cried Sandford; "and yet I could not have supposed"—

"It is a subject we cannot speak on, Sandford, therefore let us drop it."

At these words the discourse concluded.

CHAPTER IV

To the great relief of Rushbrook, Lord Elmwood that day dined from home, and he had not the confusion to see him again till the evening.—Previous to this, Sandford and he met at dinner; but as the attendants were present, nothing passed on either side respecting the incident in the morning.—Rushbrook, from the peril which had so lately threatened him, was now in his perfect cool, and dispassionate, senses; and notwithstanding the real tenderness which he bore to the daughter of his benefactor, he was not insensible to the comfort of finding himself, once more in the possession of all those enjoyments he had forfeited, and for a moment lost.

As he reflected on this, to Sandford he felt the first tie of acknowledgement—but for his compassion, he knew he should have been at that very time of their meeting at dinner, away from Elmwood House for ever—and bearing on his mind a still more painful recollection; the burthen of his kind patron's continual displeasure. Filled with these thoughts, all the time of dinner he could scarce look at his companion without his eyes swimming in tears of gratitude, and whenever he attempted to speak to him, gratitude choked his utterance.

Sandford on his part behaved just the same as ever; and to show he did not wish to remind Rushbrook of what he had done, he was just as uncivil as ever.

Among other things, he said "He did not know Lord Elmwood dined from home, for if he had, he should have dined in his own apartment."

Rushbrook was still more obliged to him for all this, and the weight of obligations with which he was oppressed, made him long for an opportunity to relieve himself by expressions.—As soon, therefore, as the servants were all withdrawn, he began:

"Mr. Sandford, whatever has been your opinion of *me*, I take pride to myself, that in my sentiments towards *you*, I have always distinguished you for that humane and disinterested character, you have this day proved."

"Humane, and disinterested," replied Sandford, "are two flattering epithets for an old man going out of the world, and who can have no temptation to be otherwise."

"Then suffer me to call your actions generous and compassionate, for they have saved me"—

"I know, young man," cried Sandford interrupting him, "you are glad at what I have done, and that you find a gratification in telling me you are; but it is a gratification I will not indulge you with—therefore say another sentence on the subject, and" (he rose from his seat) "I'll leave the room, and never come into your company again, whatever your uncle may say to it."

Rushbrook saw by the solemnity of his countenance he was serious, and positively assured him he would never thank him more; on which Sandford took his seat again, but he still frowned, and it was many minutes before he conquered his ill humour.—As his countenance became less sour, Rushbrook fell from some general topics he had eagerly started in order to appease him, and said,

"How hard is it to restrain conversation from the subject of our thoughts; and yet amidst our dearest friends, and among persons who have the same dispositions and sentiments as our own, their minds fixed upon the self-same objects, is this constraint practised—and thus society, which was meant for one of our greatest blessings, becomes insipid, nay oftentimes more wearisome than solitude."

"I think, young man," replied Sandford, "you have made pretty free with your speech to-day, and ought not to complain of the want of toleration on that score."

"I do complain," replied Rushbrook; "for if toleration was more frequent, the favour of obtaining it would be less."

"And your pride, I suppose, is above receiving a favour."

"Never from those I esteem; and to convince you of it, I wish this moment to request a favour of you."

"I dare say I shall refuse it.—However—what is it?"

"Permit me to speak to you upon the subject of Lady Matilda?"

Sandford made no answer, consequently did not forbid him—and he proceeded.

"For her sake—as I suppose Lord Elmwood may have told you—I this morning rashly threw myself into the predicament from whence you released me—for her sake, I have suffered much—for her sake, I have hazarded a great deal, and am still ready to hazard more."

"But for your own sake, do not." returned Sandford drily.

"You may laugh at these sentiments as romantic, Mr. Sandford, but if they are, to me they are nevertheless natural."

"But what service are they to be, either to her, or to yourself?"

"They are painful to me, and to her would be but impertinent, were she to know them."

"I shan't inform her of them, so do not trouble yourself to caution me against it."

"I was not going—you know I was not—but I was going to say, that from no one so well as from you, could she be told my sentiments, without the danger of her resenting the liberty."

"And what impression do you wish to give her, from her becoming acquainted with them?"

"The impression, that she has one sincere friend—that upon every occurrence in life, there is a heart so devoted to all she feels, she can never suffer without the sympathy of another—or ever can command him, and all his fortunes to unite for her welfare, without his ready and immediate compliance."

"And do you imagine, that any of your professions, or any of her necessities, would ever prevail upon her to put you to the trial?"

"Perhaps not."

"What, then, are the motives which induce you to wish her to be told of this?"

Rushbrook paused.

"Do you think," continued Sandford, "the intelligence will give her any satisfaction?"

"Perhaps not."

"Will it be of any to yourself?"

"The highest in the world."

"And so all you have been urging upon this occasion, is, at last, only to please yourself."

"You wrong my meaning—it is she—her merit which inspires my desire of being known to her—it is her sufferings, her innocence, her beauty"—

Sandford stared—Rushbrook proceeded: "It is her"—

"Nay stop where you are," cried Sandford; "you are arrived at the zenith of perfection in a woman, and to add one qualification more, would be an anti-climax."

"Oh!" cried Rushbrook with warmth, "I loved her, before I ever beheld her."

"Loved her!" cried Sandford, with astonishment, "You are talking of what you do not intend."

"I am, indeed," returned he in confusion, "I fell by accident on the word love."

"And by the same accident, stumbled on the word beauty; and thus by accident, am I come to the truth of all your professions."

Rushbrook knew he loved; and though his affection had sprung from the most laudable motives, yet was he ashamed of it, as of a vice—he rose, walked about the room, and did not look Sandford in the face for a quarter of an hour.—Sandford satisfied he had judged rightly, and yet unwilling to be too hard upon a passion, which he readily believed must have had many noble virtues for its foundation, now got up and walked away, without saying any thing in censure, though not a word in its approbation.

It was in the month of October, and just dark, at the time Rushbrook was left alone, yet from the agitation of his mind, arising from the subject on which he had been talking, he found it impossible to remain in the house, and therefore walked into the fields;—but there was another instigation, more powerful than the necessity of walking; it was the allurement of passing along that path where he had last seen Lady Matilda, and where, for the only time she had condescended to speak to him divested of haughtiness, and with a gentleness that dwelt upon his memory beyond all her other endowments.

Here he retraced his own steps repeatedly, his whole imagination engrossed with her idea, till the sound of her father's chariot returning home from his visit, roused him from the soft delusion of his trance, to dread the confusion and embarrassment he should endure, on the next meeting with his Lordship. He hoped Sandford might be present, and yet he was now, almost as much ashamed to behold him as his uncle, whom he had so lately offended.

As loath to leave the spot where he was, as to enter the house, he remained there till he considered it would be ill manners in his present humiliated situation, not to show himself at the usual supper hour, which was immediately.

As he laid his hand upon the door of the apartment to open it, he was sorry to hear by Lord Elmwood's voice, he was in the room before him; for there was something much more conspicuous and distressing, in entering where he already was, than had his Lordship come in after him.—He found himself, however reassured, by overhearing his uncle laugh and speak in a tone expressive of the utmost good humour to Sandford, who was with him.

Yet again, he felt all the awkwardness of his own situation; but making one courageous effort, opened the door and entered.—His Lordship had been away half the day, had dined abroad, and it was necessary to take some notice of his return; Rushbrook therefore bowed humbly, and what was more to his advantage, he looked humbly.—Lord Elmwood made a slight return to the salutation, but continued the recital he had begun to Sandford;—then sat down to the supper table—supped—and passed the whole evening without saying a syllable, or even casting a look in remembrance of what had passed in the morning.—Or if there was any token, that shewed he remembered the circumstance at all, it was the putting his glass to his nephew's when Rushbrook called for wine, and drinking at the time he did.

CHAPTER V

THE repulse Lord Margrave received, did not diminish the ardour of his pursuit; for as he was no longer fearful of resentment from the Earl, whatever treatment his daughter might receive, he was determined the anger of Lady Matilda or of her female friend, should not impede his pretensions.

Having taken this resolution, he laid the plan of an open violation of all right, all power, and to bear away that prize by force, which no art was likely to procure.—He concerted with two of his favourite companions, but their advice was, "one struggle more of fair means." This was totally against his Lordship's will, for he had much rather have encountered the piercing cries of a female in the last agonies of distress, than the fatigue of her sentimental harangues, or elegant reproofs, such as he had the sense to understand, but not the capacity to answer.

Stimulated, however, by his friends to one more trial; in spite of the formal dismission he had twice received, he intruded another visit on Lady Matilda at the farm.—Provoked beyond bearing at such unfeeling assurance, Matilda refused to come into the room where he was, and Miss Woodley alone received him, and expressed her surprise at the little attention he had paid to her explicit desire.

"Madam," replied the nobleman, "to be plain with you, I am in love."

"I do not the least doubt it, my Lord," replied Miss Woodley, "nor ought you to doubt the truth of what I advance, when I assure you, you have not the smallest reason to hope your love will be returned; for Lady Matilda is resolved *never* to listen to your passion."

"That man," he replied, "is to blame, who can relinquish his hopes, upon the mere resolution of a lady."

"And that Lady would be wrong," replied Miss Woodley, "who should entrust her happiness in the care of a man, who can think thus meanly of her, and of her sex."

"I think highly of them all," returned his Lordship; "and to convince you in how high an estimation I hold her Ladyship in particular, my whole fortune is at her command."

"Your absenting yourself from this house, Lord Margrave, she would consider as a much greater mark of your respect."

A long conversation, equally uninteresting as this, ensued; till the unexpected arrival of Mr. Sandford put an end to it.—He started at the sight of Lord Margrave; but his Lordship was much more affected at the sight of him.

"My Lord," said Sandford boldly to him, "have you received any encouragement from Lady Matilda, to authorise this visit?"

"None, upon my honour, Mr. Sandford; but I hope you know how to pardon a lover?"

"A rational one I do—but you, my Lord, are not such, while you persecute the pretended object of your affection."

"Do you call it persecution that I once offered her a share of my title and fortune—and even now, declare my fortune is at her disposal?"

Sandford was uncertain whether he understood his meaning— but his Lordship, provoked at his ill reception, felt a triumph in not detaining him long in doubt, and proceeded thus:

"For the discarded daughter of Lord Elmwood, cannot expect the same proposals which I made while she was acknowledged, and under the protection of her father."

"What proposals then, my Lord?" asked Sandford hastily.

"Such," replied his Lordship, "as the Duke of Avon made to her mother."

Miss Woodley quitted the room that instant.—But Sandford, who never felt resentment but to those in whom he saw some virtue, calmly replied,

"My Lord, the Duke of Avon was a gentleman, a man of elegance and breeding; and what have you to offer in recompence for your defects in these?"

"My wealth," replied he, "opposed to her indigence."

Sandford smiled, and answered,

"Do you suppose that wealth can be esteemed, which has not been able to make you respectable?—What is it which makes wealth valuable? Is it the pleasures of the table? the pleasures of living in a fine house? or riding in a fine coach?[1] These are pleasures a Lord enjoys, but in common with his valet.—It is the pleasure of being conspicuous, which makes riches desirable—but if we are conspicuous only for our vice and folly, had we not better remain in poverty?"

---

1 In the fourth and fifth editions, "or of wearing fine clothes?"

"You are beneath my notice."

"I trust I shall continue so—and that your Lordship will never again condescend to come where I am."

"A man of rank condescends to mix with any society, when a pretty woman is his object."

"My Lord, I have a book here in my pocket, which I am eager to read; it is an author who speaks sense and reason—will you pardon the impatience I feel for such company; and permit me to call your carriage?"

Saying this he went hastily and called to his Lordship's servants; the carriage drove up, the door was opened, and Lord Margrave, ashamed to be exposed before his attendants, or convinced of the uselessness of remaining any longer where he was, departed.

Sandford was soon joined by the ladies; and the conversation falling, of course, upon the nobleman who had just taken his leave, Sandford unwarily exclaimed, "I wish Rushbrook had been here."

"Who?" cried Lady Matilda.

"I do believe," said Miss Woodley, "that young man has some good qualities."

"A great many." returned Sandford, mutteringly.

"Happy young man!" cried Matilda: "he is beloved by all those, whose affection it would be my choice to possess, beyond any other blessing this world could bestow."

"And yet I question, if Rushbrook is a happy man." said Sandford.

"He cannot be otherwise," returned Matilda, "if he is a man of understanding."

"He does not want for that," replied Sandford; "although he has certainly many indiscretions."

"But which Lord Elmwood, I suppose," said Matilda, "looks upon with tenderness."

"Not upon all his faults," answered Sandford; "for I have seen him in very dangerous circumstances with your father."

"Have you indeed?" cried Matilda: "then I pity him."

"And I believe," said Miss Woodley, "that from his heart, he compassionates you.—Now, Mr. Sandford," continued she, "though this is the first time I ever heard you speak in his favour, (and I once thought as indifferently of Mr. Rushbrook as you can do) yet now I will venture to ask you, whether you do not think he wishes Lady Matilda much happier than she is?"

"I have heard him say so." answered Sandford.

"It is a subject," returned Lady Matilda, "which I did not imagine you, Mr. Sandford, would have permitted to have been lightly mentioned, in your presence."

"Lightly!—Do you suppose, my dear, we turned your situation into ridicule?"

"No, Sir,—but there is a sort of humiliation in the grief to which I am doomed, that ought surely to be treated with the highest degree of delicacy by my friends."

"I don't know on what point you fix real delicacy; but if it consists in sorrow, the young man gives a proof he possesses it, for he shed tears when I last heard him mention your name."

"I have more cause to weep at the mention of his."

"Perhaps so—But let me tell you, Lady Matilda, your father might have preferred a more unworthy object."

"Still had he been to me," she cried, "an object of envy.—And as I frankly confess my envy of Mr. Rushbrook, I hope you will pardon my malice, which is, you know, but a consequent crime."

The subject now turned again upon Lord Margrave; and all of them being firmly persuaded, this last reception would put an end to every farther intrusion from his Lordship, they treated his pretensions, and he himself, with the contempt they inspired—but not with the caution they deserved.

CHAPTER VI

THE next morning early Mr. Sandford returned to Elmwood House, but with his spirits depressed, and his heart overcharged with sorrow.—He had seen Lady Matilda, the object of his visit, but he had beheld her considerably altered in her looks and in her health;—she was become very thin, and instead of the most beautiful bloom that used to spread her cheeks, her whole complexion was of a deadly pale—her countenance no longer expressed hope or fear, but a fixed melancholy—she shed no tears, but was all sadness.—He had beheld this, and he had heard her insulted by the licentious proposals of a nobleman, from whom there was no satisfaction to be demanded, because she had no friend to vindicate her honour.

Rushbrook, who suspected where Sandford was gone, and imagined he would return that day, took his forenoon's ride, so as to meet him on the road a few miles distance from the castle; for since his perilous situation with Lord Elmwood, he was so fully convinced of the general philanthropy of Sandford's character, that in spite of his churlish manners, he now addressed him, free from that reserve to which his rough behaviour had formerly given birth.—And Sandford on his part, believing he had formed an illiberal opinion of Lord Elmwood's heir (though he took no pains to let him know that opinion was changed) yet resolved to make him restitution upon every occasion that offered.

Their mutual greetings when they met, were unceremonious but cordial; and Rushbrook turned his horse and rode back with Sandford;—yet, intimidated by his respect and tenderness for Lady Matilda, rather than by fear of the rebuffs of his companion, he had not the courage to name her, till their ride was just finished, and they came within a few yards of the house—incited then by the apprehension he might not soon again enjoy so fit an opportunity, he said,

"Pardon me, Mr. Sandford, if I guess where you have been, and if my curiosity forces me to enquire for Miss Woodley's and Lady Matilda's health?"

He named Miss Woodley first, to prolong the time before he mentioned Matilda, for though to name her gave him extreme pleasure, yet it was a pleasure intermingled with confusion and pain.

"They are both very well," replied Sandford, "at least they did not complain they were sick."

"They are not in spirits, I suppose?" said Rushbrook.

"No, indeed." replied Sandford, shaking his head.

"No new misfortune has happened, I hope?" cried Rushbrook, for it was plain to see Sandford's spirits were unusually cast down.

"Nothing new," returned he, "except the insolence of a young nobleman."

"What nobleman?" cried Rushbrook.

"A lover of Lady Matilda's." replied Sandford.

Rushbrook was petrified.—"Who? What lover, Mr. Sandford?—explain?"

They were now arrived at the house; and Sandford, without making any reply to this question, said to the servant who took his horse, "She has come a long way this morning; take care of her."

This interruption was torture to Rushbrook, who kept close to his side, in order to obtain a farther explanation; but Sandford without attending to him, walked negligently into the hall, and before they advanced many steps they were met by Lord Elmwood.

All farther information was for the present, now wholly put an end to.

"How do you do, Sandford?" said his Lordship with extreme kindness; as if he thanked him for the journey which he suspected he had been taking.

"I am indifferent well, my Lord." replied he, with a face of deep concern, and a tear in his eye, partly in gratitude for his Lordship's civility, and partly in reproach for his cruelty.

It was not now till the evening, that Rushbrook had an opportunity of renewing the conversation, which had been so barbarously interrupted.

In the evening, no longer able to support the suspense in which he was; without fear or shame he followed Sandford to his chamber at the time of his retiring, and entreated of him, with all the anxiety he suffered, to reveal to him what he alluded to, when he made mention of a lover, and insolence to Lady Matilda.

Sandford seeing his emotion, was angry he had inadvertently mentioned the subject; and putting on an air of surly importance, desired if he had any business with him, to call in the morning.

Exasperated at so unexpected a reception, and at the pain of his disappointment, Rushbrook replied, "He treated him cruelly, nor would he stir out of his room, till he had received a satisfactory answer to his question."

"Then bring your bed," replied Sandford, "for you must pass your whole night here."

He found it vain to think of obtaining any intelligence by threats, he therefore said in a timid persuasive manner,

"Did you, Mr. Sandford, hear Lady Matilda mention my name?"

"Yes." replied Sandford, a little better reconciled to him.

"Did you tell her what I declared to you?" he asked with more diffidence still.

"No." replied Sandford.

"It is very well, Sir." returned he vexed to the heart.—yet again wishing to sooth him.

"You certainly, Mr. Sandford, know what is for the best—yet I entreat you will give me some farther account of the nobleman you named?"

"I know what is for the best," replied Sandford, "and I won't."

Rushbrook bowed, and immediately left the room.—He went apparently submissive, but the moment he showed this submission, he took the resolution of paying a visit himself to the farm where Lady Matilda resided; and of learning either from Miss Woodley, the people of the house, the neighbours, or perhaps from Lady Matilda's own lips, the secret which the obstinacy of Sandford had denied him.

He saw all the dangers of this undertaking, but none appeared so great as the danger of losing her he loved, by the influence of a rival—and though Sandford had named "insolence," he was in doubt whether what had appeared such to him, was such in reality, or would be considered as such by her.

To prevent his absence being suspected by Lord Elmwood, he immediately called his groom, ordered his horse, and giving those servants concerned, a strict charge of secresy, and some frivolous pretence to apologize for his not being present at breakfast (resolving to be back by dinner) he set off that night, and arrived at an inn about a mile from the farm at break of day.

The joy he felt when he found himself so near to the beloved object of his journey, made him thank Sandford in his heart, for the unkindness which had sent him thither.—But new difficulties arose, how to accomplish the end for which he came;—he learnt from the people of the inn that a Lord with a fine equipage had visited the farm, but who he was, or for what purpose he went, no one could inform him.

Miserable to return with the same doubts unsatisfied with which he set out, and yet afraid to proceed to extremities that might be construed into presumption, he walked disconsolately (almost distractedly) about the fields, looking repeatedly at his watch, and wishing the time to stand still, till he was ready to go back with his errand compleated.

Every field he passed, brought him nearer to the house on which his imagination was fixed; but how, without forfeiting every appearance of that very respect he so powerfully felt, could he attempt to enter it?—he saw the indecorum, resolved not to be guilty of it, and yet walked on till he was within but a short orchard of the door. Could he then retreat?—he wished he could; but he now found he had proceeded too far, to be any longer master of himself.—The time was urgent; he must either be bold, and venture her displeasure; or by diffidence during one moment, give up all his hopes perhaps for ever.

With that same disregard to consequences, which actuated him when he dared to supplicate Lord Elmwood in his daughter's behalf, he at length went eagerly to the door and rapped.

A servant came—he asked to "speak with Miss Woodley, if she was quite alone."

He was shown into an apartment, and Miss Woodley entered to him.

She started when she beheld who it was; but as he did not see a frown upon her face, he caught hold of her hand, and said persuasively,

"Do not be offended with me.—If I mean to offend you, may I forfeit my life in atonement."

Poor Miss Woodley, glad in her solitude to see any one from Elmwood House, forgot his visit was an offence till he put her in mind of it; she then said with some reserve,

"Tell me the purport of your coming, Sir, and perhaps I may then have no cause to complain?"

"It was to see Lady Matilda," he replied, "or to hear of her health.—It was to offer her my services—it was Miss Woodley, to convince her, if possible, of my esteem."

"Had you no other method, Sir?" said Miss Woodley with the same reserve.

"None;" replied he, "or with joy I should have embraced it; and if you can inform me of any other, tell me I beseech you instantly, and I will immediately be gone, and pursue your directions."

Miss Woodley hesitated.

"You know of no other means, Miss Woodley." he cried.

"And yet I cannot commend this." said she.

"Nor do I.—Do not imagine because you see me here, I approve my conduct; but reduced to this necessity, pity the motives that have urged it."

Miss Woodley did pity them; but as she would not own she did, she could think of nothing else to say.

At this instant a bell rung from the chamber above.

"That is Lady Matilda's bell," said Miss Woodley; "she is coming to take a short walk.—Do you wish to see her?"

Though it was the first wish Rushbrook had, he paused, and said, "Will you plead my excuse?"

As the flight of stairs was but short, which Matilda had to come down, she was in the room with Miss Woodley and Mr. Rushbrook just as that sentence ended.

She had stept beyond the door of the apartment, when perceiving a visitor, she hastily withdrew.

Rushbrook, animated, though trembling at her presence, cried, "Lady Matilda, do not avoid me, till you know I deserve such a punishment."

She immediately saw who it was, and returned back with a proper pride, and yet a proper politeness in her manner.

"I beg your pardon, Sir," said she, "I did not know you, and I was afraid I intruded upon Miss Woodley and a stranger."

"You do not then consider me as a stranger, Lady Matilda? and that you do not, requires my warmest acknowledgements."

She sat down, as if overcome by ill spirits and ill health.

Miss Woodley now asked Rushbrook to sit—for till now she had not.

"No, Madam," replied he, with confusion, "not unless her Ladyship gives me permission."

Lady Matilda smiled, and pointed to a chair—and all the kindness which Rushbrook during his whole life had received from Lord Elmwood, never inspired half the gratitude, which this single instance of civility from his daughter excited.

He sat down with the confession of the obligation, upon every feature of his face.

"I am not well, Mr. Rushbrook," said Matilda, languidly; "and you must excuse any want of etiquette, you meet with at this house."

"While you excuse me, Madam, what can I have to complain of?"

She appeared absent while he was speaking, and turning to Miss Woodley, said, "Do you think I had better walk to-day?"

"No, my dear," answered Miss Woodley; "the ground is damp, and the air cold."

"You are not well, indeed, Lady Matilda," said Rushbrook, gazing upon her with the most tender respect.

She shook her head; and the tears, without any effort either to impel or restrain them, ran fast down her face.

Rushbrook rose from his seat, and with an accent and manner the most expressive, said, "We are cousins, Lady Matilda—in our infancy we were brought up together—we were beloved by the same mother—fostered by the same father"—

"Oh!" cried she, interrupting him, and the tears now gushed in torrents.[1]

"Nay, do not let me add to your uneasiness," resumed he, "while I am attempting to alleviate it.—Instruct me what I am to do to show my esteem and respect, rather than permit me thus unguided, to rush upon what you may misterm, cruelty or arrogance."

Miss Woodley went to Matilda, took her hand, then wiped the tears from her eyes, while Matilda reclined against her, wholly regardless of Rushbrook's presence.

---

1   In the second and third editions, "with a tone expressive of the bitterest anguish"; in the fourth and fifth editions, "with a tone which indicated the bitterest anguish."

"If I have been the least instrumental to this sorrow,"—said Rushbrook, with a face as much agitated as his mind.

"No," said Miss Woodley in a low voice, "you have not—she is often thus."

"Yes," said Matilda, raising her head, "I am frequently so weak I cannot resist the smallest incitement to grief.—But do not make your visit long, Mr. Rushbrook," she continued, "for I was just then thinking, that should Lord Elmwood hear of this attention you have paid me, it might be fatal to you."—Here she wept again, as bitterly as before.

"There is no probability of his hearing of it, Madam," Rushbrook replied; "or if there was, I am persuaded he would not resent it; for yesterday, when I am confident he knew Mr. Sandford had been to see you, he received him on his return with unusual marks of kindness."

"Did he?" said she—and again she lifted up her head; and her eyes for a moment beamed with hope and joy.

"There is something which we cannot yet define," said Rushbrook, "that Lord Elmwood struggles with; but when time shall have eradicated"—

Before he could proceed farther, Matilda was once more sunk into despondency, and scarce attended to what he was saying.

Miss Woodley observing this, said, "Mr. Rushbrook, let it be a token we shall be glad to see you hereafter, that I now use the freedom to beg you will put an end to your visit."

"You send me away, Madam," returned he, "with the warmest thanks for the reception you have given me; and this last assurance of your kindness is beyond any other favour you could have bestowed.—Lady Matilda," added he, "suffer me to take your hand at parting, and let it be a testimony that you acknowledge me for a relation."

She put out her hand—which he knelt to receive, but did not raise it to his lips—he held the boon too sacred—and only looking earnestly upon it, as it lay pale and wan in his, he breathed a sigh over it, and withdrew.

CHAPTER VII

SORROWFUL and affecting as this interview had been, Rushbrook as he rode home reflected upon it with the most inordinate delight; and had he not beheld decline of health, in all the looks and behaviour of Lady Matilda, his felicity had been unbounded.—Entranced in the happiness of her society, the thought of his rival never came once to his mind while he was with her; a want of recollection, however, he by no means regretted, as her whole appearance contradicted every suspicion he could possibly entertain, of her favouring the addresses of any man living—and had he remembered, he had not dared to have named the subject.

The time run so swiftly while he was away, that it was beyond the dinner hour at Elmwood House, when he returned.—Heated, his dress, and his hair disordered, he entered the dining room just as the desert was put upon the table.—He was confounded at his own appearance, and at the falsehoods he should be obliged to fabricate in his excuse; there was yet that which engaged his attention, beyond any circumstance relating to himself—the features of Lord Elmwood—of which his daughter's, whom he had just beheld, had the most striking resemblance; while hers were softened by sorrow, as his Lordship's were rendered austere by the self-same cause.

"Where have you been?" said his Lordship, with a frown.

"A chase, my Lord—I beg your pardon—but a pack of dogs I unexpectedly met."—For in the hacknied art of lying without injury to any one, Rushbrook, to his shame, was proficient.

His excuses were received, and the subject ceased.

During his absence that day, Lord Elmwood had called Sandford apart and said to him,—that as the malevolence which he once observed between him and Rushbrook had, he perceived, subsided; he advised him, if he was a well-wisher to the young man, to sound his heart, and counsel him not to act contrary to the will of his nearest relation and friend.—"I myself am too hasty," continued Lord Elmwood, "and, unhappily, too much determined upon what I have once (though, perhaps, rashly) said, to speak upon a topic where it is probable I shall meet with opposition.—You, Sandford, can reason with moderation.—For after all I have done for my nephew, it would be a pity to forsake him at last; and yet, that is but too likely, if he provokes me."

"Sir," replied Sandford, "I will speak to him."

"Yet," cried his Lordship sternly, "do not urge what you say for my sake, but for his—I can part from him with ease—but he may then repent, and, you know, repentance always comes too late with me."

"My Lord, I will use my endeavours for his welfare.—But what is the subject on which he has refused to comply with your desires?"

"Matrimony—have not I told you?"

"Not a word."

"I wish him to marry, that I may then conclude the deeds in respect to my estate—And the only child of Sir William Winterton (a rich heiress) was the wife I meant to propose; but from his indifference to all I have said on the subject, I have not yet mentioned her name to him; you may."

"I will, my Lord, and use all my persuasion towards his obedience; and you shall have, at least, a faithful account of what he says."

Sandford the next morning sought an opportunity of being alone with Rushbrook—he then plainly repeated to him what Lord Elmwood had said, and saw him listen to it all, and answer with the most tranquil resolution, "He would do any thing to preserve the friendship and patronage of his uncle, but marry."

"What can be your reason?" asked Sandford—though he guessed.

"A reason I cannot give to Lord Elmwood."

"Then do not give it to me, for I have promised to tell him every thing you say to me."

"And every thing I *have* said?" asked Rushbrook hastily.

"As to what you have said, I don't know whether it has made that impression on my memory, to repeat."

"I am glad it has not."

"And my answer to your uncle, is to be simply, that you will not obey him?"

"I should hope, Mr. Sandford, you would put it in better terms."

"Tell me the terms, and I will be exact."

Rushbrook struck his forehead, and walked distractedly about the room.

"Am I to give him any reason for your disobeying him?"

"I tell you again, I dare not name the cause."

"Then why do you submit to a power you are ashamed to own?"

"I am not ashamed—I glory in it—Are you ashamed of your esteem for Lady Matilda?"

"Oh! if she is the cause of your disobedience, be assured I shall not mention it, for I am forbid to name her."

"And as that is the case, I need not fear to speak plainly to you.—I love Lady Matilda—or, unacquainted with love, perhaps it is only pity—and if so, pity is the most pleasing passion that ever possessed a human heart, and I would not change it for all her father's estates."

"Pity, then, gives rise to very different sensations—for I pity you, and that sensation I would gladly exchange for approbation."

"If you really feel compassion for me, and I believe you do, contrive some means by your answers to Lord Elmwood to pacify him, without involving me.—Hint at my affections being engaged, but not to whom; and add, that I have given my word, if he will allow me a short time, a year or two only, I will, during that period, try to regain them, and use all my power to render myself worthy the lady for whom he designs me."

"And this is not only your solemn promise—but your fixed determination?"

"Nay, why will you search my heart to the bottom, when its surface ought to content you?"

"If you cannot resolve on what you have proposed, why do you ask this time of your uncle? for should he allow it you, at its expiration, your disobedience to his commands will be less pardonable than it is now."

"Within a year, Mr. Sandford, who can tell what strange unthought-of events may not occur to change all our prospects? even my passion may decline."

"In that expectation, then—the failure of which you yourself must answer for—I will repeat to his Lordship, as much of this discourse as shall be proper."

Here Rushbrook communicated his having been to see Lady Matilda, for which Sandford reproved him, but in less severe terms than his reproofs were in general delivered; and Rushbrook by his entreaties, now gained the intelligence who the nobleman was who had addrest Matilda, and on what views; but was restrained to patience by Sandford's arguments and threats.

Upon the subject of this marriage Sandford met his patron, without having determined exactly what to say, but rested on the temper in which he should find his Lordship.

At the commencement of the conversation he said, "Rushbrook begged for time."

"I have given him time, have I not?" cried Lord Elmwood, "What can be the reason of his thus trifling with me?"

Sandford replied, "My Lord, young men are frequently romantic in their notions of love, and think it impossible to have a sincere affection, where their own inclinations do not first point out the choice."

"If he is in love," answered his Lordship, "let him take the object, and leave my house and me for ever.—Nor under this destiny need he be pitied; for genuine love will make him happy in banishment, in poverty, or in sickness; it makes the poor man happy as the rich, the fool blest as the wise."—The sincerity with which Lord Elmwood had loved, was expressed more than in words, as he said this.

"Your Lordship is talking," replied Sandford, "of the passion in its most refined and predominant sense; while I may possibly be speaking of a mere phantom, that has led this young man astray."

"Whatever it be," returned Lord Elmwood, "let him and his friends weigh the case well, and act for the best—so shall I."

"His friends, my Lord?—What friends, or what friend has he on earth but you?"

"Then why will he not submit to my advice; or himself give me some substantial reason why he cannot?"

"Because there may be friendship without familiarity—and so it is between him and you."

"That cannot be; for I have condescended to talk to him in the most familiar terms."

"To condescend, my Lord, is *not* to be familiar."

"Then come, Sir, let us be on an equal footing through you.—And now speak out *his* thoughts freely, and hear mine in return."

"Why then, he begs for a respite for a year or two."

"On what pretence?"

"To me, it was preference to a single life—but I suspect it is—what he imagines to be love—and for some object whom he thinks your Lordship would disapprove for his wife."

"He has not, then, actually confessed this to you?"

"If he has, it was drawn from him by such means, I am not warranted to say so in direct words."

"I have entered into no contract, no agreement on his account with the friends of the Lady I have pointed out," said Lord Elmwood; "nothing beyond implications have passed betwixt her family and myself at present; and if the person on whom he has fixed his affections should not be in a situation absolutely contrary to my wishes, I may, perhaps, confirm his choice."

That moment Sandford's courage prompted him to name Lady Matilda, but the discretion opposed—however, in the various changes of his countenance from the conflict, it was plain to discern he wished to say more than he dared.

On which Lord Elmwood cried, "Speak on Sandford—what are you afraid of?"

"Of you, my Lord."

His Lordship started.

Sandford went on—"I know no tie—no bond—no innocence, a protection from your resentment."

"You are right." he replied, significantly.

"Then how, my Lord, can you encourage me to speak on, when that which I perhaps would say, may offend you to hear?"

"To what, and whither are you *changing* our subject?" said his Lordship.—"But, Sir, if you know my resentful and relentless temper, you surely know how to shun it."

"Not, and speak plainly."

"Then dissemble."

"No, I'll not do that—but I'll be silent."

"A new parade of submission.—You are more tormenting to me than any one I have about me—Constantly on the verge of disobeying my commands, that you may recede, and gain my good will by your forbearance.—But know, Mr. Sandford, I will not suffer this much longer.—If you choose upon every occasion we converse together (though the most remote from the subject) to think upon my daughter, you must either banish your thoughts, or conceal them—nor by one sign, one item, remind me of her."

"Your daughter did you call her?—Can you call yourself her father?"

"I do, Sir—but I am likewise the husband of her mother.—And, as such, I solemnly swear,"—He was proceeding with violence.

"Oh! my Lord," cried Sandford, interrupting him, with his hands clasped in the most fervent supplication—"Oh! do not let me draw upon her one oath more of your eternal displeasure—I'll kneel to beg you to drop the subject."

The inclination he made with his knees bent to the ground, stopped Lord Elmwood instantly.—But though it broke in upon his words, it did not alter one angry look—his eyes darted and his lips trembled with indignation.

Sandford in order to appease him, bowed and offered to withdraw; hoping to be recalled.—He wished in vain—Lord Elmwood's eyes followed him to the door, expressive of the pleasure of his absence.

CHAPTER VIII

THE companions and counsellors of Lord Margrave, who had so prudently advised gentle methods in the pursuit of his passion, while there was left any hope of their success; now, convinced there was none, as strenuously commended open violence;—and sheltered under the consideration, that their depredations were to be practised upon a defenceless woman, who had not one protector, except an old priest, the subject of their ridicule;—assured likewise from the influence of Lord Margrave's wealth, all inferior consequences could be overborne, they saw no room for fears on any side, and what they wished to execute, with care and skill premeditated.

When their scheme was mature for performance, three of his Lordship's chosen companions, with three servants, trained and tried in all the villainous exploits of their masters, set off for the habitation of poor Matilda, and arrived there about the twilight of the evening.

Near four hours after that time (just as the family were going to bed) they came up to the doors of the house, and rapping violently, gave the alarm of fire, "conjuring all the inhabitants to make their way out immediately, as they would save their lives."

The family consisted of but few persons, all of whom ran instantly to the doors and opened them; on which two men rushed in, and with the plea of saving Lady Matilda from the pretended flames, caught her in their arms, and carried her off; while all the deceived people of the house, running eagerly to save themselves, paid no regard to her being taken away, till looking for the cause for which they had been terrified, they perceived the stratagem, and the fatal consequences.[1]

Amidst the complaints, sorrow, and affright of the people of the farm, Miss Woodley's sensations wanted a name—terror and anguish give but a faint description of what she suffered—something like the approach of death stole over her senses, and she sat like one petrified with horror.—She had no doubt who was the perpetrator of this wickedness; but how was she to follow? how effect a rescue?

The circumstances of this event, as soon as the people had time to call up their recollection, were sent to a neighbouring magistrate; but little could be hoped from that.—Who was to swear to the robber?—Who undertake to find him out?—Miss Woodley thought of Rushbrook, of Sandford, of Lord Elmwood, but what could she hope from the want of power in the two former?—what from the latter, for the want of will?—Now stupefied, and now distracted, she walked about the house incessantly,

---

1 In a famous scene from Samuel Richardson's *Clarissa* (1747-48), Lovelace enters Clarissa's bedroom, using the pretext of a fire that has already been extinguished and was, presumably, also started by him. Inchbald's mother reportedly read *Clarissa* aloud to Elizabeth and her sisters. See Frances Phillips' transcription of the diary of Inchbald's sister, Ann Simpson Hunt. Folger M.s. Y.d. 592 (10), f. 1. The heroine's abduction occurs in several other eighteenth-century novels, including Frances Burney's *Evelina* (1778) and Charlotte Lennox's, *The Female Quixote* (1752).

begging for instructions what she should do, or how to forget her misery.

A tenant of Lord Elmwood's, who occupied a small farm near to that where Lady Matilda lived, and who was well acquainted with the whole history of hers and her mother's misfortunes, was returning from a neighbouring fair just as this inhuman plan was put in execution.—He heard the cries of a woman in distress, and followed the sound till he arrived at a chaise in waiting, and saw Matilda placed in it by the side of two men, who presented pistols to him as he offered to approach and expostulate.

The farmer, uncertain who this female was, yet went to the house she had been taken from (as the nearest) with the tale of what he had seen; and there, being informed Lady Matilda was her whom he had beheld, this intelligence, joined to the powerful effect her screams had on him, made him resolve to take horse immediately, and with some friends, follow the carriage till they should trace the place to which she was conveyed.

The anxiety, the firmness discovered in determining on this undertaking, something alleviated the agony Miss Woodley endured, and she began to hope timely assistance might yet be given to her beloved charge.

The man set out, meaning at all events to attempt her release; but before he had proceeded far, the few friends that accompanied him began to reflect on the improbability of their success against a nobleman, surrounded by servants, with other attendants likewise, and perhaps even countenanced by the lady's father, whom they presumed to take from him;—or if not, while Lord Elmwood beheld the offence with indifference, that was giving it a sanction, they might in vain oppose.—These cool reflections, tending to their safety, had their weight with the companions of the farmer; they all rode back rejoicing at their second thoughts, and left him to pursue his journey and prove his valour by himself.

CHAPTER IX

It was not with Sandford, as it had lately been with Rushbrook under the displeasure of Lord Elmwood—to the latter his Lordship behaved, as soon as their dissention was over, as if it had never happened—but to Sandford it was otherwise; and that resentment which he had repressed at the time of the offence, lurked in his heart and dwelt upon his mind for several days; during which, he carefully avoided exchanging a word with him, and gave every other demonstration of his anger.

Sandford, who was experienced in the cruelty and ingratitude of the world, yet could not without difficulty brook this severity, this contumely, from a man, for whose welfare, ever since his infancy, he had laboured; and whose happiness was still more dear to him, in spite of all his faults, than any other person's.—Even Lady Matilda was not so dear to Sandford as her father—and he loved her more that she was Lord Elmwood's child, than for any other cause.

Sometimes the old man, incensed beyond bearing, was on the point of saying to his patron, "How, in my age, dare you thus treat the man, whom in his youth you respected and revered?"

Sometimes instead of anger, he felt the tear, he was ashamed to own, steal to his eye, and even fall down his cheek.—Sometimes he left the room half determined to leave the house—but these were all but half determinations; for he knew him with whom he had to deal too well, not to know he might be provoked to greater anger yet; and that should he once rashly quit his house, the doors most probably would be shut to him for ever.

In this humiliating and degraded state (for even many of the domestics could not but observe their Lord's displeasure) Sandford passed three days, and was beginning the fourth, when sitting with his Lordship and Rushbrook just after breakfast, a servant entered, saying as he opened the door to somebody who followed, "You must wait till you have my Lord's permission."

This attracted their eyes to the door, and a man meanly dressed, walked in, following close to the servant.

The latter turned, and seemed again to desire the person to retire, but all in vain; he rushed forward regardless of his opposer, and in great agitation, cried,

"My Lord, if you please, I have business with you, provided you will choose to be alone."

Lord Elmwood, struck with the stranger's earnestness, bade the servant leave the room; and then said to him,

"You may speak before these gentlemen."

The man instantly turned pale, and trembled—then, to prolong the time before he spoke, went to the door to see if it was shut—returned—yet still trembling, seemed unwilling to say his errand.

"What have you done," cried Lord Elmwood, "that you are in this terror? What have you done, man?"

"Nothing, my Lord," replied he, "but I am afraid I am going to offend you."

"Well, no matter;" (answered his Lordship carelessly) "only go on, and let me know your business."

The man's distress increased—the water came to his eyes[1]—and he cried in a voice of grief and of affright—"Your child, my Lord!"—

Rushbrook and Sandford started; and looking at Lord Elmwood, saw him turn white as death.—In a tremulous voice he instantly cried,

"What of her?" and rose from his seat.

Encouraged by the question, the poor man gave way to his feelings, and answered with every sign of sorrow,

"I saw her, my Lord, taken away by force—two ruffians seized and carried her away, while she screamed in vain to me for help, and tore her hair in distraction."

"Man, what do you mean?" cried his Lordship.

"Lord Margrave," returned the stranger, "we have no doubt has formed the plot—he has for some time past beset the house where she lived; and when his visits were refused, he threatened this.—Besides, one of his servants attended the carriage; I saw, and knew him."

Lord Elmwood listened to the last part of this account with seeming composure—then turning hastily to Rushbrook, he said,

"Where are my pistols, Harry?"

Sandford rose from his seat, and forgetting all the anger between them, caught hold of his Lordship's hand, and cried, "Will you then prove yourself a father?"

---

1 The phrase "the water came to his eyes" is omitted from the second, third, fourth, and fifth editions.

Lord Elmwood only answered, "Yes." and left the room.

Rushbrook followed, and begged with all the earnestness he felt, to be permitted to accompany his uncle.

While Sandford shaked hands with the farmer a thousand times.

And he, in his turn, rejoiced as if he had already seen Lady Matilda restored to liberty.

Rushbrook in vain entreated Lord Elmwood; he laid his commands upon him not to stir from the castle; while the agitation of his own mind was too great to observe the rigour of this sentence upon his nephew.

During the hasty preparations for his Lordship's departure, Sandford received from Miss Woodley the sad intelligence of what had happened;—but he returned an answer to recompense her for all she had undergone.

Within a few hours Lord Elmwood set off, accompanied by his guide the farmer, and other attendants furnished with every requisite to ascertain the success of their enterprize—while poor Matilda little thought of a deliverer nigh, much less, that her deliverer should prove her father.

CHAPTER X

LORD Margrave, black as this incident in his story must make him to the reader, still nursed in his conscience a reserve of virtue, to keep him in peace with himself.—It was his design to plead, to argue, to implore, nay even to threaten, long before he put his threats in force;—and with this and the following reflection he reconciled—as most bad men can—what he had done, not only to the laws of humanity, but to the laws of honour.

"I have stolen a woman certainly;" said he to himself, "but I will make her happier than she was in that humble state from whence I have taken her.—I will even," said he, "now she is in my power, win her affections—and when, in fondness, she shall hereafter hang upon me, how will she thank me for this little trial, through which she will have passed to happiness!"

Thus did his Lordship hush his remorse, while he waited impatiently at home, in expectation of his prize.

Half expiring with her sufferings, in body as well as in mind, about twelve o'clock the next night Matilda arrived; and felt her spirits revive by the still greater sufferings that awaited—for her encreasing terrors now rouzed her from that death-like weakness, brought on by fatigue.

Lord Margrave's house, to which he had gone previous to this occasion, was situated in the lonely part of a well-known forest, not more than twenty miles distant from London:—this was an estate he rarely visited, and as he had but few of his servants here, it was a place which he supposed would be less the object of suspicion in the present case, than any other of his seats. To this, then, Lady Matilda was conveyed—a most superb apartment allotted her—and one of his Lordship's confidential females placed to attend upon her, with all respect, and assurances of safety.

Matilda looked in this woman's face, and seeing she bore the features of her sex, while her knowledge reached none of those worthless characters of which this person was a specimen, she imagined none of those could look as she did, and therefore found consolation in her seeming tenderness.—She was even prevailed upon (by her promises to sit by her side and watch) to throw herself on the bed, and suffer a few minutes sleep—for sleep to her was suffering; her fears giving birth to dreams terrifying as her waking thoughts.

More wearied than refreshed with her sleep, she rose at break of day, and refusing to admit of an article in the change of her dress, she persisted to sit in the torn disordered habit in which she had been dragged away; nor would she taste a morsel of all the delicacies that were prepared for her.

Her attendant for some time observed the most submissive and reverential awe; but finding this had not the effect of gaining compliance to her advice, she varied her manners, and began by less servile means to attempt an influence.—She said her orders were to be obedient, while she herself was obeyed—at least in circumstances so material as the lady's health, of which she had the charge as a physician, and expected equal compliance from her patient—food and fresh apparel she prescribed as the only means to prevent death; and even threatened her invalid with something worse, a visit from Lord Margrave, if she continued obstinate.

Now loathing her for the deception she had practised, more, than had she received her thus at first, Matilda hid her eyes from the sight of her; and when she was obliged to look, she shuddered.

This female at length thought it her duty to wait upon her worthy employer, and inform him the young lady in her trust would certainly die, unless there were means employed to oblige her to take some nourishment.

Lord Margrave, glad of an opportunity that might apologise for his intrusion upon Lady Matilda, went with eagerness to her apartment, and throwing himself at her feet, conjured her if she would save his life, as well as her own, to submit to be consoled.

The extreme disgust and horror his presence inspired, caused Matilda for a moment to forget all her weakness, her want of health, her want of power; and rising from the place where she sat, she cried, with her voice elevated,

"Leave me, my Lord, or I'll die in spite of all your care; I'll instantly expire with grief, if you do not leave me."

Accustomed to the tears and reproaches of the sex—though not of any like her—his Lordship treated with contempt those menaces of anger, and seizing her hand, carried it to his lips.

Enraged, and overwhelmed with sorrow at the affront, she cried, (forgetting every other friend she had,) "Oh! my dear Miss Woodley, why are you not here to take my part?"

"Nay," returned his Lordship, stifling a fit of laughter, "I should think the old priest, would be as good a champion as the lady."

The memory of Sandford with all his kindness, now rushed so forcibly on Matilda's mind, she shed a shower of tears, thinking how much he felt, and would continue to feel, for her situation.—Once she thought on Rushbrook too, and thought even *he* would be vext for her.—Of her father she did not think—she durst not—one single time the thought intruded, but she hurried it away—it was too bitter.

It was now quite night again; and near to that hour she came first to the house.—Lord Margrave, though at some distance from her, remained still in her apartment; while her female companion had stolen away.—His insensibility to her lamentations—the agitated looks he sometimes cast upon her—her weakly and defenseless state, all conspired to fill her mind with horror.

He saw her apprehensions pictured in her distracted face, disheveled hair, and the whole of her forlorn appearance,—yet, notwithstanding his former resolves, he could not resist the desire of fulfilling all her dreadful expectations.

He once again approached her, and was going again to take her hand; when the report of a pistol on the staircase, and a confusion of persons assembling towards the apartment deterred him.

He started—but looked more surprised than alarmed; while her alarm augmented; for she supposed this tumult was some experiment to intimidate her into submission.—She therefore wrung her hands, and lifted up her eyes to heaven in the last agony of despair, when one of Lord Margrave's servants entered hastily and cried,

"Lord Elmwood, Sir."

That moment her father entered—and with the unrestrained fondness of a parent, folded her in his arms.

Her extreme, her excess of joy on such a meeting; and from such anguish rescued, was still, in part, repressed by his awful presence.—The apprehensions to which she had been accustomed, kept her timid and doubtful—she feared to speak, or clasp him in return for his embrace, but falling on her knees clung round his legs, and bathed his feet with her tears.—These were the happiest moments she had ever known—perhaps the happiest *he* had ever known.

Lord Margrave, on whom Lord Elmwood had not even cast a look, now left the room; but as he quitted it, called out,

"My Lord Elmwood, if you have any demands on me"—

His Lordship interrupted him,—"Would you make me an executioner? The law shall be your only antagonist."

Matilda, quite exhausted, yet upheld by the sudden transport she had felt, walked, as her father led her, out of this wretched dwelling—more despicable than the cottage built with clay.[1]

---

[1] In the fourth edition, "the beggar's hovel"; in the fifth edition, "the hovel of the veriest beggar."

CHAPTER XI

OVERCOME with the want of two night's rest from her cruel fears, and all those fears now hushed; Matilda soon after she was placed in the carriage with Lord Elmwood, dropped fast asleep; and thus insensibly surprised, leaned her head against her father in the sweetest slumber imagination can conceive.

When she awoke, instead of the usual melancholy prospect before her view, she heard the voice of the late dreaded Lord Elmwood, tenderly saying,

"We will go no farther to-night, the fatigue is too much for her;—order beds here directly, and some proper persons to sit up and attend her."

She could only turn to him with a look of love and duty; her tongue could not utter a sentence.

In the morning she found her father by the side of her bed.—He inquired "If she was in health sufficient to pursue her journey, or if she would remain where she was?"

"I am able to go with you." she answered instantly.

"Nay," replied he, "perhaps you ought to stay here till you are better?"

"I *am* better," said she, "and ready to go with you."—Half afraid he meant to send her from him.

He perceived her fears, and replied, "Nay, if you stay, so shall I—and when I go, I shall take you along with me to my house."

"To Elmwood House?" she asked eagerly.

"No, to my house in town, where I intend to be all the winter, and where we shall live together."

She turned her face on the pillow to conceal her tears of joy, but her sobs revealed them.

"Come," said he, "this kiss is a token you have nothing to fear."—And he kissed her affectionately.—"I shall send too for Miss Woodley immediately." continued he.

"Oh! I shall be overjoyed to see her, my Lord—and to see Mr. Sandford—and even Mr. Rushbrook."

"Do you know him?" said Lord Elmwood.

"Yes," she replied, "I have seen him twice."

His Lordship hoping the air might be a means of re-establishing her strength and spirits, now left the room and ordered his carriage; while she arose, attended by one of his female servants, for whom he had sent to town, to bring such changes of apparel as was requisite.

When Matilda was ready to join her father in the next room, she felt a tremor seize her, that made it almost impossible to appear before him.—No other circumstance now depending to agitate her heart, she felt more forcibly its embarrassment at meeting on terms of easy intercourse, him, whom she had been used to think of, but with that distant reverence and fear, which his severity had excited; and she knew not how to dare to speak, or look on him with that freedom her affection warranted.

After several efforts to conquer these nice and refined sensations, but to no purpose, she went at last to his apartment.—He was reading; but as she entered, put out his hand and drew her to him.—Her tears wholly overcame her.—He could have intermingled his—but assuming a grave countenance, he commanded her to desist from exhausting her spirits; and, after a few powerful struggles, she obeyed.

Before the morning was over she experienced the extreme joy of sitting by her father's side as they drove to town, and receiving during his conversation, a thousand proofs of his love, and tokens of her lasting happiness.

It was now the middle of November, and yet as Matilda passed along, the fields to her delighted eye appeared green; the trees in their bloom; and every bird seemed to sing the sweetest music— Never to her, did the sun rise upon a morning such as this—never did her imagination comprehend the human heart could feel happiness so true as hers.

On arriving at the house, there was no abatement of her felicity—all was respect and duty on the part of the domestics—all paternal care on the part of Lord Elmwood;—and she seemed to be at that summit of her wishes which annihilates hope, but that the prospect of seeing Miss Woodley and Mr. Sandford, still kept this pleasing passion in existence.

CHAPTER XII

RUSHBROOK was detained at Elmwood House during all this time, more from the friendly persuasions, nay even prayers, of Sandford, than by the commands of Lord Elmwood. He had, but for Sandford, followed his uncle and exposed himself to his severest anger, rather than have endured a state of the most piercing inquietude, such as he suffered till the news arrived of Lady Matilda's safety.—He indeed had little else to fear from the known, firm, and courageous character of her father, and the expedition with which he undertook his journey; but lover's fears are like those of women, and no argument could persuade either him or Miss Woodley (who had now ventured to come to Elmwood House) but that Matilda's peace of mind might be for ever destroyed before she was set at liberty.

The summons from Lord Elmwood for their coming to town, was received by each of this party with delight; but the impatience to obey it was in Rushbrook so violent, it was painful to himself, and extremely troublesome to Sandford; who wished, from his regard to Lady Matilda, rather to delay, than hurry their journey.

"You are to blame," said he to him and Miss Woodley, "to wish by your arrival, to divide with Lord Elmwood that tender tie, with which obligations conferred ever binds the donor.[1]—At present there is no one with him to share in the care and protection of his daughter, and he is under the necessity of discharging the duty himself; accustomed to this, it may become so powerful he cannot throw it off, even if his former resolutions should urge him to it.—While we remain here, therefore, Lady Matilda is safe with her father; but it would not surprise me, if on our arrival (especially if we are precipitate) he should place her again with Miss Woodley at a distance."

To this forcible conjecture, they submitted for a few days, and then most gladly set out for town.

On their arrival, they were met, even at the door of the street, by

---

1 In the second, third, fourth, and fifth editions, "that tender bond, which ties the good who confer obligations, to the object of their benevolence."

Lady Matilda; and with an expression of joy, they did not suppose her features could have worn.—She embraced Miss Woodley! hung upon Sandford!—and to Mr. Rushbrook, who from his conscious love only bowed at an humble distance, she held out her hand with every look and gesture of the tenderest esteem.

When Lord Elmwood joined them, he welcomed them all most sincerely; especially Sandford; with whom he had not spoken for many days before he left the country, merely for his alluding to the wretched situation of his daughter—And Sandford (with his fellow travellers) now saw his Lordship treat that daughter with all the easy, natural fondness, as if she had lived with him from her infancy.—He appeared, however, at times, under the apprehension, that the propensity of man to jealousy, might give Rushbrook a pang at this dangerous rival in his love and fortune—for though his Lordship remembered well the hazard he had once ventured to befriend Matilda, yet the present unlimited reconciliation was something so unlooked for, it might be a trial too much for his generosity, to remain wholly disinterested on the event.—Slight as was this suspicion, it did Rushbrook injustice.—He loved Lady Matilda too sincerely; he loved her father's happiness, and her mother's memory too faithfully, not to be rejoiced at all he was witness of; nor did the secret hope that whispered to him "There every blessing might one day be mutual," increase the pleasure he found, in beholding Matilda happy.

Unexpected affairs in which Lord Elmwood had been for some time engaged, diverted his attention for a while from the marriage of his nephew; nor did he at this time find his disposition sufficiently severe to exact from the young man a compliance with his wishes, at the cruel alternative of being for ever discarded.—He felt his mind, by the late incident, too much softened for such harshness; he yet wished for the alliance he had proposed; for he was more consistent in his character than to suffer the sudden tenderness his daughter's danger had awakened, to derange those plans so long projected; and never for a moment did he indulge—for perhaps it had been an indulgence—the idea of replacing her exactly in that situation to which she was born, to the disappointment of all his nephew's expectations.

Milder now in his temper than he had been for years before,

and knowing he could be no longer irritated upon the subject of his daughter, his Lordship once more resolved to trust himself in a conference with Rushbrook on the subject of marriage, meaning at the same time to mention Matilda as an opponent from whom he had nothing to fear. But for some time before Rushbrook was called to this private audience, he had by his unwearied attention, endeavoured to impress upon Matilda's mind, the softest sentiments in his favour.—He succeeded—but not as he wished.—She loved him as her friend, her cousin, her softer brother, but not as a lover.—The idea of love never once came to her thoughts; and she would sport with Rushbrook like the most harmless child, while he, all impassioned, could with difficulty resist telling her, what she made him suffer.

At the meeting between him and Lord Elmwood, to which he was sent for to give his final answer on that subject which had once nearly proved so fatal to him; after a thousand fears, much confusion and embarrassment, he at length frankly confessed his "Heart was engaged, and had been so, long before his Lordship offered to direct his choice."

Lord Elmwood desired to know "On whom he had placed his affections."

"I dare not tell you, my Lord,"—returned he, infinitely confused; "but Mr. Sandford can witness their sincerity, and how long they have been fixed."

"Fixed!" cried his Lordship.

"Immoveably fixed, my Lord; and yet the object is as unknowing of it to this moment as you yourself have been; and I swear ever shall be so, without your permission."

"Name the object." said Lord Elmwood, anxiously.

"My Lord, I dare not—the last time I named her to you, you threatened to abandon me for my arrogance."

Lord Elmwood started.—"My daughter!—Would you marry her?"

"But with your approbation, my Lord; and that"—

Before he could proceed a word farther, his Lordship left the room hastily—and left Rushbrook all terror for his approaching fate.

Lord Elmwood went immediately into the apartment where

Sandford, Miss Woodley, and Matilda, were sitting, and cried with an angry voice and with his countenance disordered,

"Rushbrook has offended me beyond forgiveness.—Go, Sandford, to the library, where he is, and tell him this instant to quit my house, and never dare to return."

Miss Woodley lifted up her hands and sighed.

Sandford rose slowly from his seat to execute his office.

While Lady Matilda, who was arranging her music books upon the instrument, stopped from her employment suddenly, with her face bathed in tears.

A general silence ensued, till Lord Elmwood, resuming his angry tone, cried, "Did you hear me, Mr. Sandford?"

Sandford now, without a word in reply, made for the door—but there Matilda impeded him, and throwing her arms about his neck, cried,

"Dear Mr. Sandford, do not."

"How!" exclaimed her father.

She saw the frown that was impending, and rushing towards him, took his hand fearfully, and knelt at his feet.—"Mr. Rushbrook is my relation," she cried in a pathetic voice, "my companion, my friend—before you loved me he was anxious for my happiness, and often visited me to propose some kindness.—I cannot see him turned out of your house without feeling for him, what he once felt for me."

Lord Elmwood turned aside to conceal his sensations—then raising her from the floor, he said, "Do you know what he has asked of me?"

"No"—answered she in the utmost ignorance, and with the utmost innocence painted on her face.—"But whatever it is, my Lord, though you do not grant it, yet pardon him for asking."

"Perhaps *you* would grant him what he has requested?" said his Lordship.

"Most willingly—was it in my gift."

"It is." replied he. "And go to him in the library, and hear what he has to say;—for on your will his fate shall depend."

Like lightning she flew out of the room; while even the grave Sandford smiled at the idea of their meeting.

Rushbrook, with his fears all verified by the manner in which his uncle had left him, sat with his head reclined against a book case, and every limb extended with the despair that had seized him.

Matilda nimbly opened the door and cried, "Mr. Rushbrook, I am come to comfort you."

"That you have always done." said he, rising in rapture to receive her, even in the midst of all his sadness.

"What is it you want?" said she. "What have you asked of my father that he has denied you?"

"I have asked for that," replied he, "which is dearer to me than my life."

"Be satisfied then," returned she, "for you shall have it."

"Dear Matilda! it is not in your power to bestow."

"But his Lordship has told me it *shall* be in my power; and has desired me to give, or to refuse it you, at my own pleasure."

"O Heavens!" cried Rushbrook in transport, "Has he?"

"He has indeed—before both Mr. Sandford and Miss Woodley.—Now tell me what your petition is?"

"I asked him," cried Rushbrook, trembling, "for a wife."

Her hand that had just then taken hold of his, in the warmth of her wish to serve him, now dropped down as with the stroke of death—her face lost its colour—and she leaned against the desk by which they were standing, without uttering a word.

"What means this change?" said he; "Do you not wish me happy?"

"Yes." she exclaimed: "Heaven is my witness.—But it gives me concern to think we must part."

"Then let us be joined," cried he, falling at her feet, "till death alone can part us."

All the sensibility—the reserve—the pride, with which she was so amply possessed, returned to her that moment.—She started and cried, "Could Lord Elmwood know for what he sent me?"

"He did." replied Rushbrook—"I boldly told him of my presumptuous love, and he has yielded to you alone, the power over my happiness or misery.—Oh! do not doom me to the latter."

Whether the heart of Matilda, such as it has been described, *could* sentence him to misery, the reader is left to surmise—and if he supposes that it did not, he has every reason to suppose their wedded life was a life of happiness.

He has beheld the pernicious effects of an improper education in the destiny which attended the unthinking Miss Milner—On the opposite side, then, what may not be hoped from that school of prudence—though of adversity—in which Matilda was bred?

And Mr. Milner, Matilda's grandfather, had better have given his fortune to a distant branch of his family—as Matilda's father once meant to do—so he had bestowed upon his daughter

A PROPER EDUCATION[1]

FINIS

---

1 See Appendix C3.

Appendix A: Inchbald's Other Writings

1. Letter "To The Artist" (1807)

[Prince Hoare, dramatist, painter, and art critic, established the journal *The Artist* in 1807, subtitled "a collection of essays relative to painting, poetry, sculpture, architecture, the drama, discoveries of science, and various other subjects." *The Artist* provided a forum for Hoare's friends and colleagues to discuss the theories and techniques of their work. In this essay, Inchbald satirizes mistakes made by other novelists, but she also reveals her own belief in the novel's didactic potential.]

The ARTIST. No. XIV. Saturday, June 13, 1807.

TO THE ARTIST

SIR,

IF the critical knowledge of an art was invariably combined with the successful practice of it, I would here proudly take my rank among artists, and give instructions on the art of writing Novels.—But though I humbly confess that I have not the slightest information to impart, that may tend to produce a good novel; yet it may not be wholly incompatible with the useful design of your publication, if I show—how to avoid writing a very bad one.

Observe, that your hero and heroine be neither of them too bountiful. The prodigious sums of money which are given away every year in novels, ought, in justice, to be subject to the property tax; by which regulation, the national treasury, or every such book, would be highly benefited.

Beware how you imitate Mrs. Radcliffe, or Maria Edgeworth;[1] you cannot equal them; and those readers who most admire their works, will most despise yours.

Take care to reckon up the many times you make use of the words "Amiable," "Interesting," "Elegant," "Sensibility," "Delicacy,"

---

1 Renowned novelists of the late eighteenth and early nineteenth century. Ann Radcliffe (1764-1823) was famous for her Gothic fiction, especially her novel, *The Mysteries of Udolpho*, which is featured in Jane Austen's *Northanger Abbey*. Maria Edgeworth (1767-1849) was known for her novels and for *Practical Education*, a guide to children's education that she wrote collaboratively with her father, Richard Lovell Edgeworth (1744-1817). Both of the Edgeworths admired Inchbald's work, particularly *A Simple Story*.

"Feeling." Count each of those words over before you send your manuscript to be printed, and be sure to erase half the number you have written;—you may erase again when your first proof comes from the press—again, on having a revise—and then mark three or four, as mistakes of the printer, in your Errata.

Examine likewise, and for the same purpose, the various times you have made your heroine blush, and your hero turn pale—the number of times he has pressed her hand to his "trembling lips," and she his letters to her "beating heart"—the several times he has been "speechless" and she "all emotion," the one "struck to the soul;" the other "struck dumb."

The lavish use of "tears," both in "showers" and "floods," should next be scrupulously avoided; though many a gentle reader will weep on being told that others are weeping, and require no greater cause to excite their compassion.[1]

Consider well before you introduce a child into your work. To maim the characters of men and women is no venial offence; but to destroy innocent babes is most ferocious cruelty: and yet this savage practice has, of late, arrived at such excess, that numberless persons of taste and sentiment have declared—they will never read another novel, unless the advertisement which announces the book, adds (as in advertisements for letting Lodgings) *There are no children.*

When you are contriving that incident where your heroine is in danger of being drowned, burnt, or her neck broken by the breaking of an axle-tree—for without perils by fire, water, or coaches, your book would be incomplete—it might be adviseable to suffer her to be rescued from impending death by the sagacity of a dog, a fox, a monkey, or a hawk; any one to whom she cannot give her hand in marriage; for whenever the deliverer is a fine young man, the catastrophe of your plot is foreseen, and suspense extinguished.

Let not your ambition to display variety cause you to produce such a number of personages in your story, as shall create perplexity, dissipate curiosity, and confound recollection. But if, to show your powers of invention, you are resolved to introduce your reader to a new acquaintance in every chapter, and in every chapter snatch away his old one;

---

1 Inchbald seemed to follow this advice when she revised *A Simple Story* after its initial publication in February, 1791. In several places, she removed the tears that her characters (particularly the men) shed in the first edition. For example, in Volume three of the novel's first edition, Sandford turns to "hide his tears." In the second, third, fourth, and fifth editions, however, he turns "to conceal his feelings."

he will soon have the consolation to perceive—they are none of them worth his regret.

Respect virtue—nor let her be so warm or so violent as to cause derision:—nor vice so enormous as to resemble insanity. No one can be interested for an enthusiast—nor gain instruction from a madman.

And when you have written as good a novel as you can—compress it into three or four short volumes at most; or the man of genius, whose moments are precious, and on whose praise all your fame depends, will not find time to read the production, till you have committed suicide in consequence of its ill reception with the public.

There are two classes of readers among this public, of whom it may not be wholly from the purpose to give a slight account. The first are all hostile to originality. They are so devoted to novel-reading, that they admire one novel because it puts them in mind of another, which they admired a few days before. By them it is required, that a novel should be like a novel; that is, the majority of those compositions; for the minor part describe fictitious characters and events merely as they are in real life:—ordinary representations, beneath the concern of a true voracious novel-reader.

Such an one (more especially of the female sex) is indifferent to the fate of nations, or the fate of her own family, whilst some critical situation in a romance agitates her whole frame! Her neighbour might meet with an accidental death in the next street, the next house, or the next room, and the shock would be trivial, compared to her having just read—"that the amiable Sir Altamont, beheld the interesting Eudocia,[1] faint in the arms of his thrice happy rival."

Affliction, whether real or imaginary, must be refined,—and calamity elegant, before this novel-reader can be roused to "sympathetic sensation." Equally unsusceptible is her delicate soul to vulgar happiness. Ease and content are mean possessions! She requires transport, rapture, bliss, extatic joy, in the common occurrences of every day.

She saunters pensively in shady bowers, or strides majestically through brilliant circles. She dresses by turns like a Grecian statue and a pastoral nymph: then fancies herself as beautiful as the undone heroine in "*Barbarous Seduction;*" and has no objection to become equally unfortunate.

To the healthy, that food is nourishment, which to the sickly proves their poison. Such is the quality of books to the strong, and to the weak of understanding.—Lady Susan is of another class of readers, and has

---

1   These names are Inchbald's ironic fabrications, mocking novelistic convention.

good sense.—Let her therefore read certain well-written novels, and she will receive intimation of two or three foibles, the self-same as those, which, adhering to her conduct, cast upon all her virtues a degree of ridicule.—These failings are beneath the animadversions of the pulpit. They are so trivial yet so awkward, that neither sermons, history, travels, nor biography, could point them out with propriety. They are ludicrous, and can only be described and reformed by a humourist.

And what book so well as a novel, could show to the enlightened Lord Henry—the arrogance of his extreme condescension? Or insinuate to the judgment of Lady Eliza—the wantonness of her excessive reserve?

What friend could whisper so well to Lady Autumnal—that affected simplicity at forty, is more despicable than affected knowledge at fifteen?—And by what better means could the advice be conveyed to sir John Egotist—to pine no more at what the world may say of him; for that men like himself are too insignificant for the world to know.

A novel could most excellently represent to the valiant General B—, that though he can forgive the miser's love of gold, the youth's extravagance and even profligacy; that although he has a heart to tolerate all female faults, and to compassionate human depravity of every kind; he still exempts from this his universal clemency—the poor delinquent soldier.

The General's wife, too, forgives all injuries done to her neighbours: those to herself are of such peculiar kind, that it would be encouragement to offenders, not to seek vengeance.—The lovely Clarissa will pardon every one—except the mantua-maker who spoils her shape.—And good Sir Gormand never bears malice to a soul on earth—but to the cook who spoils his dinner.

That Prebendary is merciful to a proverb—excluding negligence towards holy things—of which he thinks himself the holiest. Certain novels might make these people think a second time.

Behold the Countess of L——! Who would presume to tell that once celebrated beauty—that she is now too wrinkled for curling hair; and her complexion too faded for the mixture of blooming pink? Should her husband convey such unwelcome news, he would be more detested than he is at present! Were her children or her waiting-maid to impart such intelligence, they would experience more of her peevishness than ever!—A novel assumes a freedom of speech to which all its readers must patiently listen; and by which, if they are wise, they will know how to profit.

The Novelist is a free agent. He lives in a land of liberty, whilst the Dramatic Writer exists but under a despotic government.—Passing over the subjection in which an author of plays is held by the Lord Chamberlain's office,[1] and the degree of dependence which he has on his actors—he is the very slave of the audience.[2] He must have their tastes and prejudices in view, not to correct, but to humour them. Some auditors of a theatre, like some aforesaid novel-readers, love to see that which they have seen before; and originality, under the opprobrious name of innovation, might be fatal to a drama, where the will of such critics is the law, and execution instantly follows judgment.[3]

In the opinion of these theatrical juries, Virtue and Vice attach to situations, more than to characters: at least, so they will have the stage represent. The great moral inculcated in all modern plays constantly is—for the rich to love the poor. As if it was not much more rare, and a task by far more difficult—for the poor to love the rich.—And yet, what author shall presume to expose upon the stage, certain faults, almost inseparable from the indigent? What dramatic writer dares to expose in a theatre, the consummate vanity of a certain rank of paupers, who boast of that wretched state as a sacred honour, although it be the result of indolence or criminality? Who dares to show to an audience, the privilege, of poverty debased into the instrument of ingratitude?—"I am poor and therefore slighted"—cries the unthankful beggar: whilst his poverty is his sole recommendation to his friends; and for which alone, they pay him much attention, and some respect.

What dramatist would venture to bring upon the stage—that which so frequently occurs in real life—a benefactor living in awe of the object of his bounty; trembling in the presence of the man whom he supports, lest by one inconsiderate word, he should seem to remind him of the predicament in which they stand with each other; or by an involuntary look, seem to glance at such and such obligations?

Who, moreover, dares to exhibit upon the stage, a benevolent man, provoked by his crafty dependant—for who is proof against ungrate-fulness?—to become that very tyrant, which he unjustly had reported him?

---

1 According to the 1737 Licensing Act, only government-sanctioned plays could be performed. The act was passed in part because Henry Fielding (1707-54) wrote plays ridiculing political figures.
2 The late eighteenth-century taste tended to be for moral, sentimental comedies.
3 During the middle decades of the eighteenth century, the Licensing Act affected risk-taking on the part of theatre managers, so the mid- to late eighteenth century often reproduced known, established plays instead of producing new ones.

Again.—The giver of alms, as well as the alms-receiver, must be revered on the stage.—That rich proprietor of land, Lord Forecast, who shall dare to bring him upon the boards of a theatre, and show—that, on the subject of the poor, the wily Forecast accomplishes two most important designs? By keeping the inhabitants of his domain steeped in poverty, he retains his vast superiority on earth; then secures, by acts of charity, a chance for heaven.

A dramatist must not speak of national concerns, except in one dull round of panegyrick. He must not allude to the feeble minister of state,[1] nor to the ecclesiastical coxcomb.

Whilst the poor dramatist is, therefore, confined to a few particular provinces; the novel-writer has the whole world to range, in search of men and topics. Kings, warriors, statesmen, churchmen, are all subjects of his power. The mighty and the mean, the common-place and the extraordinary, the profane and the sacred, all are prostrate before his muse. Nothing is forbidden, nothing is withheld from the imitation of a novelist, except—other novels.

E.I.

2. From Inchbald's Daily Pocket Diaries (1788)

[Inchbald kept daily records throughout her life, using the popular *Ladies' Own Memorandum Book*. The extant diaries (1776, 1780, 1782, 1783, 1788, 1793, 1807, 1808, 1814, and 1820) are held by the Folger Library, in Washington, DC. A sample entry has been reproduced from 1788, by permission of the Folger Shakespeare Library.]

a. Facsimile of two week's diary entries [see pages 348-49]

b. Transcription of a typical week's diary entries

[Inchbald's diary entries resemble stage directions, as if they were written as notes to remind her of significant events in her own life. Just two weeks are reprinted here (April 8 to April 14, 1776, and February 25 to March 2, 1788) to exemplify the diaries. Some of these entries (such as her visit with the publisher Robinson) are directly related to the composition of *A Simple Story*. Other entries (such as her attendance at the Hastings trial) are more tenuously connected to the novel, but nev-

---

1 Fielding's plays were credited with helping to bring down Robert Walpole, prime minister of England from 1722-42.

ertheless deepen our understanding of its cultural contexts. Throughout 1776, Inchbald kept careful accounts of her expenses and earnings, but in 1788, she limited her entries to her social and professional life. Entries for the year 1788, in particular, demonstrate how fully Inchbald was involved in the theatre.]

April 8, to Account of Cash	April 14, 1776 Memorandums and Remarks
Washing—0.39	M 8 After I came from Prayers called at the House on Mr. Inchbald—then was at my part. After dinner wrote French at ten received a Letter from my Brother. While Mr. Inchbald was playing in *Rule a Wife*[1] I worked all time …
a letter—00.10	Tu After I came from Prayers called at the house … then walked a little with Mr. Inchbald and wrote French. In the afternoon wrote to my brother. After tea Mr. Inchbald walked—I was at Rosalind[2] all the Evening.
my shoe's covering 00.60	W While Mr. Inchbald was at rehearsal I was at Rehearsal—Then walked then called at the House—Bob[3] dined—in the afternoon I wrote French—while Mr. Inchbald was playing in *Macbeth* … behind the curtains I was at my part … Mr. Inchbald called between his scenes …

1 The comedy, *To Rule a Wife and Have a Wife* (1624), by Beaumont and Fletcher. Inchbald was to review this play later in *The British Theatre* (1808) and conclude that "though it has an unpleasing fable, with female characters utterly detestable, yet it is so constituted with parts so ably written, so forcible in sentiment and humour, that actors of a certain class of excellence must ever give it powerful effect in the exhibition."

2 Inchbald played Rosalind in Shakepeare's *As You Like It*.

3 Robert Inchbald, Joseph Inchbald's son.

Week 2]	Account of CASH	Received.
	Brought over £	

Washing

Pins

a Letter _Mr_ Inchbald
received from a Son

My Letter

fruit after Dinner

Cakes when my Book finish
was here

fruit in the Evening

At the Chapel

fruit in the afternoon

| | Cash in Hand | |
| | Total £ | |

Typical diary entry.

JANUARY 14, 1776.

Paid.			MEMORANDUMS and REMARKS.
0	3	6	M.
0	0	1	
0	0	1	T.
0	0		
0	0	1	W.
0	0		
0	0		
0	0	1	Th.
			F.
			Sa.
0	0	1	Su.
0	0	1	

| to my French Master 1.10 | Th |
| | I was at rehearsal of Rosamond then walked by my self—after dinner wrote French ... then saw the last act of *All in the Wrong*[1] and Bob was in Mr. Duffy's Box.... |

| to the seamstress 44 | Fri |
| | I was at Rehearsal—a windy day and I took no walk—... |

| my black gown's mending 0.09 pins 0.01 | Sa |
| | I was at Rehearsal then walked a little and sat with Mr. Inchbald.... |

| at the chapel 0.01 | Su |
| | A very Windy Day—after I came from prayers walked by my self and was angry with Mr. Inchbald he was not kind—in the afternoon wrote French—Bob drank tea here—after Mr. Inchbald walked—I was at the French c & c- |

| **February 25, to Account of Cash** | **March 2, 1788 Memorandums and Remarks** |

| *Monday* | M. 25 |
| "Love in the East"[2] with Mr. Marlowe[3] | Was from nine till four at the Trial of Mr. Hastings.[4] Met Sir Charles as I |

1 A comedy by Arthur Murphy, which Inchbald praised in *The British Theatre*, remarking that "the dialogue of 'All in the Wrong' is of a species so natural, that it never in one sentence soars above the proper standard of elegant life; and the incidents that occur are bold without extravagance or apparent artifice, which is the criterion on which judgment should be formed between comedy and farce."

2 A comic opera (1788) by James Cobb.

3 William Marlow, painter (1740/41-1813). Inchbald's friend who occasionally attended the theatre with her.

4 Warren Hastings was governor general of Fort William in Bengal. His ambitious plans for expansion laid the foundation for British power in India, but he was impeached under charges including corruption, oppression, and unauthorized wars. Inchbald's play, *Such Things Are* (1788) addresses explicitly issues surrounding expansion and trade in India. (See Bolton, 202-30 and Green, "'You Should Be

our play *Capricious Lady*[1] &
Pantomime[2]—Davis[3] supped
here—My face poorly[4] for
fourscore days

Dinner and all the Evening
reading the French Manuscript
Mr. Twiss[5] Left me in the
Morning—Play *Robin Hood*[6]
& *Midnight Hour.*[7]

returned in a Chair. He called here
while I was at the new Opera.

Tu.
Fatigued with yesterday. Worked
& read. Mr. Topham[8] called. Then
Nanny and Mrs. Hunt.[9] Received
a letter from Mr. Colman[10] which
pleased me—after read and was dull.

Wednesday
Mr. Twiss called for his comedy
— my face poorly—all evening
working and surprised at my

W.
My hair dresser came last—heard the
King came to the play,[11] tomorrow
then heard he did not. Mrs. Hunt here,

My Master': Imperial Recognition Politics in Elizabeth Inchbald's *Such Things Are*").
In *A Simple Story*, Miss Milner's unnecessary purchases of expensive china and books
may be a reference to the excess and greed associated with the East India Trade
Company.

1   A comedy by William Cooke.
2   A pre-show performance using gestures and body movements without words.
    Inchbald often performed in the trendy pantomimes.
3   Davis was a hairdresser and costumier as well as a long-time friend of Inchbald's.
4   Inchbald complained of pain in her face for several months. Jenkins speculates that
    the pain may have been caused by a toothache (239).
5   Francis Twiss (bap. 1759, d. 1827) was a circuit judge and friend of Inchbald's who
    read and critiqued her writing, possibly including *A Simple Story*.
6   A comic opera (1784) by Irish dramatist Leonard MacNally.
7   A comedy (1787) by Inchbald, bought by Thomas Harris.
8   Edward Topham (1751-1820), founder, along with Charles (Parson) Este (1753-1829),
    of *The World and Fashionable Advertiser*. After the collaboration between Topham and
    Este ended in 1790, Inchbald sold *A Simple Story* to Robinson on 11 November 1790.
9   Inchbald's sister, Dolly Hunt.
10 George Colman, the younger, (1762-1836), a dramatist and friend of Inchbald's.
11 King George III enjoyed the theatre and attended often.

disappointment—wrote to Mr. Harris[2]—at nine called on Mr. Whitfield[3]—Davis supped with me told me of the Irish Lady mending for him.

then Mrs. Carter[1] called—after read and was dull.

Th.
....
—played in Recruiting Officer.[4] My head and face very bad...

Friday
....
—nanny a new maid came— Sir Charles[6] here most of the evening I worked. Read after & expected Davis—my face poorly.

Fr.
A dirty day—read—received a note from Mr. Lewis[5] that he would take the part of Malinda from me—then Mr. and Mrs. Marlow thru Mr. Texier[7] called to bill.

Sa. March 1.
A fine warm day—Mrs. Harris here.

Su.
Warm and Cloudy—House chambers then at Robinson's[8] Then Mr. Le Texier, Mrs. Taylor[9] and then Mr. Marlowe here some time.

---

1   Mrs. Carter was a friend of Inchbald's.
2   Thomas Harris (d. 1820) bought Inchbald's first play and maintained a professional relationship with her for many years in spite of the famous incident when she escaped his amorous attentions by pulling his hair.
3   John and Mary Whitfield were actors and friends of Inchbald's. Mary Whitfield (nee Lane), also a singer, was known for her eccentric performances of songs and plays. Inchbald was inconsolable after Mary died in 1795.
4   A 1706 comedy by George Farquhar (1676/7-1707).
5   William Thomas Lewis (1748-1811) was manager of the Covent Garden Theatre.
6   Charles Bunbury (1740-1821) was Inchbald's friend and probably lover. See Jenkins, 233, 238, 509.
7   Anthony A. LeTexier (c. 1737-1814) French actor and friend of Inchbald's.
8   George Robinson (1736-1801) publisher of several of Inchbald's plays and *A Simple Story*.
9   Possibly Susannah Taylor (nee Cook) (1755-1823).

3. From Selected Plays

[In addition to *A Simple Story*, Inchbald wrote approximately twenty-one plays, at least one other novel, and a collection of critical prefaces to popular plays, *The British Theatre* (1808). Because her career was multi-faceted, it is difficult if not impossible to separate her career as a dramatist from her careers as an actress, a novelist, and a critical essayist. In her writing, she often compares the subject matter, goals, and methods of her various crafts. (See the discussion of Inchbald's *British Theatre* Preface to *Wives as they Were and Maids as they Are* in the headnote to the following section.)]

a. From Wives as They Were and Maids as They Are *(1797)*

[In Inchbald's Preface to this play in *The British Theatre*, she refers to herself in the third person and, as she commonly does, discusses the craft of writing. Inchbald claims that "the writer of this drama seems to have had a tolerable good notion of that which a play ought to be; but has here failed in the execution of a proper design." Despite Inchbald's criticism that the play fails to live up to its comic potential, she concludes her essay by praising the character, Miss Dorrillon, the "most prominent and interesting one in the piece." Miss Dorrillon's power, like that of Miss Milner in *A Simple Story*, stems from her complex nature. Miss Dorrillon "appears to have been formed of the same matter and spirit as compose the body and mind of the heroine of the 'Simple Story'—a woman of fashion with a heart—a lively comprehension, and no reflection:—an understanding, but no thought.—Virtues abounding from disposition, education, feeling:—Vices obtruding from habit and example."]

ACT ONE

. . . .

Mr. NORBERRY.
　　Depend upon it, my dear friend, that miss Dorrillon, your daughter, came to my house just the same heedless woman of fashion you now see her.
Sir WILLIAM [impatiently].
　　Very well—'Tis very well.—But, when I think on my disappointment—

Mr. NORBERRY.

There is nothing which may not be repaired. Maria, with you for guide—

Sir WILLIAM.

Me! She turns me into ridicule—laughs at me! This morning, as she was enumerating some of her frivolous expences, she observed me lift up my hands and sigh; on which she named fifty other extravagances she had no occasion to mention, merely to enjoy the pang which every folly of hers sends to my heart.

Mr. NORBERRY.

But do not charge this conduct of your daughter to the want of filial love:—did she know you were Sir William Dorrillon, did she know you were her father, every word you uttered, every look you glanced, would be received with gentleness and submission;—but your present rebukes from Mr. Mandred (as you are called), from a perfect stranger, as she supposes, she considers as an impertinence which she has a right to resent.

Sir WILLIAM.

I wish I had continued abroad. And yet, the hope of beholding her, and of bestowing upon her the riches I acquired, was my sole support through all the toils by which I gained them.

Mr. NORBERRY.

And, considering her present course of life, your riches could not come more opportunely.

Sir WILLIAM.

She shall never have a farthing of them. Do you think I have encountered the perils of almost every climate, to squander my hard-earned fortune upon the paltry vicious pleasures in which she delights? No.—I have been now in your house exactly a month—I will stay but one day longer—and then, without telling her who I am, I will leave the kingdom and her for ever—Nor shall she know that this insignificant merchant whom she despises, was her father, till he is gone, never to be recalled.

Mr. NORBERRY.

You are offended with some justice: but, as I have often told you, your excessive delicacy and respect for the conduct of the other sex, degenerate into rigour.

Sir WILLIAM.

True—for what I see so near perfection as woman, I want to see perfect. We, Mr. Norberry, can never be perfect; but surely women, women, might easily be made angels!

Mr. NORBERRY.

And if they were, we should soon be glad to make them into women again.

Sir WILLIAM [inattentive to Mr. NORBERRY].

She sets the example. She gives the fashion—and now your whole house, and all your visitors, in imitation of her, treat me with levity, or with contempt.—But I'll go away to-morrow.

Sir NORBERRY.

Can you desert your child in the moment she most wants your protection? That exquisite beauty just now mature—

Sir WILLIAM.

There's my difficulty!—There's my struggle!—If she were not so like her mother, I could leave her without a pang—cast her off, and think no more of her.—But that shape! That face! Those speaking looks! Yet, how reversed!—Where is the diffidence, the humility—where is the simplicity of my beloved wife? Buried in her grave.

....

Miss DORRILLON.

I have now lost all my money, and all my jewels, at play; it is almost two years since I have received a single remittance from my father; and Mr. Norberry refuses to advance me a shilling more.—What I shall do to discharge a debt which must be paid either to-day or to-morrow, heaven knows!—Dear Lady Mary, you could not lend me a small sum, could you?

Lady MARY.

Who? I! [*with surprise*]—My dear creature, it was the very thing I was going to ask of you: for when you have money, I know no one so willing to disperse it among her friends.

Miss DORRILLON.

Am not I?—I protest I love to part with my money; for I know with what pleasure I receive it myself, and I like to see that joy sparkle in another's eye, which has so often brightened my own. But last night ruined me—I must have money somewhere.—As you can't assist me, I must ask Mr. Norberry for his carriage, and immediately go in search of some friend that can lend me four, or five, or six, or seven hundred pounds. But the worst is, I have lost my credit—Is not that dreadful?

b. From Every One Has His Fault *(1793)*

[Published in 1793 and performed 29 January 1793, *Every One Has His Fault* was extremely popular despite complaints that it revealed Inchbald's transgressive, Jacobin sympathies. As Inchbald pointed out in her preface to the play in *The British Theatre*, however, the play was "productive to both the manager and the writer, having, on its first appearance, run, in the theatrical term, near thirty nights; during which, some of the audience were heard to laugh, and some were seen to weep." Thematically, the play resembles *A Simple Story* in its representation of a despotic father figure. (See the Introduction for a more detailed discussion.)]

ACT V.

SCENE I. *An apartment at Lord* Norland's.
Enter HAMMOND, followed by Lady ELEANOR.

HAMMOND.
My Lord is busily engaged, Madam; I do not suppose he would see any one, much less a stranger.
LADY ELEANOR.
I am no stranger.
HAMMOND.
Your name then, Madam?
LADY ELEANOR.
That, I cannot send in. But tell him, Sir, I am the afflicted wife of a man, who for some weeks past has given many fatal proofs of a disordered mind. In one of those fits of phrensy, he held an instrument of death, meant for his own destruction, to the breast of your Lord (who by accident that moment passed), and took from him, what he vainly hoped might preserve his own life, and relieve the wants of his family. But his paroxysm over, he shrunk from what he had done, and gave the whole he had thus unwarrantably taken, into a servant's hands to be returned to its lawful owner. The man, admitted to his confidence, betrayed his trust, and instead of giving up what was so sacredly delivered to him, secreted it; and, to obtain the promised reward, came to this house, but to inform against the wretched offender; who now, only resting on your Lord's clemency, can escape the direful fate he has incurred.

HAMMOND.

Madam, the account you give, makes me interested in your behalf, and you may depend, I will repeat it all with the greatest exactness.

[*Exit* Hammond]

LADY ELEANOR,
Looking around her.

This is my father's house! It is only through two rooms and one short passage, and there he is sitting in his study. Oh! in that study, where I (even in the midst of all his business) have been so often welcome; where I have urged the suit of many an unhappy person, nor ever urged in vain. Now I am not permitted to speak for myself, nor have one friendly voice to do that office for me, which I have so often undertaken for others.

[*Re-enter* Hammond, Edward *following.*]

HAMMOND.

My Lord says, that any petition concerning the person you come about, is in vain. His respect for the laws of his country demands an example such as he means to make.

LADY ELEANOR.

Am I, am I to despair then? [*To* Hammond] Dear Sir, would you go once more to him, and humbly represent—

HAMMOND.

I should be happy to oblige you, but I dare not take any more messages to my Lord; he has given me my answer.—If you will give me leave, madam, I'll see you to the door.

[*Crosses to the other side, and Exit.*]

LADY ELEANOR.

Misery—Distraction!—Oh, Mr. Placid! O, Mr. Harmony! Are these the hopes you gave me, could I have the boldness to enter this house? But you would neither of you undertake to bring me here!—neither of you undertake to speak for me!

[*She is following the Servant; Edward walks softly after her, till she gets near the door; he then takes hold of her gown, and gently pulls it; she turns and looks at him.*]

EDWARD.

Shall I speak for you, Madam?

LADY ELEANOR.

Who are you, pray, young Gentleman? Is it you, whom Lord Norland has adopted for his son?

EDWARD.

I believe he has, Madam; but he has never told me so yet.

LADY ELEANOR.

I am obliged to you for your offer; but my suit is of too much consequence for *you* to undertake.

EDWARD.

I know what your suit is, Madam, because I was with my Lord when Hammond brought in your message; and I was so sorry for you, I came out on purpose to see you—and, without speaking to my Lord, I could do you a great kindness—if I durst.

LADY ELEANOR.

What kindness?

EDWARD.

But I durst not—No, do not ask me.

LADY ELEANOR.

I do not. But you have raised my curiosity; and in a mind so distracted as mine, it is cruel to excite one additional pain.

EDWARD.

I am sure I would not add to your grief for the world.—But then, pray do not speak of what I am going to say.—I heard my Lord's lawyer tell him just now, "that as he said he should not know the person again, who committed the offence about which you came, and as the man who informed against him was gone off, there could be no evidence that he did the action, but from a book, a particular pocket-book of my Lord's, which he forgot to deliver to his servant with the notes and money to return, and which was found upon him at your house: and this, Lord Norland will affirm to be his."—Now, if I did not think I was doing wrong, this is the very book—[*Takes a pocket-book from his pocket*] I took it from my Lord's table;—but it would be doing wrong, or I am sure I wish you had it.

[*Looking wishfully at her.*]

LADY ELEANOR.

It will save my life, my husband's and my children's.

EDWARD, trembling.

But what is to become of me?

LADY ELEANOR.

That Providence, who never punishes the deed, unless the *will* be an accomplice, shall protect you for saving one, who has only erred in a moment of distraction.

EDWARD.

I never did any thing to offend my Lord in my life;—and I am in such fear of him, I did not think I ever should.—Yet, I cannot refuse *you*;—take it.—[*Gives her the book.*] But pity me, when my Lord shall know of it.

LADY ELEANOR.

Oh! should he discard you for what you have done, it will embitter every minute of my remaining life.

EDWARD.

Do not frighten yourself about that.—I think he loves me too well to discard me quite.

LADY ELEANOR.

Does he indeed?

EDWARD.

I think he does;—for often, when we are alone, he presses me to his bosom so fondly, you would not suppose.—And, when my poor nurse died, she called me to her bed-side, and told me (but pray keep it a secret)—she told me I was—his grandchild.

LADY ELEANOR.

You are—you are his grand-child—I see,—I feel you are;—for I feel that I am your mother. [*Embraces him.*] Oh! take this evidence back [*returning the book*]—I cannot receive it from thee, my child;—no, let us all perish, rather than my boy, my only boy, should do an act to stain his conscience, or to lose his grand-father's love.

EDWARD.

What do you mean?

Lady ELEANOR.

The name of the person with whom you lived in your infancy, was Heyland?

EDWARD.

It was.

LADY ELEANOR.

I am your mother; Lord Norland's only child, [*Edward kneels*] who, for one act of disobedience, have been driven to another part of the globe in poverty, and forced to leave you, my life, behind. [*She embraces and raises him.*] Your father, in his struggles to support us all, has fallen a victim;—but Heaven, which has preserved my child, will save my husband, restore his sense, and once more—

EDWARD, *starting.*

I hear my Lord's step,—he is coming this way:—Begone, mother, or we are all undone.

LADY ELEANOR.

No, let him come—for though his frown should kill me, yet must I thank him for his care of thee.

[*She advances toward the door to meet him.*]

[*Enter Lord* Norland.]

[*Falling on her knees.*] You love me,—'tis in vain to say you do not: You love my child; and with whatever hardships you have dealt, or still mean to deal to me, I will never cease to think you love me, nor ever cease my gratitude for your goodness.

LORD NORLAND.

Where are my servants? Who let this woman in?

[*She rises, and retreats from him alarmed and confused.*]

EDWARD.

Oh, my Lord, pity her.—Do not let me see her hardly treated— Indeed I cannot bear it.

Enter HAMMOND.

LORD NORLAND, to LADY ELEANOR.

What was your errand here? If to see your child, take him along with you.

LADY ELEANOR.

I came to see my father;—I have a house too full of such as he already.

LORD NORLAND.

How did she gain admittance?

HAMMOND.

With a petition, which I repeated to your Lordship.

[Exit HAMMOND.]

LORD NORLAND.

Her husband then it was, who—[*To Lady Eleanor*] but let him know, for this boy's sake, I will no longer pursue him.

LADY ELEANOR.

For that boy's sake you will not pursue his father; but for whose sake are you so tender of that boy? 'Tis for mine, for my sake; and by that I conjure you—[*Offers to kneel.*]

LORD NORLAND.

Your prayers are in vain—[*To Edward.*] Go, take leave of your mother *for ever*, and instantly follow me; or shake hands with me for the last time, and instantly begone with her.

[Edward *stands between them in doubt for some little time: looks alternately at each with emotions of affection; at last goes to his grand-father, and takes hold of his hand.*]

EDWARD.

Farewell, my Lord,—it almost breaks my heart to part from you;— but, if I have my choice, I must go with my mother.

[*Exit Lord* Norland *instantly.*]
[*Lady* Eleanor *and her Son go off on the opposite side.*]

4. Remarks in *The British Theatre* (1808)

[A series of popular plays along with Inchbald's prefaces appeared periodically beginning in 1806 and was assembled in 1808, under the title, *The British Theatre*. The following are representative of Inchbald's thoughts about methods and goals for acting as well as writing for the stage.]

a. *Hannah Cowley,* The Belle's Stratagem *(1780)*

[Inchbald played the part of Lady Frances Touchwood in *The Belle's Stratagem* several times. Other critics, including Terry Castle, have noticed thematic similarities between *A Simple Story* and *The Belle's Stratagem*. The masquerade scene in *The Belle's Stratagem* may have been the model for the masquerade in *A Simple Story*, and certainly Dorriforth's name in *A Simple Story* resembles Doricourt's name in *The Belle's Stratagem*.[1] See Appendix C4 for an excerpt from *The Belle's Stratagem*.]

THIS comedy appeared on the stage in 1780; it was extremely attractive for two seasons, and still holds a place in the catalogue of those plays which are generally performed every year.

Its greatest charm is, that it is humorous, without ever descending

---

1 Castle, 319.

to that source of humour, easy of access, and which is placed among characters in low life.

The persons of importance in this drama are all elegant, or, at least, well-bred; and while they excite mirth, they create also an interest in their behalf, which is assisted to the end of the piece by a variety of forcible and pleasing occurrences.

The incident, from which the play takes its title, is, perhaps the least pleasing, and the least probable, of any amongst the whole; still, this stratagem, as the foundation of a multiplicity of others, far better conceived and executed, has a claim to the toleration of the reader, and will generally obtain admiration from the auditor, by the skill of the actress who imitates a simpleton.

The dialogue of this play is very good; abounding in excellent satire, with a most perfect description of the modes and manners of the fashionable world.

If Doricourt should remind the reader of Sir Harry Wildair, or Valentine in "Love for Love,"[1] it is the only character in the work that does not appear original—Sir George and Lady Frances Touchwood are more particularly new than the rest.

The second plot, in which they are the principals, is, to many spectators and readers, much more interesting than the first. It is assuredly more refined and more natural, though neither so bold nor so brilliant.

The love of Sir George and his wife is fervent, yet reasonable; they are fond, but not foolish; and with all their extreme delicacy of opinions, never once express their thoughts, either in ranting, affected, or insipid sentences.

Lady Frances, being protected at the masquerade, delights some auditors, as much as Doricourt's falling violently in love there: and though neither of these events, traced through all their meanders, may appear strictly within the bounds of likelihood, yet dramatic probability is seldom for a moment lost; which is the happy art of alluring the attention of an audience, from the observation of every defect, and of fixing it solely upon every beauty which the dramatist displays.

To explain this remark—who does not scorn that romantic passion, which is inflamed to the highest ardour, by a few hours conversation with a woman whose face is concealed? And yet, who does not here sympathize with the lover, and feel a strong agitation, when Letitia,

---

1   *Love for Love*, William Congreve's adaptation of Shakespeare's *Anthony and Cleopatra* opened at Lincoln's Inn Theatre on 30 April 1695. Its popularity continued throughout the eighteenth century.

going to take off her mask, exclaims in a tremulous voice,—"This is the most awful moment of my life!"

"The Belle's Stratagem" certainly classes amongst modern plays; and yet the mention of powder worn by the ladies,[1] their silk gowns, and other long-exploded fashions, together with the hero's having in Paris "danced with the queen of France[2] at a masquerade," gives a certain sensation to the reader, which seems to place the work on the honourable list of ancient dramas.

But the period of the last twenty-six years, which has produced in the world more wonderful changes in fashions, manners, opinions, and characters, than, many a century had done before, has yet preserved one illustrious character,[3] named in the play, free from alteration;—and, at the present moment her eulogium is heard in the midst of crowded theatres, with all that glow of veneration and love, which heretofore it inspired; and which now, more than ever, becomes due to those virtues—which time has proved to be stedfast.

b. Robert Jephson, The Count of Narbonne (1781)

[Inchbald's friend John Philip Kemble (who trained for the priesthood before becoming an actor) played the lead in the Irish production of *The Count of Narbonne*. J.M.S. Tompkins suggests in her introduction to *A Simple Story* (vii-xvi) that Lord Elmwood (Dorriforth) may have been modeled on Kemble's performance in *The Count of Narbonne*. See Appendix C1 for a portrait of Kemble.]

THIS tragedy was brought upon the stage in 1780; it was extremely admired, and exceedingly attractive.

Neither "The Winter's Tale," nor "Henry VIII" by Shakspeare, were at that time performed at either of the theatres; and the town had no immediate comparison to draw between the conjugal incidents in "The Count of Narbonne," and those which occur in these two very superior dramas.

The Cardinal Wolsey[4] of Shakspeare is, by Jephson, changed into a holy and virtuous priest: but his importance is, perhaps, somewhat di-

---

1 Hair powder was a popular fashion until 1795 when the hair powder tax took effect and unpowdered hair became trendy.
2 The French queen was executed on 14 October 1793.
3 Queen Charlotte (1714-1818), renowned for her virtue.
4 Cardinal Wolsey (1470/71-1530), The chief aid to Henry VIII who tried to help the King end his marriage with Catherine of Aragon so that he could marry Anne

minished by a discovery, which was intended to heighten the interest of his character; but which is introduced in too sudden and romantic a manner to produce the desired consequence upon a well-judging auditor.

One of the greatest faults, by which a dramatist can disappoint and fret his auditor, is also to be met with in this play.—Infinite discourse is exchanged, numberless plans formed, and variety of passions agitated, concerning a person who is never brought upon the stage.—Such is the personal nonentity of Isabel, in this tragedy, and yet the fable could not proceed without her.—Alphonso, so much talked of, yet never seen, is an allowable absentee, having departed to another world; and yet, whether such invisible personages be described as alive, or dead, that play is the most interesting, which makes mention of no one character, but those which are introduced to the sight of the audience.

The lover of romances, whose happy memory, unclouded by more weighty recollections, has retained a wonderful story, by the late Lord Orford,[1] called "The Castle of Otranto," will here, it is said, find a resemblance of plot and incidents, the acknowledged effect of close imitation.

Lord Orford (at that time Mr. Horace Walpole) attended some rehearsals of this tragedy, upon the very account, that himself was the founder of the fabric.

The author was of no mean reputation in the literary world, for he had already produced several successful dramas. "The Count of Narbonne" proved to be his last and his best composition.—Terror is here ably excited by descriptions of the preternatural; horror, by the portraiture of guilt; and compassion, by the view of suffering innocence.—These are three passions, which, divided, might each constitute a tragedy; and all these powerful engines of the mind and heart are here most happily combined to produce that end,—and each forms a lesson of morality.

c. *William Shakespeare,* The Winter's Tale *(1611)*

[Inchbald particularly admired Hermione and Paulina, both of whom, she argues, confer "honour and interest upon Leontes, merely by his keeping such excellent company." Boaden compares *The Winter's Tale*'s two-part structure to that of *A Simple Story.* See the Introduction (33-34) for a more detailed discussion.]

Boleyn. Unfortunately for Wolsey, Anne Boleyn held him responsible for the long delay in settling her status, and she used her influence to discredit him with the King.

1 Horace Walpole (1717-97), author of *The Castle of Otranto* (1765), was named the fourth Earl of Orford in 1791.

Although the reader of the following play may have read it frequently, he will dwell upon many of its beauties with a new delight; and, if the work is wholly unknown to him, or its fable, incidents, and poetry, have been but slightly impressed upon his memory, he will sometimes be surprised into a degree of enthusiastic admiration!

The "Winter's Tale" was very successful at Drury Lane Theatre a few years ago; and yet, it seems to class among these dramas that charm more in perusal than in representation. The long absence from the scene of the two most important characters, Leontes and his wife, and the introduction of various other persons to fill their places, divert, in some measure, the attention of an audience; and they do not so feelingly unite all they see and all they hear into a single story, as he who, with the book in his hand, and neither his eye nor ear distracted, combines, and enjoys the whole grand variety.

Besides the improbability of exciting equal interest by the *plot* of this drama, in performance as in the closet; some of the poetry is less calculated for that energetic delivery which the stage requires, than for the quiet contemplation of one who reads. The conversations of Florizel and Perdita have more of the tenderness, than the fervour, of love; and consequently their passion has not the force of expression to animate a multitude, though it is properly adapted to steal upon the heart of an individual.

Shakspeare has said in his tragedy of Othello, that a man is "jealous, because he is jealous." This conceit of the poet seems to be the only reason that can possibly be alleged, for the jealousy of the hero of the present work; for the unfounded suspicion of Leontes in respect to the fidelity of Hermione, is a much greater fault, and one with which imagination can less accord, than with the hasty strides of time, so much censured by critics, between the third and fourth acts of the play. It is easier for fancy to over-leap whole ages, than to overlook one powerful demonstration of insanity in that mind which is reputed sane.

The mad conduct of Leontes is however the occasion of such noble, yet such humble and forbearing demeanour on the part of his wife, that his phrenzy is rendered interesting by the sufferings which it brings upon her: and the extravagance of the first is soon forgotten through the deep impression made by the last.

High as this injured queen ranks in virtue and every endearing quality, she has a faithful attendant, who in that lowly capacity, reaches even the summit of her majesty's perfection. Paulina, in nature, and the best of all nature, tenderness united with spirit, has such power over the scenes in which she is engaged for the protection of the new-born child, that, like the queen, she confers honour and interest upon Leontes, merely by his keeping such excellent company.

In the barbarous transaction of this jealous King of Sicilia, and in the patient dignity of his queen, it has generally been supposed that the author meant to gratify the reigning Queen of England (Elizabeth,) by an allusion, which her majesty was certain to observe in this conjugal mistrust, to the wronged innocence of her mother, the accused and condemned Anne Boleyn.[1]

One commentator on "The Winter's Tale," even traces the language of the Queen of Sicilia upon her trial—the words used also in the recommendation of her infant daughter to the love of her cruel father—and other sentences pronounced on the same pitiable subject, to similar expressions made use of by the mother of Queen Elizabeth, in her similar state.

If Shakspeare really meant, in the characters of Leontes and Hermione, to give a portrait of Henry the Eighth and his second unfortunate wife—and to produce such pictures as the queen on the throne should admire, it was perfect good policy, rather than want of skill, to make the king jealous without one apparent motive. But still, even more of a courtier than in this point, did the great bard prove himself, in his forming the person of the king's discarded daughter! Perdita, the representative of Elizabeth, is here given by poetry, more beauty than painting could bestow; and thus the renowned Queen of Great Britain is assailed on the only feeble part of her understanding—that vanity, which proclaimed her sex.

There are two occurrences in this drama, quite as improbable as the unprovoked jealousy of the Sicilian king—the one, that the gentle, the amiable, the tender Perdita, should be an unconcerned spectator of the doom which menaced her foster, and supposed real, father; and carelessly forsake him in the midst of calamities. The other disgraceful improbability is—that the young prince Florizel should introduce himself to the court of Sicilia, by speaking arrant falsehoods.

There is a scene in this play which is an exception to the rest, in being far more grand in exhibition than the reader will possibly behold in idea. This is the scene of the Statue, when Mrs. Siddons[2] stands for Hermione.

---

1   Anne Boleyn (c. 1500-36), Henry VIII's second wife and the mother of Queen Elizabeth. When she failed to produce a son, she was executed on charges of witchcraft, incest, and adultery on 19 May 1536.

2   Sarah Siddons (1755-1831), actress and friend of Inchbald and the sister of John Kemble.

Appendix B: Eighteenth-Century Reception of A Simple Story

I. Reviews of *A Simple Story*

[Critical reception of *A Simple Story* was generally positive. The following published reviews reveal much about contemporary attitudes toward the novel, which was usually expected to be didactic as well as intellectual. The reviews probably influenced Inchbald's later revisions of her novel.]

a. Anna Laetitia Barbauld, The British Novelists, *Vol. 28 (1810) i-iv*

[This essay appears in Barbauld's highly influential 50-volume collection of British novels, which included the final editions of Inchbald's *A Simple Story* and *Nature and Art*. Barbauld's inclusion of Inchbald's work is one indication of how important her novels were considered at the time.]

To the readers of taste it would be superfluous to point out the beauties of Mrs. Inchbald's novels. The *Simple Story* has obtained the decided approbation of the best judges. There is an originality both in the characters and the situations which is not often found in similar productions. To call it a *simple story* is perhaps a misnomer, since the first and second parts are in fact two distinct stories, connected indeed by the character of Dorriforth, which they successfully serve to illustrate.

Dorriforth is introduced as a Romish priest of a lofty mind, generous, and endued with strong sensibilities, but having in his disposition much of sternness and inflexibility. His being in priest's orders presents an apparently insurmountable obstacle to his marriage; but it is got over, without violating probability, by his becoming heir to a title and estate, and on that account receiving a dispensation from his vows. Though slow to entertain thoughts of love, as soon as he perceives the partiality of his ward, it enters his breast like a torrent when the flood-gates are opened. The perplexities in which he is involved by Miss Milner's gay unthinking conduct bring them to the very brink of separating for ever; and very few scenes in any novel have a finer effect than the intended parting of the lovers, and their sudden, immediate, unexpected marriage.

It is impossible not to sympathize with the feelings of Miss Milner, when she sees the corded trunks standing in the passage; or again, when after their reconciliation she sees the carriage, which was to take away her lover, drive empty from the door. The character of the ward of Dorriforth is so drawn as to excite an interest such as we seldom feel for more faultless characters. Young, sprightly, full of sensibility, gay and thoughtless, we feel such a tenderness for her as we should for a child who is playing on the brink of a precipice. The break between the first and second parts of the story has a singularly fine effect. We pass over in a moment a large space of years, and find everything changed: scenes of love and conjugal happiness are vanished; and for the young, gay, thoughtless, youthful beauty, we see a broken-hearted penitent on her death-bed.

This sudden shifting of scene has an effect which no continued narrative could produce; an effect which even the scenes of real life could not produce; for the curtain of futurity is lifted up only by degrees, and we must wait the slow succession of months and years to bring about events which are here presented close together. The death-bed letter of Lady Milner is very solemn, and cannot be perused without tears.

Dorriforth in these latter volumes is become, from the contemplation of his injuries, morose, unrelenting, and tyrannical. How far it was possible for a man to resist the strong impulse of nature, and deny himself the sight of his child residing in the same house with him, the reader will determine; but the situation is new and striking.

It is a particular beauty in Mrs. Inchbald's compositions, that they are thrown so much into the dramatic form. There is little of mere narrative, and what there is of it, the style is careless; but all the interesting parts are carried on in dialogue:—we see and hear the persons themselves; we are but little led to think of the author, and it is only when we have done feeling that we begin to admire.

[A discussion follows of Inchbald's later novel, *Nature and Art*.]

b. The Critical Review; or, Annals of Literature 2 *(February 1791): 207-13, 435*

A WORK of invention, bearing the name of Mrs. Inchbald, cannot but excite the curiosity and raise the hopes of the public. The entertainment her theatrical pieces have so frequently afforded is a pledge that the exertions of the same mind must afford a certain degree of satisfaction and delight. It is true that Fielding[1] and Smollett,[2] excellently as many of their novels are written, were indifferent dramatic poets: but we recollect no instance of a successful theatrical writer having failed in the less difficult composition of novels; and either we are mistaken, or Mrs. Inchbald has discovered the true path which she ought to pursue.

Entertaining these sentiments, after having read her book, we turn back to her preface with considerable pain. She there asserts that "during the writing of it, she has suffered every quality and degree of weariness and lassitude, into which no other employment could have betrayed her—that she has the utmost detestation to the fatigue of inventing; and that necessity is her only motive for being an author."—She deceives herself. Necessity most probably was the grand stimulative which induced her to submit to that length of labour, and that reiterated strength of effort, which alone can enable even genius itself to write successfully: but the pleasure resulting from labour so great, and efforts so unremitting, amply repays the pain. The mind is enamoured with the repeated discoveries of its own powers, and congratulates itself while it contemplates its beauteous offspring. Let Mrs. Inchbald reflect how often she has experienced such delight, such rapture, and forbear to complain of the labour by which it was preceded.

The merits of the Simple Story are many. Character is accurately delineated and faithfully preserved, with few exceptions: the most delicate feelings are continually excited: the incidents are natural; and, what is more extraordinary in the present state of novel-writing, they are new. Invention never flags, except from the author's impatience; and though this work is composed of two stories, and of two heroines, it has a peculiar unity; superior to that of some even of our best novels; of which there are two sources. The first is, there is but one hero, Dorriforth; whose consistency of character charms, offends, agitates, and astonishes: but the still more intimate link of connection is the unremitting attention which the fable and principal characters command. The mind never loses sight of the first heroine, till she no longer occupies the scene, but gives place to Matilda: and the reader's thoughts are then as intensely fixed on the daughter, as they before had been on her mother. The manner in which the principal persons are so constantly kept in view is eminently remarkable; and the workings of the passions are inimitably displayed.

---

1   Henry Fielding (1707-54), novelist and dramatist and author of *Tom Jones* (1749), *Joseph Andrews* (1742), and *Amelia* (1751).
2   Tobias George Smollett (1721-71), novelist and dramatist.

Having spoken with so much pleasure of the parts which are meri-
torious, we are sorry to be obliged to notice errors; one of which is
indeed glaring. This error is abruptness; and in two places it is painfully
conspicuous. The first is at the beginning of the third volume; where,
indulging that impatience before hinted at, a void of seventeen years
is left; and a few unsatisfactory hints, instead of that fulness of narrative which probability requires, introduces a totally new story. Here,
however, the power of that unity which we described above is fully
displayed; for, though nothing can be more disjointed than these two
stories in the present mode of connecting them, no sooner do the original hero and the second heroine possess the scene than attention is rivet-
ted to them; and the pain of vacancy, so lately experienced, is totally
lost. But the second specimen of abruptness is by far the greatest error
in the work; and this is the imperfect manner in which it ends. Never
was an impatience to conclude more manifest than in this novel: and
we are persuaded that it was under the latent influence of those feelings
of impatience, and of the bad effects of them on her denouement, that
Mrs. Inchbald wrote her preface. It was one of those attempts which the
human mind is always making to palliate its own imperfections.—But
we prophesy there will be more than one edition; and we persuade
ourselves she will not permit a second to appear with the same *crying fin*,
the same disappointment of expectation artfully raised and as suddenly
defeated, and left in a state of irritation, to imagine what the writer was
too weary to relate.[1]

The style of Mrs. Inchbald is in general clear and unaffected; but
sometimes it is obscure and ungrammatical.[2] There are many obvious
errors of the press; and we cannot help suspecting that some of the mistakes of grammar and language originate in this source, and not with
the author. The mind of Mrs. Inchbald is attentive, perspicuous, and
acute; we, therefore, suspect she never could write—"A conversation
in which no other but themselves *partook a part*,"[3] vol. i. p. 202. At page
187 of the same volume, we have a lord Edward,[4] though no such person

---

1 In the second edition, Inchbald did attempt to prepare her readers for the sudden
   changes between the novels' two parts by adding references to the West Indies so that
   Elmwood's absence might be less startling.
2 Inchbald was especially sensitive about errors in her writing, and she worked diligently after *A Simple Story*'s initial publication to correct errors and raise the diction
   throughout the novel.
3 Whether or not the mistake was an "obvious error of the press," Inchbald revised the
   phrase in the second and later editions to "took a part."
4 Inchbald corrected this clerical error (to Elmwood) for the second and later editions.

exists among the dramatis personae. Rusbrook,[1] in the first volume, changes his name in the third and fourth to Rushbrook; and, if there be not some erratum, the word countenance (vol. i. p. 16) is used in a manner totally unauthorized.[2]

....

To the readers of circulating libraries we need not recommend this work; its being a novel is sufficient to command their attention: but to those who delight in tracing the struggles and bursts of passion, we announce a degree of pleasure, which seems to be the greater because the power of communicating it is uncommon.

[The following review appeared later the same year, in the April 1791 issue of the same publication.]

In our Review for February we prophesied that there would be more than one edition of this work, and are glad to find our prediction already verified.[3] In the same confidence we now venture to give our opinion that the demand of the public will not let it rest here.

We recommended it to Mrs. Inchbald to fill up the void of seventeen years at the beginning of the third volume. Perhaps the shortness of the time may be the reason why she has not complied with our advice; but candour now requires that we should say, she will do well to consider this point maturely, as what at first appeared to us as a blemish, has been approved of by many critics of taste, as a new and artful way of conducting a story. It may likewise be true, that Mrs. Inchbald's delicacy revolted from a minute description of the falling off from virtue, and the progress of vice. Still it is for her consideration whether such scenes, represented with the nice touches of an elegant pencil, will not improve the moral of her work.—It is with pleasure that we see that several inaccuracies, which had escaped from her pen, are removed in the present edition. If this writer continues to revise her works with the same attention to friendly advice, we may pronounce that the beauties of her style will soon be as much admired as the elegance of her sentiments.

---

1   In the second and later editions, Inchbald regularized the spelling of "Rushbrook," which was her mother's maiden name. These corrections have been maintained in this edition.

2   In later editions of the novel, Inchbald continued to use the word "countenance" in this "unauthorized" manner. The *OED* lists "face" or "visage" as a possible definition for "countenance," beginning as early as 1303. Godwin uses the term in *Caleb Williams*: "I fixed my eye upon his countenance as he said this" (276).

3   The second edition of *A Simple Story* was published in March 1791, a month after the first edition.

c. The Gentleman's Magazine and Historical Chronicle 61 *(1791): 255*

Among our ancestors it appears to have been thought a piece of gallantry to admire every thing that was the literary production of a lady. The Sapphos and the Corinnas[1] of a hundred years ago were flattered and panegyrised for no mortal reason but because they wore a petticoat. At present, the case is altered; the fair sex has asserted its rank, and challenged that natural equality of intellect which nothing but the influence of human institutions could have concealed for a moment. One of the good effects of this revolution is, that Criticism becomes once more the office of Reason, and Gallantry surrenders the sceptre to Justice and Truth.

Speaking with the frankness which these authorities dictate, we are ready to confess that we were not pleased with the dramatical productions of Mrs. I. [Inchbald] There are in them some ingenuity of structure, and some merits of an inferior sort; but we search in vain for the glowing impressions of character, and the fervent enthusiasm of passion. What we wanted in the plays of this lady, we have found in the *Simple Story*. She has struck out a path entirely her own. She has disdained to follow the steps of her predecessors, and to construct a new novel, as is too commonly done, out of the scraps and fragments of earlier inventors. Her principal character, the Roman Catholic lord, is perfectly new; and she has conducted him, through a series of surprizing and well-contrasted adventures, with an uniformity of character and truth of description that have rarely been surpassed. The novel, in reality, consists of two distinct histories; and the talisman by which they are united is this unity of character in its hero. We do not recollect an instance of an invention so happily calculated for the purpose of uniting events in their own nature unconnected and opposite.

Every writer of a novel, in his moments of diffidence, will be inclined to tremble lest his production should be lost and forgotten amidst the immense lumber of trash that is hourly published under this description. This, however, is a difficulty, and not a discouragement; it should waken exertion, not incline to despondence. When conquered, the triumph is so much the more illustrious; and there are few records more honourable in the archives of literature than those of the labours of Richardson.[2] Turgot,[3]

---

1 Lyric poets of Ancient Greece.

2 Samuel Richardson (fl. 1637-58), novelist who sought to instill a moral purpose into his writings. His *Pamela* (1740) is often credited with being the first English novel.

3 Jacques Turgot (1727-81), French economist and statesman. Louis XVI named him comptroller general of France in 1774. His efforts to help the poor were unpopular with the privileged class.

the virtuous and penetrating statesman of France, has asserted, that the science of morals is more impartially and effectually taught by romances than by any other species of composition. We predict that Mrs. Inchbald, especially if she can be prevailed upon to persist in the path she has so honourably begun, will rank amongst the first classes of those who, through this enchanting vehicle, have communicated instruction and improvement to mankind.

In the midst of admiration we forgot censure; but we cannot stand excused to ourselves in omitting to notice, in spite of the beauties of this charming production, the painful sentiment excited by the catastrophe. It is so huddled and imperfect, that the feeling left upon the mind of the reader, when he closes the volumes, is that of embicility; the strength of stamina in the novel is for a moment forgotten; and it is not till after a pause that he can call back his mind to recollect the eminent excellences by which this defect is so gloriously atoned.

d. Impartial Review 5 *(February 1791): 66-71*

One of the greatest drawbacks on our pleasures, as *Impartial Reviewers of New Publications*, is the absolute necessity we are under of reading with attention whatever is laid before us. No species of professional drudgery can be more tiresome; for many are the productions, both in prose and verse, which in no sense compensate a perusal: but certainly none of Mrs. Inchbald's critics can refuse her this indulgence. The impulse under which she accosts us, rather conciliates, than forbids a nearer acquaintance. Indeed, her delicate situation is so well depicted, her principal instigation in writing is so honestly avowed, and the oddity of her fortunes is so forcibly expressed, that though criticism were in the habit of combining all the surliness of Sandford, the obstinacy of Dorriforth, and the gaiety of his ward, her Preface would disarm it.[1] Humility has often softened the sternest asperity, and supplicating Innocence unnerved the arm uplifted to strike.

There is much of nature, of sensibility, and of those almost imperceptible ties which entwine around the heart, and constitute the chief happiness or misery of life, in these volumes. It is a domestic scene throughout; and the fair authoress, like one of the family, a counselor, a confidante, or an oracle, to every individual by turns, divulges all the hidden springs on which the whole economy or management depends.

---

1   For a discussion of "humility" in the Preface, see the Introduction (15-16).

Here is no double or subordinate plot. The fable, carried on to the conclusion of the work, is but one....

[A plot summary, which has been omitted here, follows in the original.]

These are the leading features of the story, which, from the paucity of characters described and occupied, the want of a plot, and inattention to the bustle of incident, and all the customary resources of modern novel-writers, is denominated *simple*. We own too, the construction of the fable is not any where perplexed or involved. The whole is luminous, and conveyed to our minds in a language easy, unaffected, and perfectly intelligible. Mrs. Inchbald deals no where in tropical declamation. The business in hand is never out of sight: we are always aware of what is going forward, and rarely disappointed by the issue. Yet every page we read is interesting. The scene is so managed as, on no occasion, to lose its attraction. Some concern of one or other of the parties is constantly uppermost, constantly in hazard, and constantly an object of the reader's solicitude. This is the true magic of writing, and the charm which all sorts of readers, with or without taste, if they have but a heart, must feel.

A vein of the sweetest sensibility enriches the whole work. And we must say, the reader, whether male or female, who can peruse but the first chapter of this *simple story*, and not betray a tear, is an unfound link in the chain of being, and blessed with such a stock of apathy as renders him a match for Big Ben,[1] or even the late heavy Editor of Shakespeare.[2] Ah! Mrs. Inchbald, these are touches which none but genius can give. They come warm from the heart, and by the heart alone are cognizable.

Her opinion of the celebrated question, whether a man of strict morals, or a man of gallantry, makes the best husband, is more to the purpose than volumes written professedly on the subject. "Put," says she, "in competition the languid love of a debauchee with the vivid affection of a sober man, and judge which has the dominion. Oh! In my calendar of love a solemn Lord Chief Justice, or a devout Archbishop, ranks before a licentious King."

The characters who accomplish the fiction are but few, but have all much to do, and are strongly marked. *Sandford*, who is the confessor

---

1   Ben Jonson (1572-1637), dramatist, actor, poet, and critic.
2   Samuel Johnson (1709-84), writer, editor, critic, and lexicographer.

of the family, appears to be severe in his morals, unaccommodating in his manners, a harsh satirist, proud, turbulent, and acrimonious. His sarcasms are, in general, at once bitter and impertinent; his conduct, on some occasions, seems even savage to every one not wretched; but in him, every creature not happy finds a friend.

Miss Milner, the heroine of the tale, has also great sensibility. She is happy in relieving the misfortunes of others, but careless in preventing her own. All her dispositions are liberal, all her virtues humane, all her inclinations pure. But she was not bred a Roman Catholic. Her guardian, his confessor, and even her best friend, the gentle-hearted *Woodley*, who never abandons her or hers, look upon her as an heretic, and conclude all the defects of her character and all their painful consequences to originate in this primary bias in her education.

Dorriforth, who afterwards assumes the title of *Lord Elmwood*, is described as virtuous in his principles, stately in demeanour, and of the most inflexible resolution:—this last trait of this character is, in the course of this narrative, carried, in some instances, to the utmost extremity. He affects, on all occasions, to be above passion, to act from dictates of the soundest reason, and to be influenced only by what is most just and honourable; but, like all mankind, he is often weakest where he thinks his chief strength lies, and duped by the very feelings he would disguise. His system of ethics seems too exalted and refined for common life and common use: the application of them on every crisis of importance, renders him awkward; and, as we get acquainted with him, he becomes less amiable. His presence is always serious, forbidding, gloomy, austere, and humiliating; and though exhibited at first as a man of the most disinterested and noble views, generous, benevolent, and susceptible of the tenderest friendship, we cannot help regarding him, before we part, as a proud, overbearing, selfish, ferocious, and hateful despot, who takes a pleasure in rendering those miserable whom it is his interest and his duty to make happy.

It is said, and with some justice, of Shakspeare, that he never introduces a lady on the stage, but with a view to depreciate the female character.—The illness of Desdemona, the lunacy of Olivia, the cruelty of Macbeth, and the obvious bad qualities which his other female worthies are distinguished, give at least some colouring to this censure. We would charitably hope Mrs. Inchbald has not willingly copied this imperfection in our great bard. But why does the lovely Miss Milner suffer so much? Her giddiness and vivacity merit no such punishment. She often errs, but as often repents; and on no occasion is either hardened in folly or impenitent in vice. Is there not something unnatural in coupling two persons of such opposite sentiments? May not many of her indiscretions be ascribed to the unaccommodating humour of a phlegmatic husband? Does she not seem the only undesigning person in the family? And is she not at last a victim of a conduct in Lord Elmwood which struck her as mysterious, and therefore insulting, at least disrespectful. Except in this single instance of gross criminality, which, by the by, is incongruous to the character, she uniformly acts the most innocent part, wherever we see her in action: her love, indeed, for this unlovely guardian, produces frequent consultations with the faithful *Woodley*; but none of these ever amount to any thing like intrigue. In absence of all, as in their presence, she is always candid; and her language is as free of scandal as her heart is of deceit.

They reverse her conduct in every particular. Her guardian and lover not only suffers her to be insulted in his presence by the grossest sarcasms, but often joins in the insult. And when she is absent, how is she treated? Is there not always some scheme in execution, to mortify and chagrin her? And whence this harshness?—It is certainly unaccounted for by any thing she does or says. They are all her enemies; and we know not for what. She is in our opinion the least guilty, yet ultimately made the greatest wretch!

Much stress, by our fair authoress, is every where put on the wrong education of Miss Milner. This her father regrets on his death-bed, and this is seriously impressed on the reader as the great lesson to which the whole relation refers: but, in the conduct of this lady it is no where specified, or even very apparent, except in that criminality which we conceive an absurdity, as justified, indicated, or countenanced in the least degree by any feature in her character. This is the great defect in the fable. The conclusion is not warranted by the premises. Her *protestantism* seems to us the only cause of all her misfortunes.

Here it is impossible not to remark the partiality of a pious mind for its first impressions; but we notice it with no illiberal intention to fix any thing like blame on her choice of religion, and knowing the worst to be better than none, and that the selection of a good heart cannot, materially, be bad.

Mrs. Inchbald gives various proofs of judgment as well as of genius and taste in the conduct of the work. For many of Lord Elmwood's actions, she pretends not to account. Though her apologies for the effrontery and rudeness of Sandford are never successful, the tenderness he discovers for Lady Elmwood, in her state of penitence and remorse, more than atones for all his former harshness. But the artifices which ruin Lady Elmwood, the various black passions which led to that event, the conflict between guilt and fear, and the infinite distress in such a breast as hers, which it implicated, she attempts not once to describe! Either she felt herself unequal to the task, or was unwilling to appear familiar with these *mysteries of inequity.*

We are hardly made acquainted with the depravity of Lady Elmwood, till her contrition and sufferings disarm all the resentment which it is natural to feel against her: and the very next chapter plunges her into the jaws of eternity. No spectacle can be more affecting, than this delicate creature, reduced from all the gaieties of life, dead to every mortal wish, but alive to all the agonies of past folly, and dividing her last pangs between maternal fondness and holy resignation. The scene is finely imagined, and derives its best effect from its simplicity and brevity.

Frequent occasions are afforded the writer, of showing her attention to the mysterious and delicate workings of the heart and passions. She somewhere puts the question, *What can make good people so skilled in all the weaknesses of the bad?* The observation could be suggested only by deep and tried experience of human life. The very essence of virtue consists in such a marked attention to the obliquities and temptations of vice, as most effectually to avoid and resist them. Innocence, however pure, is a mere negative excellence, and often derives all its merit from a fine face, and an elegant make. She is the real virtuous woman, who, knowing what *evil* is, had the resolution to prefer what is *good*; or having even for once made a wrong choice, and fallen from her honour, recollects her situation, and rises yet more honourable from her fall.

This, upon the whole, is a beautiful and interesting, as well as a *simple story*; and we frankly acknowledge our obligations to Mrs. Inchbald for the pleasure it has afforded us. The sentiments are all natural and rich, neither far-fetched, nor wire-drawn, nor over-wrought.—They arise from the subject, or are suggested by the circumstances with which it is connected. The diction is every where correct, perspicuous, and pleasing; and the work will always give satisfaction to an intelligent and feeling reader, because it treats of no concern but those of the heart, and delineates no scenes but those of a domestic nature, in which every parent, every child, and every friend, are interested, as they are all more or less liable to be called upon to act a part.

e. Lady's Magazine 21 *(February 1791): 59-61*

"Account of *A Simple Story*"
To this lady the public are indebted for the following dramatic pieces, which have all been stamped with general approbation. "I'll Tell You

What," "Such Things Are," "The Child of Nature," "Appearance is Against Them," "The Widow's Vow," "The Married Man," and "The Midnight Hour." Various reasons, of which, in the preface to the work before us, we have a transient hint, induced this lady to withdraw her pen from the stage, a circumstance the more to be regretted because it occurs at a time when dramatic writers of merit are exceedingly scarce—perhaps never more so.

Genius, however, is industrious. Mrs. Inchbald determined not to be idle, and she has now presented the world with the produce of her leisure hours in the form of a novel, entitled "A Simple Story"—It is but seldom that we notice performances under the title of novels, unless, indeed, we discover in them a tendency which we can approve, or find them holding forth an example which we can recommend. And we can give no better reason for reviewing "A Simple Story" than that which Fielding assigns for his being so lavish in his praise of Sophia,[1] "because, says he, we are not only in love with her ourselves, but wish that our readers may be so too."—In a word, we have read this novel with impartiality and attention, and as we can honestly pronounce upon its superior merits, so we would wish to recommend them to the notice of our readers.

Throughout the whole our authoress manifests an accurate knowledge of the human heart. She traces the working of a passion with justice and minuteness, places it in every *setting*, if we may use the expression, and exhibits its luster and its dimness, its brilliancy and its specks, precisely as we may observe in real life. But as few can observe, so there are still fewer who can describe a variety of feelings arising from the same passion, and operated upon by the varieties of accident, time, place, and person.—In all this Mrs. Inchbald excells; and the result of the whole is, as may naturally be supposed, an instructive as well as an entertaining narrative.—And here, by the bye, we would beg leave to say to such of our readers as have felt an itch for novel-writing, that they are exceedingly much to blame in storing their memories with the incidents and characters of other writers, since an examination of their own hearts, and an observation of the actions of others in real life, will not only furnish them with what is new and interesting, but convince them that the human heart is an exhaustless fund, from whence the novelist, and poet, the philosopher, and the moralist, may always draw sums that have never been claimed before.

---

1 Sophia Western, virtuous heroine of Henry Fielding's *Tom Jones* (1749). Fielding patterned Sophia after his wife, Charlotte, who died in 1744.

f. Mary Wollstonecraft, Analytical Review 10 *(May 1791): 101-02*

[This essay was first attributed to Mary Wollstonecraft by Ralph Wardle, in "Mary Wollstonecraft, 'Analytical Reviewer'" (*PMLA*, 62:4 [December 1947], 1000-09). Her signature, "M," was the next to appear after this article, and internal evidence (including Inchbald's defensive response when Wollstonecraft died) suggests the essay was Wollstonecraft's.]

The plan of this novel is truly dramatic, for the rising interest is not broken, or even interrupted, by any episode, nor is the attention so divided, by a constellation of splendid characters, as to make the reader at a loss to say which is the hero of the tale.

Mrs. I. [Inchbald] had evidently a very useful moral in view, namely to show the advantage of a good education; but it is to be lamented that she did not, for the benefit of her young readers, enforce it by contrasting the characters of the mother and daughter, whose history must warmly interest them. It were to be wished, in fact, in order to insinuate a useful moral into thoughtless unprincipled minds, that the faults of the vain, giddy miss Milner had not been softened, or rather gracefully withdrawn from notice by the glare of such splendid, yet fallacious virtues, as flow from sensibility. And to have rendered the contrast more useful still, her daughter should have possessed greater dignity of mind. Educated in adversity she should have learned (to prove that a cultivated mind is a real advantage) how to bear, nay, rise above her misfortunes, instead of suffering her health to be undermined by the trials of her patience, which ought to have strengthened her understanding. Why do all female writers, even when they display their abilities, always give a sanction to the libertine reveries of men? Why do they poison the minds of their own sex, by strengthening a male prejudice that makes women systematically weak? We allude to the absurd fashion that prevails of making the heroine of a novel boast of a delicate constitution; and the still more ridiculous and deleterious custom of spinning the most picturesque scenes out of fevers, swoons, and tears.

The characters in the Simple Story are marked with a discriminating outline, and little individual traits are skillfully brought forward, that produce some natural and amusing scenes. Lively conversations abound, and they are, in general, written with the spirited vivacity and the feminine ease that characterizes the conversation of an agreeable well-bred woman. The author has even the art to render dialogues interesting that appear to have only the evanescent spirit, which mostly evaporates in description, to recommend them....

2. Exchange of Letters between William Godwin and Elizabeth Inchbald on the Day of Mary Wollstonecraft's Death (10 September 1797)

[The following letters exemplify the tension between Godwin and Inchbald, based in part on Wollstonecraft's disreputable reputation (see the Introduction, 20-21). Much of Inchbald's defensive posture, however, stems from Wollstonecraft's negative response to *A Simple Story*. The letters here are reprinted from C. Kegan Paul, *William Godwin: His Friends and Contemporaries* (London: Henry S. King, 1876).]

a. Godwin's Letter to Inchbald

My wife died at eight this morning. I always thought you used her ill, but I forgive you. You told me you did not know her. You have a thousand good and great qualities. She had a very deep-rooted admiration for you.

Yours, with real honour and esteem,
W. Godwin.

b. Inchbald's First Reply to Godwin

You have shocked me beyond expression, yet, I bless God, without exciting the smallest portion of remorse. Yet I feel most delicately on every subject in which the good or ill of my neighbours is involved.

I did not know her. I never wished to know her; as I avoid every female acquaintance, who has no husband, I avoided her. Against my desire you made us acquainted. With what justice I shunned her, your present note evinces, for she judged me harshly.[1] *She* first thought I used her ill, for you would not. I liked her—I spoke well of her. Let Charlotte Smith[2] be my witness, who received her character from me, such as I gave of her to everybody.

Be comforted. You *will* be comforted. Still I feel for you at present. Write to me again. Say what you please at such a time as this; I will excuse and pity you.

---

1 A reference to Wollstonecraft's dislike of Inchbald's work.
2 Charlotte Smith (1749-1806), novelist and poet.

c. Inchbald's Second Reply to Godwin, Later the Same Day

The ceremony of condolence is an impertinence, but if you consider mine superior to ceremony, you will accept it.

I have too much humility to offer consolation to a mind like yours. I will only describe sensations which nearly a similar misfortune excited in me.

I felt myself for a time bereft of every comfort the world could bestow, but these opinions passed away, and gave place to others, almost the reverse.

I was separated from the only friend I had in the world, and by circumstances so much more dreadful than those which have occurred to you, as the want of warning increases all our calamities,[1] but yet I have lived to think with indifference to all I then suffered.

You have been a most kind husband, I am told. Rejoice,—the time might have come when you would have wept over her remains with compunction for cruelty to her.

While you have no self-reproaches to wound you, be pacified. Every ill falls short of that.

I lament her as a person whom you loved. I am shocked at the unexpected death of one in such apparent vigour of mind and body; but I feel no concern for any regret she endured at parting from this world, for I believe she had tact and understanding to despise it heartily. Mr. Twiss received the news with sorrow, and Mrs. Twiss[2] shed many tears. They were not prepared, any more than myself, for the news, for they had not heard of her illness. I showed them your note to me, and if you had seen the manner in which they treated your suspicion of my influence with them (and that was certainly your only meaning), you would beg my pardon.

I shall be glad to hear of your health, and that your poor little family are well, for believe me concerned for your welfare.

E.I.

---

1 Inchbald's husband died suddenly on 6 June 1779.
2 Francis Twiss (bap. 1759, d. 1827) was a circuit judge and friend of Inchbald's who read and commented on her writing. His wife (1759-1822), formerly Frances Kemble, was a sister of Sarah Siddons and John Philip Kemble.

3. Maria Edgeworth, Letter to Elizabeth Inchbald (14 January 1810)

[Maria Edgeworth (1768-1849), novelist, educational philosopher, and author of children's books, admired all of Inchbald's work, but especially, as the following letter indicates, *A Simple Story*. Inchbald and Edgeworth met and became friends near the end of Inchbald's life, and their correspondence indicates that although Inchbald's social circle toward the end of her life was much smaller than it had been while she was writing and acting on the stage, she remained engaged in intellectual activities and conversations with a few close friends. The letter is reprinted from Boaden, *Memoirs of Mrs. Inchbald*, I, 151-56.]

Edgeworth's Town, Jan. 14, 1810.

I am going to do a very bold thing. Personally a stranger to Mrs. Inchbald myself, I am going to take the liberty of introducing one of my brothers to her. Your kindness to my brother Lovell[1] will perhaps incline you more in Sneyd's[2] favor than any thing I could urge. If you should be so good as to let him be in your society, I think you will find in him the same affectionate temper and good dispositions which characterized his brother—and abilities, of which I will say nothing, lest I should say too much.

I hope you will not suspect me of the common author practice of returning praise for praise, when I tell you that I have just been reading, for the third—I believe for the fourth time—the "Simple Story." Its effect upon my feelings was as powerful as at the first reading; I never read any novel—I except *none*—I never read any novel that affected me so strongly, or that so completely possessed me with the belief in the real existence of all the people it represents. I never once recollected the author whilst I was reading it; never said or thought, *that's a fine sentiment*—or *that is well expressed*—or *that is well invented*. I believed all to be real, and was affected as I should be by the real scenes if they had passed my eyes: it is truly and deeply pathetic. I determined, this time of reading, to read it as a critic—or rather, as an author, to try to find out the secret of its peculiar pathos. But I quite forgot my intention in the

---

1 Maria Edgeworth's brother, who directed a school for boys from both Catholic and Protestant families and from different social classes. He succeeded his father as owner of the family estate, Edgeworthstown, but he was so unskilled at maintaining the property that Maria had to take over its management in 1826.

2 Charles Sneyd Edgeworth, Maria's brother. After his father's death, he became a poet, abandoning his profession as a lawyer.

interest Miss Milner and Dorriforth excited: but *now it is all over*, and I can coolly exercise my judgment, I am of opinion that it is by leaving more than most other writers to the imagination, that you succeed so eminently in affecting it. By the force that is necessary to repress feeling, we judge of the intensity of the feeling; and you always contrive to give us by intelligible but simple signs the measure of this force. Writers of inferior genius waste their words in describing feeling; in making those who pretend to be agitated by passion describe the effects of that passion, and talk of the *rending of their hearts, &c.* A gross blunder! as gross as any Irish blunder;[1] for the heart cannot feel, and describe its own feelings, at the same moment. It is *"being like a bird in two places at once."*

What a beautiful stroke is that of the child who exclaims, when Dorriforth lets go his hands, *"I had like to have been down."*

I am glad I have never met with a Dorriforth, for I must inevitably have fallen desperately in love with him; and destitute of Miss Milner's powers of charming, I might have died in despair. Indeed I question, whether my being free from some of her faults would not have made my chance worse; for I have no doubt that, with all his wisdom and virtue, he loved her the better for keeping him in a continual panic by her coquetry. I am excessively sorry you made her end *naughtily*; though I believe this makes the story more moral; Your power as a pathetic writer is even more conspicuous in the second volume, however, than in the first: for notwithstanding the prodigious and painful effort you require from the reader to jump over, at the first page, eighteen years,[2] and to behold at once Dorriforth old, and Miss Milner a disgraced and dying mother, with a grown-up daughter beside her; notwithstanding the reluctance we feel to seeing Dorriforth as an implacable tyrant, and Sandford degraded to a trembling dependent; yet against our will, and absolutely against our resolution to be unmoved, you master our hearts, and kindle a fresh interest, and force again our tears. Nothing can be finer than the scene upon the stairs, where Dorriforth meets his daughter, and cannot unclasp her hand, and when he cannot call her by any name but Miss Milner—dear Miss Milner.

I wish Rushbrooke had not been a liar. It degrades him too much for a hero. I think you sacrificed him too much to the principle of the pyramid. The mixture of the father's character in the daughter is beautiful. As to Miss Woodley, who can help loving her, and thinking she is like their best friend, whoever that may be?

---

1 Because Edgeworth's own heritage was Irish, the joke here is at her own expense.
2 The time elapsed is actually 17 years.

Mrs. Horton is excellent comic. Her moving all the things about in the room, to lessen the embarrassment, and her wishing (without being ill-natured) to see a quarrel, that she might have some sensations, is admirable. Did you really draw the characters from life?[1] or did you invent them? You excel, I think, peculiarly in avoiding what is commonly called *fine writing*—a sort of writing which I detest; which calls the attention away from the *thing* to the *manner*—from the feeling to the language; which sacrifices every thing to sound, to the mere rounding of a period; which mistakes *stage effect* for *nature*. All who are at all used to writing, know and detect the *trick of the trade* immediately; and, speaking for myself, I *know* that the writing which has least the appearance of literary *manufacture* almost always pleases me the best. It has more originality; in narration of fictitious events, it most surely succeeds in giving the idea of reality; and in making the biographer, for the time, pass for nothing. But there are few who can in this manner bear the *mortification* of staying behind the scenes. They peep out, eager for applause, and destroy all illusion by crying, "*I* said it; *I* wrote it; *I* invented it all! Call me on the stage and crown me directly."[2]

I don't know whether you have ever met with a little book called "Circumstances respecting the Life of the late Charles Montford, Esq. by George Harley, Esq."[3] When you have half an hour's leisure, do me the favour to look at it; for I think it possesses something of the same kind of merit as the "Simple Story," though it has many faults; and, except now and then, nothing like its pathos. But it resembles it in creating the belief of its being real. I often thought, while I was reading

---

1   In a letter from Edgeworth to her father's sister, Margaret Ruxton (1746-1830), Edgeworth relayed Inchbald's response to this question: "She says they were all invention except that she once knew a man who would she thinks have acted just like Sandford had similar occurrences fallen in his way—He was a Jesuit and her first confessor—so you see she is a catholic—Mrs. Horton's love of a quarrel she declares she took from her own disposition—she says she has often in London been so solitary, so longing for something to break the uniformity of life & to create a sensation that she has enjoyed a high wind, or a thunderstorm or even, (though in perfect charity,) a chimney on fire." National Library of Ireland MS. 10, 166-67, letter of Maria Edgeworth on 2 March 1810 to Mrs. Ruxton. Quoted in Sigl, 253.

2   Edgeworth's admiration of Inchbald's ability to stay "behind the scenes" of her novel calls to mind Keats's concept of "negative capability," where "a man is capable of being in uncertainties, mysteries, doubts, without any irritable reaching after fact and reason" (1817 letter to his brothers). The concept is in direct contradiction to Henry Fielding's notoriously intrusive narration style.

3   *Circumstances Respecting the late Charles Montford, esq. By George Harley esq.* (1804), written by George Davies Harley (d. 1811), was purportedly a biography, although the narrative may have been, as Edgeworth suggests, fiction.

it, This might have been better written; but I am glad the circumstances did not fall into the hands of a professed novel-writer, who might perhaps have made more of them for common readers, but who would have spoiled them for me by the manufacture. It must be true, I thought, and the biographer must be a real friend, because he cares so little about himself and his own writing, so that he does justice to the memory of his friend.

I have lately been told that it is a mere fiction, and that it was written by a gentleman whose name I forget—a brother of Mrs. Trench's;[1] perhaps you know the name.

My father and Mrs. Edgeworth beg to be kindly remembered to you, and wish you would come here and see us, as we cannot go to England at present. Can you? Will you?

Affectionately yours,

MARIA EDGEWORTH.

---

1 Probably Melesina Trench, Irish author (1768-1827).

Appendix C: Cultural Contexts

1. Portrait of John Philip Kemble

[Beginning with Boaden (I: 274-75), readers have assumed that Inchbald based the character of Dorriforth on the actor John Philip Kemble. Because Kemble had trained for the priesthood, and because Inchbald's theatrical colleagues assumed a romantic interest between the two, readers assumed that the novel was at least partially an autobiographical account of their relationship. Inchbald herself, however, denied basing her characters on anyone she knew, and, recently, Jenkins has argued that the "if the readers in the spring of 1791 wanted to discuss a possible 'romance' between Kemble and Inchbald, they did so with no evidence except speculation, speculation that has, following Boaden, been repeated as a 'romantic' story that is certainly fiction within fiction" (277). Kemble was, however, a close associate of Inchbald's, and his life and career shed light on the context within which *A Simple Story* was composed. Although this portrait is not full length (as is Elmwood's portrait in the second half of *A Simple Story*), it is probably similar in style and medium to the portrait of Elmwood.]

John Philip Kemble by Gilbert Stuart, National Portrait Gallery, London.

2. Gender and the French Revolution

[Although much of *A Simple Story* may have been composed long before the events leading up to the French Revolution, several critics have examined the novel in the context of Inchbald's growing concern with public conflicts, and especially conflicts in France. That *A Simple Story* anticipates overt "representations of revolution" has been suggested by Gary Kelly, who claims the novel should be classified as "pre-Jacobin"[1] and Ronald Paulson, who argues that "the situation *A Simple Story* dramatizes is remarkably appropriate to the time without being related allegorically or analogically to what was happening in France" (or even was about to happen since it was largely written before 1789).[2] The following passages exemplify concerns with gender and power that were central to revolutionary rhetoric and, more generally, to concerns of the period.]

a. From Mary Wollstonecraft, A Vindication of the Rights of Woman (1792), 1-38

[Wollstonecraft's relationship with Inchbald was tense, but their overall philosophies were similar. Wollstonecraft's concern with the means by which women have traditionally gained power is reminiscent of Inchbald's discomfort with Miss Milner's almost despotic power over Dorriforth/Elmwood. Of Miss Milner's ambition to be beloved "in spite of her faults," Inchbald's narrator exclaims, "unthinking woman! ... But what female is not fond of experiments? to which, how few are there, that do not fall a sacrifice!"]

INTRODUCTION

AFTER considering the historic page, and viewing the living world with anxious solicitude, the most melancholy emotions of sorrowful indignation have depressed my spirits, and I have sighed when obliged to confess, that either nature has made a great difference between man and man, or that the civilization which has hitherto taken place in the world has been very partial. I have turned over various books written on the subject of education, and patiently observed the conduct of parents and the management of schools; but what has been the result?—a

---

1   Kelly, 64-93.
2   Paulson, 229.

profound conviction that the neglected education of my fellow-creatures is the grand source of the misery I deplore; and that women, in particular, are rendered weak and wretched by a variety of concurring causes, originating from one hasty conclusion. The conduct and manners of women, in fact, evidently prove that their minds are not in a healthy state; for, like the flowers which are planted in too rich a soil, strength and usefulness are sacrificed to beauty; and the flaunting leaves, after having pleased a fastidious eye, fade, disregarded on the stalk, long before the season when they ought to have arrived at maturity.—One cause of this barren blooming I attribute to a false system of education, gathered from the books written on this subject by men who, considering females rather as women than human creatures, have been more anxious to make them alluring mistresses than rational wives;[1] and the understanding of the sex has been so bubbled by this specious homage, that the civilized women of the present century, with a few exceptions, are only anxious to inspire love, when they ought to cherish a nobler ambition, and by their abilities and virtues exact respect.

In a treatise, therefore, on female rights and manners, the works which have been particularly written for their improvement must not be overlooked; especially when it is asserted, in direct terms, that the minds of women are enfeebled by false refinement; that the books of instruction, written by men of genius, have had the same tendency as more frivolous productions; and that, in the true style of Mahometanism,[2] they are only considered as females, and not as a part of the human species, when improvable reason is allowed to be the dignified distinction which raises men above the brute creation, and puts a natural sceptre in a feeble hand.

Yet, because I am a woman, I would not lead my readers to suppose that I mean violently to agitate the contested question respecting the equality or inferiority of the sex; but as the subject lies in my way, and I cannot pass it over without subjecting the main tendency of my reasoning to misconstruction, I shall stop a moment to deliver, in a few words, my opinion.—In the government of the physical world it is observable that the female, in general, is inferior to the male. The male pursues, the female yields—this is the law of nature; and it does not appear to be suspended or abrogated in favour of woman. This physical superiority cannot be denied—and it is a noble prerogative! But not content with this natural pre-eminence, men endeavour to sink us still lower, merely

---

1 Wollstonecraft refers here to the educational literature of Jean-Jacques Rousseau, which she challenged in her other writings.
2 The religion of Islam.

to render us alluring objects for a moment; and women, intoxicated by the adoration which men, under the influence of their senses, pay them, do not seek to obtain a durable interest in their hearts, or to become the friends of the fellow creatures who find amusement in their society.

...

My own sex, I hope, will excuse me, if I treat them like rational creatures, instead of flattering their *fascinating* graces, and viewing them as if they were in a state of perpetual childhood, unable to stand alone. I earnestly wish to point out in what true dignity and human happiness consists—I wish to persuade women to endeavour to acquire strength, both of mind and body, and to convince them that the soft phrases, susceptibility of heart, delicacy of sentiment, and refinement of taste, are almost synonymous with epithets of weakness, and that those beings who are only the objects of pity and that kind of love, which has been termed its sister, will soon become objects of contempt.

Dismissing then those pretty feminine phrases, which the men condescendingly use to soften our slavish dependence, and despising that weak elegancy of mind, exquisite sensibility, and sweet docility of manners, supposed to be the sexual characteristics of the weaker vessel, I wish to shew that elegance is inferior to virtue, that the first object of laudable ambition is to obtain a character as a human being, regardless of the distinction of sex; and that secondary views should be brought to this simple touchstone.

...

The education of women has, of late, been more attended to than formerly; yet they are still reckoned a frivolous sex, and ridiculed or pitied by the writers who endeavor by satire or instruction to improve them. It is acknowledged that they spend many of the first years of their lives in acquiring a smattering of accomplishments: meanwhile strength of body and mind are sacrificed to libertine notions of beauty, to the desire of establishing themselves,—the only way women can rise in the world,—by marriage. And this desire making mere animals of them, when they marry they act as such children may be expected to act:—they dress; they paint, and nickname God's creatures.—Surely these weak beings are only fit for a seraglio! Can they govern a family, or take care of the poor babes whom they bring into the world?

If then it can be fairly deduced from the present conduct of the sex, from the prevalent fondness for pleasure which takes place of ambition and those nobler passions that open and enlarge the soul; that the instruction which women have received has only tended, with the constitution of civil society, to render them insignificant objects of desire—mere propagators of fools!—if it can be proved that in aiming to accomplish them, without cultivating their understandings, they are taken out of their sphere of duties, and made ridiculous and useless when the short-lived bloom of beauty is over,[1] I presume that *rational* men will excuse me for endeavouring to persuade them to become more masculine and respectable.

Indeed the word masculine is only a bugbear: there is little reason to fear that women will acquire too much courage or fortitude; for their apparent inferiority with respect to bodily strength, must render them, in some degree, dependent on men in the various relations of life; but why should it be increased by prejudices that give a sex to virtue, and confound simple truths with sensual reveries?

Women are, in fact, so much degraded by mistaken notions of female excellence, that I do not mean to add a paradox when I assert, that this artificial weakness produces a propensity to tyrannize, and gives birth to cunning, the natural opponent of strength, which leads them to play off those contemptible infantine airs that undermine esteem even whilst they excite desire. Do not foster these prejudices, and they will naturally fall into their subordinate, yet respectable station, in life.

It seems scarcely necessary to say, that I now speak of the sex in general. Many individuals have more sense than their male relatives; and, as nothing preponderates where there is a constant struggle for equilibrium, without it has naturally more gravity, some women govern their husbands without degrading themselves, because intellect will always govern.

....

[Chapter I, "The Rights and Involved duties of mankind" has been omitted.]

CHAPTER II
The prevailing opinion of a sexual character discussed.

To account for, and excuse the tyranny of man, many ingenious arguments have been brought forward to prove, that the two sexes, in the acquirement of virtue, ought to aim at attaining a very different character: or, to speak explicitly, women are not allowed to have sufficient strength of mind to acquire what really deserves the name of virtue. Yet

---

1 A lively writer, I cannot recollect his name, asks what business women turned of forty have to do in the world? [A reference, perhaps, to Lord Merton in Burney's *Evelina*, who remarks, "I don't know what the devil a woman lives for after thirty: she is only in other folk's way" (405).]

it should seem, allowing them to have souls, that there is but one way appointed by Providence to lead *mankind* to either virtue or happiness.

If then women are not a swarm of ephemeron triflers, why should they be kept in ignorance under the specious name of innocence? Men complain, and with reason, of the follies and caprices of our sex, when they do not keenly satirize our headstrong passions and groveling vices.—Behold, I should answer, the natural effect of ignorance! The mind will ever be unstable that has only prejudices to rest on, and the current will run with the destructive fury when there are no barriers to break its force. Women are told from their infancy, and taught by the example of their mothers, that a little knowledge of human weakness, justly termed cunning, softness of temper, *outward* obedience, and a scrupulous attention to a puerile kind of propriety, will obtain for them the protection of man; and should they be beautiful, every thing else is needless, for, at least, twenty years of their lives.

Thus Milton describes our first frail mother; though when he tells us that women are formed for softness and sweet attractive grace,[1] I cannot comprehend his meaning, unless, in the true Mahometan strain, he meant to deprive us of souls, and insinuate that we were beings only designed by sweet attractive grace, and docile blind obedience, to gratify the senses of man when he can no longer soar on the wing of contemplation.

How grossly do they insult us who thus advise us only to render ourselves gentle, domestic brutes! For instance, the winning softness so warmly, and frequently, recommended, that governs by obeying. What childish expressions, and how insignificant is the being—can it be an immortal one? who will condescend to govern by such sinister methods! "Certainly," says Lord Bacon, "man is of kin to the beasts by his body; and if he be not of kin to God by his spirit, he is a base and ignoble creature."[2] Men, indeed, appear to me to act in a very unphilosophical manner when they try to secure the good conduct of women by attempting to keep them always in a state of childhood. Rousseau[3] was more consistent when he wished to stop the progress of reason in both sexes, for if men eat of the tree of knowledge, women will come in for a taste; but, from the imperfect cultivation which their understandings now receive, they only attain a knowledge of evil.

---

1   Compare to John Milton's description of Eve in *Paradise Lost* (IV): "For softness she and sweet attractive grace; / He for God only, she for God in him" (lines 298-99).

2   Compare to Francis Bacon's essay, "Of Atheism" (1601): "They that deny a God destroy man's nobility; for certainly man is of kin to the beasts by his body."

3   Jean-Jacques Rousseau (1712-78), French educational philosopher and novelist.

Children, I grant, should be innocent; but when the epithet is applied to men, or women, it is but a civil term for weakness. For if it be allowed that women were destined by Providence to acquire human virtues, and by the exercise of their understandings, that stability of character which is the firmest ground to rest our future hopes upon, they must be permitted to turn to the fountain of light, and not forced to shape their course by the twinkling of a mere satellite. Milton, I grant, was of a very different opinion; for he only bends to the indefeasible right of beauty, though it would be difficult to render two passages which I now mean to contrast, consistent. But into similar inconsistencies are great men often led by their senses.

> To whom thus Eve with *perfect beauty* adorn'd,
> My Author and Disposer, what thou bidst
> *Unargued* I obey; so God ordains;
> God is *thy law, thou mine*: to know no more
> Is Woman's *happiest* knowledge and her *praise*.[1]

These are exactly the arguments that I have used to children; but I have added, your reason is now gaining strength, and, till it arrives at some degree of maturity, you must look up to me for advice—then you ought to think, and only rely on God.

Yet in the following lines Milton seems to coincide with me; when he makes Adam thus expostulate with his Maker.

> Hast thou not made me here thy substitute,
> And these inferior far beneath me set?
> Among *unequals* what society
> Can sort, what harmony or true delight?
> Which must be mutual, in proportion due
> Giv'n and receiv'd; but in the *disparity*
> The one intense, the other still remiss
> Cannot well suit with either, but soon prove
> Tedious alike: of *fellowship* I speak
> Such as I seek, fit to participate
> All rational delight—[2]

---

1 Eve's subservient response to Adam in Milton's *Paradise Lost* (IV), lines 634-38.
2 *Paradise Lost* (VIII), lines 381-84.

In treating, therefore, of the manners of women, let us, disregarding sensual arguments, trace what we should endeavour to make them in order to co-operate, if the expression be not too bold, with the supreme Being.

By individual education, I mean, for the sense of the word is not precisely defined, such an attention to a child as will slowly sharpen the senses, form the temper, regulate the passions, as they begin to ferment, and set the understanding to work before the body arrives at maturity; so that the man may only have to proceed, not to begin, the important talk of learning to think and reason.

To prevent any misconstruction, I must add, that I do not believe that a private education can work the wonders which some sanguine writers have attributed to it. Men and women must be educated, in a great degree, by the opinions and manners of the society they live in. In every age there has been a stream of popular opinion that has carried all before it, and given a family character, as it were, to the century. It may then fairly be inferred, that, till society be differently constituted, much cannot be expected from education. It is, however, sufficient for my present purpose to assert, that, whatever effect circumstances have on the abilities, every being may become virtuous by the exercise of its own reason; for if but one being was created with vicious inclination, that is positively bad, what can save us from atheism? or if we worship a God, is not that God a devil?

Consequently, the most perfect education, in my opinion, is such an exercise of the understanding as is best calculated to strengthen the body and form the heart. Or, in other words, to enable the individual to attain such habits of virtue as will render it independent. In fact, it is a farce to call any being virtuous whose virtues do not result from the exercise of its own reason. This was Rousseau's opinion respecting men: I extend it to women, and confidently assert that they have been drawn out of their sphere by false refinement, and not by an endeavour to acquire masculine qualities. Still the regal homage which they receive is so intoxicating, that till the manners of the times are changed, and formed on more reasonable principles, it may be impossible to convince them that the illegitimate power which they obtain, by degrading themselves, is a curse, and that they must return to nature and equality, if they wish to secure the placid satisfaction that unsophisticated affections impart. But for this epoch we must wait—wait, perhaps, till kings and nobles, enlightened by reason, and, preferring the real dignity of man to childish state, throw off their gaudy hereditary trappings: and if then women do not resign the arbitrary power of beauty—they will prove that they have *less* mind than man.

b. From *Mary Wollstonecraft,* An Historical and Moral View of the
Origin and Progress of the French Revolution *(1794), 420-23*

[Inchbald's portrayal of Lord Elmwood's near-tragic tyranny seems to
anticipate Mary Wollstonecraft's later retrospective portrayal of Louis
XVI as desperately maintaining the illusion of father-like authority and
adoration.]

On the first of October, in consequence of these fresh machinations, a
magnificent entertainment was given in the name of the king's body-
guards; but really by some of their principal officers, at the opera-house
of the castle. The affectation of excluding the dragoons, distinguished
for their attachment to liberty, seemed to show, but too plainly, the end
in view, rendered still more conspicuous by the unusual familiarity of
persons of the first rank with the lowest soldiers.

When their heads were heated by a sumptuous banquet, by the tumult of an immense crowd, and the great profusion of delicious wines
and *liqueurs,* the conversation, purposely turned into one channel,
became unrestrained, and a chivalrous scene completed the folly. The
queen, to testify her satisfaction for the homage paid to her, and the
wishes expressed in her favour, exhibited herself to this half-drunken
multitude; carrying the dauphin in her arms, whom she regarded with a
mixture of sorrow and tenderness, and seeming to implore in his favour
the affectation and zeal of the soldiers.

This acting, for it is clear that the whole was a preconcerted business,
was still more intoxicating than the wine.—The exclamation *vive le roi,*
vive la reine, resounded from all sides, and the royal healths were drunk
over drawn swords, whilst that of the nation was rejected with contempt by the body-guards. The music, the choice could not have been
the effect of chance, played the well known air—O Richard! O my
king! the universe abandons thee![1] and during this moment of fascination some voices, perhaps bribed for the occasion, mingled execrations
against the assembly. A grenadier even darted from the midst of his
comrades, and accusing himself of having been unfaithful to his prince,
endeavoured several times to plunge his sword into his bosom. His held
arm was not indeed allowed to search for the disloyal heart; but some
blood was permitted to flow—and this theatrical display of sensibility,
carried to the highest pitch, produced emotions almost convulsive in

---

1   "O Richard, O mon roi, / L'univers t'abandonne!" [Song from André Ernest
     Modeste Grétry's *Richard Coeur de Lion,* first produced in 1771.]

the whole circle, of which an English reader can scarcely form an idea. The king, who is always represented as innocent, though always giving proofs that he more than connived at the attempts to recover his power, was likewise prevailed on to show himself at this entertainment. And some of the same soldiery, who had refused to second the former project of the cabal, were now induced to utter insults and menaces against the very authority, they then supported. "The national cockade," exclaimed Mirabeau,[1] "that emblem of the defenders of liberty, has been torn in pieces, and stamped under foot; and another ensign put in it's place.—Yes; even under the eye of the monarch, who allowed himself to be styled—*Restorer of the rights of his people*, they have dared to hoist a signal of faction."

The same scene was renewed two days after, though with less parade; and invitations for a similar treat were given for the following week.

c. From Edmund Burke, Reflections on the Revolution in France, and on the Proceedings in certain Societies in London, Relative to that event in a letter intended to have been sent to a gentle man in Paris *(1790), 111-13*

[Burke's concern with "generous loyalty to rank and sex" brings to mind Miss Milner's insistence on Elmwood's servitude.]

Although this work of our new light and knowledge, did not go to the length, that in all probability it was intended it should be carried; yet I must think, that such treatment of any human creatures must be shocking to any but those who are made for accomplishing Revolutions. But I cannot stop here. Influenced by the inborn feelings of my nature, and not being illuminated by a single ray of this new-sprung modern light, I confess to you, Sir, that the exalted rank of the persons suffering, and particularly the sex, the beauty, and the amiable qualities of the descendant of so many kings and emperors, with the tender age of royal infants, insensible only through infancy and innocence of the cruel outrages to which their parents were exposed, instead of being a subject of exultation, adds not a little to by sensibility on that most melancholy occasion.

I hear that the august person,[2] who was the principal object of our

---

1   Honore Gabriel Riquetti, comte de Mirabeau (1749-91), French revolutionary and political leader.
2   Louis XVI (1754-93) King of France from 1774-92.

preacher's triumph,[1] though he supported himself, felt much on that shameful occasion. As a man, it became him to feel for his wife and his children, and the faithful guards of his person, that were massacred in cold blood about him; as a prince, it became him to feel for the strange and frightful transformations of his civilized subjects, and to be more grieved for them, than solicitous for himself. It derogates little from his fortitude, while it adds infinitely to the honour of his humanity. I am very sorry to say it, very sorry indeed, that such personages are in a situation in which it is not unbecoming to us to praise the virtues of the great.

I hear, and I rejoice to hear, that the great lady,[2] the other object of the triumph, has borne that day (one is interested that beings made for suffering suffer well) and that she bears all the succeeding days, that she bears the imprisonment of her husband, and her own captivity, and the exile of her friends, and the insulting adulation of addresses, and the whole weight of her accumulated wrongs, with a serene patience, in a manner suited to her rank and race, and becoming the offspring of a sovereign distinguished for her piety and her courage; that like her she has lofty sentiments; that she feels with the dignity of a Roman matron; that in the last extremity she will save herself from the last disgrace, and that if she must fall, she will fall by no ignoble hand.

It is now sixteen or seventeen years since I saw the queen of France, then the dauphiness, at Versailles; and surely never lighted on this orb, which she hardly seemed to touch, a more delightful vision. I saw her just above the horizon, decorating and cheering the elevated sphere she just began to move in,—glittering like the morning-star, full of life, and splendor, and joy. Oh! And what a heart must I have, to contemplate without emotion that elevation and that fall! Little did I dream that, when she added titles of veneration to those of enthusiastic, distant, respectful love, that she should be obliged to carry the sharp antidote against disgrace concealed in that bosom; little did I dream that I should have lived to see such disasters fallen upon her in a nation of gallant men, in a nation of men of honour and of cavaliers. I thought ten thousand swords must have leaped from their scabbards to avenge even a look that threatened her with insult.—But the age of chivalry is gone.—That of

---

1 Reference to a sermon by Richard Price (1723-91), "Discourse on the Love of our Country" (1789), to which Burke's essay is a response.

2 Marie Antoinette (1755-93), queen of France and wife of Louis XVI. Daughter of the Austrian Archduchess Maria Theresa and the holy Roman Emperor Francis I, she was known for her frivolous extravagance during an insolvent period in France's history.

sophisters, oeconomists, and calculators,[1] has succeeded; and the glory of Europe is extinguished for ever. Never, never more, shall we behold that generous loyalty to rank and sex, that proud submission, that digni-fied obedience, that subordination of the heart, which kept alive, even in servitude itself, the spirit of an exalted freedom. The unbought grace of life, the cheap defence of nations, the nurse of manly sentiment and heroic enterprise is gone! It is gone, that sensibility of principle, that chastity of honour, which felt a stain like a wound, which inspired cour-age whilst it mitigated ferocity, which ennobled whatever it touched, and under which vice itself lost half its evil, by losing all its grossness.

d. *From William Godwin,* Enquiry Concerning Political Justice and Its Influence on Morals and Happiness, *vol I (1793), 94-96*

[When Dorriforth (who later gains the title of Lord Elmwood) partici-pates in several duels, he acts according to the dictates of masculinity proscribed by his culture, but, at the same time, he violates expectations that a man possess sensitivity, or as Inchbald expresses it, "genuine feel-ing." (See "Elizabeth Inchbald, Letter to William Godwin" in section 5b of this Appendix.) Inchbald's own concern with dueling became personal when her brother, George Simpson, was killed in a duel in 1795.]

Appendix, No. II.
Of Duelling.
Motives of duelling.—I. Revenge.—2. Reputation for courage.—
Fallacy of this motive.—Objections answered.—Illustration.

It may be proper in this place to bestow a moment's consideration upon a trite, but very important case of dueling. A very short reflection will suffice to set it in its true light.

This despicable practice was originally invented by barbarians for the gratification of revenge. It was probably at that time thought a very happy project, for reconciling the odiousness of malignity with the gal-lantry of courage.

But in this light it is now generally given up. Men of the best under-standing who lend it their sanction, are unwillingly induced to do so,

---

1   Probably a reference to the *philosophes*, scientists and intellectuals of eighteenth-cen-tury France and England, including John Locke (1632-1704), Jean-Jacques Rousseau (1712-78), and François Marie Arouet (pseudonym, Voltaire) (1694-1778).

and engage in single combat merely that their reputation may sustain no slander.

In examining this subject we must proceed upon one of two suppositions. Either the lives of both the persons to be hazarded are worthless, or they are not. In the latter case, the question answers itself, and cannot stand in need of discussion. Useful lives are not to be hazarded, from a view to the partial and contemptible obloquy that may be annexed to the refusal of such a duel, that is, to an act of virtue.

Which of these two actions is the truest test of courage: the engaging in a practice which our judgment disapproves, because we cannot submit to the consequences of following that judgment; or the doing what we believe to be right, and chearfully encountering all the consequences that may be annexed to the practice of virtue?

"But the refusing a duel is an ambiguous action. Cowards may pretend principle to shelter themselves from a danger they dare not meet."

This is partly true and partly false. There are few actions indeed that are not ambiguous, or that with the same general outline may not proceed from different motives. But the manner of doing them, will sufficiently show the principle from which they sprung.

He, that would break through universally received custom because he believes it to be wrong, must no doubt arm himself with fortitude. The point in which we principally fail, is in not accurately understanding our own intentions, and taking care beforehand to purify ourselves from every alloy of weakness and error. He, who comes forward with no other idea but that of rectitude, and who expresses, with the simplicity and firmness which conviction never fails to inspire, the views which which he is impressed, is in no danger of being mistaken for a coward. If he hesitate, it is because he has not an idea perfectly clear of the sentiment he intends to convey. If he be in any degree embarrassed, it is because he has not a feeling, sufficiently generous and intrepid, of the demerit of the action in which he is urged to engage.

If there be any meaning in courage, its first ingredient must be the daring to speak truth at all times, to all persons, and in every possible situation. What is it but the want of courage that should prevent me from saying, "Sir, I will not accept your challenge. Have I injured you? I will readily and without compulsion repair my injustice to the uttermost mite. Have you misconstrued me? State to me the particulars, and doubt not that what is true I will make appear to be true. Thus far will I go. He that holds this language with a countenance in unison with his words, will never be suspected of acting upon the impulse of fear.

3. Literature on Education

[The final statement in *A Simple Story* that Matilda has received what her mother did not, "a proper education," invites readers to consider eighteenth-century debates about female education. Many conduct book writers, including Hannah More, Mary Wollstonecraft, and Catharine Macaulay Graham encouraged young women to reject "the precious sovereignty of an hour" (Macaulay) that beauty and rank provide, and pursue instead the wisdom that would confer "those established rights which, independent of accidental circumstances, may afford protection to the whole sex."]

a. From Hannah More, Strictures On The Modern System of Female Education *(1799), 62-87*

[An evangelical philanthropist, Hannah More's social and political views tended to be much more conservative than those of Mary Wollstonecraft and Catharine Macaulay Graham. Her condemnation of frivolous and inconsequential female behavior, manners, and dress, however, aligns her with many of her more liberal contemporaries.]

Chap. II.

On the education of women.—The prevailing system tends to establish the errors which it ought to correct.—Dangers arising from an excessive cultivation of the arts.

I T is far from being the object of this slight work to offer a regular plan of female education, a task which has been often more properly assumed by far abler writers; but it is intended rather to suggest a few remarks on the reigning mode, which, though it has had many panegyrists, appears to be defective, not only in certain particulars, but as a general system. There are indeed numberless honourable exceptions to an observation which will be thought severe; yet the author questions if it be not the natural and direct tendency of the prevailing and popular system, to excite and promote those very defects which it ought to be the main end and object of Christian education to remove; whether instead of directing this important engine to attack and destroy vanity, selfishness, and inconsideration, that triple alliance in league against female virtue; the combined powers of instruction are not sedulously confederated in confirming their strength and establishing their empire?

If indeed the *material* substance; if the body and limbs, with the organs and senses, be really the more valuable objects of attention, then there is little room for animadversion and improvement. But if the immaterial and immortal mind; if the heart, "out of which are the issues of life,"[1] be the main concern; if the great business of education be to implant right ideas, to communicate knowledge, to form a correct taste and a sound judgment, to resist evil propensities, and, above all, to seize the favourable season for infusing principles and confirming habits; if education be a school to fit us for life, and life be a school to fit us for eternity; if such, I repeat it, be the chief work and grand ends of education, it may then be worth inquiring how far these ends are likely to be effected by the prevailing system.

Is it not a fundamental error to consider children as innocent beings, whose little weaknesses may perhaps want some correction, rather than as beings who bring into the world a corrupt nature and evil dispositions, which it should be the great end of education to rectify? This appears to be such a foundation-truth, that if I were asked what quality is most important in an instructor of youth, I should not hesitate to reply, *such a strong impression of the corruption of our nature, as should insure a disposition to counteract it; together with such a deep view and thorough knowledge of the human heart, as should be necessary for developing and controlling its most secret and complicated workings.* And let us remember that to *know the world*, as it is called, that is to know its local manners, temporary usages, and evanescent fashions, is not to *know human nature*: and that where this prime knowledge is wanting, those natural evils which ought to be counteracted will be fostered.

Vanity, for instance, is reckoned among the light and venial errors of youth; nay, so far from being treated as a dangerous enemy, it is often called in as an auxiliary. At worst, it is considered as a harmless weakness, which subtracts little from the value of a character; as a natural effervescence, which will subside of itself, when the first ferment of the youthful passions shall have done working. But those know little of the conformation of the human, and especially of the female heart, who fancy that vanity is ever exhausted, by the mere operation of time and events. Let those who maintain this opinion look into our places of public resort, and there behold if the ghost of departed beauty is not to its last flitting fond of haunting the scenes of its past pleasures; the soul, unwilling (if I may borrow an allusion from the Platonic mythology) to quit the spot in which the body enjoyed its former delights, still continues to hover about the same place, though the same pleasures are

---

1   Proverbs IV: 23.

no longer to be found there. Disappointments indeed may divert vanity into a new direction; prudence may prevent it from breaking out into excesses, and age may prove that it is "vexation of spirit;" but neither disappointment, prudence, nor age can *cure* it: for they do not correct the principle. Nay, the very disappointment itself serves as a painful evidence of its protracted existence.

Since then there is a season when the youthful must cease to be young, and the beautiful to excite admiration; to grow old gracefully is perhaps one of the rarest and most valuable arts which can be taught to woman. It is for this sober season of life that education should lay up its rich resources. However disregarded they may hitherto have been, they will be wanted now. When admirers fall away, and flatterers become mute, the mind will be driven to retire into itself, and if it find no entertainment at home, it will be driven back again upon the world with increased force. Yet forgetting this, do we not seem to educate our daughters, exclusively, for the transient period of youth, when it is to maturer life we ought to advert? Do we not educate them for a crowd, forgetting that they are to live at home? for the world, and not for themselves? for show, and not for use? for time, and not for eternity?
....

[A discussion follows of the dangers of "excessive cultivation of the arts."]

It is of the essence of human things that the same objects which are highly useful in their season, measure, and degree, become mischievous in their excess, at other periods, and under other circumstances. In a state of barbarism, the arts are among the best reformers; and they go on to be improved themselves, and improving those who cultivate them, till having reached a certain point, those very arts which were the instruments of civilization and refinement, become instruments of corruption and decay; enervating and depraving in the second instance as certainly as they refined in the first. They become agents of voluptuousness. They excite the imagination; and the imagination thus excited, and no longer under the government of strict principle, becomes the most dangerous stimulant of the passions; promotes a too keen relish for pleasure, teaching how to multiply its sources, and inventing new and pernicious modes of artificial gratification.

May we not rank among the present corrupt consequences, the unchaste *costume*, the impure style of dress, and that indelicate statue-like exhibition of the female figure, which by its artfully-disposed folds, its wet and adhesive drapery, so defines the form as to prevent covering itself from becoming a veil? This licentious mode, as the acute Montesquieu[1] observed on the dances of the Spartan virgins, has taught us "to strip chastity itself of modesty."

May the author be allowed to address to our own country and our own circumstances, to both of which they seem peculiarly applicable, the spirit of that beautiful apostrophe of the most polished poet of antiquity to the most victorious nation? "Let us leave to the inhabitants of *conquered countries* the praise of carrying to the very highest degree of perfection, sculpture and the sister arts; but let *this* country direct her own exertions to the art of governing mankind in equity and peace, of shewing mercy to the submissive, and of abasing the proud among surrounding nations."[2]

b. From Catharine Sawbridge Macaulay Graham, Letters on Education (1790)

[Catharine Sawbridge Macaulay Graham was best known for her 18-volume history of England during the English Civil War and the Restoration, *The History of England from the Accession of James I to that of the Brunswick Line*. Her *Letters on Education* was written in 1790, two years before Mary Wollstonecraft's *A Vindication of the Rights of Woman*. Addressing Hortensia, a fictional correspondent, Macaulay argues in *Letters on Education* that a false notion of "female excellence" stemmed from the separate education given to girls and boys.]

Letter XXIII.
Coquettry.

THOUGH the situation of women in modern Europe, Hortensia, when compared with that condition of abject slavery in which they have

---

1   Charles-Louis de Secondat, baron de le Brede et de Montesquieu (1689-1755), French writer and philosopher.

2   [More's note] Let me not be suspected of bringing into any sort of comparison the gentleness of British government with the rapacity of Roman conquests, or the principles of Roman dominion. To spoil, to butcher, and to commit every kind of violence, they call, says one of the ablest of their historians, by the lying name of *government*, and when they have spread a general desolation they call it *Peace*. (Tacitus' *Life of Agricola*, speech of Galgaous to his soldiers.)

    With such *dictatorial*, or, as we might now read *directorial* inquisitors, we can have no point of contact; and if I have applied the servile flattery of a delightful poet to the purpose of English happiness, it was only to shew wherein true national grandeur consists, and that every country pays too dear a price for those arts and embellishments of society which endanger the loss of its morals and manners.

always been held in the east, may be considered as brilliant; yet if we withhold comparison, and take the matter in a positive sense, we shall have no great reason to boast of our privileges, or of the candour and indulgence of the men towards us. For with a total and absolute exclusion of every political right to the sex in general, married women, whose situation demand a particular indulgence, have hardly a civil right to save them from the grossest injuries; and though the gallantry of some of the European societies have necessarily produced indulgence, yet in others the faults of women are treated with a severity and rancour which militates against every principle of religion and common sense. Faults, my friend, I hear you say; you take the matter in too general a sense; you know there is but one fault which a woman of honour may not commit with impunity; let her only take care that she is not caught in a love intrigue, and she may lie, she may deceive, she may defame, she may ruin her own family with gaming, and the peace of twenty others with her coquettry, and yet preserve both her reputation and her peace. These are glorious privileges indeed, Hortensia; but whilst plays and novels are the favourite study of the fair, whilst the admiration of men continues to be set forth as the chief honour of woman, whilst power is only acquired by personal charms, whilst continual dissipation banishes the hour of reflection, Nature and flattery will too often prevail; and when this is the case, self preservation will suggest to conscious weakness those methods which are the most likely to conceal the ruinous trespass, however base and criminal they may be in their nature. The crimes that women have committed, both to conceal and to indulge their natural failings, shock the feelings of moral sense; but indeed every love intrigue, though it does not terminate in such horrid catastrophes, must naturally tend to debase the female mind, from its violence to educational impressions, from the secrecy with which it must be conducted, and the debasing dependancy to which the intriguer, if she is a woman of reputation, is subjected. Lying, flattery, hypocrisy, bribery, and a long catalogue of the meanest of the human vices, must all be employed to preserve necessary appearances. Hence delicacy of sentiment gradually decreases; the warnings of virtue are no longer felt; the mind becomes corrupted, and lies open to every solicitation which appetite or passion presents. This must be the natural course of things in every being formed after the human plan; but it gives rise to the trite and foolish observation, that the first fault against chastity in woman has a radical power to deprave the character. But no such frail beings come out of the hands of Nature. The human mind is built of nobler materials than to be so easily corrupted; and with all the disadvantages of situation and education, women seldom become entirely abandoned till they are thrown into a state of desperation by the venomous rancour of their own sex.

...

[Two paragraphs follow, discussing Rousseau's argument that women's defects in physical strength are compensated for by their superiority in "art and ingenuity."]

These agreeable talents, as the author expresses it, are played off to great advantage by women in all the courts of Europe; who, for the arts of female allurement, do not give place to the Circassian. But it is the practice of these very arts, directed to enthrall the men, which act in a peculiar manner to corrupting the female mind. Envy, malice, jealousy, a cruel delight in inspiring sentiments which at first perhaps were never intended to be reciprocal, are leading features in the character of the coquet, whose aim is to subject the whole world to her own humour; but in this vain attempt she commonly sacrifices both her decency and her virtue.

By the intrigues of women, and their rage for personal power and importance, the whole world has been filled with violence and injury; and their levity and influence have proved so hostile to the existence or permanence of rational manners, that it fully justifies the keeness of Mr. Pope's satire on the sex.[1]

...

To do the sex justice, it must be confessed that history does not set forth more instances of positive power abused by women, than by men; and when the sex have been taught wisdom by education, they will be glad to give up indirect influence for rational privileges; and the precarious sovereignty of an hour enjoyed with the meanest and most infamous of the species, for those established rights which, independent of accidental circumstances, may afford protection to the whole sex.

Letter XXIV.
Flattery—Chastity—Male Rakes.
A F T E R all that has been advanced, Hortensia, the happiness and perfection of the two sexes are so reciprocally dependant on one another that; till both are reformed, there is no expecting excellence in either. The

---

1   Pope satirized women in works such as *Epistle to a Lady* (1735) and *The Rape of the Lock* (1712, 1714).

candid Addison[1] has confessed, that in order to embellish the mistress, you must give a new education to the lover, and teach the men not to be any longer dazzled by false charms and unreal beauty. Till this is the case, we must endeavour to palliate the evil we cannot remedy; and, in the education of our females, raise as many barriers to the corruptions of the world, as our understanding and sense of things will permit.

As I give no credit to the opinion of a sexual excellence, I have made no variation in the fundamental principles of the education of the two sexes; but it will be necessary to admit of such a difference in the plan as shall in some degree form the female mind to the particularity of its situation.

The fruits of true philosophy are modesty and humility; for as we advance in knowledge, our deficiencies become more conspicuous; and by learning to set a just estimate on what we possess, we find little gratification for the passion of pride. This is so just an observation, that we may venture to pronounce, without any exception to the rule, that a vain or proud man is, in a positive sense, an ignorant man. However if it should be our lot to have one of the fair sex, distinguished for any eminent degree of personal charms, committed to our care, we must not attempt by a premature cultivation to gather the fruits of philosophy before their season, nor expect to find the qualities of true modesty and humility make their appearance till the blaze of beauty has in some measure been subdued by time. For should we exhaust all the powers of oratory, and all the strength of sound argument, in the endeavour to convince our pupil that beauty is of small weight in the scale of real excellence, the enflamed praises she will continually hear bestowed on this quality will fix her in the opinion, that we *mean* to keep her in ignorance of her true worth. She will think herself deceived, and she will resent the injury by giving little credit to our precepts, and placing her confidence in those who tickle her ears with lavish panegyric on the captivating graces of her person.

Thus vanity steals on the mind, and thus a daughter, kept under by the ill exerted power of parental authority, gives a full ear to the flattery of a coxcomb. Happy would it be for the sex did the mischief end here; but the soothings of flattery never fail to operate on the affections of the heart; and when love creeps into the bosom, the empire of reason is at an end. To prevent our fair pupils therefore from becoming the

---

1 Joseph Addison (1672-1719), poet, essayist, and statesman. Founder, along with Richard Steele, of *The Spectator* (1711-12, 1714) and *The Tatler* (1709-11), periodicals containing essays designed to provide instruction and light entertainment, particularly for women.

prey of coxcombs, and serving either to swell their triumph, or repair their ruined fortunes, it will be necessary to give them a full idea of the magnitude of their beauty, and the power this quality has over the frail mind of man. Nor have we in this case so much to fear from the intimations of a judicious friend, as from the insiduous adulation of a designing admirer. The haughty beauty is too proud to regard the admiration of fops and triflers; she will never condescend to the base, the treacherous, the dangerous arts of coquettry; and by keeping her heart free from the snares of love, she will have time to cultivate that philosophy which, if well understood, is a never failing remedy to human pride.

But the most difficult part of female education, is to give girls such an idea of chastity, as shall arm their reason and their sentiments on the side of this useful virtue. For I believe there are more women of understanding led into acts of imprudence by the ignorance, the prejudices, and the false craft of those by whom they are educated, than from any other cause founded either in nature or in chance. You may train up a docile idiot to any mode of thinking or acting, as may best suit the intended purpose; but a reasoning being will scan over your propositions, and if they find them grounded in falsehood, they will reject them with disdain. When you tell a girl of spirit and reflection that chastity is a sexual virtue, and the want of it a sexual vice, she will be apt to examine into the principles of religion, morals, and the reason of things, in order to satisfy herself on the truth of your proposition. And when, after the strictest enquiries, she finds nothing that will warrant the confining the proposition to a particular sense, she will entertain doubts either of your wisdom or your sincerity; and regarding you either as a deceiver or a fool, she will transfer her confidence to the companion of the easy vacant hour, whose compliance with her opinions can flatter her vanity. Thus left to Nature, with an unfortunate biass on her mind, she will fall a victim to the first plausible being who has formed a design on her person. Rousseau is so sensible of this truth, that he quarrels with human reason, and would put her out of the question in all considerations of duty. But this is being as great a fanatic in morals, as some are in religion; and I should much doubt the reality of that duty which would not stand the test of fair enquiry; beside, as I intend to breed my pupils up to act a rational part in the world, and not to fill up a niche in the seraglio of a sultan, I shall certainly give them leave to use their reason in all matters which concern their duty and happiness, and shall spare no pains in the cultivation of this only sure guide to virtue. I shall inform them of the great utility of chastity and continence; that the one preserves the body in health and vigor, and the other, the purity and independence of the mind, without which it is impossible to possess virtue or happiness. I shall intimate, that the great difference now beheld in the external consequences which follow the deviations from chastity in the two sexes, did in all probability arise from women having been considered as the mere property of the men; and, on this account had no right to dispose of their own persons: that policy adopted this difference, when the plea of property had been given up; and it was still preserved in society from the unruly licentiousness of the men, who, finding no obstacles in the delicacy of the other sex, continue to set at defiance both divine and moral law, and by mutual support and general opinion to use their natural freedom with impunity. I shall observe, that this state of things renders the situation of females, in their individual capacity very precarious; for the strength which Nature has given to the passion of love, in order to serve her purposes, has made it the most ungovernal propensity of any which attends us. The snares therefore, that are continually laid for women, by persons who run no risk in compassing their seduction, exposes them to continual danger; whilst the implacability of their own sex, who fear to give up any advantages which a superior prudence, or even its appearances, give them, renders one false step an irretrievable misfortune. That, for these reasons, coquettry in women is as dangerous as it is dishonorable. That a coquet commonly finds her own perdition, in the very flames which she raises to consume others; and that if any thing can excuse the baseness of female seduction, it is the baits which are flung out by women to entangle the affections, and excite the passions of men.

I know not what you may think of my method, Hortensia, which I must acknowledge to carry the stamp of singularity; but for my part, I am sanguine enough to expect to turn out of my hands a careless, modest beauty, grave, manly, noble, full of strength and majesty; and carrying about her an aegis sufficiently powerful to defend her against the sharpest arrow that ever was shot from Cupid's bow. A woman, whose virtue will not be of the kind to wrankle into an inveterate malignity against her own sex for faults which she even encourages in the men, but who, understanding the principles of true religion and morality, will regard chastity and truth as indispensible qualities in virtuous characters of either sex; whose justice will incline her to extend her benevolence to the frailties of the fair as circumstances invite, and to manifest her resentment against the underminers of female happiness; in short, a woman who will not take a male rake either for a husband or a friend. And let me tell you, Hortensia, if women had as much regard for the virtue of chastity as in some cases they pretend to have, a reformation would long since have taken place in the world; but whilst they continue to cherish immodesty in the men, their bitter persecution of their own sex will not save them from the imputation of those concealed propensities with which they are accused by Pope,[1] and other severe satirists on the sex.

c. From *Mary Wollstonecraft,* Thoughts on the Education of Daughters *(1788), 93-103*

[*Thoughts on the Education of Daughters* was intended partially to advertise the school for girls Wollstonecraft established with the help of her two sisters and her friend, Fanny Blood. In *Thoughts on the Education of Daughters*, Wollstonecraft advocates a rational education for girls, who, she believed, should learn to support themselves economically.]

MATRIMONY

Early marriages are, in my opinion, a stop to improvement. If we were born only "to draw nutrition, propagate, and rot,"[2] the sooner the end of creation was answered the better; but as women are here allowed to have souls, the soul ought to be attended to. In youth a woman endeavours to please the other sex, in order, generally speaking, to get married, and this endeavour calls forth all her powers. If she has had a tolerable education, the foundation only is laid, for the mind does not soon arrive at maturity, and should not be engrossed by domestic cares before any habits are fixed. The passions also have too much influence over the judgment to suffer it to direct her in this most important affair; and many women, I am persuaded, marry a man before they are twenty, whom they would have rejected some years after. Very frequently, when the education has been neglected, the mind improves itself, if it has leisure for reflection, and experience to reflect on; but how can this happen when they are forced to act before they have had time to think, or find that they are unhappily married? Nay, should they be so fortunate as to get a good husband, they will not set a proper value on him; he will be found much inferior to the lovers described in novels, and their want of knowledge makes them frequently disgusted with the man, when the fault is in human nature.

---

1   Alexander Pope (1688-1744), poet and essayist known for his satire of women writers such as Eliza Haywood and Lady Mary Wortley Montagu in *The Dunciad* (1728).
2   Alexander Pope, *Essay on Man* (1732-34), Epistle ii, line 63: "Fixed like a plant on his particular spot / to draw nutrition, propagate, and rot."

When a woman's mind has gained some strength, she will in all probability pay more attention to her actions than a girl can be expected to do; and if she thinks seriously, she will chuse for a companion a man of principle; and this perhaps young people do not sufficiently attend to, or see the necessity of doing. A woman of feeling must be very much hurt if she is obliged to keep her children out of their father's company, that their morals may not be injured by his conversation; and besides, the whole arduous talk of education devolves on her, and in such a case is not very practicable. Attention to the education of children must be irksome, when life appears to have so many charms, and its pleasures are not found fallacious. Many are but just returned from a boarding-school, when they are placed at the head of a family, and how fit they are to manage it, I leave the judicious to judge. Can they improve a child's understanding, when they are scarcely out of the state of childhood themselves?

....

[Two paragraphs follow on "dignity of manners" and "proper pride."]

Reason must often be called in to fill up the vacuums of life; but too many of our sex suffer theirs to lie dormant. A little ridicule and smart turn of expression, often confutes without convincing; and tricks are played off to raise tenderness, even while they are forfeiting esteem.

Women are said to be the weaker vessel, and many are the miseries which this weakness brings on them. Men have in some respects very much the advantage. If they have a tolerable understanding, it has a chance to be cultivated. They are forced to see human nature as it is, and are not left to dwell on the pictures of their own imaginations. Nothing, I am sure, calls forth the faculties so much as the being obliged to struggle with the world; and this is not a woman's province in a married state. Her sphere of action is not large, and if she is not taught to look into her own heart, how trivial are her occupations and pursuits! What little arts engross and narrow her mind! "Cunning fills up the mighty void of sense;"[1] and cares, which do not improve the heart of understanding, take up her attentions. Of course, she falls a prey to childish anger, and silly capricious humors, which render her rather insignificant than vicious.

In a comfortable situation, a cultivated mind is necessary to render

---

1   Misquoted from Pope, *An Essay on Criticism* (1711): "Pride, where wit fails, steps in to our defence, / And fills up all the mighty void of sense!" 208-09.

a woman contented; and in a miserable one, it is her only consolation. A sensible, delicate woman, who by some strange accident, or mistake, is joined to a fool or a brute, must be wretched beyond all names of wretchedness, if her views are confined to the present scene. Of what importance, then, is intellectual improvement, when our comfort here, and happiness hereafter, depends on it.

4. Masquerade

[The ubiquitous masqued balls (masquerades) were considered exciting and dangerous because of their potential to blur categories of social class and even gender. By 1791, however, when *A Simple Story* was published, the parties had become common-place enough to have lost some of their anarchic potential, as Jenkins suggests when she remarks that the masquerade incident in *A Simple Story* is "of no great importance; it would have been read simply as a young lady going to a party without an escort" (286). The following excerpts demonstrate changing attitudes toward the masquerade, beginning with strict warning against the masquerade's dangers in Eliza Haywood's *The Female Spectator* (1744-46), and ending with the unapologetic advertisements for masquerade costumes in the eighteenth-century newspaper, *The World* (1787-90).]

a. From Eliza Haywood, The Female Spectator, *vol. 1, book V (1744-46)*

[*The Female Spectator*, published anonymously by Haywood, was the first English periodical written by and for women. Letters published in *The Spectator* were supposedly derived from actual letters, although the correspondents were given pseudonyms.]

THIS is indeed a crisis which calls for the utmost precaution in a parent: I am told by persons who are always consulted on every occasion that relates to pleasure, that, a subscription is intended, some say actually on foot, for ridottos and masquerades at Ranelagh[1] next winter; and if so, our young ladies will probably live there all night as well as all day. Whether Mr. Heidegger[2] will have interest enough to prevent

---

1 Opened in 1742, Ranelagh Pleasure Gardens was a fashionable resort in London, South of the Royal Hospital, on the River Thames. Ranelagh's attractions included an ornamental lake and a rotunda larger in diameter than the Coliseum in Rome.

2 The masquerade tradition was first introduced in England by James Heidegger, a Swiss Count who arrived in England in 1708. He sponsored the first masquerade ball at Haymarket Opera House. See Castle, 10-11.

this invasion of his province, I know not; but if it should go on, one may venture to pronounce, without being any great conjurer, that those nocturnal rambles will be found of more dangerous consequence at Chelsea, than they have proved at the Haymarket.

I COMMUNICATED this piece of intelligence to a young lady, who at present passes the greatest part of her time at Ranelagh, and never in my life did I see a creature so transported:—her eyes sparkled, her lips quivered, all her frame was in agitation, through eagerness to know something farther of this important affair; and when I mentioned the apprehensions I had, that if such a design should take place, it might be prejudicial to the health of those who should venture themselves, in the damps of winter, in a place so near the water,—"O madam, cried she, one cannot catch cold at Ranelagh!"—I could not forbear, after this, giving her some broad hints of other inconveniencies, which might probably attend being so far from home, at hours that might encourage attempts, no way agreeable to the modesty of our sex; on which she only said, "Lard, madam, how you talk!"—And all my admonitions had no other effect, than to make her shorten her visit; no doubt to impart the discourse we had together to some of her acquaintance, and to ridicule my want of taste.

SHE has one motive, as I have been told by the men, which, notwithstanding, she would be very unwilling to acknowledge, for her preferring masquerades to all other public diversions; which is, that she never had a handsome thing said to her out of a vizard;—nature, it is certain, having not been over-curious in the formation of her features, and that cruel enemy to beauty, the small-pox, has rendered them yet less delicate; but with the help of new stays[1] once a month, and strait lacing, she has a tolerable shape; but then her neck suffers for it, and confesses in scarlet blushes, the constraint upon her waist:—this misfortune, however, she conceals under a handkerchief, or pelerine, and high tucker, and never trips it in the walks without some share of admiration from those who follow, and are nimble enough to overtake her.

A MASQUERADE may, therefore, well be the delight of her heart, where the advantageous part of her only is revealed; yet, though she cannot be insensible of what is amiable in herself, and what the contrary, as she looks so often in her glass, she was weak enough last winter to lay herself open to a rebuff at the masquerade, which occasioned a good deal of raillery among those who heard it.

To display all her perfections in the best light she could, she assumed

---

1 Corsets.

the habit of a Diana.[1] A green velvet jacket, fringed with silver, made so straight, that, as I heard, her chambermaid sprained both her thumbs with buckling it on, very much added to her natural slenderness:—a silver crescent glittered on her head, which had no other covering than her hair, of which indeed she has a great deal, and well coloured, braided with rows of pearl and flowers interspersed; the vizard on, it must be owned she made a very complete figure, and attracted the eyes of a good part of the assembly who were there that night.

B U T that which flattered her ambition most was, that the great Imperio[2] took notice of her, and imagining that a real Venus might be hid under the fictitious Diana, ordered a nobleman who stood near him, to go to her, and prevail with her to come to the beaufet[3] and unmask. He, who was not unaccustomed to such employments, readily flew to execute his commission, and, after having brought her to the highest pitch of vanity by the most extravagant compliments, to crown all, let her know who it was that sent him, and on what errand. Charmed as she was with the praises he gave, it was some time before she yielded to do as he desired; but at last her resolution was subdued, by the reflection that she ought not to refuse any thing to Imperio; and she suffered herself to be conducted by him to the beaufet, near which Imperio stood, who presented her with a glass of wine with his own hand, accompanied with many compliments; both which she received with a low obeisance, and at the same time plucked off her mask.

B U T fatal was this complaisance to all her hopes:—Imperio started back, and above the necessity of concealing the disappointment of his expectations,—"It will not do, my lord, said he to the nobleman, it will not do, and I am sorry I gave you so much trouble."

S E V E R A L of the company, whom this adventure had drawn to that part of the room, saw her face before she could be quick enough to replace her mask; and a much greater number heard the words Imperio spoke, as he turned from her; so that the whole time she staid afterwards, she was saluted with nothing but, "It will not do," and a loud laugh.

H A D she been mistress of resolution enough to have resisted the importunities of the emissary-lord, and the commands of Imperio, she would doubtless have heard many praises of the charming Diana repeated afterwards in company; whereas now the mystery was revealed, and

---

1 Diana is the goddess of the hunt as well as the goddess of chastity. Inchbald's Miss Milner wears this costume when she attends her masquerade.
2 The leader of the masquerade (derived from the Romance Language word for emperor or empire).
3 Side table or buffet.

the real Diana known, her greatest intimates could not forbear laughing at the mortification she had received; and on every little dispute with any of them, the way they took to be revenged was to cry, "It will not do."

MUCH more lovely women than the person I have been speaking of, have sometimes met with little indignities and slights, which their pride could ill sustain: and, indeed, how should it be otherwise! The men are so censorious, that they look on all those of our sex, who appear too much at these public places, as setting themselves up for sale, and therefore taking the liberty of buyers, measure us with their eyes from head to foot; and as the most perfect beauty may not have charms for all who gaze upon her in this scrutinous manner, few there are, if any, who have not found some who will pass by her with a contemptuous toss, no less significant than the most rude words could be.

O WHEREFORE then will not women endeavour to attain those talents which are sure of commanding respect!—No form so faultless, but the enquiring eyes of wanton and ungenerous men may find a blemish in. But she who has not the least pretence to beauty, has it in her power, would she but once be prevailed upon to exert it, to awe the boldest, or most affectedly nice libertine into submission, and force him to confess her worthy of a serious attachment. If even by indigence of circumstances, or the unjust parsimony some parents are guilty of, she is denied the means of cultivating her genius, and making herself mistress of those expensive accomplishments, which might render her what we call a shining figure in the world, innocence and modesty are still her own; they were born with her, they will cost nothing to preserve, and, without the aid of any other charm, will be a sure defence from all insults.

b. "Historical Account of Masquerades," Lady's Magazine *(May 1775)*

[This essay chronicles the development of the masquerade from its earliest English origins during the reign of Edward III[1] to its current status in 1775. See Castle, 19-20.]

Sir,

As the masquerade is become a favourite entertainment, many of your fair readers may, perhaps, be amused with the following particulars

---

1 King of England from 1327 to 1377, who led England into the Hundred Years' War (1337-1453) with France.

relating to its progress in this kingdom from a state of extreme simplicity, collected from the writings of various authors.

As far back as the reign of Edward the Third we are told of a masquerade or mumming, made by the citizens for disport of the young prince, Richard, son to the Black Prince.[1] This mummery however, was, probably, an innocent Christmas gambol. It does not appear that any intrigues were carried on during the celebration of it. An hundred and thirty citizens went to court masked, with great shew and finery, and returned home after much feasting, music, and dancing, in good order. There could have been nothing criminal, surely, in such a masquerade.

A similar kind of Christmas entertainment was made for Henry the Fourth[2] at Eltham. "Twelve aldermen and their sons rode in a mumming, to the great satisfaction of the court." There is no mention of their wives and daughters.

Henry the Eighth[3] was himself a notorious masquerader. By this time love-affairs were mingled with the disguises of the night. The masquerade which was made for him and the king of France, by Anne Bolin, at Calais, forwarded the consummation of an intended marriage. We are well assured, however, that before this marriage, wit and gallantry had made no small advances in our island. At the commencement of the jolly monarch's reign an act of parliament passed to suppress masquerades, setting forth, that "forasmuch as lately within this realm, divers persons have disguised and appareled themselves, and covered their faces with visors or other things, in such manner as they should not be known, and divers of them in a company together, naming themselves mummers, have come to the dwelling place of divers men of honour, and substantial persons, and so departed unknown: whereupon murders, felony, rape, and other great hurts and inconveniences have afore-time grown, and hereafter be like to come by the colour thereof, if the said order should continue not reformed, &c."

The masquerade in the reign of James the First[4] do [sic] not give us an encouragement to believe that rapes were committed in them....

---

1 A reference to Edward, the Black Prince (1330-1376), son and heir apparent of Edward III of England.

2 King of England from 1399 to 1413, Henry IV was the first of three 15th-century monarchs from the house of Lancaster.

3 King of England from 1509 to 1547. After attaining an annulment of his marriage to Catherine of Aragon, he married Anne Boleyn. When she did not produce a male heir, he had her beheaded in 1536 on charges of witchcraft and adultery.

4 First Stuart king of England and Ireland from 1603 to 1625 and king of Scotland (as James VI) from 1567 to 1625.

In the reign of Charles the Second,[1] masquerades were much in the modern style. Burnet,[2] in his History of his Own Times, attributes them to the great dissolution of morals in the court, and gives the following account of them—"At this time the court fell into much extravagance in masquerading, both king and queen, and all the court, went about masked, and came into houses unknown, and danced there with a great deal of wild frolick. In all this people were so disguised, that without being in the secret, none could distinguish them. They were carried about in Hackney chairs[3]—Once the queen's chairmen, now knowing who she was, went from her, so she was alone, and was much disturbed, and came to Whitehall[4] in a hackney coach: some say it was a cart."— This proceeding of her majesty, it seems, gave great scandal. We are told, by the same historian, that Buckingham, taking advantage of her behaviour, proposed to the king "that he would give him leave to steal her away, and send her to a plantation, where she should be well and carefully looked to, but never heard of more." Buckingham intended by this proposal to pave the way to divorce; but the king rejected it with horror.—The queen, informed of the indecency of her conduct, thought proper to give over such wild frolick. Were the good bishop now alive, however, he might be pained at the sight of our present masquerades, he would, undoubtedly, be pleased to see that they do not originate from "a great dissolution of morals in the court."

    I am, Sir,

        Your very humble servt.

          Antiquarius

c. "An Essay on Masquerades," Lady's Magazine *(December 1777)*

[This satirical essay articulates the masquerade's blurring of social distinctions, a result that caused the omnipresent masquerade balls to be both feared and appreciated.]

WHOEVER knows the meaning and intention of a masquerade, must be highly pleased to hear that the nation is this winter (notwithstanding

---

1   King of Great Britain and Ireland (1660-85), who was restored to the British throne after years of exile during the Puritan Commonwealth.

2   Bishop of Salisbury (1643-1715). He wrote History of my Own Times (1724-34) about the Glorious Revolution.

3   Portable, enclosed chairs mounted on horizontally placed parallel poles and carried by men or animals.

4   Street in the City of Westminster, London. The name Whitehall also applies to the cluster of short streets, squares, and governmental buildings adjoining the street.

the American war) blessed with its revival. Its tendency to diffuse a *spirit of liberty*, by reducing all men to an equality; to encourage population by the innocent freedoms which it allows; to accumulate wealth and enlarge estates, by the rage of gaming which it creates, must endear it to every lover of his country. In this nocturnal assembly rank and distinction cease to insult us with their superiority; the noble peer is confounded with the ignoble peasant; the order of things is inverted, the first is put last, and the last first. Every one divests himself of his borrowed feathers, and following his natural propensity, assumes the character which suits him best. In short, everyone humours his own genius so exactly, that whoever are well acquainted with the temper and disposition of our nobility in public life, will have no difficulty in tracing them out under the disguise of their masks; and those who are not, will here meet with an opportunity of penetrating into the inmost recesses of their hearts, and have a proper clue to unravel their national conduct. I verily believe that a man of any sagacity, who has studied human nature, will find it much easier to decipher every mask in such an assembly, than to unfold the character of one single modern politician on the stage of common life.

It is well known to all adept in ancient history, that the first grand masquerade happened when the gods were so hard pressed by the giants, that in order to escape their fury, they put on the masks of bulls, rams, and goats, and by this stratagem triumphed at last over their brutal enemies. Tho fear and necessity first suggested this idea to the gods, they found the artifice so convenient in their future dealings with men, or rather women, that it was continued for a series of ages, and would not, in all probability, have been dropt, had not mortals aped them, and brought the practice into disgrace. The pranks of Jupiter, Venus, and other celestial beings, were personated by mere terrestrial pretenders, and have ever since been emulated in different countries, according to their different genius. But of all nations, none, except our own, have carried masquerades to such a high degree of perfection as a certain set in India, who, at stated times of the year, assemble themselves, enter the masquerade room, put out every light, and mingle with each other as familiarly and indiscriminately as our nobility can possibly do.

d. Sample Advertisements for Masquerades and Costumes, The World *(30 January 1788)*

[The newspaper, *The World; or, Fashionable Advertiser* (1787-90) was established by Inchbald's friends, Edward Topham (1721-1820) and Charles (Parson) Estes (1753-1829). The paper, appealing to "the fashionable

WEDNESDAY, JANUARY 30, 1788.

For the BENEFIT of Mr. SEDGWICK.
ROYALTY THEATRE.
ON THURSDAY, January 31, 1788, the Audience will be presented with the following performances,
A new MUSICAL PASTICCIO, (the 32d time) called
APOLLO TURNED STROLLER;
Or, THEREBY HANGS A TALE,
As a CONCERT. The Vocal Parts by
Mr. BANNISTER, &c. as usual.
(The 26th time) a New Pantomimic Dance, called
THE DESERTER OF NAPLES.
Or, ROYAL CLEMENCY.
Under the direction of Mr. DELPINI.
The Deserter by Mr. PALMER.
A GRAND MASQUERADE JUBILEE.
With elegant Illuminations, and Decorations; a variety of Airs, Duets, &c. will be introduced by Messrs. Bannister, Leoni, Delpini, Chapman, Arrowsmith, Gaudry, Master Braham, and Mr. Sedgwick; Mrs. Fox, Miss Burnett, and Miss George, with dancing by Mons. Malter, Mr. Holland, and Mr. Bourk, Mademoiselle Constance, Mr. Delpini, and Miss Rithmire. The Jubilee to conclude with a Comic Song by Mr. Delpini. And Mr. Sedgwick, will introduce some of the most favourite Airs, sung by him in the Opera of
ARTAXERXES.
Boxes 5s. Pit 3s. First Gallery 2s. Second Gallery 1s.
Tickets to be had of Mr. Sedgwick, No. 21, Canterbury-row, Lambeth; of Messrs. Longman and Broderip, Cheapside, and the Haymarket; and of Mr. Clark, at the Theatre, where places for the Boxes may be taken.

PANTHEON.
January 30, 1788.
THE Nobility and Gentry are respectfully acquainted, that the First
MASQUED BALL,
at this place, will be TO-MORROW EVENING. There will be a SUPPER as usual, with WINES, &c. &c. Tickets, at ONE GUINEA each, may be had at the Office. The Doors will be opened at Ten o'Clock, and the Supper Rooms at One.

MASQUERADE WAREHOUSE. FARN, Successor to Mrs. Atkinson, removed from Pall-Mall, to No. 346, Oxford-street, near the Pantheon, The Nobility and Gentry are respectfully informed, that a great variety of rich dominos with hoods and cloaks, great choice of black and coloured Venetian and fancy masks, also an elegant and new assortment of rich feathers, flowers, ribbons, gloves, &c. &c. are now ready for their inspection.

RICHMAN, real Hat-Maker, and Masquerade Warehouseman to His Royal Highness the Prince of Wales, No. 261, two doors from the Pantheon, Oxford-street, respectfully acquaints the Nobility and Gentry, that his Wardrobe of elegant Masquerade Dresses, is opened to-day, till To-morrow Evening; and on Monday next will be opened again for the Opera Masquerade, with every article in great variety suitable for entertainment. The Warehou-

The World; or Fashionable Advertiser, 1 January 1788, Shelfmark: Burney. Reproduced with permission of the British Library.

world and polite circles" (The World, 3 January 1787), included work by caricaturist Henry William Bunbury (1750-1811) and short contributions by actors and dramatists including Mary Robinson (1756/58?-1800), Hannah Cowley (1743-1809), Robert Merry (1755-98), Mary Wells (1762-1829), and Elizabeth Inchbald. The excerpts above are typical of the many fashionable advertisements included in the newspaper.

One of the masquerades advertised above was to be held at the Pantheon, a building on Oxford Street designed by architect James Wyatt (1746-1815) and built in 1769. Inspired by the Pantheon in Italy, a temple in Ancient Rome, the Pantheon provided a venue for masquerades, exhibitions, and concerts. In Correspondence, Horace Walpole (1717-97) pronounced that the building was "the most beautiful edifice in England" (1773, pp.101-02, letter to Rev. William Mason (1725-97).]

e. From Hannah Cowley, The Belle's Stratagem *(1780)*

[The ball in this play, one of Inchbald's favorites,[1] may well have inspired the masquerade in *A Simple Story*. In Act IV, Doricourt has rejected Letitia as a potential love interest, and she attends a masquerade in hopes that, not knowing who she is, he will fall in love with her. The stratagem works, and, when Letitia reveals her face, Doricourt assures her that "nothing can be captivating that you are not."]

DORICOURT.
    By Heaven, the same sweet creature!
LETITIA.
    You have chosen an odd situation for study. Fashion and taste preside in this spot:—they throw their spells around you:—ten thousand delights spring up at their command;—and you, a Stoic—a being without senses, are wrapt in reflection.
DORICOURT.
    And you, the most charming being in the world, awake me to admiration. Did you come from the Stars?
LETITIA.
    Yes, and I shall reascend in a moment.
DORICOURT.
    Pray shew me your face before you go.
LETITIA.
    Beware of imprudent curiosity; it lost Paradise.
DORICOURT.
    Eve's curiosity was rais'd by the Devil;—'tis an Angel tempts mine.—So your allusion is not in point.
LETITIA.
    But *why* would you see my face?
DORICOURT.
    To fall in love with it.
LETITIA.
    And what then?
DORICOURT.
    Why, then—Aye, curse it! there's the rub. [Aside.]
LETITIA.
    Your Mistress will be angry;—but, perhaps, you have no Mistress?

---

1   See Jenkins, 285.

DORICOURT.
  Yes, yes; and a sweet one it is!
LETITIA.
  What! is she old?
DORICOURT.
  No.
LETITIA.
  Ugly?
DORICOURT.
  No.
LETITIA.
  What then?
DORICOURT.
  Pho! don't talk about *her*; but shew me your face.
LETITIA.
  My vanity forbids it;—'twould frighten you.
DORICOURT.
  Impossible! Your Shape is graceful, your Air bewitching, your bosom
  transparent, and your Chin would tempt me to kiss it, if I did not see
  a pouting red Lip above it that demands—
LETITIA.
  You grow too free.
DORICOURT.
  Shew me your face then—only half a glance.
LETITIA.
  Not for worlds.
DORICOURT.
  What! you will have a little gentle force?
  [Attempts to seize her mask.]
LETITIA.
  I am gone for ever!

                                                              [Exit.]

DORICOURT.
  'Tis false;—I'll follow to the end.

                                                              [Exit.]
….

[An exchange follows in which the married Lady Frances Touchwood
is rescued from her would-be suitor, Sir Courtall.]

[DORICOURT and LETITIA come forward.]

DORICOURT.

By Heavens! I never was charm'd till now.—English beauty—French vivacity—wit—elegance. Your name, my Angel!—tell me your name, though you persist in concealing your face.

LETITIA.

My name has a spell in it.

DORICOURT.

I thought so; it must be *Charming.*

LETITIA.

But if reveal'd, the charm is broke.

DORICOURT.

I'll answer for its force.

LETITIA.

Suppose it Harriet, or Charlotte, or Maria—or—

DORICOURT.

Hang Harriet, and Charlotte, and Maria—the name your Father gave ye!

LETITIA.

That can't be worth knowing, 'tis so transient a thing.

DORICOURT.

How, transient?

LETITIA.

Heav'n forbid my name should be *lasting* till I am married.

DORICOURT.

Married! The chains of Matrimony are too heavy and vulgar for such a spirit as yours.—The flowery wreaths of cupid are the only bands you should wear.

LETITIA.

They are the lightest, I believe: but 'tis possible to wear those of Marriage gracefully.—throw 'em loosely round, and twist 'em in a True-Lover's knot for the bosom.

DORICOURT.

An Angel! But what will you be when a Wife?

LETITIA.

A Woman.—If my Husband should prove a Churl, a Fool, or a Tyrant, I'd break his heart, ruin his fortune, elope with the first pretty Fellow that ask'd me—and return the contempt of the world with scorn, whilst my feelings prey'd upon my life.

DORICOURT.

Amazing! [*Aside.*] What if you lov'd him, and he were worthy of your love?

LETITIA.

Why, then I'd be any thing—and all!—Grave, gay, capricious—the soul of whim, the spirit of variety—live with him in the eye of fashion, or in the shade of retirement—change my country, my sex;—feast with him in an Esquimaux hut,[1] or a Persian pavilion[2]—join him in the victorious war-dance on the borders of Lake Ontario,[3] or sleep to the soft breathings of the flute in the cinnamon groves of Ceylon[4]—dig with him in the mines of Golconda,[5] or enter the dangerous precincts of the Mogul's[6] Seraglio[7]—cheat him of his wishes, and overturn his empire to restore the Husband of my Heart to the blessings of Liberty and Love.

DORICOURT.

Delightful wildness! Oh, to catch thee, and hold thee for ever in this little cage!

[Attempting to clasp her.]

LETITIA.

Hold, Sir! Though cupid must give the bait that tempts me to the snare, 'tis Hymen must spread the net to catch me.

DORICOURT.

'Tis in vain to assume airs of coldness—Fate has ordained you mine.

LETITIA.

How do you know?

DORICOURT.

I feel it *here*. I never met with a Woman so perfectly to my taste; and I won't believe it form'd you so, on purpose to tantalize me.

LETITIA.

This moment is worth a whole existence. [Aside.]

DORICOURT.

Come, shew me your face, and rivet my chains.

---

1 Eskimo hut.
2 Allusion to the eighteenth-century fascination with India and the East.
3 The lake in North America was a site of a canoe-based trading empire.
4 Modern Sri Lanka, Ceylon is a large island in the Indian Ocean at the tip of India.
5 Fortress in Southern India.
6 A mogul was a member of the Muslim dynasty that ruled India until 1857.
7 Harem.

LETITIA.

To-morrow you shall be satisfied.

DORICOURT.

To-morrow! and not to night?

LETITIA.

No.

DORICOURT.

Where then shall I wait on you to-morrow?—Where see you?

LETITIA.

You shall see me in an hour when you least expect me.

DORICOURT.

Why all this mystery?

LETITIA.

I like to be mysterious. At present be content to know that I am a woman of Family and Fortune. Adieu!

….

[An exchange follows in which Dorricourt attempts to discover Letitia's identity.]

ACT V

DORICOURT.

It was! Base and ungenerous! Well, Sir, you shall be gratified. The possession of my heart was no object either with You, or your Daughter. My fortune and name was all you desired, and these—I leave ye. My native England I shall quit, nor ever behold you more. But, Lady, that in my exile I may have one consolation, grant me the favour you denied last night;—let me behold all that mask conceals, that your whole image may be impress'd on my heart, and chear my distant solitary hours.

LETITIA.

This is the most awful moment of my life. Oh, Doricourt, the slight action of taking off my Mask, stamps me the most blest or miserable of Women!

DORICOURT.

What can this mean? Reveal your face, I conjure you.

LETITIA.

Behold it.

DORICOURT.

Rapture! Transport! Heaven!

5. Female Transgression

[As is evident in *A Simple Story*, sexual transgression was ruinous to women, and Inchbald carefully preserved her virtuous reputation. As Jane Spencer argues, in spite of various rumors about Inchbald's relationships with various men, "mud never stuck to her" (ix).]

a. From William Godwin, Memoirs of the Author of a Vindication of the Rights of Woman *(1798), 124-26*

[After Mary Wollstonecraft's death, Godwin wrote an account of her controversial life. In the following excerpt, he philosophizes about her attachment to Gilbert Imlay (1754-1828), an attachment that resulted in public humiliation when she had a daughter out of wedlock.]

Why did she [Wollstonecraft] thus obstinately cling to a passion, at once ill-assorted, and unpromising? Because it is of the very essence of affection, to seek to perpetuate itself. He does not love, who can resign this cherished sentiment, without suffering some of the sharpest struggles that our nature is capable of enduring. Add to this, Mary had fixed her heart upon this chosen friend; and one of the last impressions a worthy mind can submit to receive, is that of the worthlessness of the person upon whom it has placed its esteem. Mary had struggled to entertain a favourable opinion of human nature; she had unweariedly fought for a kindred mind, in whose integrity and fidelity to take up her rest. Wounded affection, wounded pride, all those principles which hold most absolute empire in the purest and loftiest minds, urged her to still further experiments to recover her influence, and to a still more poignant desperation, long after reason would have directed her to desist, and resolutely call off her mind from thoughts of so hopeless and fatal a description. Mr. Imlay undertook to prove, in his letters written immediately after their complete separation, that his conduct towards her was reconcileable to the strictest rectitude; but undoubtedly Mary was of a different opinion. Whatever the reader may decide in this respect, there is one sentiment that, I believe, he will unhesitatingly admit: that of pity for the mistake of the man, who, being in possession of such a friendship and attachment as those of Mary, could hold them at a trivial price, and, "like the base Indian,[1] throw a pearl away, richer than all his tribe."[2]

---

1   Misquote from William Shakespeare's *Othello* (5:2): "one whose hand, / Like the base Indian, threw a pearl away" (lines 355-56).

2   A person, whom Mary saw frequently about this time, was Archibald Hamilton

b. Elizabeth Inchbald, Letter to William Godwin, 18 September 1805
(Oxford, Bodleian Library, [Abinger Deposit] Dep. c. 509.)[1]

[As a woman, Inchbald felt that she could not afford to be seen publicly with Godwin, who was known to have been married to Mary Wollstonecraft. As the following letter indicates, Godwin continued to pursue Inchbald's friendship, apparently until her death in 1821.]

My Dear Sir

The moment I received your letter I was in a great hurry of being just come to town, and I thought I had a thousand things to say to you, but to day I find I was mistaken and in reality I had but one—and that one I find a difficulty, a *Pain* in renewing so—but as evasion and equivocation are more detestable than even this Repeating of this grievance, I boldly fly to the Last, rather than cheat you by the former.

I have a letter or two of yours in my possession[2]—the contents of which I perfectly forgive, and perfectly do *excuse*, or I had been the meanest wretch on earth to have asked a favor of you this spring.

Still, these letters must ever prevent any *premeditated* renewal of our personal acquaintance—my manners, or my conversation even, so much deceived you to my disadvantage, that I cannot knowingly or willingly risk the possibility of such rather disgraceful mortification.

In your invitation to me Last Spring, to meet Mr. Edgeworth,[3] you alluded to this circumstance with great propriety and delicacy. I had another reason at that time (fully as forcible as I painted it to you) and I wished not to call to mind the other. It has occurred to me since, to examine, whether it is a point ever to be overcome while you are in the selfsame predicament which gave rise, to your former error—the seeing through the eyes, and feeling through the heart of another.[4]

I revere the person which can Blind you, and I revere Blindness as

---

Rowan, who had lately become a fugitive from Ireland, in consequence of a political prosecution, and in whom she found those qualities which were always eminently engaging to her, great integrity of disposition, and great kindness of heart.

1 This letter has been reproduced by the kind permission of Lord Abinger and granted through the Bodleian Library.

2 Godwin had proposed marriage to Inchbald before he married Mary Wollstonecraft, and it is conceivable that the "letter or two" might have contained a renewal of his suit.

3 Richard Lovell Edgeworth (1744-1817), educational philosopher and father of Maria Edgeworth.

4 Presumably refers to Godwin's love for Mary Wollstonecraft, a passion that Inchbald was never able to understand or condone.

the sole proof that can be given of the *genuine* passion, but, so few men are gifted with refined sensibility like yours, that I have never yet been obliged to practice the art of pleasing them through those they Love, and I dare not hazard the want of this power with *you*.

I hate the appearance of evasion as much as the evasion itself or I might solely have answered in respect to Mr. Prince Hoare[1] & the company I met at his house—they were all persons which chance throws in my way almost every day in the streets.—Mrs. Opie & so forth[2]—You I have not seen in many a year—but that I once was acquainted with you is a source of great pleasure to me; and it would grieve me very much if I thought I should never see you again.

E. Inchbald

c. From Trials for Adultery: Or, The History of Divorces. Being Select Trials At Doctors Commons, For Adultery, Fornication, Cruelty, Impotence, &C. From the Year 1760, to the present Time. Including the whole of the Evidence on each Cause. Together With The Letters, &c. that have been intercepted between the amorous Parties. The whole forming a complete History of the Private Life, Intrigues, and Amours of many Characters in the most elevated Sphere: every Scene and Transaction, however ridiculous, whimsical, or extraordinary, being fairly represented, as becomes a faithful Historian, who is fully determined not to sacrifice Truth at the Shrine of Guilt and Folly. Taken in Short-Hand, by a Civilian *(1779)*

[*Trials for Adultery* was published in 1779 with the dual purpose of dissuading potential adulterers and publicly humiliating those who had already violated their marriage vows. However, as George E. Haggerty has pointed out, these tales of adultery focus almost exclusively on *female* violators: "six and a half of the seven volumes contain tales of female infidelity luridly told and brutally concluded. In each of these, as brutally preemptive as they are, it becomes clear how 'simple' a woman's story can be when it is subjected to the rigors of patriarchal law" (662).]

---

1 Prince Hoare (1755-1834), dramatist, actor, and editor of *The Artist*, a journal to which Inchbald contributed.
2 Amelia Opie (1769-1853), poet and novelist.

i. Preface

Conjugal Infidelity is become so general that it is hardly considered as criminal; especially in the fashionable world. Sensible of the consequences resulting from illicit love, a Right Reverend Prelate has·endeavoured to introduce a new law,[1] for the punishment of those who are convicted of Adultery; his intention was praise-worthy, though perhaps a better act than he proposed, might possibly have been framed. It however passed the House of Lords, but it did not meet with the concurrence of the Lower House. It is indeed a difficult matter to deter those of an abandoned disposition, from the commission of crimes where the punishment is trivial: a separation is generally the worst consequence that can ensue in adulterous cases, and that is but too often what the offending parties devoutly wish. This publication may perhaps effect what the law cannot: the transactions of the adulterer and the adulteress will, by being thus *publickly circulated*, preserve others from the like crimes, from the fear of shame, when the fear of punishment may have but little force.

It requires little or no apology for the publication of these trials. It may, perhaps, (as already observed) deter the wavering wanton from the completion of her wishes; it may be of service to the practicers in the law, as they may have recourse to these trials for information, which will answer the same purpose in this, as the Law and Equity Reports in other courts; it will shew to the world in general by what gradual steps affection sinks into indifference, indifference into disgust, and disgust into aversion: the consequences of which are but too apparent from the perusal of these volumes. When a woman (especially of the superior class) has lost that inestimable jewel, virtue; alas! how is the fallen! her nobility no longer claims our reverence; her coronet ceases to be enviable; her birth (which she has disgraced) but adds to her offence; as, from her situation, it was incumbent on her to have been an example of purity to the rest of her sex: she is indeed become the object of scorn, pity, and derision of her relations, her former associates, and the public.

June 19, 1779

---

1 In 1779 legislation was introduced by Dr. Shute Barrington, bishop of Durham (1734-1826) that would have prevented divorced women from marrying their lovers.

ii. Lord Ligonier, Against Lady Ligonier 1771.

[Deposition of Thomas Johnson (Volume III)]

15th July, 1771.
The Deposition of Thomas Johnson.

THOMAS JOHNSON, of Barnet, in the county of Middlesex, post-boy, aged sixteen years and upwards, a witness produced and sworn, saith, that in the month of March last, the deponent was a post-boy at the Griffin Inn, at Kingston upon Thames, in the county of Surry; and in or about the latter end of the said month of March, (but what day in particular he does not recollect) a foreign gentleman came to the Griffin Inn, aforesaid, about eleven o'clock in the forenoon, as he now best recollects; and he had a servant with him who was also a foreigner, and who ordered a post-chaise at the said inn, for Cobham, in the said county of Surry: and the deponent drove the said foreign gentleman, (whom he hath since been informed, and believes, was Count Vittorio Armadeo Alsieri) and his said servant in such chaise, to the White-Lion Inn, at Cobham aforesaid, where such gentleman ordered the deponent to wait; and he went from the said Inn, and was absent for about two hours: in which time he went and viewed Lord Ligonier's gardens, as the deponent believes, by reason that the servants at the White-Lion Inn, were talking among themselves about the said gentleman's going to Lord Ligonier's, and the deponent over-heard them: that, when the said gentleman returned to the inn, the deponent drove him and his servant to the said Griffin Inn at Kingston, and from thence to London, and set them down at the end of Suffolk Street, near the Hay Market.

He also saith, that, in the afternoon of Sunday the fifth of May last, about eight o'clock, the same foreign gentleman, whom the deponent had before drove to Cobham, and whom he believes was the articulate Count Vittorio Armadeo Alsieri, came again in a chaise to the Griffin Inn, at Kingston, and ordered a chaise for Cobham; but he had then no servant with him, and was much disguised in his dress, having on an old blue cloth great coat, with a round post-boy's hat, and one of his arms bound up in a black crape sling: but, notwithstanding this disguise, the deponent well knew him to be the same foreign gentleman, whom he had before drove to Cobham; and particularly by his having very red or carrotty hair: and the deponent also observed that, under his old blue great coat, he had a very handsome coat, and was particularly smart about his legs and feet, having clean white silk stockings, and neat shoes and buckles on: that the deponent then again drove the said gentleman in a chaise from Kingston, and he ordered the deponent to set him down at a small distance from the Tartar, a little public house on the road side, leading from Kingston to Cobham, within about half a mile from Cobham: and, when the deponent set him down there, agreeable to such directions, it was about nine o'clock in the evening: that the deponent told the said gentleman there were no stables at the Tartar, but he replied, he knew there were, and he ordered the deponent to wait for him at the Tartar; and told the deponent he would return in three or four hours: that the said gentleman got out of the chaise on the top of the hill, before he came to the Tartar, and went across the road over a stile, at the end of the garden belonging to the Tartar; and went towards Church Cobham, the nearest way to Lord Ligonier's house; and the deponent went to the Tartar, and put up his horses there: that, between three and four o'clock the next morning (Monday the sixth of May last) the said gentleman came back to the Tartar, and ordered the deponent to be called up, and to get the chaise ready: that the deponent got up and prepared the chaise, and offered to pay for the horses, but he said, as well as he could in broken English, that he would pay for all; and he paid for all accordingly: that, about four o'clock that morning, the gentleman set off in the chaise, from the Tartar, for Kingston, and the deponent drove him; and he gave the deponent three shillings and sixpence for himself on arriving at Kingston; and, in the deponent's hearing, ordered the boy who drove him from thence to London, to set him down at Charing Cross.

THOMAS JOHNSON

[Deposition of Nathanial Sandy (Volume III)]

16th July, 1771.
The Deposition of Nathaniel Sandy.

NATHANIEL SANDY, of North Audley Street, in the parish of St. George, Hanover Square, in the county of Middlesex, servant to Lord Ligonier, aged thirty-years and upwards, a witness produced and sworn, saith, that he well knows the Right Hon. Penelope Lady Viscountess Ligonier, party in this cause, by means of his having lived with her husband, the Right Hon. Edward Lord Viscount Ligonier, the other party in this cause, as his footman, for about nine months past: that he verily believes Lady Ligonier to be a person of a vicious and lewd disposition, and that she hath, for some time past, given herself up to a very lewd, vicious, debauched and adulterous life.

This deponent further saith, that, on Sunday Morning, the fifth of May last, Penelope Lady Viscountess Ligonier went from London, to the house of Edward Lord Viscount Ligonier, her husband, at Cobham, in the county of Surry, attended by a young lady, whose name was Miss Graham; and Lord Ligonier was prevented from, and did not go with her at that time, he being obliged as aid-de-camp to the King, to attend a review made by his Majesty, on Monday the sixth of the said month of May last: that there then was, and still is, a gate in the gardens of the said Lord Viscount Ligonier, which opens at the bottom of a lawn, into the road, and which is usually kept locked, and of which William Fletcher, Lord Ligonier's house-steward, and John Whitely, his gardener, only have keys; that Lady Ligonier, soon after the arrived at Cobham, on Sunday morning, the fifth of May last, asked the said John Whitely for his key of the said garden gate, and he gave it to her ladyship, and she kept it till she went away from thence, on the Tuesday next following; when the said John Whitely asked her for it, and she returned it to him, as the deponent has been informed and believes: that in the evening of the said Sunday, the fifth of May last, the deponent happening to be walking out in the fields, near Lord Ligonier's house, at Cobham, between eight and nine o'clock, he saw a post-chaise stop at the top of the hill, before it came to the Tartar, a small public house on the road side, leading from Kingston, to Cobham; and he observed a person get out of such chaise, and thereupon the deponent went down to the Tartar, and the post-boy soon after came up to the Tartar, and the deponent enquired of the boy who he had brought in the chaise, and whither such person was going in the presence of George Pope, the landlord of the Tartar: that the post-boy answered, that the person he had brought in the chaise, was a foreign gentleman, who had ordered him to wait at the Tartar for him, for three or four hours, and that he believed such foreigner was going to Lord Ligonier's, at Cobham: that the person who so got out of the chaise, went immediately across the road, over a gate, at the end of the garden belonging to the Tartar, towards Church Cobham; and on the post-boy's saying, that he believed he was going to Lord Ligonier's, the deponent immediately followed him, overtook him, and passed him; and then observed that such gentleman was disguised in his dress, for he had got on an old blue cloth great coat, and a round post-boy's hat; but, under such great coat, the deponent saw a very handsome coat, and he was particularly smart about the legs and feet, and had neat shoes and buckles; and the deponent took as much notice of his person as possible: that the deponent thereupon went forward towards Church Cobham, in order to acquaint William Fletcher, Lord Ligonier's steward, with what he had heard and seen, relative to the said foreign gentleman in disguise; and, on his road thither, the deponent met with William Wood, groom to Lord Ligonier, and told him what he had observed, and desired the said William Wood to go to watch such person in disguise, whilst the deponent went on to Mr. Fletcher's: that the said William Wood went to watch accordingly, and he saw the person in disguise, before described, and watched him for some time; but, at last, when it grew almost dark, lost him, as the said William Wood informed the deponent, and which information he believes to be true: that the deponent having seen the said Mr. Fletcher, at Church Cobham, and acquainted him with the circumstances beforementioned, as to the foreign gentleman, he returned to Lord Ligonier's house, where he arrived about half an hour after nine o'clock on the said Sunday evening; and he then acquainted William Pepper, Lady Ligonier's footman, with what he had observed, and he desired William Pepper, when he carried up candles, to fasten the doors and windows as usual, Lord Ligonier's directions being always to do so, when candles were brought up: and the deponent particularly desired William Pepper to do so that night, as he suspected that the person he had watched, was somewhere about the house: that William Pepper accordingly, when he carried up candles, went round the house, and shut and bolted all the windows and doors, except the south-entrance door, and particularly shut the north entrance door, which opens out of the garden into the saloon, and which is half door and half window, the window shutting down upon the door; and he put the shutters to, and put the large iron bar quite across, and hasped it, as the said William Pepper informed the deponent; and which information he believes to be true: and it was particularly taken notice of by the servants, that Lady Ligonier was walking out in the pleasure grounds that evening till it was quite dark, contrary to her usual custom: that about ten, or a little after ten o'clock of the said Sunday evening, the fifth of May last, the deponent, being very anxious to find out where the person he had watched, and who was disguised, could be gone, he went to Cobham, and enquired at the White Lion and the George, the only two inns there, whether any person, of the description of the person whom he had seen get out of the chaise and walk towards Lord Ligonier's house, was at either of the said inns, or if he had ordered lodgings at either of them; but the deponent could hear nothing of him, nor was the said person at either of the said inns, as the deponent believes, any part of the said night.

He further saith, that he doth verily and in his conscience believe, that the said Penelope, Lady Viscountess Ligonier, after it was dark, in the evening of the said fifth of May last, let the said person in disguise before particularly mentioned (and whom the deponent verily believes and is well convinced was the articulate Count Vittorio Armadeo Alsieri) into the said Lord Ligonier's house, at Cobham, and that she secreted him therein for some time; and that the said Lady Ligonier and Count Alsieri lay together, and had the carnal use and knowledge of each other's bodies, and committed the crime of adultery together at that time; for the deponent, on Monday morning the sixth of May last, about one o'clock, having strong suspicions that such person was in or about the house, he went round the house with William Pepper, Lacy Ligonier's footman, to see whether the doors and windows were all fast; and they found the south-entrance door fast; but on going to the north-entrance door, which opens into the salloon, they found the iron bar which goes across, unhasped, and taken down; the window-shutters were close, but the windows not down by about an inch and an half; notwithstanding the said William Pepper had completely fastened the same the evening before, as he then again asserted to the deponent: that they then shut the window quite down, put the shutters close, and the bar across and hasped it again, and then went to bed.

This deponent further saith, that, about eight o'clock of the said Monday morning, the sixth of May last, the deponent told William Fletcher what had passed the night before, and particularly the circumstance of the window and door having been found open, and then the deponent and William Wood, the groom, determined to see if they could track any person upon the sand walks in the garden; and they accordingly went and viewed the same, and then and there observed the print of a lady's foot, and the print of a man's foot, whereupon the deponent went and told William Fletcher thereof; and then William Fletcher, the deponent, and William Wood, went altogether and observed that the said prints were fresh; which they could plainly discover, by reason that the walks had been new laid down, and swept over on the Saturday before, against Lord and Lady Ligonier's coming down; and they observed the like prints of the feet, as well of the lady as of the man, at the garden-gate that opens from the lawn to the road.

This deponent further saith, that, about eleven o'clock of the said Monday morning, the sixth of May last, the deponent went to the said public house called the Tartar, and enquired of the landlord what time the person went away in the chaise, that came there the night before; and the landlord informed the deponent, that such person went away between three and four o'clock in the morning; and that he behaved very well on going away; and also said, he could not tell what the gentleman had been about; that he had no buckles in his shoes when he came in the morning: that the deponent thereupon grew more suspicious than ever, and immediately returned to Lord Ligonier's house, and went up stairs into the saloon, and looked at the north-entrance door, and found the window again not shut down by about an inch and half: this induced him to look further, and accordingly he went into the bed-room, which adjoins to the salloon, and wherein is the state-bed, but no one had lain in the said room, nor had there been a fire therein for upwards of three months next before: that, on the said Sunday morning, the fifth of May last, Elizabeth Chilton, one of the maid-servants, had dusted the bed, and counterpain, and left the said room, bed, and carpet, at the foot thereof, all clean and smooth, as she informed the deponent: and which information he believes to be true: that, on going into the said room, the deponent opened one of the window-shutters, and found the carpet at the bottom of the bed much rumpled, and there were then two large dints at the bottom of the bed, as if two persons had been sitting on it; and the bed in the middle appeared as if some person had been lying upon it; and, a little above the middle of the bed, there was a round place about the size of a person's head, all covered with powder: that, on the deponent's observing these circumstances, he fetched up William Fletcher, and William Pepper, who saw the bed in the same condition.

He further saith, that, on the said Monday, the sixth of May last, Lord Ligonier arrived at his house at Cobham, and on Tuesday morning the seventh of the said month of May, the deponent having consulted with William Fletcher, the steward, came to a resolution to mention the aforesaid matters to his lordship, and he mentioned them accordingly: that Lord Ligonier on the same day, and after the deponent had related to him the circumstances before-mentioned, ordered a chaise to be got ready to carry Lady Ligonier to her father, Mr. George Pitt, at his house at Stratfield Say, in the county of Hants; and Lord Ligonier ordered another chaise to be got ready for him to come to town; and he came to town immediately, and the deponent with him.

He further saith, that the said Lord Viscount Ligonier arrived from Cobham, at his house in North-Audley Street, on the said Tuesday the seventh of May last, between seven and eight o'clock in the evening, and the deponent was with him: that his lordship, on getting out of the chaise, immediately went from his house towards Bond Street, and in Bond Street he took a sword from a sword cutler's, and he afterwards went to the Opera House, and found Count Alsieri, and they went together into the Green Park, and fought a duel; when Lord Ligonier wounded Count Alsieri in the arm: and afterwards Count Alsieri confessed to his lordship, that he had been at his lordship's house at Cobham, the Sunday night before, and had lain with Lady Ligonier in his lordship's bed; as the said Lord Ligonier informed the deponent; and such information he is well convinced was the truth: and the next day the deponent, by his lordship's directions, carried back the sword to the cutler's in Bond Street, of whom his lordship had borrowed it.

The deponent further saith, that, after the circumstances last mentioned, he twice saw a foreign gentleman, whom he was informed was Count Alsieri, and knew him to be the same person that he had seen in the fields near Lord Ligonier's house at Cobham, disguised as before-mentioned, on Sunday evening, the fifth of the said month of May.

NATHANIEL SANDY.

Select Bibliography

Anderson, Misty G. *Female Playwrights and Eighteenth-Century Comedy: Negotiating Marriage on the London Stage*. New York: Palgrave, 2002.

Armstrong, Nancy. *Desire and Domestic Fiction: A Political History of the Novel*. New York: Oxford UP, 1987.

Backscheider, Paula R. *Spectacular Politics: Theatrical Power and Mass Culture in Early Modern England*. Baltimore: Johns Hopkins UP, 1993.

—. ed. *The Plays of Elizabeth Inchbald*. 2 vols. New York: Garland, 1980.

Balfour, Ian. "Promises, Promises: Social and Other Contracts in the English Jacobins (Godwin/Inchbald)." *New Romanticisms: Theory and Critical Practice*. Ed. David L. Clark and Donald C. Goellnicht. Toronto: U of Toronto P, 1994. 225-50.

Barker-Benfield, G.J. *The Culture of Sensibility: Sex and Society in Eighteenth-Century Britain*. Chicago and London: U of Chicago P, 1992.

Berger, John. *Ways of Seeing*. Harmondsworth: Penguin, 1990.

Boaden, James. *Memoirs of Mrs. Inchbald: Including her Familiar Correspondence with the Most Distinguished Persons of her Time*. 2 vols. London: Richard Bentley, 1833.

—. *Memoirs of Mrs. Siddons*. London: Gibbings, 1893.

—. *Memoirs of the Life of John Philip Kemble*. 2 vols. London: Longman, Hurst, Rees, Orme, Brown, and Green, 1825.

Boardman, Michael. "Inchbald's *A Simple Story*: An Anti-Ideological Reading." *Ideology and Form in Eighteenth-Century Literature*. Ed. David H. Richter. Lubbock, TX: Texas Tech UP, 1999. 207-22.

Bolton, Betsy. *Women, Nationalism and the Romantic Stage: Theatre and Politics in Britain, 1780-1800*. Cambridge: Cambridge UP, 2001.

Bossy, John. *The English Catholic Community, 1570-1850*. London: Darton, Longman, and Todd, 1975.

Breashears, Caroline. "Defining Masculinity in *A Simple Story*." *Eighteenth-Century Fiction* 16:3 (April 2004): 451-70.

The British Theatre: Or, A Collection of Plays, Which are Acted at the Theatres Royal, Drury Lane, Covent Garden, and the Haymarket, with Biographical and Critical Remarks, by Mrs. Inchbald. 25 vols. London: Longman, Hurst, Rees, and Orme, 1808.

Burney, Frances. *Evelina, or, a Young Lady's Entrance into the World*. Ed. Susan Kubica Howard. Peterborough, ON: Broadview, 2000.

Burroughs, Catherine B. *Closet Stages: Joanna Baillie and the Theater Theory of British Romantic Women Writers*. Philadelphia: U of Pennsylvania P, 1997.

Butler, Marilyn. *Jane Austen and the War of Ideas*. Oxford: Clarendon P, 1975. Rev. ed. 1987.

Byrne, Paula. "*A Simple Story:* From Inchbald to Austen." *Romanticism: The Journal of Romantic Culture and Criticism* 5:2 (1999): 161-71.

Carlson, Julie. "Remaking Love: Remorse in the Theatre of Baillie and Inchbald." *Women in British Romantic Theatre: Drama, Performance, and Society, 1790-1840*. Ed. Catherine B. Burroughs. Cambridge: Cambridge UP, 2000. 285-310.

Carlson, Marvin. "Elizabeth Inchbald: A Woman in her Theatrical Culture." *Women in British Romantic Theatre: Drama, Performance, and Society, 1790-1840*. Ed. Catherine B. Burroughs. Cambridge: Cambridge UP, 2000. 207-22.

Castle, Terry. *Masquerade and Civilization: The Carnivalesque in Eighteenth-Century English Culture and Fiction*. Stanford: Stanford UP, 1986.

Clemit, Pamela. Introduction. *A Simple Story*. Harmondsworth: Penguin, 1996.

Clery, E.J. *The Rise of Supernatural Fiction, 1762-1800*. Cambridge: Cambridge UP 1995.

Conway, Alison. *Private Interests: Women, Portraiture, and the Visual Culture of the English Novel, 1709-1791*. Toronto: U of Toronto P, 2001.

Craft-Fairchild, Catherine. *Masquerade and Gender: Disguise and Female Identity in Eighteenth-Century Fictions by Women*. University Park, PA: Pennsylvania State UP, 1993.

Donkin, Ellen. *Getting into the Act: Women Playwrights in London, 1776-1829*. London and New York: Routledge, 1995.

Fielding, Henry. *Joseph Andrews*. Ed. Jane Stabler. Oxford: Oxford UP, 2003.

—. *Tom Jones*. Ed. John Bender and Simon Stern. Oxford UP, 1996.

Ford, Susan Allen. "A Name More Dear: Daughters, Fathers, and Desire in *A Simple Story, The False Friend*, and *Mathilda*." *Revisioning Romanticism: British Women Writers, 1776-1837*. Ed. Joel Haefner and Carol Shiner. Philadelphia: U of Pennsylvania P, 1994. 51-71.

Godwin, William. *Caleb Williams*. Ed. Gary Handwerk and A.A. Markley. Peterborough, ON: Broadview, 2000.

Green, Katherine S. "Mr. Harmony and the Events of 1793: Elizabeth Inchbald's *Every One Has His Fault*." *Theatre Journal* 56:1 (March 2004): 47-62.

—. "'You Should be My Master': Imperial Recognition Politics in

Elizabeth Inchbald's *Such Things Are.*" *CLIO: A Journal of Literature, History, and the Philosophy of Ideas* 27:3 (Spring 1998): 387-414.

Haggerty, George E. "Female Abjection in Inchbald's *A Simple Story.*" *Studies in English Literature, 1500-1900* 36:3 (Summer 1996): 655-71.

Haydon, Colin. *Anti-Catholicism in the Eighteenth Century: A Political and Social Study.* Manchester: Manchester UP, 1994.

Haywood, Eliza. *The Female Spectator.* 2nd ed. London: T. Gardner, 1748.

Hoagwood, Terence Allan. "Elizabeth Inchbald, Joanna Baillie, and Revolutionary Representation in the 'Romantic' Period." *Rebellious Hearts: British Women Writers and the French Revolution.* Ed. Adriana Craciun and Kari E. Lokke. Albany, NY: State U of New York P, 2001. [AU: page extent?]

Hunter, J. Paul. *Before Novels: The Cultural Contexts of Eighteenth-Century English Fiction.* New York: W.W. Norton, 1992.

Inchbald, Elizabeth. Diary and Account Book. Folger Library MS M.a. 149, 1776. M.a. 150, 1780. M.s. 151, 1782. M.a. 152, 1783. M.a. 153, 1788. M.a. 154, 1807. M.a. 155, 1808. M.a. 156, 1814. M.a. 157, 1820. W.a. 240, 1782 and 1793.

——. Letter to William Godwin. Oxford, Bodleian Library [Abinger Deposit]. Dep. c. 509.

——. *Nature and Art.* London: G.G. and J. Robinson, 1796.

Jenkins, Annibel. *I'll Tell You What: The Life of Elizabeth Inchbald.* Lexington: UP of Kentucky, 2003.

Johnson, Samuel. *Essays from the Rambler, Adventurer, and Idler.* Ed. W.J. Bate. New Haven: Yale UP, 1963.

Kelly, Gary. *The English Jacobin Novel 1780-1805.* London: Clarendon, 1976.

Littlewood, Samuel Robinson. *Elizabeth Inchbald and her Circle: The Life Story of a Charming Woman.* London: D.O. Connor, 1921.

Lott, Anna. "Sexual Politics in Elizabeth Inchbald." *Studies in English Literature* 34:3 (Summer 1994): 635-48.

Manvell, Roger. *Elizabeth Inchbald: England's Principal Woman Dramatist and Independent Woman of Letters in 18th Century London.* New York and London: UP of America, 1987.

Martin, Mary Patricia. "Reading Reform in Richardson's *Clarissa.*" *Studies in English Literature* 37:3 (Summer 1997): 595-614.

Mathew, David. *Catholicism in England: The Portrait of a Minority, its Culture and Tradition.* London: Eyre & Spottiswoode, 1955.

Maurer, Shawn Lisa. Introduction. *Nature and Art.* London: Pickering and Chatto, 1997.

—. "Masculinity and Morality in Elizabeth Inchbald's *Nature and Art*." *Women, Revolution, and the Novels of the 1790s*. Ed. Linda Lang-Peralta. East Lansing, MI: Michigan State UP, 1999. 155-76.

—. *Proposing Men: Dialectics of Gender and Class in the Eighteenth-Century English Periodical*. Stanford: Stanford UP, 1998.

McCrea, Brian. *Impotent Fathers: Patriarchy and Demographic Crisis in the Eighteenth-Century Novel*. Newark: U of Delaware P; London; Cranbury, NJ: Associated University Presses, 1998.

McKee, William. *Elizabeth Inchbald, Novelist*. Washington, DC: Catholic U of America, 1935.

McKeon, Michael. *The Origins of the English Novel, 1600-1740*. Baltimore: Johns Hopkins UP, 1987.

Moody, Jane. "Suicide and Translation in the Dramaturgy of Elizabeth Inchbald and Anne Plumptre." *Women in British Romantic Theatre: Drama, Performance, and Society, 1790-1840*. Ed. Catherine B. Burroughs. Cambridge: Cambridge UP, 2000. 257-84.

More, Hannah. *Strictures on the Modern System of Female Education*. London: T. Cadell and W. Davies, 1799.

Nachumi, Nora. "'Those Simple Signs': The Performance of Emotion in Elizabeth Inchbald's *A Simple Story*." *Eighteenth-Century Fiction* 11:3 (April 1999): 317-38.

Nelson, Bonnie. "*Emily Herbert*: Forerunner of Jane Austen's *Lady Susan*." *Women's Writing* 1:3 (1994): 317-23.

Osland, Diane. "Heart-Picking in *A Simple Story*." *Eighteenth-Century Fiction* 16:1 (October 2003): 79-101.

O'Quinn, Daniel. "Inchbald's Indies: Domestic and Dramatic Re-Orientations." *European Romantic Review* 9:2 (Spring 1998): 217-30.

—. "'Scissors and Needles': Inchbald's *Wives as They Were, Maids as They Are*, and the Governance of Sexual Exchange." *Theatre Journal* 51:2 (May 1999): 195-225.

—. "Elizabeth Inchbald's The Massacre: Tragedy, Violence and the Networks of Political Fantasy." *British Women Playwrights around 1800* <http://www-sul.stanford.edu/mirrors/romnet/wp1800/essays/massacre_intro.html>.

Parker, Jo Alyson. "Complicating *A Simple Story*: Inchbald's Two Versions of Female Power." *Eighteenth-Century Studies* 30:3 (Spring 1997): 255-70.

Paul, Charles Kegan. *William Godwin: His Friends and Contemporaries*. 2 vols. London: Henry S. King, 1876.

Paulson, Ronald. *Representations of Revolution, 1789-1820*. New Haven: Yale UP, 1983.

Perry, Ruth. *Novel Relations: The Transformation of Kinship in English Literature and Culture, 1748-1818.* Cambridge: Cambridge UP, 2004.

Pointon, Marcia R. *Hanging the Head: Portraiture and Social Formation in Eighteenth-Century England.* New Haven, CT: Yale UP, 1993.

Poovey, Mary. *The Proper Lady and the Woman Writer: Ideology as Style in the Works of Mary Wollstonecraft, Mary Shelley, and Jane Austen.* Chicago: U of Chicago P, 1984.

Ribeiro, Aileen. *The Art of Dress: Fashion in England and France, 1750 to 1820.* New Haven, CT: Yale UP, 1995.

Richardson, Samuel. *Clarissa, or, The History of a Young Lady.* Ed. Angus Ross. Harmondsworth: Penguin, 1986.

—. *Pamela, or, Virtue Rewarded.* Ed. Thomas Keymer and Alice Wakely. Oxford: Oxford UP, 2001.

—. *The History of Charles Grandison.* Ed. Joselyn Harris. London: Oxford UP, 1972.

Rogers, Katherine M. "Inhibitions on Eighteenth-Century Women Novelists: Elizabeth Inchbald and Charlotte Smith." *Eighteenth-Century Studies* 11:1 (Autumn 1977): 63-78.

—. *Feminism in Eighteenth-Century England.* Brighton: Harvester Press, 1982.

Scheuermann, Mona. *Her Bread to Earn: Women, Money, and Society from Defoe to Austen.* Lexington: UP of Kentucky, 1993.

Schoch, Richard W. "'We Do Nothing But Enact History': Thomas Carlyle Stages the Past." *Nineteenth-Century Literature* 54 (June 1999): 27-52.

Schofield, Mary Anne. *Masking and Unmasking the Female Mind: Disguising Romances in Feminine Fiction, 1713-1799.* Newark: U of Delaware P, 1990.

Schofield, Mary Anne and Cecilia Macheski, eds. *Curtain Calls: British and American Women and the Theatre, 1660-1820.* Athens: Ohio UP, 1991.

Shaffer, Julie. "The High Cost of Female Virtue: The Sexualization of Female Agency in Late Eighteenth- and Early Nineteenth-Century Texts." *Misogyny and Literature: An Essay Collection.* Ed. Katherine Ackley. New York: Garland, 1992. 105-42.

Sigl, Patricia. *The Literary Achievement of Elizabeth Inchbald.* Ph.D. thesis. University of Wales, Swansea. 1980.

Smallwood, Angela. "Introduction to volume six of *Eighteenth-Century Women Playwrights*: Elizabeth Inchbald." *British Women Playwrights around 1800.* Section Editor, Catherine Burroughs. General Editors: Thomas C. Chrocunis and Michael Eberle-Sinatra. August 15, 2001.

<http://www.etang.umontreal.ca/bwp1800/essays/smallwood_in-troPC.html>.

Spacks, Patricia Ann Meyer. *Desire and Truth: Functions of Plot in Eighteenth-Century English Novels*. Chicago: U of Chicago P, 1990.

Spencer, Jane. Introduction. *A Simple Story*. Oxford: Oxford UP, 1998.

—. *The Rise of the Woman Novelist: From Aphra Behn to Jane Austen*. Oxford: B. Blackwell, 1986.

Spender, Dale. *Mothers of the Novel*. London: Pandora; New York: Methuen, 1986.

—. ed. *Living by the Pen: Early British Women Writers*. New York: Teachers College P, Columbia University, 1992.

Taylor, John. *Records of My Life*. London: Edward Bull, 1832.

Taylor, Patricia M. "Authorial Amendments in Mrs. Inchbald's *Nature and Art*." *Notes and Queries* 25 (February 1978): 68-70.

Todd, Janet. *Mary Wollstonecraft: A Revolutionary Life*. New York: Columbia UP, 2000.

—. *The Sign of Angellica: Women, Writing and Fiction*. Columbia UP, 1989.

Tomalin, Claire. *The Life and Death of Mary Wollstonecraft*. New York: Harcourt Brace Jovanovich, 1974.

Tompkins, J.M.S. Introduction. *A Simple Story*. Oxford: Oxford UP, 1967.

Ty, Eleanor. *Unsex'd Revolutionaries: Five Women Novelists of the 1790s*. Toronto: U of Toronto P, 1993.

Ward, Candace. "Inordinate Desire: Schooling the Senses in Elizabeth Inchbald's *A Simple Story*." *Studies in the Novel* 31:1 (March 1999): 1-18.

Wardle, Ralph M. "Mary Woolstonecraft: Analytical Reviewer." *PMLA* 62:4 (December 1947): 1000-09.

Watt, Ian. *The Rise of the Novel: Studies in Defoe, Richardson, and Fielding*. Berkeley and Los Angeles: U of California P, 1957.